DESTRUCTIVE REASONING

THE AUTHORITIES: BOOK TWO

BOOKS BY SCOTT MEYER:

THE AUTHORITIES SERIES:

The Authorities
Destructive Reasoning

MAGIC 2.0 SERIES:

Off to Be the Wizard
Spell or High Water
An Unwelcome Quest
Fight and Flight
Out of Spite, Out of Mind
The Vexed Generation

Master of Formalities
Run Program
Grand Theft Astro

BASIC INSTRUCTIONS COLLECTIONS:

Help Is on the Way
Made with 90% Recycled Art
The Curse of the Masking-Tape Mummy
Dignified Hedonism

More information about Scott's novels can be found
at scottmeyer.rocks.
More of Scott's comics can be found at basicinstructions.net.

DESTRUCTIVE REASONING

SCOTT MEYER

DESTRUCTIVE REASONING

Published by Rocket Hat Industries
Text copyright © 2022 by Scott Meyer
All rights reserved.
Cover design by Missy Meyer

ISBN-13: 978-1-950056-07-1

DESTRUCTIVE REASONING

ONE

Rutherford clenched his jaw, gripping a wooden match between his teeth as he said, "Julius Clearman, you're under arrest."

"What?!" Clearman sputtered. "Here?! Now?!" He sat on one end of a bench seat in the last car of a long tram. His wife sat at the other end, and their nine-year-old daughter sat between them, holding a red balloon and looking confused.

Rutherford grimaced, almost apologetically. "Yeah. Look, really, there's no convenient time or place to get arrested." He and Sloan sat in the row behind Clearman: a scruffy man in a leather jacket doing all the talking and a woman dressed all in black, her features concealed by a black full-face helmet and her black-gloved hands resting on the handle of her black-and-silver cane, utterly motionless and seemingly emotionless.

Clearman's eyes darted wildly, looking for any means of escape. The tram drove between two high walls, leaving only about three feet on each side. A fake rock texture half-heartedly tried to make it look as if the tram was driving through a cave. The walls curled inward toward the tram roof before shooting straight up, blocking all but a sliver of light on each side.

If Clearman jumped off the tram, he'd either have to run toward the rear of the tram, and Rutherford could grab him as he passed, or he could run forward, the same direction as the tram, and Rutherford would only have to wait until he got tired, then grab him.

During the few seconds it took for Clearman to weigh his limited options, an old-timey voice from the PA system said, "Welcome folks, to Varmit Valley, where the small live large!"

Sloan turned her helmet slightly to look at Rutherford. Rutherford groaned and said, "Forget it, Clearman. You've got nowhere to run . . . unless you plan to climb up on the roof."

Julius Clearman's eyes widened, as if he'd just had a great idea. He stood up, stepped on the front of the tram car, and shimmied through the gap between the roof of their car and the one ahead. Clearman's weight made the fiberglass above the passengers' heads buckle with a loud *thunk*.

Rutherford said, "As predicted."

In his earpiece, the computer-generated voice Sloan used to communicate said, "You didn't predict it. You suggested it."

Also in his earpiece, he heard Terri, the team leader, monitoring the situation from the van. "After him, Rutherford."

"Is it really necessary, Terri?"

"For you to do what I tell you? Yes. It is."

Albert, the team tech expert, also listening in from the van, said, "Deploying camera drones."

Sloan turned to look at Rutherford. "That's your cue."

Rutherford stood up, bending at the waist to keep from bashing his head on the underside of the tram's roof. He said, "Excuse me," and started to climb over the seats in front of him to follow Clearman, but the look on the faces of Mrs. Clearman and her daughter made it clear that him stepping between them would not be excused.

Rutherford muttered, "Right. Sorry." He turned around and clambered over the back of his and Sloan's bench, stepping on the seat between two more of his teammates: Max, a jolly, bearded

Dutchman in a cardigan, and Professor Sherwood, a dignified black man in his sixties wearing a blue nylon windbreaker with "B-9" written on the back in vinyl letters.

The ride narrator said, "Most are called pests. A few are called pets. They're all called varmints, and they call this valley home."

Rutherford maneuvered himself over the back of the last row of seats, onto the rear of the tram and turned himself around to climb up onto the roof. He heard the buzz of Albert's camera drones, rushing in to capture whatever would happen next. Below that he could make out the ride's recorded narration explaining that small furry rodents survived the asteroid that wiped out the dinosaurs. On either wall, illustrations meant to look like cave paintings showed rats playing around a T. rex skeleton.

As his head rose above the edge of the roof, Rutherford saw Clearman crouching, preparing to leap off the back.

Seeing the man he was trying to escape literally pop up between him and freedom caused Clearman to recoil and scramble toward the front of the tram car.

Rutherford shouted, "Give it up, Clearman. You're going to jail."

Clearman bawled, "It was an accident!"

"Of course it was. Nobody plans to run over a nun who fosters sick kittens while she's out delivering Meals on Wheels."

Clearman spun around and said, "I didn't mean to hit her! I was looking at a text! That doesn't make me a bad guy!"

"Maybe not, but driving away, after rolling her body into a ditch, covering her with brush, and taking the dessert from the meal she was delivering does."

"I never!"

"We searched your car in the parking lot. The dents match, and we found crumbs!"

"It was carrot cake! I love carrot cake!"

"Well, you're not the first criminal brought down by their love for . . . a baked good."

Clearman skittered forward onto the next tram car in line, employing a move that was a weird combination of a dive and a hop.

Rutherford pictured himself doing the same thing in video on the internet, and said, "Maybe this is a job for the bees."

Sherwood said, "My hive is in the van, but I don't think it's practical to release the bees in this situation. Of course, if you had let me bring Her Majesty—"

Terri said, "We're not going to argue about this right now, Professor."

As Rutherford clawed his way onto the tram roof, the ride narrator said, "All of the mammals that exist today, including the cows and pigs we eat, the horses and camels we ride, the dogs and cats we keep as pets, and us, came from the lowly varmint!"

Rutherford grumbled, "We could've just picked him up at work, but no, we decide to grab him at the zoo."

Terri said, "We wanted him somewhere he'd be off balance, and the zoo makes an interesting background. It's a good place to make our move."

Rutherford ran forward, leaping to the next tram car. "I understand all of that, except your use of the word *our*."

The walls rolling past the tram on both sides made Rutherford feel as if he was moving much faster than he knew he was. He saw Clearman two cars ahead, jumping from roof to roof, permanently denting each one and terrifying the families beneath.

"Where's he gonna go?" Rutherford asked. "He gets to the front and then what, jumps down and spends five minutes getting slowly run over by the entire train?"

"Not if you catch him first."

The drones grew louder as they took up positions behind and above Rutherford to document the pursuit.

Albert said, "Drones in position. Recording."

Rutherford ran into the wind, leaping from car to car every third step.

Terri said, "Rutherford, don't flap your arms like that when you jump. It looks ridiculous."

"I'm trying to keep my balance!"

"Well try not to flap your arms as you do it."

"How long do these walls go on for?!"

Albert said, "Another hundred yards."

"Really?!"

Sloan said, "The humble varmint has a long and noble history. We only just got to the plague."

"Why do zoos have to make everything into a ride or a guided experience these days?" Sherwood asked. "What was wrong with just walking around, looking at animals?"

Max said, "Once the corporations that run these places mastered controlling the animals, it was only a matter of time before they turned their attention to controlling the people. Governments will pay handsomely for either of those services."

Clearman perched on the roof of the diesel tractor pulling the tram, searching for somewhere to jump off. The walls on either side and the road directly in front of the tram offered no options.

Rutherford, now only one car behind him, shouted, "Nowhere to go!"

Clearman let out a pained cry and rushed Rutherford, grabbing him around the throat with both hands. Rutherford put his hands up between Clearman's arms and pushed outward, trying to break his grip, but failed. He attempted to spin himself free, and when that also didn't work, tried spitting his matchstick in Clearman's face. In desperation, Rutherford dug his thumbs into Clearman's mouth, executing a move the other boys at his elementary school had called *the double fishhook.*

The two of them stood there, Rutherford struggling for a breath, Clearman's mouth stretched open, tongue lolling as he bellowed in outrage and discomfort as the drones captured the whole thing from three angles.

At last, Clearman let go. Rutherford gratefully gasped for air, too distracted by how good it felt to breathe to wonder why Clearman dropped to lay flat on his belly on the roof of the tram. The drones following the tram shot straight up, and in his ear five voices shouted his name in unison. He spun around just in time to collide with a catwalk that stretched between the two walls.

The handrail hit him square in the gut, knocking the wind out of him. He rolled gracelessly over the railing and tumbled headfirst onto the walkway.

Clearman passed beneath the bridge, then rose to his hands and knees, looked back, and smiled at Rutherford, who was still lying on the catwalk, losing ground.

Rutherford climbed over the front catwalk railing down onto the tram again; he was now several cars back. He could see that the walls on either side of the track would end soon. "Looks like there's someplace for him to go! What's ahead?"

Clearman waved at Rutherford and leapt off the side of the tram, out of sight.

Albert said, "Animal habitats."

"Great!" Rutherford said. "We have him in a cage, then!"

Rutherford finally passed the end of the wall and saw Clearman below, limping in a simulated forest clearing. Small dark shapes moved around the outside of the space.

Terri said, "Go in after him before he finds a way out!"

Rutherford ran backward on the tram to hold his position above Clearman. "What animals are in there?"

"Varmints! Now get in there!"

Rutherford, cursing under his breath, leapt from the moving tram, over the edge of the plexiglass wall, and landed hard on the Astroturf-covered concrete floor, rolling to break the fall. He rose to his feet and turned to face the only other human in the enclosure.

Clearman pressed his back against the plexiglass wall.

Rutherford asked, "What's your problem?" Then he looked around.

Raccoons dotted the sides and rear of the enclosure. They had probably scattered when Clearman fell from the sky into their midst. Now they formed a semicircle around Clearman and Rutherford, blocking the path to the exit, on the other side of which a surprisingly worried looking zookeeper fumbled with the lock.

Rutherford didn't get it. He looked down at the furry little creatures with their cute bandit masks. For a moment he thought about getting one as a pet.

Rutherford grabbed Clearman by the shoulder and took a step toward the exit. All of the raccoons bared their yellow teeth and hissed. Rutherford and Clearman instinctively leapt back against the window, the place farthest from all the raccoons.

Rutherford gasped, "Jeez!"

Clearman said, "I know, right?!"

Rutherford attempted to draw in closer to Clearman, instinctively looking to his fellow human for security when surrounded by slowly advancing animals, but Clearman started climbing onto Rutherford's back. As the raccoons came within striking range, Rutherford drew his sidearm: a modern replica of the TP-82, a massive handgun with three barrels, two for shotgun cartridges and a third for pistol rounds underneath, originally designed for cosmonauts to use in fighting off wolves and bears after landing in the Kazakhstani wilderness, thus making it one of the most badass objects on earth. He fired a shotgun round straight up into the sky. The raccoons withdrew a few feet. Clearman shouted, "Agh! My ears!"

For a moment everything in the enclosure was still, as if frozen in a diorama. Clearman clung to Rutherford's shoulders and waist like a living backpack. As Rutherford pointed his gigantic smoking gun at the small furry creatures, he glanced back over his shoulder. The last car of the tram rolled past.

Clearman's family and Rutherford's teammates stared at them. Max smiled and stepped off the moving tram as if it were no more difficult than stepping down from a barstool.

Clearman regained his senses after the shock of Rutherford's shotgun blast and resumed his frantic climbing, using Rutherford as a ladder. Rutherford grunted, "Will you stop that!?"

The raccoons began advancing again, hissing and baring their teeth. Clearman's weight lifted from Rutherford's shoulders as he pulled himself up to the top of the enclosure's plexiglass viewing wall. Once Clearman was solidly perched, Rutherford reached up. "Now pull me up!"

Clearman looked down at Rutherford, then at the raccoons. "Sorry, man."

Rutherford jumped as high as he could and barely managed to get a few fingers hooked on the wall's edge. Beyond the glass, Max stretched his arms up toward Clearman. "Sir, I will help you down."

"No. Just—get out of the way."

"No, please," Max insisted. "Come down. I'll help you."

Clearman started to lower himself down the other side of the glass wall. Max rushed forward and grabbed Clearman by the hips. "Here we go. Careful now."

Clearman said, "Let go. I don't nee—"

To the normal observer, what Max gave Clearman looked like *help*, but Rutherford knew better. Even as he was occupied by his attempt to scale a smooth plexiglass wall, he marveled at the efficiency and subtlety of the beating Max provided.

Holding his hips *for support*, Max yanked Clearman down off the wall. He then set Clearman down on his feet at an ungainly angle, with a twist in a direction the human ankle found unpleasant.

"Oh," Max said. "Careful."

Clearman fell to the ground. Max said, "Watch it now," holding him by both hands, slowing his descent, but also preventing him from in any way breaking his own fall. Max let go in time for Clearman to fall the last foot or so to the ground, just enough to knock the wind out of him. Clearman lay on the ground, gasping. He tried to roll over and spring to his feet, but Max knelt beside him and pressed down reassuringly on his sternum, pinning him down.

"Just rest," Max said. "You're safe now."

Clearman thrashed and struggled but couldn't knock Max's hand away, leaving him captured and helpless.

Max said, "Good work, Rutherford."

Rutherford had one elbow hooked over the top of the wall but was having difficulty getting a good grip with the other hand. He struggled for traction on the smooth plexiglass and kicked his feet just out of range of the half-dozen angry raccoons gathered beneath. "Thanks, Max. You too."

TWO

The hotel conference center rang with laughter as the gathered press watched the already-famous clip taken just hours earlier, of Julius Clearman standing on Rutherford's shoulder and head, pulling himself to the top of the clear wall while Rutherford pointed his immense firearm at the approaching raccoons.

As the clip ended, the screen split up into multiple boxes, each showing some different still or moving image related to the case. There were photos of the victim, Clearman's mug shot, Rutherford chasing Clearman along the top of the tram, a black Audi with a dented fender, Clearman falling to the ground *despite* Max's help, an adorable raccoon, and a piece of carrot cake.

The press's attention returned to the man of the hour, billionaire innovator Vincent Capp, standing behind a podium on a raised stage. The team stood in a line beside the stage. They had done their part: capturing the guilty party and getting some attention in the process. Now it was Capp's turn to do his job: bask in that attention.

"Fortunately," Capp said, "the zookeepers were able to neutralize the situation before any raccoons were harmed.

Mr. Clearman has confessed to hitting the late Sister Elaine Camacho with his car, and while that does appear to have been an accident, hiding her body and fleeing the scene were not. The mayor and the chief of police have both issued letters of congratulations and gratitude, which I have added to the stack. As to the matter of the fifty-thousand-dollar reward for information leading to the capture of Sister Elaine's killer, my team, dubbed by some in the press as *the Authorities*, has certainly earned it. But they have decided not to file a claim."

As the press applauded, Sloan used the team's earpieces to say, "This is the first I've heard of it. Still, nice of us. Who offered that reward? I doubt it was her Meals on Wheels recipients, or her foster kittens."

Terri, the team's manager—a small black woman with bright eyes and a luminous smile—covered her mouth, speaking just loud enough for her team to hear. "It was offered by a nonprofit, founded by Mr. Capp."

Rutherford laughed and covered his own mouth. "He's turning down his own money."

Sloan said, "It costs him nothing and he looks like a hero twice. Even when he's magnanimous he comes out ahead. Laughing. Laughing."

Terri asked, "Albert, have you looked at modifying Sloan's voice synthesizer to make a laughing noise instead of just saying 'laughing'?"

Albert leaned closer to Terri and muttered, "Yes, but a flat, robotic *ha ha ha* sounds too sarcastic."

Max asked, "How about *ho ho ho*?"

Albert said, "Too jolly."

Capp said, "That concludes my planned remarks. Do any of you have any questions?"

Countless arms shot up, so many that Rutherford wondered if some of the reporters had raised both hands to double their odds of getting picked.

Capp pointed at a reporter, who asked, "Detective Rutherford, would you really have shot those raccoons?"

Terri leaned forward slightly and looked down the line at Rutherford, making sure he remembered the conversation they'd had earlier, the one in which she had told him to stop going on and on about how frightening the small, furry, woodland creatures had been, and then coached him what to say if asked a question like this.

Rutherford glanced at her to let her know he was going to play ball and clenched his jaw around the wooden match in his mouth. "Raccoon leaves me alone, I leave the raccoon alone. Raccoon wants trouble, it'll get trouble."

The next question was also for Rutherford. "This is the fifth high-profile crime in the Pacific Northwest your team has solved. All of them have involved some sort of foot chase. Detective Rutherford, is there something you're doing that causes people to run?"

Rutherford said, "I don't make them run. They make me chase them."

Capp said, "And I'd remind you that the serial billboard vandal in Bellingham didn't run. He fell. The doctors agreed that our man, *Cement Shoes* Rutherford, probably saved him from serious injury, like a human airbag. You know that. We've all seen the video online. I could show it right now if that'd be helpful."

Rutherford said, "I don't think we need to."

Capp laughed. "Oh, let's go ahead anyway. I know the techs keep it cued up."

On the screen behind Capp, Rutherford ran toward a billboard shouting, "Come down! Come down right now! No! Be careful! Hold on! OOF!"

Any further dialog from the screen was drowned out by the reporters laughing as the footage showed Rutherford struggling, first to hold the vandal up, then, after they both fell, to push the vandal off of him, then finally to catch the vandal as he sprinted away. The perpetrator stopped after a few seconds as he was swarmed by Professor Sherwood's famous crime-fighting bees.

* * *

The team filed out of the conference room, down the hall into a smaller room set aside as a place for them to hide while the reporters left, sparing them the risk of answering any unsanctioned questions outside of Capp and his publicity team's supervision.

Rutherford muttered, "I don't see the big deal. They guy was hanging from the railing before he slipped. He only fell two feet before I caught him."

"It's not the hanging or the falling," Sloan said. "It's the catching. It's the way he landed on your face with his arms and legs flailing, and you stumbling around trying to keep from dropping him."

Sherwood said, "And the way you both were yelling the whole time. No words, just you both going *whoa, ohh, oohwoa!*"

Albert laughed, "Yeah, but Rutherford's voice was muffled by the guy's butt."

"His butt wasn't in my face. It was his lower back by that point. Like, the love handle, tramp-stamp area."

Sloan asked, "Is that better?"

"It's more accurate."

"I think that went well," Capp said, sweeping into the room behind them, drawing a small army of handlers, flacks, facilitators, and security along in his wake. "The killer's in jail, the arrest went viral, and no raccoons were harmed. All in all, a fine job. Professor, it would have been nice to get your bees involved more visibly, but I understand why we couldn't. The zoo was the wrong place for them. People react one way when they see footage of bees swarming a person. They'd react very differently seeing bees swarm an animal. People care about animals."

Sloan said, "Makes you feel good and bad about humanity at the same time, doesn't it?"

"Yes, an uncontrolled swarm was out of the question," Sherwood said. "But if we had deployed *Her Majesty*—"

Terri's smile briefly became gritted teeth before relaxing into a smile again. "Professor, I've told you, I'm not comfortable using your new invention without more field testing."

"And today would have been an excellent field test."

"No, Professor, when I say field testing, I mean testing out in a field, far from where anyone can get hurt."

Capp said, "Hey Professor, I wanted to ask you, have you ever thought about bedbugs?"

"No," Sherwood said. "I try not to."

Capp said, "Quite right. I do think about them though."

Sloan said, "Exterminating all of them, I hope."

"Tempting, but shortsighted," Capp said. "I think bedbugs could have tremendous applications. They're small enough to be virtually invisible, cause tremendous discomfort and emotional distress, and are next to impossible to get rid of."

Professor Sherwood shook his head. "All reasons I really don't want to work with them, sir."

"I understand that, Professor, but do think about it. Science is worth suffering for, after all. In the meantime, I might just leak the idea that you're experimenting with crime-fighting bedbugs as an experiment in psychological warfare. Once you suspect you have bedbugs, you feel them even if they aren't there. We could have criminals turning themselves in to stop the psychosomatic itching. Rutherford, I'm very happy with how today went, but I do have a couple of notes to discuss. First, the match, it isn't working. Why'd we get rid of the cigar again?"

Rutherford said, "Cancer."

Albert said, "At first people thought vaping might not be bad for you, but now it looks like that wasn't the case. It turns out it's not a good idea to breath anything you can see."

"Okay," Capp said. "I see where we might want to avoid having Rutherford inhale any carcinogens."

Rutherford said, "Might?"

Capp said. "Does the match have any special gadgets built in? Any purpose?"

"It can start a fire." Albert shrugged, a bit embarrassed. "I'm working on some ideas, but the best thing I've got is to make it a much more potent match, like a super incendiary thermite match, but Rutherford didn't like the sound of that."

Rutherford shook his head. "Carrying an explosive in my mouth? No. I didn't like the sound of that one bit."

Sloan asked, "How about a toothpick?"

Albert said, "Maybe I could make the toothpick out of titanium, colored to look like wood. I could make the ends razor sharp. He could take it out of his mouth and flick it at people, as a weapon."

"Yeah," Rutherford said. "Or I could just spit blood at them from the cuts I'd have on my gums and tongue."

Max asked, "How about a lolly?"

Professor Sherwood said, "Yeah! A lollipop! Like Kojak."

Capp asked, "Albert, can you make anything out of that?"

"Hmm. There are some new plastic explosives that are transparent and can come in bright colors. Maybe I could put a detonator in the stick."

"No! I'm sorry, but no," Rutherford blurted. "I don't want anything that explodes or burns in my mouth."

Sloan said, "That explains why we never have Mexican for lunch when it's his turn to pick."

Capp looked Rutherford in the eye and smiled. "The other thing I want to discuss—Terri says that you're doing everything she tells you to do."

Rutherford smiled. "Good."

Capp's smile faded. He shook his head. "No. Not really. Terri shouldn't be having to tell you what to do. We didn't hire you because we wanted you to be an extension of Terri. We hired you because we wanted you."

Rutherford stammered for a moment, at a loss, and looked down at the soiled T-shirt, jeans, and leather jacket they'd given him to wear instead of the tailored suits he preferred. "Which me do you want? The fictional me who wants to do the stuff you order me to, or the real me, who thinks almost all of it is a terrible idea? Look, I get it. I mean, I think I get it. You want me to do the kinds of things that cops on TV and in movies do, but real cops almost never do that stuff. They train us not to, and I sailed right through the training because I didn't want to do any of that in the first place. I'm a real cop. Every instinct I have tells me not to do the things Terri tells me to do."

"But you do it when you're told to," Terri said. "And you do it well."

Capp said, "We just have to coach you up to where you don't need to be told."

Rutherford shook his head. "I have some very clear ideas about what's right and what's wrong, and you're asking me to do things I know are wrong."

Capp said, "No."

Terri agreed. "Not at all."

Capp shrugged. "But in a sense, yes."

Terri nodded. "Exactly."

Rutherford squinted at them.

Capp said, "We like it that you have a brain, and that you know right from wrong. When a situation pops up that calls for you to take action, we want you to use your brain, determine what's right and what's wrong, but then to go a step further. Look at the course of action that you think is wrong. Ask yourself if there's a course of action that is right, but looks wrong, or one that's wrong, but *the right kind of wrong*. The kind of wrong that will work."

"You're asking me to ignore my instincts."

"Not at all. The opposite. I want you to listen well to what your instincts tell you to do, then do something else. Your job is to generate press and fight crime, preferably at the same time. Today on top of the tram you did that, but Terri can't always be talking you through it; you need to take the initiative. And for the record, fighting on top of anything that looks like a train is a plus. The marketing stooges say it adds a sense of danger while also being reassuringly familiar."

Capp paused, leaving an opening for Rutherford to say that he understood.

Rutherford didn't say anything.

Capp said, "I can see on your face that I've overcomplicated this and freaked you out. It'll be okay, son. You'll get the idea."

Rutherford relaxed a bit.

Capp continued. "Or you won't, and we'll replace you with someone who does."

Rutherford cringed.

Capp gripped his shoulder, "But either way, you need to understand—it'll be all right in the end."

Rutherford said, "Yeah."

Capp said, "For me and the team. We'll be fine either way. For you, it'd be a huge wasted opportunity that would haunt you for the rest of your life."

THREE

Rutherford applied the absolute minimum pressure he could manage to the throttle of the van, causing the tires to barely break loose around the corner into the marina parking lot, emitting only the slightest chirp on the usually-wet road. He had read that some race car drivers in the forties and fifties used to drive with their right foot bare so they could operate the throttle with more subtlety. Rutherford considered driving his company-issued, dangerously torque-heavy prototype steam-powered van that way, but the idea of having to either chase a perp in one shoe or give them a head start while he laced up was a non-starter. He had proposed those running shoes designed to make it feel as if one was running barefoot, but when Terri looked them up online the first ones she saw were the kind with separated toes, and that ended that.

The van fit into his assigned parking space with only a few inches to spare, which wouldn't have been a problem if his neighbors on either side drove small cars. One drove an SUV that took up even more room than the van, and the other drove a crew-cab pickup, which also took up all of the space in their slot. This meant neither Rutherford nor his neighbors could open their doors. The neighbors blamed him for this, even though he didn't paint the lines on the pavement, and their vehicles were larger than his. The heavily modified seventies vintage van was different, and as such attracted the blame. Of course, one of the ways the van was different was that he could pass between the front seats and the swiveling captain's chairs in the second row, over the back of the rear bench seat, and out the back door more easily than the SUV driver could, or than the pickup driver could slither out the cab's rear window.

The fact that the parking space problem inconvenienced Rutherford less than it inconvenienced his neighbors did little to make them feel better about it.

Rutherford walked across the parking lot and onto the dock, past the houseboats lining both sides so tightly one could scarcely see the water between them. He found it ironic that people who lived on boats tended to have a lot of house pride. Curb appeal mattered tremendously to those who had no curbs.

Some of the homes looked like beautifully maintained boats in which someone chose to live. Others looked like pleasantly eccentric, well-kept houses that someone chose to float on the water. Most had at least one occupant at home, near enough to a window to glare at Rutherford as he passed, and Rutherford would have to pass all of them since his home—what looked to be a dilapidated Airstream trailer lashed to an old barge—occupied the slip at the very end. He had the best view of Lake Union and the parts of Seattle that surrounded it, and everyone else had the best view of his faux-derelict vessel, between them and the scenery. Furthermore, anyone floating past on a boat couldn't help noticing Rutherford's rust heap and anyone walking down the dock was forced to look at it.

The smell of salt air and seaweed filled his nose. The feeling of cold dampness seemed to seep through his clothes and into his bones. The sound of wood creaking and waves slapping the pilings pattered quietly behind everything else. Rutherford had always heard about the romance of the sea and the soothing effect the nautical life had on the human spirit. Before he lived on the water he simply didn't get it, but now he understood that it was a complete crock of crap.

Rutherford reached the end of the dock and walked down the short plank to his rusty, oil-stained barge and artistically grime-covered Airstream trailer. As he put the key in the door, he heard a familiar voice bark, "Hey, pal."

Rutherford said, "Hi, Brian," as he turned to face his neighbor, a man with gray hair, gray skin, and a light-blue cap with an embroidered captain's wheel on the crown.

Brian said, "I thought we'd agreed that you would get your place cleaned up."

"I never agreed to that."

"Well, I told you that if you didn't, I'd have to contact the marina owners and file a complaint."

"And I said that was fine. Oh, I think I see the confusion. You thought I was saying I was fine with cleaning the place up, but I meant that I was fine with you complaining to the marina owners. Sorry for the confusion. My fault entirely."

Rutherford smiled at Brian, who slunk back into his houseboat, grumbling with disgust. Rutherford was polite and pleasant by nature. He had learned that when someone dressed like a walking attitude problem, but behaved in a cheerful and positive manner, it was taken as extreme sarcasm— a quirk of human nature that had already saved his job more than once.

The idea of Brian complaining about his behavior didn't worry Rutherford at all, since the marina was owned by a long trail of shell companies and dummy corporations that led to Vince Capp. The complaint would actually help Rutherford maintain good favor with his boss. If Rutherford were to clean up his barge and behave like a model neighbor, he'd probably get fired and lose his rent-free houseboat on Lake Union, a perk that saved him more money in rent every month than he used to get paid as a patrol officer for the Seattle Police Department.

Once inside the trailer, Rutherford drew his arms in close to his body, trying to keep his faux-weathered leather jacket from touching any of the walls or built-in furnishings. Despite the trailer's outward appearance, the interior had come to him in pristine, brand-new condition, and for the most part he had managed to keep it that way. Unfortunately, while the fake weathering rubbed off of the jacket with minimal friction, he'd learned the hard way that it was nearly impossible to clean off of teak veneer.

He peeled off the jacket and his work clothes beneath. He tossed the clothes straight into the hamper and hung the jacket in the special closet he set aside for his work uniform to keep it separate from the clothes he purchased himself and actually enjoyed, but never got to wear.

After a quick shower, Rutherford slipped into his favorite pair of baby-blue Egyptian cotton pajamas and made himself a cup of coffee, thinking about his day as he used a long-spouted kettle to carefully wet the grounds in the cone filter evenly and at the perfect rate for maximum flavor extraction. He had a sip and looked at the mug, satisfied. When he saw that he'd grabbed the mug that read, "I'm having coffee because I can't drink meth," his satisfaction diminished.

Before going back outside to unwind, he threw on an ancient, stained terry-cloth bathrobe some thrift-store donor had long ago stolen from the Stardust Hotel and Casino in Las Vegas before it was demolished. He put on a pair of old, unlaced Reebok high-tops with wool-lined slippers hidden within for comfort and went outside. He sat on a lawn chair on his barge deck, watching floatplanes land on the lake and evening commuters pour into and out of downtown on the Ship Canal Bridge.

He looked down at his phone. He had a text from his older sister, consisting of three periods, her signal that he should call her. She wanted to talk, but she never called him, or at least she never called him unless he'd ignored one too many prompts to call her. When she did call under those circumstances, the conversation seldom went well.

After a few rings, she picked up. "Sinclair, what's up?"

"You texted me to call you, Vanessa."

"Yes, because I wanted to ask you what's up. What, a sister can't take an interest in her little brother's life?"

"Sure she can. It's great that she does. Her brother just wished she'd be less confrontational about it."

"Can't help you with that."

"Actually, you're the only one who can."

"Well, I'm not gonna. I saw your latest video, the one where you were pointing your gun at the raccoons."

"Yeah, not my finest moment."

"I'll say. Why didn't you take the shot?"

"I didn't want to kill the raccoons. And kids were watching. They'd have been horrified."

"Isn't doing that kind of thing part of your job? Besides, the kids would have thought it was cool. Their parents would have been horrified."

"Maybe Capp hired the wrong Rutherford."

"Don't be silly, Sinclair. I couldn't do what you do."

"No?"

"Never. I have my pride. Look, what's wrong? Isn't Capp happy with your work today? I mean, sure, you went soft on the raccoons, but you looked pretty cool running on the top of that tram."

"Really?"

"Yeah, kinda. I mean, it was a tram. There was only so cool you could look, but you looked that cool, at least."

"Yeah, well, Capp's happy with what I'm doing, he's just not happy about how I'm doing it. It's like it's not enough that I follow orders I think are wrong, they want me to do these things on my own because I've convinced myself they're right."

"Well maybe if you keep doing the stuff they want you to, it'll start coming natural. In the meantime you could just throw in some things on your own. Little flourishes, you know, to show them you're trying."

"Like what?"

"I dunno. Cop stuff. Oh, you could run real fast then slide across the hood of the car! That's a cool cop move."

"No it isn't. Real police never do that. It isn't any faster than running around the nose of the car, you risk turning an ankle when you land, and it's bad for the paint. Besides, I drive a van. It has no hood."

Rutherford caught sight of his neighbor Brian, sitting on his own deck, glaring back at him. Out of instinct, Rutherford raised his pro-meth coffee mug in greeting. Coffee slopped out and landed down the front of the bathrobe. Brian looked away as Rutherford surveyed the damage, groaning.

"What's the matter?" Vanessa asked.

"Oh, I spilled coffee on my robe. I'm going to have to go spray it."

"Is that what your boss would want you to do?"

"No, he wouldn't. But he wants me to be rebellious, so I'm gonna do it anyway."

"This isn't the kind of rebelliousness he wants."

"Sticking to the kind of rebelliousness your boss wants isn't really rebelliousness, now is it?"

FOUR

Rutherford steered the van through pre-dawn traffic. The night before, he and every other member of the team had gone to bed believing that they would wake at the normal time and go about a normal day. Instead, they'd been awakened by phone calls at five twenty with the news that they would be getting up at that moment and flying to Los Angeles immediately, for a stay of indeterminate length. This led all of them to pack hastily, with limited information, while still bleary with sleep—circumstances that are not conducive to underpacking. Now they sat in the van surrounded by their luggage, including a gigantic, old, mint-green Samsonite suitcase Professor Sherwood held on his lap. A grid of haphazardly drilled holes perforated one side of its scuffed exterior, and to nobody's surprise, it emitted a constant buzz.

Sloan swiveled her captain's chair to look at Albert and Sherwood in the back of the van. "You made him a portable hive to carry around?"

Albert said, "I did not make that."

Sherwood smiled and rubbed the side of the suitcase like he was petting a beloved dog. "Yes, this is all me. Don't get me wrong, Albert does some great things with 3D printers and machined aluminum, but all you really need is a thrift-store find to modify, and some particle board. I spent twenty bucks on materials and got a portable apiary with enough extra storage to carry Her Majesty."

Terri twisted around in the front passenger seat to look back at him. "Professor, I didn't tell you to bring Her Majesty."

"I took the initiative."

"Well don't take any more initiative. You've had enough." She settled back down into her seat and sipped at her coffee, trying to will herself into full consciousness.

Rutherford glanced at her. She noticed and held up her cup. "Thanks for the coffee, Rutherford. It's delicious."

Rutherford said, "Thanks. It's a blend from a shop in Fremont. It can be a bit harsh, but I use the pour-over method. That knocks down the more discordant notes. And I do realize that what I just said wasn't very in character."

Terri shrugged. "No it wasn't, so don't talk like that in public. But please keep the coffee coming."

Max, back in one of the two rotating captain's chairs that constituted the van's second row, smiled. "Caffeine is an addictive substance. We drink it in the mornings because we think it gives us energy and makes us feel better, but tell me this, when you don't have your coffee how is it you feel, specifically? Do you have headaches? Are you irritable? Do you feel as if you can't think straight?"

He paused for someone, anyone to answer. Everyone glared straight ahead silently, which was all the answer he needed.

"Would it surprise you to learn," Max continued, "that I have just described the symptoms of caffeine withdrawal? Drinking coffee every morning creates an addiction that in turn generates the need to drink coffee every morning. We think we are not morning people, when in fact what we are is drug addicts."

Professor Sherwood said, "You're drinking coffee too, Max."

"Yes, but I know I am an addict and am at peace with it. I think of it as a sacrament that gives me powers, but at a cost, like your . . . What was his name? . . . Popeye! With his canned spinach, yes? He gets great strength, but at the cost of having to eat wet leaves and living with freakishly bulging forearms."

Sloan's artificial voice remained bright and cheerful regardless of how she felt. "See, I always liked to think that the spinach wasn't really good for Popeye. I figure he's like the Hulk, and choking down a can of spinach was just a surefire way to make himself angry."

Albert looked back down to his phone. "I know it would tick me off. Okay everyone, we've got the videoconference set up. If you'll all look at the screen in the dashboard, we should have Mr. Capp any second."

The screen—really just a tablet mounted as if it were a car stereo—displayed a progress bar for a moment, then cut to an image of Vince Capp in pajamas, sitting at a table, eating a bowl of cereal, while members of his executive team stood around in full business attire.

Capp said, "Good morning."

The entire team said good morning back, more or less in unison.

Capp asked, "Can you see me okay?"

Terri said, "Yes, sir. Can you see us?"

"Don't need to. First off, thanks for getting rounded up and on the road so early on such short notice, everyone. I wouldn't have made you do it without a good reason. I've got something exciting to tell you, gang. It hasn't hit the news yet, but Emery Hindman has been murdered."

Terri frowned.

Max tilted his head to the side. "Was he someone you dislike?"

Rutherford said, "He's an actor. He's been on a few TV shows."

Albert said, "Yeah, he's on some period piece. An old-timey detectives kinda thing."

Capp said, "It's called *Deer Stalker*. It's a reworked version of Sherlock Holmes. I'll have my tech guy George put a picture of him up on the screen here."

The team sat silently for a few seconds while one of Capp's hangers-on frantically stabbed a finger at a tablet. The dashboard screen displayed a promotional image from the show. Rutherford glanced down at the picture of a beefy, blandly good-looking white guy in his midthirties with a bushy mustache that merged with his sideburns.

Sloan said, "I've seen a few episodes. The show takes place in the 1890s. Their version of Holmes is a Native American named Deer Stalker who lives at the Smithsonian."

"What is he, a caretaker?" Rutherford asked.

Sloan said, "An exhibit. Which is awful, but it's the kind of thing they used to do. Anyway, he solves crimes in Washington, DC, using logic, and he's an outsider so he sees things the police don't. He's escorted by a burly know-it-all anthropologist named Watson."

Capp said, "Played by our victim. Was he any good?"

"I guess. His main job was to be condescending early in each episode, then astonished at the end, and occasionally he'd strip to the waist and shout 'Put up your dukes, sir!' I assume you're happy because this is the high-profile, national-scale crime you've been waiting for?"

"I am, and it is, but you don't know the half of it. The *LA Times* and all of the major cable news channels got an email this morning just after the murder took place. George, please put the email on their screen."

Again, after some panicked screen poking, the letter came up. The team in the van fell silent as they read.

Rutherford said, "I don't wanna take my eyes off the road here. What does it say?"

Sloan said, "I just killed a Watson. Tomorrow, I will do it again, and again, and again. Every day from now on a Watson will die until there are no Watsons left. None of the Sherlocks you people seem to love so much can stop me."

Capp said, "Albert, could you work on getting Sloan a less cheerful tone of voice to use when she reads this kind of thing out loud? That gave me the willies."

Sloan said, "I won't use it."

"So, what's that mean?" Rutherford asked while frantically head checking to merge into the right lane before an off-ramp. "He's going to kill someone named Watson every day until he's caught?"

Capp said, "No. The first victim wasn't named Watson, he played Watson. See, Sherlock Holmes is as famous a character as Superman or Mickey Mouse, but Sherlock's in the public domain. Any screenwriter who's out of ideas, which is most of them on any given day, can just tweak Holmes's situation a bit and call it a new creation."

"But how often can they actually do that and get away with it?"

Capp said, "Right now there are four different TV and film adaptations of Sherlock Holmes in production in the United States alone, including *Deer Stalker*. There are three more scripts in various stages of development, but none of them have a solid cast locked in, and I doubt any actors will sign on to play Watson until this killer is captured."

Max said, "Have you ever gotten to know an actor?"

Capp said, "No. Dated a few, but I didn't really talk to them much. There's also a series in Japan, the title translates to something like *Days Gone By Crime Sniffer*. And a pilot a couple of years back that didn't get picked up called *Holmes-Boy*, about a rapper who solved crimes. His sidekick was his hype man, a white kid who kept shouting 'What-son?!' Typical middle-aged Caucasian's idea of black youth culture kind of stuff. We don't think that actor's in danger."

Professor Sherwood said, "That's a shame."

"The point," Capp continued, "is there are three more Watsons in Hollywood at the moment, and in the note he said *again* three times. I doubt that's a coincidence. And that's why I had to get you all out of bed and ship you to Los Angeles."

Sloan said, "That means we have one day before he kills again, and after that, three more days before the last Watson's dead and the killer disappears. We need to catch the murderer as quickly as possible."

"Yes," Capp said, "and I want the record to show that I stated clearly that catching the murderer before anyone else was killed would be the best possible outcome. I mean, in theory, if you don't catch the killer today, and he goes on to kill another Watson tomorrow, that would only get that much more attention, and make it a bigger deal when you do get them. It'd be terrible for the victims and their families of course, but probably better for us."

Sloan said, "Sometimes you amaze me."

Capp said, "Thanks."

"That wasn't a compliment."

"You decide what you say. I decide how I take it."

Professor Sherwood said, "So the first victim is in Los Angeles. Where do the other shows film?"

Capp said, "Same. All of them are made in Los Angeles."

"Then really this isn't a national case," Sherwood said. "It's just a local case in Los Angeles."

"National news is made up of medium or large stories that take place in Los Angeles, New York, or Washington, DC, and horrifying disasters that take place anywhere else. The LAPD knows to expect you, and they've agreed to allow you access to their crime scenes, the ability to question suspects after they've had first crack at them, and to share certain basic information. But you can't count on any further cooperation than that, so no access to their CSI findings."

Terri said, "That's a problem."

"No," Capp said. "It's an opportunity to create a corporate partnership with the CartFulls corporation."

"CartFulls?" Terri asked. "The superstores?"

"Yup. I'm sure you're all familiar. You must have seen their ads."

"Yes," Max nearly shouted. "The ones with the animated shopping cart that's always complaining about the big, heavy loads of savings the customers pile into him."

Albert said, "Cary the Cart! I love those commercials."

Rutherford imitated the overly enthusiastic delivery of an actor portraying a shopper. "Look at the low price on these fifty-pound bags of dog food! I'm gonna buy three!"

He, Albert, and Max, all in unison, imitated the cart's depressive voice. "Three bags? Oooh nooo!"

Sloan said, "The best part is at the end when they show the CartFulls logo, and Cary rolls by straining under the weight. I can't explain it, but I love watching that cart suffer."

"We enjoy the misery of cartoon mascots because we know it is not real," Max said. "The Trix rabbit is eternally denied the cereal he craves. The Lucky Charms leprechaun is tenaciously pursued by greedy children. The Hamburger Helper talking glove assists in the making of a meal he can feel, but never taste."

"How, exactly, will CartFulls be helping us?" Terri asked. "Are we getting a discount on supplies?"

"No," Capp said. "It's a little-known fact, but CartFulls happens to operate one of the finest independent forensics labs in the country. They started it to help solve theft cases in their stores, but over the years they've grown the operation and now they regularly sell their services to other companies looking to root out theft or industrial espionage. They have a large lab in Los Angeles, and have assigned a team to help with the case. Their leader is a Dr. Claire Romero. She'll meet you at the crime scene."

Rutherford said, "We're here," as he pulled up next to an airplane hangar. One of Capp's private jets sat out front; like all of the jets in Capp's fleet, its bare aluminum skin was buffed to a high sheen. The reflective surface and rounded shape of the plane meant that some facet of the jet would invariably reflect the sun directly into an onlooker's eyes, forcing them to either look away or put on dark glasses—unless the plane was in Seattle, as it was this morning. The reflected early-morning cloud cover made the plane look as if it were cast from solid pewter.

A small army of white-gloved baggage handlers in smart-looking black coveralls swarmed the van, opening the sliding side door and taking the team's luggage away to the plane's hold. The team started unbuckling their seat belts and opening their doors, but Capp stopped them. "Hang on a second. There's still one more thing to cover."

As the attendants reached into the van and took hold of the buzzing suitcase, Sherwood said, "That goes in the passenger compartment, please."

Terri asked, "Does it have to?"

"Yes. It's the only safe way for them to travel."

Terri said, "Safe for the bees. Not necessarily for us."

The professor shook his head. "If the plane jostles hard enough to break that suitcase open, we'll have much bigger problems than bees in the cabin. The bees will be a welcome distraction to get your mind off the fiery plane crash."

Capp turned to his assistants. "Make a note. I never fly anywhere with them." He turned back to the camera. "You need to know; your transportation will be waiting for you at the airport when you land. You won't have your van. You'll be traveling in a loaner van, from a company I'm a major investor in called TurkMO."

Albert said, "Really? I didn't know you were involved with TurkMO."

"I'm keeping it quiet for now, you know, in case there are any accidents or injuries."

Terri narrowed her eyes. "Accidents *or* injuries? We're going to get transportation from something that might cause injuries?"

"Injuries that might not be accidental?" Sloan added.

Capp shook his head and waved his hands, trying to erase the last few seconds. "Of course, any injuries will be accidental.

TurkMO has a new angle on ride sharing and autonomous cars. People don't trust computers to drive, so the TurkMO vans use all of the sensors and safeguards of a self-driving car, but the control goes to a person driving from a remote location. The name comes from an industry term, "Mechanical Turk." It refers to when you make a human's work look like a machine is doing it. It's primarily a rideshare system right now, but when they go into wide release, it'll be an option on new cars. If you're tired or drunk, you can just hit a button and they'll drive your car home, with you in it."

Rutherford asked, "A stranger who's not there driving your car. Won't that be weird?"

"Yes, but not as weird as a stranger who *is* there driving your car. You'll have a minivan with a button on the dash to engage the service, but Rutherford's the only member of the team that can sit in the driver's seat."

"In case there's a high-speed chase?"

"It's a minivan. High-speed anything won't be an option. No, it's a legal thing. Since it's a commercial trial, I had to have you legally registered as a cabbie, so there's more good news. If you don't solve this case and I have to break up the team, that'll be another career option for you to fall back on."

FIVE

The victim's car remained in place while the police examined the crime scene, meaning that they had to cordon off part of three rows of parking spaces, block all through traffic, and rob the studio parking lot of nearly a third of its capacity. Cars clogged the rest of the lot, trolling along the remaining aisles in first gear like vultures circling. Drivers grumbled or shouted curses at their own dashboards while following the car in front of them as close as they could, living in fear of a space becoming available just ahead, and the slowpoke in front of them reversing to claim it, or even worse, as they passed, only to get snapped up by the bastard tailgating them.

Of course, once the drivers learned that their inconvenience was caused by someone's horrible death, they would feel terrible for having been angry. This wouldn't end their anger, just add a counterpoint of guilt.

Rutherford drove straight to the front of the lot and pulled up next to the crime scene tape in their loaner vehicle, which was either a surprisingly small full-sized van or the largest minivan Rutherford had ever seen. The interior reminded him of a dinner at Olive Garden: uninteresting but plentiful. It contained one hundred and seventy cubic feet of cloth seating and cargo space, and its three rows of seats carried the entire team in comfort, if not style. From the inside, the only clue that the van was not an average fleet vehicle was an extra LCD screen on the dash displaying the TurkMO logo: a large TM with a tiny TM in the corner, legally establishing that the larger TM was TurkMO's trademark.

Rutherford twisted around to look at the team: Terri riding shotgun as usual, and the others spread out in the second and third row of seats. "You all get out here. I'll find a parking spot and come join you as fast as I can."

Albert called out from the back seat, "That'll take forever. Just let the remote driver find a spot."

Rutherford winced. "Eh, I don't know. I don't really like that idea. When I was a kid I had a remote-controlled car, and I remember how I drove it."

Terri said, "Fair point, but TurkMO isn't hiring kids, I hope. The team needs you. Let the car park. That's an order."

Rutherford pressed the TM logo, which dissolved into a straight line extending across the screen. A few pleasant notes played, more than a chime but not quite a jingle, as the straight line warped and scribbled into the kind of graph that clearly represented the sound's waveform without telling the viewer any useful information.

A somewhat high-pitched male voice, cracking and clearly nervous, said, "Thank you for using TurkMO. I'm Toby, your remote driver. Where can I take you?"

Rutherford said, "Nowhere. I'm hoping you can just park the car."

"Absolutely, sir."

The team climbed out of the vehicle. Rutherford started to exit, but stopped and leaned in toward the dashboard. "Hey,

Toby, just promise me you'll be careful. I'm sorry. I'm just nervous. This is new to me."

"You have nothing to apologize for, sir. And nothing to worry about. I mean, even if I do crash, you won't be in the vehicle."

"No, but I'll be out there, where you might crash into me."

"That's unlikely."

"But not impossible."

"When you're ready to leave, the TurkMO app can lead you to the car, or you can just use the app to summon the car, and we'll drive it to you."

Rutherford muttered, "Like a guided missile," as he got out.

The outside of the van literally looked generic, with white paint and black plastic trim, except for the sensor pods on each corner and the mass of boxes, cables, and cameras covering the rooftop luggage rack.

Once everyone was out, the van pulled away slowly, traveled a distance roughly twice its own length, and waited to edge into traffic, which was not moving.

The team turned toward the crime scene. Photographers and officers swarmed around a black luxury car that sat with its driver's-side door open, blood dripping from every interior surface. Yellow plastic tape surrounded the car. Uniformed police officers surrounded the tape. Just inside the tape stood a woman in her late twenties, brown hair pulled back in a ponytail, with bright brown eyes and a professional smile. She carried a tablet computer and wore a crisp lab coat in t he signature purple color of the CartFulls corporation. A small image of Cary, the CartFulls shopping cart, was embroidered on the breast pocket. She talked to two police detectives: a younger man in a nice brown suit and a blue vest that didn't match but definitely did *go*, and an older man wearing a gray wool suit just expensive enough and just well cared for enough to tell the world that he cared about his professional appearance, but only just enough.

The detectives and the woman in the purple lab coat noticed their arrival and came forward to meet them at the yellow tape line.

As they approached, Rutherford saw a silver bracelet peeking out from the cuff of the woman's lab coat. Her black Mary Jane shoes were cute and of very high quality, not particularly expensive or showy, but unquestionably business appropriate. This was a woman after his own heart.

The woman scanned the team as they approached, but her gaze seemed to lock onto Rutherford. She glanced over his ratty sneakers, tattered jeans, rumpled T-shirt, and leather jacket, and finally looked him in the eyes. When she saw that he was watching her too she turned away, all trace of a smile erased instantly.

"Hello," she said, looking only at everyone but Rutherford. "You must be the Authorities. I'm Dr. Claire Romero. I was told to ask for Terri Wells?"

Terri shook Dr. Romero's hand and introduced herself, then the rest of the team. Everyone got a friendly greeting, including Sloan, whose helmet didn't seem all that out of place outdoors, in the middle of a parking lot. The only exception was Rutherford, whom she barely glanced at and greeted with a quick "Hi."

The younger of the two plainclothes cops came over to the group. "I'm Detective Frederick. This is my partner, Detective Burski. I gotta say, I'm impressed you got here from Seattle so fast."

Terri smiled as she shook their hands. "We flew nonstop, then drove directly from the airport to here. We wanted to get access to the scene while it's as fresh as possible."

Dr. Romero said, "The LAPD CSI team is just finishing up, then my team will get access. They aren't officially cooperating with us, but I spoke to their leader and I think they'll work with me. They're curious about my techniques, and a few CartFulls fifty-percent-off coupons didn't hurt."

Detective Burski said, "We've been told to cooperate with you up to a point. I look forward to us all finding that point together."

After Terri introduced the team, Professor Sherwood held up his scanner, a black wand, similar to a handheld metal detector, only buzzing, as it contained live bees. "I'll go scan the scene." He stepped over the caution tape, already waving his wand while carrying his buzzing thrift-store suitcase in the other.

Detective Burski lifted up the crime scene tape so the team could pass beneath.

The piano-black luxury car sat with its mangled passenger door violently pried open, exposing the tan leather interior that was splattered and stained on every surface with blood. More blood spilled out from the open door and mixed with shattered glass from the driver's-side window.

Detective Frederick looked down at his notepad. "The victim was Emery Hindman. Actor, thirty-one years old. Costar of the television series *Deer Stalker*. Ever seen it?"

Rutherford said, "No."

Frederick looked Rutherford over, sneered for half a second, and looked at Dr. Romero. "He was probably watching wrestling."

Dr. Romero made a tiny smirk.

Rutherford smiled as well. He knew what this was. Detective Frederick was interested in Dr. Romero and perceived Rutherford as a competitor. Now Frederick was trying to change the dynamic from one where Frederick and Rutherford compete for Romero to one where Frederick and Romero make fun of Rutherford for not being as smart, or well read, or classy as they are. This didn't worry Rutherford. He came to solve a murder, not to meet women. Also, he had tried the gambit himself and knew that it never worked.

Besides, Frederick had no idea whom he was dealing with.

Rutherford said, "Actually, I'm working through re-watching the films of Wes Anderson."

Dr. Romero said, "What?"

"Yeah, last night was *Moonrise Kingdom*, which is good, but not my favorite. Tonight's *The Grand Budapest Hotel*, so I'm looking forward to that."

Dr. Romero looked at Rutherford. She seemed confused.

Terri said, "Rutherford's just messing with you. He was at a strip club last night. Isn't that right?"

Rutherford reminded himself that Terri was his boss and that he liked his job. He gritted his teeth. "Yes."

"A really cheap one," Terri said.

Rutherford nodded, grudgingly. "Who doesn't love a bargain?"

Detective Frederick smiled. Dr. Romero didn't. "You know," she said, "some of us like Wes Anderson. I guess it's easy to mock things you don't understand."

Sloan asked, "Are Wes Anderson's films really all that hard to understand? I've seen a few, and usually the only question I have is: Why is Bill Murray depressed this time?"

Unable to hear Sloan's comment, Detective Frederick went back to his notes. "The victim drove himself to work as usual. There were two witnesses, sort of. A security guard, and the victim's personal trainer, who it just so happens is Amanda Hogan."

"Should I have heard of her?" Rutherford asked.

Detective Frederick said, "She's pretty high-profile herself. You just hit town, so you might not have noticed her billboards yet, but you will."

Terri said, "She's aggressive about getting her name and face out there, eh?"

Detective Burski said, "Not her face."

Detective Frederick said, "She was here to work with him on set. Neither witness saw the beginning of the killing; they just heard a shout and saw a ton of blood, with Hindman pounding on the car window. He couldn't get the door to open. The handprints show that he tried. They couldn't open it from the outside either. They had to break the window with the guard's nightstick, but by then it was too late. Even then it wouldn't unlock. We had to crowbar the passenger door to get access. The victim was locked in the car, alone and dead."

Rutherford noticed Claire looking at him. He glanced back at her, but the instant he made eye contact she looked away.

Max said, "The poor man bled to death trapped in his own car, freedom and help just on the other side of the glass, but out of reach. Awful. So, what exactly is it that happened in the car?"

Detective Burski said, "He bled to death, as you probably figured. His left wrist was shredded."

Claire said, "Yes. Multiple lacerations. The artery was obliterated. No hope of any meaningful clotting. He had dozens of cuts, some shallow, some deep, some less than an inch long, some over five inches, running up the inside of his left wrist."

Sloan said, "Right where he'd wear a watch."

Rutherford nodded sagely and repeated for the non-team members who had no earpiece and couldn't hear Sloan, "Right where he'd wear a watch."

Claire smiled. "That's right." She looked at Rutherford, the smile held for half a second, then died as she looked away and cleared her throat.

Detective Frederick said, "We've already sent someone to break the news to the widow and ask her some questions. Today Mr. Hindman wore a new watch, given to him last night. It was delivered to his home, labeled as a gift from the executive producer. His widow says he made a point of wearing it. He wanted to look grateful."

Detective Burski said, "Of course, the watch was booby-trapped. The car door locks too. There was a small circuit board spliced into the car's wiring harness to prevent the doors from opening. He was killed by his luxury watch while he was trapped in his luxury car. The shiny baubles he used to impress others and make himself feel important in the end kept him isolated and bled him dry. It's always awful to contemplate another person's thoughts and emotions as they die, but it's made worse in this case by the fact that we all know, to some extent, how he felt. Even as he pounded on the blood-smeared windows, his cries for help contained by the car's impeccable build quality and ample soundproofing, his situation was just an exaggerated example of the modern way of life. We know that feeling because we all feel that way, every day of our lives."

After a long silence so thick Rutherford could almost see it, Sloan said, "Wow. He just managed to bring down the mood at a murder scene."

SIX

Claire cleared her throat and got on with business. "The circuit board we found was custom printed, so it will either be very easy to trace, or impossible." She poked and swiped at her tablet screen, then turned it around to show the team a grid of photos depicting a small, yellow triangle hanging from some wires. As is the case in most circuit boards, a series of capacitors, transistors, and other doodads sprouted from one side connected by dull gray lines. But the lines looked strange to Rutherford; he expected them to be straight with hard angles, but these curved gracefully, nesting into each other unevenly, as if they'd been drawn by hand.

Max leaned in close to the photo. "Thank you. May I please have a copy of this image?"

"Sure. I also have several pictures of the murder weapon, the watch." She swiped to an image of a chunky steel watch on a matching metal bracelet, and started to show it to Max. "It's a really interesting piece of engineering."

Max chuckled. "Oh, I am sorry. I've given you the wrong idea. I am not very technically inclined."

Terri said, "Albert is our tech expert."

Everyone turned to Albert, whose attention had drifted; he was watching a grubby Chinese take-out box someone had crumpled into a ball. Now it was rolling across the crime scene, blown by the light breeze.

Albert noticed the silence and looked around. "What? Pardon me. I zoned out there for a second. You were talking about the watch?"

"It's the murder weapon, and it's been modified in a really interesting way." Claire turned the tablet for Albert to see. Rutherford leaned in to look over Albert's shoulder. The pictures showed a gray steel analog watch, with a dark-green dial and bezel and a small magnifying window over the date display. A crown logo and tiny white text on the dial said that the watch was a Rolex Submariner. The next photo showed the watch's serial number and a decorative filigree etched into the case back. Down near the bracelet clasp, at least a foot of stiff wire, originally the same color as the watch but now stained with blood, trailed away from the clasp and hung in the air, supported by its own rigidity.

Albert asked, "Is that memory wire?"

Claire nodded. "Right on the first try. It was tightly wound around the clasp. It looked like some sort of decoration. The original movement was pulled out and replaced with the smaller quartz module from a kids' watch. A little radio receiver sent a current to the wire, causing it to violently unwind itself from the clasp, grinding between the bracelet and the victim's arm with each loop. It was fast and violent, and the last four inches of the wire are razor sharp."

Max said, "The poor man's wrist turned into a showerhead, but for blood. At first he probably worried about ruining his car's interior, then when he couldn't open the doors, he'd start furiously trying to tear and smash his way out."

Terri said, "Which just made the blood flow out faster, making him less strong but more afraid. It's awful."

"But," Albert said, "ingenious."

In their earpieces, Sloan said, "Not just technically. The social engineering of it. The expensive gift to an egotistical actor, knowing that he'd certainly wear it the very next morning to curry favor with the producer or rub it in his costars' faces. Whoever did this knew what they were doing."

Burski said, "It's a lot of trouble to go to for a suicide."

Rutherford blinked and furrowed his brow. "How can you possibly think this is a suicide?"

"I didn't say that I think it's a suicide. I said this would be a lot of trouble to go to for one."

"Oh."

"I'm just not willing to rule a suicide out yet."

Terri grimaced. "Who would kill themselves in public, in such a weird, gruesome way, and send a note saying it was a serial killer?"

"Someone who wants their death to be remembered, but not as a suicide. Someone with a flair for the dramatic, likes to show off, wants attention but wants to control that attention. What did our victim do for a living again?"

Detective Frederick said, "He was an actor."

"There you go."

Sloan said, "Tell him this isn't a suicide."

Rutherford said, "This isn't a suicide."

Burski shrugged. "You're probably right, but I always start by assuming any death by foul play is probably a suicide. The two things you look for in a killer are motive and opportunity: a reason to want the victim dead, and private access to the victim. Nobody on earth has more of both of those than the victim themselves. Once I rule out suicide, I move on to the person with the second most motive and opportunity. Their spouse."

Rutherford said, "Sometimes, I suppose."

"Every time, and the fact that you don't agree tells me you've never been married."

Sloan said, "You have to admit, that's some pretty good detective work."

Max said, "It should be easy to trace the watch. Rolex is an expensive brand. Surely records are kept."

Rutherford said, "It's a fake."

Claire looked at him, surprised. "What makes you so sure?"

Rutherford made a sucking noise against his teeth. "Well, a few things. A Submariner is crazy expensive, and this is the green-dialed variant. They call it the Hulk. It costs even more. The MSRP is something over nine grand, but you can't buy it for that unless the jeweler owes you a favor. It's more like fifteen thousand new, and they often get more expensive used, not less. I don't see anyone spending that on a watch just to hollow it out. Also, the back. Rolex doesn't put any branding or decoration on the back. Just a flat stainless disk with the serial number stamped in, not etched."

The team looked at Rutherford in silence. Sloan said, "Nice!"

Claire tilted her head slightly and stared at Rutherford, stunned. After a moment, her expression darkened again. "Well, I suppose they had to teach you to look for that kind of thing for when you bust guys selling counterfeit watches out of a trench coat."

Rutherford laughed. "I wasn't trained in the nineteen forties. I mean, do you also picture me calling people *Mac*, and threatening to take them to *the slammer*?"

Detective Frederic gently reached over and used the end of his pen to lift the left cuff of Rutherford's jacket. "I can see you're a watch expert from the fine Casio digital you're sporting there."

"What, this?" Rutherford said. "They make me wear this."

Frederick looked Rutherford over, shaking his head slightly. "Figures. Late so often they had to buy you a watch."

"No, I had a watch of my own. They just didn't want me to wear it on the job."

Claire asked, "Why not?"

Rutherford started to describe the German-built Bauhaus chronometer he'd bought with his first paycheck from Vince Capp, but Terri cut him off.

"It had a picture of a naked woman on it."

Claire, Frederick, and Rutherford all cringed.

"Ugh. Really?" Claire asked.

Rutherford started to speak, but Terri cut him off again, looking him straight in the eye as she said, "Yes. Really. Her breasts were the hour and minute hands."

Frederick laughed.

Claire asked, "How does that work? Were they different lengths?"

"Yes," Terri said. "They were."

Claire scrunched her face. "Why on earth would anyone wear such a thing?"

Rutherford tried to claw back some dignity. He quickly concocted a story about a partner who taught him everything and died tragically in the call of duty. "It was a gift from—"

Terri cleared her throat. She and Rutherford made eye contact and over the course of three seconds engaged in a battle of wills, which Rutherford lost, forfeiting what dignity he had hoped to regain.

Rutherford continued, "—my mother."

Sloan said, "Slick!"

Frederick kept laughing as Claire looked at Rutherford, disgusted. "I have to go check on my team." She walked away.

Detectives Burski and Frederick also excused themselves and returned to their police work.

Rutherford watched Dr. Romero go. "Thanks for that, Terri."

Terri said, "You're more than welcome."

In his earpiece, Rutherford heard Sloan's synthesized voice say, "Laughing. Laughing."

Albert said, "I'll have the drones record the scene, but first I should talk to LAPD's forensics team and see if I can get a look at the watch in person. Maybe there's a real brand name inside the case, or the electronics might have some clue."

Max said, "The circuit board that sabotaged the door locks. I have seen one like it before."

Albert asked, "Do you remember where?"

"All too well. That circuit board matches very closely the boards made by a man who went by many names but was known to the espionage community as *the Inventor of Antwerp*. He was a contract killer. And a Belgian."

"And it sounds like he invented Antwerp," Rutherford said.

Sloan said, "I assume his name sounded cooler in French."

Max shook his head. "In Belgium they speak three languages, and his title doesn't sound cool in any of them. It's hard to make a name that includes *Antwerp* seem dashing. The Inventor specialized in elaborate deaths, usually creating or modifying some piece of equipment. Most of his jobs were made to look like accidents, but occasionally if his client wanted to make some sort of statement, he'd do something like this. The kinds of components he needed were not available off the shelf. One does not walk into Best Buy and purchase a radio-controlled door-lock inhibitor. On the rare occasion that he left any evidence, there would often be weird triangular circuit boards with strangely flowing patterns."

Rutherford asked, "Why would he use such a distinctive circuit board? Was it like a calling card?"

"No, my boy. Only in the movies and bad novels do criminals use calling cards. In real life, the goal of the criminal is to not get credit for their crimes. The calling card of the true professional is their total lack of a calling card. His boards usually were destroyed in whatever explosion or violent accident befell the target, so he wasn't worried about them being distinctive, and on the rare occasion the board would be found, he knew they weren't traceable, because he made them himself from scraps he had lying around. He was notoriously cheap, and deadly."

"Where is he now?" Sloan asked.

"Supposedly he died in a tragic accident involving a high shelf and a ten-gallon bucket of acid. It poured down on his face, mouth, and the fronts of his hands." Max mimed looking up in horror, mouth open to scream while shielding his face with his hands. "It made a positive identification impossible, of course. I'll contact a few people. Ask some unwanted questions."

"You don't think the corpse was really him?" Rutherford asked.

"When you're in the business as long as I was, you stop thinking any corpse was ever really anyone. But being dead and pretending to be dead are functionally the same thing. If a person is pretending to be dead, he isn't going to bother you. And if he ever turns up alive, he'll probably be genuinely dead within a few hours anyway. That's why I never bothered to fake my death."

Albert said, "That and there's nobody out there who wants you dead, I hope."

"There's somebody who wants everybody dead, and everybody wants somebody dead."

Rutherford said, "I don't want anybody dead, and I don't think anybody wants me dead."

"Not yet, dear boy, but don't worry. Someday you'll meet the wrong person."

SEVEN

The steering wheel and turn indicator levers moved on their own. Rutherford sat in the driver's seat with his hands and feet pulled back as if the controls were radioactive.

Sloan, sitting in the middle seats with Max, turned and looked over her shoulder at Albert and Professor Sherwood sitting in the van's back row. "Man, Professor, that bellhop was not happy that you insisted on carrying your own suitcase."

Max said, "But he changed his tune when he found out it was full of bees."

Albert said, "Then he got unhappy again fast when he got his tip."

Professor Sherwood said, "Fresh honey is better than cash. It's delicious, calorie dense, shelf stable, and I even put it in a squeeze bottle shaped like a bear."

Rutherford gritted his teeth and emitted a high nervous moan, clearly fighting the urge to stomp on the brakes and take back over as the van worked its way through traffic without his input. His head swiveled as he frantically checked the front window, side window, all three mirrors, and the instrument panel.

"Where are you going to set up the hive at night?" Albert asked.

"The hotel manager gave me access to the roof after I offered to put it on my balcony over the pool."

"That wasn't an offer," Sloan said. "It was a threat."

"Either way, it worked."

Terri looked down at her phone and announced to the entire team, "I have an email from Dr. Romero over at the CartFulls lab. They should have their preliminary results in an hour or two."

The remote driver's voice boomed from the van's sound system. "I heard you mention CartFulls? I could swing by one if you need to pick up a few things."

"No thanks" Terri said. "That won't be necessary."

"Let me know if you change your mind. There are three CartFulls superstores along your route."

"We will. Thanks."

"I love their commercials with that whiny cart," the driver said. "*The prices are so low, let's throw in two more thirty-pound bags of potting soil!*"

In unison, the remote driver and Albert cried out, "*Two more bags?! Oh no!*"

Terri glared at Albert, who smiled and shrugged back at her.

The turn indicator activated as the minivan began drifting to the left. Rutherford looked in the side-view mirror, then turned to check the blind spot, pressing his face against the glass. "Careful! Car there! Be careful, there's a car there!"

The remote driver said, "I see the car, sir, better than you do. I have a 3D lidar map of the traffic. I can see openings you can't."

"If I can't see an opening, how open can it be?"

Terri said, "Rutherford, the driver will probably find it easier to concentrate if you don't engage him in complex logical arguments."

"Am I really the only one bothered by this?" Rutherford asked, staring down at the steering wheel as it made minor course corrections seemingly on its own. "How is this not freaking you all out?"

Professor Sherwood said, "We're accustomed to you driving us everywhere in an overpowered van you can barely control."

Albert added, "Which generates superheated steam."

Max said, "And contains live bees."

"We're desensitized to all risks, and we've made peace with the idea that we'll die in a van," Sloan said.

Terri said, "Enough. You've all had your fun; now stop teasing Rutherford about all of us dying horribly. Wow, maybe we really have become desensitized. Anyway, Claire says she'll email us the results."

Albert said, "You could send Rutherford around to pick the lab results up in person. It'll give him more time to get used to the remote driver."

Terri said, "No. That would be counterproductive."

Sloan agreed. "What's the fun of making Rutherford squirm if we're not there to see it?"

Terri said, "I think it would be best to keep Rutherford away from Claire; there was some kind of weird energy going on with them and Detective Frederick. We're here to do a job. We don't want Rutherford trying to impress her and breaking his cover, or making an ass of himself, or probably both."

"Why do you think I'd make an ass of myself?"

"You're a man. All men make asses of themselves eventually. It's just a matter of how badly they do it, and whether or not they've built up enough goodwill for the people they're trying to impress to put up with it."

The remote driver said, "Sorry. I couldn't help overhearing. It sounds like one of you has a girl you're after, but you can't get any traction, yeah? I can help with that. There's a Reddit page I go to with what they call *seduction techniques*. There's a lot of really great tips in there."

Max said, "I'm sorry, young man, but seduction techniques are a hoax. They were invented by women as a trick to make men who aren't worth bothering with identify themselves through certain telltale behaviors."

"That's not true!"

Max laughed. "They've convinced you to try to interest women by being rude, ignoring them, and insulting them. They're fooling you into isolating yourself."

"But I have a friend who negs and blows off girls all the time. It works for him," the driver said. "I've seen it."

"Tell me, is your friend, by any chance, very good looking and confident?"

"Yeah, but that's not . . . Huh."

Terri asked, "Pardon me, driver. Is it possible to turn off the microphone?"

"Sure. There should be a button on the touchscreen."

"Ah," Terri said. "I see it. Thank you." She reached forward, pressed the button, and settled back into her seat.

Sloan said, "Thank you. Now we can concentrate less on catching a woman and more on catching our killer."

Professor Sherwood said, "Our killer might be a woman."

Sloan said, "Possible, but not likely. If it really is a serial killer we're dealing with, the standard profile is someone who's angry at the world and blames society for his lowly place in it. Someone who feels like he should be important, admired, but deep down knows he never will be. The tension between those two things drives him to antisocial behavior and eventually murder."

"Anything else?" Terri asked.

Sloan said, "The vast majority of the time, the serial killer is a white male."

"Why is that?" Sherwood asked.

"Hard to say for sure. Some think white men feel a greater societal expectation to succeed since the game is tilted in their favor, and they suffer more shame for it when they fail. Or that they feel cheated, like success was promised to them and was never delivered. I like to think it's just that women and non-Caucasians are forced to become stronger and wiser by the pressure of growing up in a society dominated by white men. The Caucasian patriarchy has been the crucible in which we, the sword that will one day smite them, has been forged. It's made us too evolved to kill for pleasure, or at least too smart to get caught."

Terri said, "I like that theory."

Albert said, "A lot!"

Professor Sherwood said, "Hell yeah!"

"Still," Terri said, "we're looking for an unsuccessful, entitled white guy; that doesn't narrow it down much. There are a lot of those in Hollywood."

Rutherford said, "Our perp isn't a normal serial killer, though. If Max's lead here pans out, he hired a professional killer to do the job for him. What's that tell us?"

Professor Sherwood said, "That he's feckless."

Rutherford asked, "What's that word mean? *Feckless.*"

Sloan said, "I'll use it in a sentence. *Rutherford was too feckless to look up the word himself.* Does that help?"

"No," Rutherford said. "That wasn't helpful at all."

Terri said, "It means lazy and weak, and it still doesn't narrow things down."

Max said, "The Inventor of Antwerp's services do not come cheap. Assuming he himself doesn't have a grudge against the victim, we can assume the client is a man of some means."

Terri said, "A white, angry, disenfranchised *rich* guy. That does add a twist. Might narrow things down, a little."

Rutherford said, "We're here," as he reached forward and pressed the button deactivating the remote driver. A pleasant yet somehow downbeat chime played, and the driver thanked them and wished them a good day as Rutherford took the wheel and slowed to a stop next to an empty parallel-parking space.

Terri said, "I'm sure he could have parked the car."

"Yeah," Rutherford said, "but I feel better handling the difficult part myself."

Rutherford backed up, turned in, backed in further, turned the other direction to pull the van's nose in, stopped before hitting the car behind them, turned the wheel hard, pulled forward, turned the wheel, backed up, turned the wheel, pulled forward, turned the wheel, backed up, turned, pulled forward, turned, backed up, pulled forward a little bit, then killed the engine and got out of the car without saying a word.

EIGHT

As the team piled out, Terri looked down at the wide and uneven gap between the tires and the curb. "Not your best parking job, Rutherford."

Rutherford shrugged. "You want me to act like a rough-and-tumble *cop on the edge*. Here you go. I took command of the situation and I parked by my own rules."

Terri frowned down at the gutter. "It's a start. A small, bad start."

Their actual destination was still half a block away, part of an unbroken line of shabby storefronts. Max walked ahead, pointing up at the sign over one of the shops. "There it is."

A cheap vinyl banner drooped over the storefront—the kind meant to be tied up temporarily, but it had clearly been hanging in place for at least ten years. Letters that probably started as bright red on a white background, but now resembled pastel orange on a dingy gray, read "Electronics: Sony JVC Repairs."

"Cheap," Max muttered. "Cheap and deadly."

Terri glanced back at the rest of the team, did a double take, and shook her head. "Professor, you brought Her Majesty?"

"Yes," Sherwood said, lugging the large suitcase.

Terri waved a hand. "Okay, you wanna carry it around, fine. But don't use it."

"I won't . . . unless I have a good reason."

Albert looked through the filthy windows at rows of outdated camcorders and portable CD players propped up in front of their sun-faded packaging. "How does a store like this even stay in business?"

"The government supports this one," Max said. "It's a perfect place for an electronics expert who is in the witness relocation program to work. It seems like a legitimate business, but there is no chance whatsoever that someone will come in who might accidentally recognize him, because nobody ever comes in, except for us, right now. Okay, friends, I must ask that you let me do all the talking. Please just answer any direct questions I might ask you, and otherwise try to be seen and not heard."

Terri asked, "Are you sure you really want us to come in at all?"

"Yes. It is necessary."

Rutherford nodded. "To let him know you have backup."

"Very much no. It is to make it clear to him that you all are under my protection. Shall we?"

Sloan said, "I guess." Her artificial voice sounded more positive than her word choice suggested.

Max pushed open the door. The whole store smelled of hot dust. The wear patterns on the thin, hard carpet and the logos woven into its pattern showed the place used to be a video rental store. Now the entire center of the shop was empty. Low glass cases like in a jewelry store lined both sides and the back, but instead of rings and necklaces, the displays held personal stereos, boom boxes, and cameras.

Behind the rear counter a young woman with red hair and a magnifying visor jumped in surprise at the sound of the little tin bell on a springy wire connected to the door. She looked up from the partially dismantled stereo component and her soldering iron, her magnified eyes looking alarmed. "Who are you?"

Max approached the counter. "Customers."

She lifted the visor, narrowed her eyes, and looked at Professor Sherwood's briefcase. "What's that?"

Max said, "Nothing you need to worry about."

She tilted her head, listening. "Is it buzzing?"

Max said, "Yes."

"It's probably malfunctioning. I could open it up and take a look at it for you."

Max said, "Believe me, you don't want to do that. We're here to talk to Mr. Boris DeBeul."

She leaned back and shouted over her shoulder at a door to the back room, "You have a visitor."

A distant French accented voice shouted, "Who are you talking to, apprentice?"

The young woman rolled her eyes. "Come on, man. Not in front of people."

"It's even more important in front of people. Who are you talking to?"

"You, Maestro."

"Very good. Now see if you can get them to go away."

The apprentice looked to Max, who said, "You cannot."

"Sorry, Maestro, I cannot."

"Ask them who they are."

Before the apprentice could relay the question, Max, loud enough to be heard in the back, said, "Max Warmenhoven."

After some crashing and scrabbling sounds, the door opened, and a man's head poked around the corner. He was pale and bald, the skin smooth and shiny on his scalp but loose and rough on his face. Boris DeBeul looked toward Max and the rest of the team. He stepped out into the showroom and brought up a pair of tortoiseshell glasses with large, smudged lenses that hung from a too-shiny gold-plated chain around his neck.

He took a moment to compose himself, then turned to his apprentice. "You almost done with that CD player?"

"Yes, Maestro. I don't see why you're making me repair this old piece of junk."

DeBeul said, "Because this is a repair shop. Were you unaware of what it is we do here?"

"But why repair this? It's worthless."

"It's not worthless. It's undervalued. There's a world of difference. I'll explain. I am a renowned technician with a reputation the world over, who is sought out by the top people in their fields." DeBeul gestured toward Max. "And yet I waste my time in this awful little shop, a filth-clogged pore in the skin on the devil's anus. I am undervalued. You are an apprentice who argues with her maestro and can't be counted on to do a simple belt-and-capacitor replacement in less than two hours. You are worthless. Now get back to work. Mr. Warmenhoven and I must talk."

Max said, "Boris DeBeul, I hope I'm pronouncing your assumed name correctly."

DeBeul smiled. "If you're saying it wrong, I am too, Max."

"Can we speak freely in front of your assistant?"

"I have no assistant. An assistant is of assistance. Someday I hope she may learn enough to become an assistant. But you have a point, this conversation will push the limits of her comprehension. Go get me my lunch. Normal order."

The apprentice took off her magnifying goggles. "Gotcha. One appetizer as a main course, a side of free mints from the bucket by the cash register, and a large water, hold the tip." She walked across the shop and out the front door, glaring at her boss, Max, all of the team members, and the world as she went.

Max asked, "You're not alarmed to see me at all?"

DeBeul shrugged. "You, Max? No. Nobody would send you to kill me. To apprehend me, maybe, but as you see, I'm already a prisoner."

Rutherford said, "You didn't mention that you knew each other."

Max said, "We don't. We've never met before. But we know *of* each other very well."

DeBeul said, "In my former line of work, one way to stay alive was to learn about those who might try to kill you. I see you've had just as much bad luck with your apprentice as I've had with mine, Max."

"He's not an apprentice. He's a colleague."

"Worse luck still. What can I do for you?"

"I'm hoping you can explain something. An actor was killed this morning. A modified wristwatch cut open his wrist and he bled to death in his own locked car."

"Sounds messy and ugly. Why would I know anything about it?"

Max lifted the tablet in his hand and pulled up a picture of the strange, triangular circuit board. "Because this is the device that kept the poor man's doors locked. I trust it looks familiar."

DeBeul looked at the image. "Yes, of course it does. It looks like the boards I used to make."

"But you didn't make this one."

"No. What can I tell you? My work has been influential in my former industry. There is no shortage of imitators. If you suspect me, I can assure you, my current benefactors keep very close tabs on me. They can provide ample evidence that I've never been anywhere near this victim of yours."

"I'm sure they can, and I will check. I'm curious if you would look at the images of the board and the modified watch, just to give us your impressions. Maybe you will see something we don't."

DeBeul said, "Almost certainly," and brought the tablet close to his face as he swiped through the pictures.

"Inspired by my work," DeBeul muttered. "Minimally proficient. Wasteful layout. Clumsy assembly. No élan. The watch is a clever idea, if brutal. Used more memory wire than needed. Half as much would have achieved the same result faster. Max, the person you're looking for has few skills and limited originality. Beyond that, I don't know what to tell you. I'll think about it further, but I wouldn't hold out much hope."

"I understand. Here's my card." Max placed a business card on the counter. "I'll be in touch. Good day, Boris."

As the team walked to the door, DeBeul picked up the card, examining it with a sly grin. "You know, Max, I have an acquaintance who'll be interested to hear that you're in town."

Max glanced back over his shoulder. "I hope I bump into them."

DeBeul said, "You shouldn't."

Max stopped, turned, and looked at DeBeul, who arched an eyebrow. Max walked out the door, DeBeul smiling at his back as he left. Rutherford tried to give DeBeul the stink eye on his way out the door, but he only made the older man laugh.

As they walked back to the minivan, Max said, "I can check with my contacts. If DeBeul has done anything suspicious in the last few days, they would know."

Sloan said, "Please do check, but I don't think a man in his position is likely to embark on some sort of high-profile killing spree."

"Yeah," Rutherford agreed. "He seemed kind of offended at the idea. So, what do we do now?"

Sloan said, "I've been thinking about this. We have pretty much nothing and we're left waiting for the lab results or a new note to fall in our laps. Meanwhile, the clock is ticking. I think we should stop concentrating on catching this guy before he strikes again and try to catch him when he strikes again. The killer promised another murder tomorrow, right? And there are three more productions based on Sherlock Holmes, meaning three more Watsons. I say we split up into three teams and spend the day tomorrow, all day, embedded with them. That way we have a chance of being there to foil the next attempt. With any luck, we may be able to prevent a death and capture the killer in one go."

Terri said, "Yeah, that makes sense. It won't be a problem getting each team their own TurkMO van for the day. We should be smart about assigning teams, though. Albert, what are the two next most popular Sherlocks after *Deer Stalker*?"

Albert did a little quick typing on his smartphone, waited a moment, and muttered to himself as he skimmed and assimilated the information he received. "That's the weird thing. *Deer Stalker* was number two. The most popular one is a show called *No Matter How Improbable*. A modern-day Holmes and Watson solve supernatural crimes and kill monsters of the week. Watson's a skeptic while Holmes refuses to rule anything out. Second place was *Deer Stalker*. Third is a kids' movie called *Nose for Crime 2*. A cartoon, sequel to *Nose for Crime*. Watson's a cop and Holmes is his police dog."

Sloan said, "A bloodhound, I assume."

"No," Albert said. "A German shepherd. More realistic. The dog does talk and wear a hat, though. Then after that there's a Sherlock-themed recurring segment on a late-night talk show, *The Wee Smalls with Mia Paul*."

Terri said, "So Sloan takes one team, Rutherford takes another, and I'll take the third wherever the killer seems least likely to strike. Who goes where?"

Sloan said, "I'll take the cartoon. We want Rutherford to apprehend the killer if possible, just for the footage, and it feels more likely that the killer would go after a TV star than a voice-over artist."

Terri said, "Makes sense. How about you, Max?"

"I'll accompany Sloan, so if Rutherford does have an altercation, Albert will be there to film it."

Terri said, "And Professor Sherwood and I will take the talk show, as it's least likely to see any action."

"But if it does, we'll have Her Majesty, and you'll be present to authorize her use."

"Sure," Terri said. "Good plan. Be on your toes, though, Max. DeBeul might be calling whoever it is who is looking for you right now."

"Oh, I wouldn't worry about that if I were you."

"You figure he was bluffing."

"Oh, no. He's already alerted whomever it is. Even now, he or she is plotting our reunion. But, I assure you, the odds of it being the one person I actually fear are exceedingly low."

NINE

A young woman with a *No Matter How Improbable* baseball cap on her head and an ID lanyard around her neck walked at a pace just shy of jogging between the huge beige soundstages that constituted the bulk of the studio lot. Rutherford and Albert managed to keep up, Albert carrying his aluminum briefcase computer. Its size allowed for a larger screen, powerful and easily replaceable desktop components, and built-in storage for his drones.

The woman glanced back over her shoulder. "Still with me, guys?"

Albert said, "No problem. Don't slow down for us."

"What exactly do you do on the show?" Rutherford asked.

The woman said, "I'm a PA. A production assistant."

Rutherford asked, "So, how do you assist the production?"

"I confer with the showrunner, the director, and the principal actors, and I remember their orders."

"Their orders for the crew?"

"Their orders for food. In the morning I get them all their coffee and pastries. When that's done, I start arranging lunch. Then afternoon snacks, and dinner when shooting goes long. It's in the production's best interest to give expensive talent no reason to ever wander off the set. Anyway, an army travels on its stomach. Napoleon knew it; Kubrick knew it; I know it."

They entered a soundstage through the side door. A uniformed police officer examined the PA's pass before letting them through. Inside, Rutherford's eyes took a moment to adjust, and even after they did, he needed a second to make sense of what he saw. Around the cavernous space, artificial representations of places designed to feel real in an idealized sort of way sat waiting for eventual use. Rutherford recognized an apartment, a bedroom, and an interrogation room.

The PA led Rutherford and Albert to a large folding table covered with a cheap plastic tablecloth, and wicker baskets full of granola bars and bags of chips. The far end of the table held fruit, vegetables chopped into dippable chunks, and a tub of ranch dressing with some little plastic cups to the side.

"We have two soundstages," the PA said. "We're filming on the other one today. Ugh, where is he?"

Albert looked at the table of snacks. "You set this up?"

"What?" the PA asked, visibly annoyed.

Albert pointed at the table full of snacks. "This food. Part of your job is putting this out?"

"No! This is craft services. It's for the people who don't have an assistant to get them food."

"People like you," Rutherford asked.

She laughed. "I get my own food when I get my boss's. It's a perk of the job."

"You order and retrieve your own food, and that's a perk?"

"Yeah. It's a hell of a business. Okay, here comes Randy. He's going to show you two around."

As she spoke, a wiry-looking man in his late thirties wearing jeans and a shiny nylon jacket walked up to the table. He peeped over the top of bent aviator glasses at the food, taking no notice of the PA, Rutherford, or Albert. Instead, he tore open a bag of chips.

The PA continued, "We thought Randy would be perfect to help you guys. Since he's our full-time police consultant, he should understand both how we work and how you work."

Randy continued picking up and tearing open bags of chips, putting the open bags on the table in front of him.

The PA raised her voice to make sure that Randy could hear her. "And it's a nice chance for Randy to earn his pay, since he doesn't do anything else useful at all, ever."

Randy glanced at her just long enough to let her know that he found her disdain amusing. Then he picked up all the opened bags in one large clump and squeezed, shattering all of the chips and producing a cloud of seasoning dust and a shower of flying crumbs. He tipped the open bags over the tub of ranch dressing, leaving a thick layer of assorted chip shards on the surface of the dressing and drifts of the bits that missed the tub around it on the table. He picked up the tub and pulled out the small plastic ladle, which he stuck in his mouth, stretching his cheeks in the process. He pulled the ladle from his mouth, stripping off some of the ranch and chip crumbs, then flung it down on the table where it landed with a splat in the basket of fruit. He hugged the tub of dressing and crushed chips to his nylon bomber jacket with his left arm, extended two fingers on his right hand as if giving the Boy Scout salute, then dipped them into the tub like a spoon. The fingers came out encrusted with ranch and chip chunks. He stuck the fingers in his mouth and smiled at the PA as he chewed and swallowed.

She sneered down at the ranch tub. "That isn't all for you, you know."

Randy feigned innocence. "What? I'm sorry. How thoughtless of me. You want some?" He thrust his fingers back into the dressing, pulled them out, and offered them to the PA.

She recoiled. "No!"

"Then what's the problem?" Randy put his fingers back in his mouth, winking at her over the top of his sunglasses.

The PA turned to Rutherford and Albert. "Randy, this is Mr. Mok and Detective Rutherford. Mr. Mok, Detective Rutherford, I'm sorry, but I have to leave you with Randy."

Albert started to offer a handshake but pulled back when he realized the condition Randy's hand was in. Randy didn't mind. He barely glanced at Albert in his three-piece suit. He looked at Rutherford's ratty and rumpled outfit and nodded. "Hey."

Rutherford responded by jutting out his chin in a sort of upward nod the way he'd seen some guys greet each other, but never him. "Hey."

The PA said, "If you need anything, tell Randy and he'll pass it along. Good luck."

Rutherford and Albert tried to thank her, but she had already turned and walked away. She waved back over her shoulder as she went out the door.

Randy sucked some ranch off of his fingers with a loud smacking sound. "So, someone's gonna try to kill Russell, huh?"

Albert said, "Maybe. We think someone's going to try to kill someone who plays Watson today. We don't know that it'll be your Watson."

"We can hope. C'mere. I'll give you the nickel tour, introduce you to the future victim. Whatever you do, don't ask about his mother."

"He doesn't like to talk about her?"

"He doesn't like to talk about anything else, so why make it easy for him? Occasionally I time it to see how long it takes him to bring her up if nobody else does."

Randy led Rutherford and Albert past the darkened sets and out a back door, past another uniformed police officer. The tall buildings and early hour meant the road remained cast in shadow. A long row of soundstages stretched off to the left and right, but across the street was a four-story office building: a wall of mirrored windows with welded-steel louvers cantilevered out over each floor. Randy turned left, walking around the outside of a large travel trailer. An Astroturf rug and a little set of metal stairs led up to the closed trailer door.

Randy licked some ranch off his fingers and swallowed. "The show has two soundstages; that one was for the permanent sets. Today they're filming on the other stage they use for stuff they only need for one or two episodes. This trailer is hair and makeup."

Randy showed his pass to the officer guarding the second soundstage, then pulled a door open, ranch dressing mixed with saliva squishing out from under his fingers as he gripped the handle. It was the most disgusting thing Rutherford had ever seen until Randy let go of the door, leaving a gooey white handprint behind, only to immediately dip that hand back into the chips and ranch, scoop up another serving, and shove it directly into his mouth.

In this soundstage Rutherford saw a perfect re-creation of a cluttered scientific laboratory, only missing two full walls and lit far more brightly than any human lab worker could tolerate. Around the periphery people stood still, looking pensive while watching the actors or staring at monitors. On the set, several people hunched around or behind the camera as it recorded three men talking. One wore a long coat and a hat cut in the style of a traditional two-billed deerstalker cap but made of a modern microfiber material. A second wore a rumpled suit. The third wore a police uniform.

The actor in the hat, clearly the Sherlock of the production, said, "Captain Lestrade, I agree with you that the prints are too large to be a dog."

The actor in the police uniform said, "Far too large."

The man in the hat went on, "And Watson, of course I agree that they can't possibly be from a werewolf."

The man in the suit said, "I'm glad to hear that you understand that, Holmes."

"Of course. The creature walked on all fours. Werewolves walk on two legs."

"They don't walk at all. They don't exist."

"We'll have that argument later, Watson. We have no time to lose, given what we're up against. As I always say, if you eliminate the impossible, whatever's left, no matter how improbable, must be the case. It can't be a dog, and it can't be a werewolf. What we're dealing with, clearly, must be a dog that was bitten by a werewolf!"

Watson said, "That's preposterous!"

"There's no reason to believe werewolves can't bite animals, Watson."

"I can think of one very good reason: they don't exist."

"The prints disagree. Lestrade, where did you say the trail leads?"

"To the aquarium, Holmes."

"Exactly, and dogs are excellent swimmers. We have no time to waste!"

The director shouted, "Cut! We'll use that one. On to the next setup." She was a walking study in contrast: jet-black hair against pale white skin, fire-engine-red lipstick on a face otherwise devoid of obvious makeup, and a casual sweater and capri pants worn with the precision and bearing of a military dress uniform. At her go-ahead, the room exploded into hectic activity, everyone moving with great haste and purpose.

Randy led Rutherford and Albert toward the director. "Kyndra, these are the guys they sent to catch whoever kills Russell."

She shook their hands firmly and quickly, as if she wanted to greet them once, greet them well, and then never have to greet them again. "Yes, yes. From Capp's Authorities. Cement Shoes Rutherford and Albert Mok. I was warned you were coming."

Randy said, "Guys, this is Kyndra Perrin, the showrunner and director for this episode."

Albert said, "Thanks for having us. Is it common for a showrunner to direct the show too?"

Kyndra said, "It is when the series is over budget for the season. I think it's important that you both know that I don't want you here. I have orders from upstairs to let you on the set, and now I have. I'd really appreciate it if you took off. You'll only be in the way."

Albert said, "We don't want to be any trouble."

"Then leave."

"We'll hang back. You won't even know we're here."

"Then you might as well not be here."

Rutherford arched an eyebrow. "You don't want your actor to be protected?"

"Of course I do. That's why there are police officers stationed at every door."

"But what if he's attacked by someone who's already in here?"

"Like who? Look around. These people all work with Russell every day. Not one of them wants to see any harm come to him. They'd be out a job. Besides, if someone tries something in here we'll just shout for help. As I said, there are police officers just outside the door. Now, if you aren't going to leave, I have to ask you to at least leave me alone. I have work to do."

Rutherford and Albert tried to thank her for her time, but before they got the words out she had already turned around, taken three steps, and started shouting at someone on the far side of the set.

Rutherford said, "Wow."

Albert shook his head. "Seriously."

"I know, hot, right?" Randy stuck two ranch-covered fingers in his mouth and waggled his eyebrows suggestively. Once he'd sucked his fingers clean, he said, "Come on, I'll introduce you to the victim."

The three actors stood off to the side of the set, leaning on various trunks and tables, looking over their scripts. The actor playing Holmes said, "Russell, I don't know how you make this material sound so natural."

The man playing Watson said, "All I do is react as if I'm listening to nonsense. It's easy, since that's what I'm actually doing. You have the hard part. You have to pretend to believe this stuff."

Randy looked at his watch. "So this is Chris Wolfberg, Alex Milius, and Russell Byrne. They play Holmes, Lestrade, and Watson. Guys, Detective Rutherford and Mr. Mok are here to catch whoever kills Russell today."

Rutherford said, "We're here to stop anyone who tries."

Randy said, "Yeah, right, of course. I'm sure you'll give it a shot."

The three actors shook hands with Rutherford and Albert. Wolfberg said, "I was told the police were already here to protect Russell."

"Yes," Rutherford said. "LAPD and studio security are patrolling the lot and guarding the entrances."

"We're just here as a precaution," Albert said. "Odds are, nobody will even make an attempt anyway."

Byrne said, "I suspect they will. I'm the obvious next target, on account of my mother."

Randy said, "Ha! Twenty-four seconds!"

Rutherford asked, "What would this have to do with your mother? You don't think she's behind it, do you?"

Byrne stiffened while the other two actors cringed. Randy laughed, scooping two fingers of ranch into his mouth. The actors cringed even harder.

Russell Byrne said, "I really don't think so. She's been dead since I was a child."

"Oh," Rutherford said. "I'm sorry."

Wolfberg said, "His mother was Catalina Byrne."

Rutherford's eyes grew wide. "Oh! Oh, of course! I'm so sorry!"

Albert said, "Oh, yeah! I see it now. You've got her eyes."

Byrne said, "And her talent, I like to think."

Randy smiled as he dipped his fingers in his ranch tub. "Yeah, here's hoping you didn't get her luck, eh?"

Byrne glared at Randy. Rutherford and Albert looked at their shoes. Rutherford said, "Sorry. We didn't mean to be insensitive. It must have been difficult for you."

Randy nodded. "Yeah, to grow up knowing that most men in the country have seen your mom's boobs."

Rutherford said, "I meant losing your mother like that."

"Such an awful accident," Albert said. "You had to be pretty young."

Byrne said, "You're right on both counts, and being constantly reminded of it doesn't help. It's bad enough that instead of her work, my mother's remembered for how she died. Now it seems that I'm doomed to be remembered for it too."

"She's also remembered for that topless scene," Randy said.

Rutherford said, "Horrible luck that she played an ambulance dispatcher on TV, and died in an ambulance accident. It kinda made the whole thing into a legend."

"But you didn't know," Russell said. "I have to say, it doesn't give me a lot of confidence that the people who are here to protect me weren't aware of something as important as this."

Albert said, "In our defense, we've only been on the case for twenty-four hours, and we've been focusing on other things."

"Like what?" Russell asked.

Rutherford said, "The man who got murdered yesterday."

Russell said, "Oh. Fair enough. Uh, guys, could I please have a moment to talk to the detectives alone?"

The other two actors said "of course" and excused themselves. Randy stayed right where he was, smiling and licking ranch dressing from his fingers.

Russell asked, "Randy, would you mind going somewhere else?"

"Why?"

"Because I don't want you here."

Randy said, "Normally I'd stay even longer after you say something like that, but I see that hot new camera chick they hired is between shots, and if I go talk to her I might get some."

Byrne said, "She hates you, because you never learned her name and call her 'the hot new camera chick.'"

Randy scoffed. "I'm honest about my feelings. Chicks dig that. Besides, if I wrote off every girl who thinks they hate me, I'd never hit on anyone. I'm going for it. Wish me luck."

Randy slapped Rutherford on the back and walked off toward the unlucky woman.

Rutherford looked at Albert. "I have ranch dressing on my back now, don't I?"

Albert nodded gravely and turned back to Russell Byrne. "I'm not so much a detective as a surveillance and equipment specialist. I should go set up my gear while they're prepping for the next shot."

Russell Byrne said. "That's fine, and Mr. Mok, thanks for being here."

"You're welcome." Albert waited a moment for Russell to either suggest a place or point him to someone who could help him.

Byrne waited a moment for Albert to leave.

Finally, Albert said, "I'll go find a spot," and walked away.

Byrne focused on Rutherford, who had removed his jacket and was holding it up, looking at the back and grimacing.

"Look, Detective, two things," Byrne said. "First, if someone's trying to kill me, shouldn't I be in hiding?"

Rutherford carefully rolled his jacket inside out to contain the mess and tucked it under his arm as he answered. "We don't know that anybody is trying to kill you, we just think someone *might*. But if you hide, that means a limited police presence. If whoever's behind this finds you, they'll actually have a much better chance at getting to you and getting away."

"That makes sense, I suppose. The other thing is, see, uh, I play a detective."

"I thought Watson was a doctor."

"In this version he has a PhD in criminology, so in that sense he's a doctor of detective-ing. Look, you're a detective. Like, a real detective, or they wouldn't have sent you on a case like this, right?"

"I work with a private team of specialists, but I am a fully sworn detective with the Seattle Police Department."

"Great! I'd love to pick your brain sometime, you know, for research, after you're done preventing my murder. It's just . . . this character's very different from me, and I would appreciate any insights you could provide."

Rutherford thought for a moment. "Mr. Byrne, I'm no actor. I don't know how it works, but let's say you decided to base your character on me. How would you do it? Are there certain questions you'd ask?"

"I'd try to find out about your life. I'd ask about your parents, your childhood, your love life, but really, the main thing would be to spend time with you. Shadow you. Learn your reactions. Steal your soul."

"And that works?"

"Yeah. I mean, it sometimes takes forcing your own natural instincts down, but if you put the time in, you can get to where you just naturally react to a situation the way they would."

"I'd be happy to help, but why me? I thought Randy's job was to advise you about police work."

"So did I. So does everybody, except Randy. I tried going to him for help. He was not receptive. He's not really the kind of cop I want to base anything on, anyway. Apparently he was kicked off of the force before he landed this job."

"Really?"

"They say he refused to follow orders. Played by his own rules. Made a lot of noise. Stepped on the wrong toes. All the things he still does here. He's just the worst."

"Yeah," Rutherford said. "Sounds terrible."

Byrne said, "The last person anyone would want to emulate."

"Yeah," Rutherford said. "You'd think."

TEN

The toolbox weighed a ton but lugging it around was no inconvenience. Like many of the trappings of the sniper's particular vocation, his heavy toolbox and stiff coveralls felt glamorous, romantic, though they were very much neither of those things. Ignoring discomfort. Acting causal while on high alert. Walking slowly in plain sight while infiltrating a secure location just in time for his limited window of opportunity. It all embodied a strange combination of macho and Zen. If pressed to describe it, the sniper would have simply called it "badass."

The coveralls and box of tools acted as an invisibility cloak. He had learned long ago that when trying not to be noticed, it was wise to dress as someone nobody wants to see. A grease-smeared repairman fit that bill nicely. The person who needs a repairman is happy to see them, but to everyone else, his presence serves as an unwelcome reminder that the machines they depend on will eventually break and that they themselves will be incapable of fixing them; a powerful double whammy of doubt that most people don't want to deal with. The only better disguise he'd ever found was to dress as a hippie gathering signatures for a petition. In that disguise people made a point of not seeing him, often going so far as to literally hide from his view.

The sniper looked at his watch. He had entered the studio lot with almost twenty minutes to spare. More than enough time, but not too much.

In his line of work there was a temptation to arrive hours early and wait for the window of opportunity to open, but he was paid to kill people, not time. Loitering around in the target zone just gave the adversary more opportunity to catch you there. That said, he did have plenty of time for a nice, unhurried, serpentine stroll around the lot, which was also good. Ambling around seemingly at random served the dual purpose of making it obvious if he was being followed and preventing competing snipers from anticipating his route.

Thieves worry about getting robbed. Lawyers worry about getting sued. He worried about getting assassinated.

With five minutes to go before the window of opportunity opened, he approached the building where he would set up shop. For the most part, studio lots are surprisingly unglamorous, blue-collar environments. But among the solid-walled, windowless soundstages surrounded by asphalt, there was one building: four stories with lots of glass and fancy awnings, surrounded by grass, trees, and shaded paths. This building, much more comfortable than the cavernous boxes where the paying work got done, was set aside for admin staff and executives, the people whose work was to do the paying.

At the far end of the building's side wall he saw an unmarked steel door with a single keyhole and a metal flange to pull it open instead of a knob: the emergency exit at the bottom of a rear stairwell.

He put down his fake toolbox, pulled a slim packet containing his real tools out of his pocket, knelt in front of the door, and began to pick the lock.

Again, his repairman disguise worked to his advantage. Anyone who saw him would assume he was simply working on the lock, which, in fact, he was. All the best lies are mostly true. The only thing that worried him was some office stooge sneaking out the door as he tried to open it, but the odds of that were low.

The tumblers clicked. The lock turned. The bolt retracted. He pulled the door open, picked up his toolbox, and entered, doing his best to look like he was not sneaking. It would be easy to disable the lock so he wouldn't need to pick it again. A piece of duct tape would do the trick, but he let it close and latch normally. Tampering further with the lock would be an unnecessary precaution, and in his line of work, unnecessary precautions were often referred to as "physical evidence."

Four floors of stairs didn't take long to climb. He emerged on the roof, the only living soul in sight. The client's intel was accurate. The rear stairwell provided a great means of entry and would serve well as an exit when the job was done, or if everything went to hell.

He made a point of not running around the air handlers, over the ducts and conduits to the building's edge. He found hurrying was like taking laxatives: useful when you needed to, counterproductive when you didn't.

He looked over the roof's edge. The vantage point was just as good as the client promised. He looked down on the two soundstages where they made *No Matter How Improbable*. A police officer lurked next to the door watching everyone who came or went. In a way, he pitied the cop, assigned to prevent the target's death. Instead, he would witness it.

Crew and other staff milled in and out, but at some ill-defined point in the next few minutes the target, Russell Byrne, would leave for the day and walk into the makeup trailer, putting himself out in the open for approximately twenty seconds. After makeup removal, Byrne would be exposed again as he stepped out of the trailer and around the corner, but only for a second and with no advance warning. Not enough time to put Byrne's head in the crosshairs. The trip from the soundstage to the makeup trailer was his window.

He couldn't know for sure when that window would open, but he knew it would be soon. The actors arrived at different times each morning depending on when they were needed. Usually they left at different times as well, but Byrne had an engagement, some sort of performance art piece. It gave Byrne what they called a "hard out."

He rolled the term around in his head as he put down his toolbox. He loved the sound of it. *Hard out.* He thought it might make a great name for his future memoirs, which would be published either anonymously, posthumously, or from prison. After this job he had no doubt there would be a market for the book. This was the kind of job that made a hit man famous if caught, and infamous if not. By offing Byrne he was fulfilling the final act of a classic Hollywood story. First the mother: young, famous, beautiful, survives an OD just to die in an accident on the ambulance ride to the hospital, taking a paramedic and driver with her. Years later, her son fights his way to fame and success just to die under equally tragic circumstances, snuffed out in a single shot by a highly skilled master assassin.

His pulse quickened and a smile crossed his lips as he opened the toolbox and lifted out the top tray full of greasy tools. The beauty of working in an industry that adheres to the Han Solo reimbursement plan (half now, half when we get to Alderaan) was that he could spend part of the take from the job on equipment needed to complete that same job.

The toolbox alone was a joy to behold, with its perfectly hidden compartment lined with custom-cut foam padding. Nestled inside, the blackened steel components of a top-of-the-line, custom-made, low-velocity, suppressed sniper rifle, a tool perfectly suited to the job. For very long distances, a higher velocity would be preferable. But with speed and range came noise and muzzle flash, a showy display that drew attention he did not want. For a situation like this, where the target was only a hundred or so meters away, this new rifle would prove accurate and deadly while producing no flash and less noise than a hearty cough. The loudest sound involved in the murder would be the surprised shouts of anyone in the splash zone.

After he had removed all three foam inserts, lining them up neatly on the roof deck, he lifted the buttstock and ran his fingers across the knurled grip. He picked up a black steel spring and pressed it into place. While keeping the spring compressed, he slid the main assembly of the gun, called the lower receiver, into its exquisitely machined groove. The scope popped into place with a click that satisfied on an almost spiritual level. He took great pleasure in assembling his weapon. Before him he had no batteries, no motors, no computers. Just an assortment of inanimate objects made of metal, wood, and glass, each one harmless on its own. When assembled like a puzzle they worked together to form a precision engineered instrument of death. It was more than a tool; it was a metaphor, an object imbued with great symbolism and multiple important life lessons about human ingenuity, potential, and the importance of being part of the team rather than its target.

Reverently, as if handling a sacred relic, he lifted the barrel. He took a moment to look through it, noting the sharpness and precision of the spiral rifling of its inner bore. Driven by a reflex he couldn't suppress, he moved the barrel back and forth, then down slowly, while peering through it and humming the James Bond theme. Laughing at himself, he pressed the barrel to the receiver assembly. A loose circular bezel slid down along the barrel until its threads caught on a matching set on the receiver. He held the rifle upright, its barrel sticking up like an antenna while he screwed the bezel down.

He fitted the suppressor onto the end of the barrel, where it would serve its dual paradoxical purposes of drawing less attention and making the gun look about a thousand times cooler.

He cradled the rifle in the crook of his elbow, still pointed upward as he inserted a fully loaded magazine, completing the rifle's transformation from a collection of parts into a powerful machine designed for the discreet delivery of death.

He thought about the phrase *the discreet delivery of death*. It might be an even better title than *Hard Out*. Maybe he'd use it for a follow-up. After all, he had no intention for Byrne to be his last high-profile job.

Down at ground level, the soundstage door opened. A young woman with a tablet walked out at a brisk pace. A second person followed her, then a third. He knew that eventually Byrne would emerge.

The door closed for a moment, then opened again. A slight young man in a leather jacket walked out, head on a swivel, looking for any ground-level attacks. The target, Byrne, followed behind him.

This was it. The moment of his success, his reward for being patient, being careful, doing things right way, the first time, every time.

A grim smile crossed the sniper's lips as he lowered his weapon and peered down the scope. The smile disappeared when the rifle's barrel drooped two inches at the muzzle, stopping with a distinct clunk.

He blinked, then waggled the gun back and forth. The barrel lolled from side to side. In an instant he knew what was wrong. He looked to the black foam inserts beside him and saw a black metal washer lying almost invisible in its custom-cut depression.

He unscrewed the bezel as quickly as he could. The barrel came loose and nearly fell.

Below, Byrne was now fully out in the open. The guy in the leather jacket walked ahead of him. An Asian guy in a suit followed behind, then a few steps back there was a guy in the kind of crappy nylon jacket one buys at a surplus store. All of them looked to be on high alert, walking fast.

He placed the washer in its intended mount, between the receiver and the barrel. He pressed the barrel back in place, no longer caring about making noise. In his haste he nearly cross threaded the bezel, but he finally got it seated right, tightened it down, and lifted the rifle back into position.

The crosshairs centered on the back of Byrne's head just as the makeup trailer door closed, blocking the target from view before he could squeeze off a shot. The guys in the leather and nylon jackets stayed outside, looking out for possible threats. He silently seethed at them until the one in the nylon jacket glanced toward the roofline. The assassin dropped to all fours, hiding himself from view, he hoped. He squeezed his eyes shut and moaned, "Oh, fudge."

ELEVEN

Rutherford stood in the corner, trying to decide how he felt about what he saw. Luckily, he was at an art gallery, so that's what he was supposed to be doing.

The art gallery looked exactly as one would picture an art gallery. Wood floors, white walls—Rutherford suspected that he could ask a random person to close their eyes and imagine any gallery they'd ever seen in any movie and they would picture the room in which he stood. By the same token, aside from the plainclothes police, the people gathered to watch Russell Byrne's performance piece looked and dressed exactly as one would expect people who would gather in an art gallery to look and dress; so much so that Rutherford wondered if the space had been made by a set designer and populated with actors. Then he realized he was in Los Angeles. Odds were very good that the space had been designed by someone who also worked as a set designer, and that many of the people were, or at some point had hoped to be, actors.

A quick glance at the beat-up Casio watch on his wrist told him it was time to find an unobtrusive spot for a phone call. He weaved his way around the gallery patrons and out the door to the street. The gallery's glass storefront radiated a warm yellow light out onto the sidewalk. At the corner of the building, Albert stood, talking into his phone.

"I know it's a lot of files, but you have a lot of 3D printers and mills. If you put multiple machines on it, you can easily get it done tonight. Then you can deliver it tomorrow morning with the other two prototypes."

Rutherford pointed to his watch. Albert shrugged apologetically and shook his head.

Rutherford mouthed, *Okay*.

Albert smiled. "Assembly won't be hard either. I'll send instructions. It's essentially a sandwich of four thin layers. All you'd do is glue and fold it. No soldering. I'll handle the software installation. Seriously, it's all down to whether the prints come out right."

Rutherford turned around and looked into the gallery, satisfied that he could see inside well enough to get involved if anyone made an attempt on Byrne's life.

A TV hanging sideways in the gallery window to give the impression of a poster displayed the words: *Solar Eclipse by Russell Byrne*. Slowly, a picture of a full eclipse faded in, a fiery ring around a pitch-black circle in a black sky. Below the picture, more words appeared:

"*When a vital, luminous star is obscured from view by a dark, lifeless body.*"

Finally, below that, a review faded in. "A challenging work with multiple layers of meaning."

As Rutherford reflected on the fact that the review didn't include the word *good*, he heard the tone in his earpiece that announced a conference call beginning. He pulled out his phone, accepted the call, and saw the icons for Terri, Sloan, Max, and Professor Sherwood pop up on his screen.

The first voice he heard was Terri. "That's almost everyone."

Rutherford said, "I'm afraid it is everyone. Albert's tied up on a call with a rapid-prototyping workshop. He'll join when he can, and if not, I'll fill him in."

Terri said, "Fair enough. Let's get started then. So, as you're all aware, there was no attempt on any of the Watsons today. Professor Sherwood and I have seen ours safely home and left the surveillance to the local police. Where are the rest of you?"

Rutherford said, "Filming at the studio was uneventful. I'm probably off ranch dressing for life, but that's a story for another time. The showrunner was weirdly hostile. She made it clear that she didn't want us there."

Terri asked, "Did you apologize for her inconvenience?"

"No."

Terri said, "Good. You might just be getting the hang of your job."

"Thanks. Now Albert and I are at the art gallery where Byrne does his performance piece. When he's done we'll accompany him home and leave him to LAPD, like you did."

Sloan said, "Max and I are at our Watson's home. We intend to keep him under our protection for a few more hours."

Terri said, "That's very thorough of you."

Max said, "Mac, our Watson, is a lovely man. He and his wife invited us home for dinner and schnapps. We're doing a jigsaw puzzle."

Sloan said, "And keeping him under our protection. A man can make some dangerous decisions while drinking schnapps."

"Sounds good," Terri said. "So, we got a note promising a dead Watson every day, and the very next day, no dead Watson. Any theories?"

Sloan said, "Most likely the note was a hoax, sent by someone who had nothing to do with the murder. Or it could have been sent by the killer hoping we'd get too distracted trying to prevent the next crime to solve the first one. Also, it could be that the killer tried to kill a Watson today and failed without anyone noticing."

Max said, "All the security and police surrounding all the Watsons, and as well organized as serial killers usually are, that seems unlikely."

Terri said, "Whatever the reason that nobody was killed today, we still have yesterday's murder to solve. Good news on that front. Claire and her team at CartFulls were able to trace the memory wire used in the booby-trapped watch."

"Was it sold by CartFulls?" Sloan asked. "Please tell me it was sold by CartFulls."

Sherwood popped into his impression of Cary the shopping cart. "A fifty-pound spool of memory wire?"

In unison, he, Rutherford, and Max said, "Oh no!"

"It was not sold by CartFulls," Terri said. "Though that would have made things even easier. Not many places make or sell that stuff, and they tend to keep records. A company that produces that specific formulation sold a spool of wire in that gauge to an electronics shop in Los Angeles operated by one Boris DeBeul."

Max pursed his lips. "Suspicious."

"Very suspicious," Sloan said, "almost verging on being ironclad proof of guilt. It's so suspicious that it breaks on through to the other side and makes me think he didn't do it."

"Exactly," Max said. "DeBeul wouldn't leave such a clear chain of evidence."

Sherwood said, "Solid evidence that DeBeul—our chief suspect—made the murder weapon . . . makes you two think he's innocent?"

Max said, "I may well be wrong. I'm just saying that the man known as the Inventor of Antwerp would not make such a rudimentary mistake."

Terri said, "Tomorrow morning we'll ask him about it and see what he has to say. All right, everyone. Good work today. Sloan, Max, I hope you have fun tonight."

Max said, "We fully expect to."

"Rutherford," Terri said, "you and Albert enjoy the performance art."

Rutherford said, "I am less confident."

The call ended. Rutherford put his phone away and went back into the gallery. After a moment, Albert joined him. Rutherford started to fill him in on what was discussed in the conference call, but the lights went down and all conversation hushed. Everyone looked to the corner of the gallery floor and the door to a back room that had been cordoned off with velvet ropes for Russell Byrne's performance.

After a pregnant pause, a projector hanging from the ceiling covered the wall with what appeared to be a national news broadcast from the early nineties. A middle-aged man with fantastic hair stared into the camera. "Tragedy struck today, as television and film star Catalina Byrne perished in a freak traffic accident." As the anchorman tossed to the field reporter, a second national news report about the death of Catalina Byrne was projected on the ceiling. After a few seconds, a third appeared on the floor. All three had their full soundtracks, playing at equal volume, creating an unintelligible cacophony. After ten seconds of this, the door opened, and Russell Byrne stepped out carrying a notebook and wearing a suit and top hat that were covered with old smartphones and tablets, all of which played various news stories, documentaries, and retrospectives about Catalina Byrne at full volume. Russell Byrne looked around the gathered audience, bowed to them politely, opened his notebook, and in a normal, conversational volume barely audible over the din, began to read aloud.

"Review of touring company production of *Les Misérables*, June of two thousand three. Quote, 'Newcomer Russell Byrne brings welcome energy and enthusiasm to the role of Marius.' Review of *ER* episode 'Never Ever, Yet.' Quote, 'Russell Byrne manages to somehow draw focus from the stars while lying motionless with his eyes closed.' Article in a trade publication about a Dr Pepper commercial featuring Russell Byrne. Quote, 'the forgettable concept is uplifted by the talent of the actor.'"

Rutherford and Albert stood, their heads cocked to get at least one ear closer to Byrne, both grimacing with the effort of making out his words.

Rutherford said, "He doesn't have to keep saying 'quote' like that."

Albert said, "So, it's about how he feels overshadowed by his mother?"

"On the surface, I guess."

They struggled to listen for a moment as he read more positive reviews amid the jumble of accounts of his mother's death.

Rutherford said, "It's ironic. He's mad that everyone fixates on his mom, and he complains by calling attention to his mom."

Albert nodded. "And it's not even his mom or her work he's being drowned out by. It's the news, other people talking about how she died."

Rutherford realized he was squinting and holding a hand to his ear to hear better. He looked at Albert, and all the rest of the audience members, and saw they were doing the same thing. "Huh," he said. "The review they posted was totally accurate. Byrne's piece is challenging, it has multiple layers of meaning, and they never claimed it was good."

TWELVE

The minivan veered on its own into the next lane, inserting its front driver's-side fender between two slow-moving cars like a wedge, forcing itself into a crack in the bumper-to-bumper LA morning commute. The car behind slowed, making room for the minivan to merge by pulling up uncomfortably close to the back of a semi. Rutherford sat in the driver's seat, one hand squeezing the door handle, the other clawing at the armrest while the soles of his feet and back of his neck pressed against the floor and headrest.

Terri said, "Rutherford, please, try to calm down."

Rutherford forced a laugh. "What? I'm calm. I'm just, you know, kicking back."

"I'm sorry, but Mr. Capp wants us to evaluate TurkMO's service, and to do that we have to use it."

Rutherford said, "I don't know what you're talking about. I'm good."

The brakes applied rather sharply, causing Rutherford to tighten his grip and increase his pressure on the floor and headrest. He clenched his teeth as the minivan narrowly avoided rear-ending the truck in front of them. He saw Terri observing his reactions and said, "I'm just, you know, shocked at the sexist imagery on that truck's mud flaps."

Max laughed, "Yes, the infamous chrome woman. The female form, idealized by people who are themselves less than ideal. It is the perfect woman as pictured by people with the taste level required to buy or make decorative mud flaps in the first place."

"If that's their perfect woman, what's their idea of a perfect man?" Sloan asked.

"Isn't it obvious? Yosemite Sam, guns drawn, masking his vulnerability, warning anyone getting too close to, as he says, 'Back off.'"

Rutherford continued staring at the truck's rear bumper in front of them. As the ebb and flow of traffic caused the bumper to draw closer, Rutherford's eyes bulged, his lips drew back into a rictus grin, and he emitted an elongated grunt. He noticed Terri looking at him and tried to cover. "I was laughing at Max's joke."

Max said, "I wasn't joking. The male inability to accept healthy intimacy is one of the world's primary problems."

Terri rolled her eyes and leaned in toward the touchscreen set into the dash. "Pardon me, driver?"

How can I help you, ma'am? And please, call me Clark."

"Clark, it might help my associate relax if you described your driving setup to him, so he can know how much more information and control you have than a normal driver."

"I'd love to, ma'am, but I can't. I'm not allowed to describe the workings of our system with any non-TurkMO employees."

Rutherford asked, "Why not? What aren't you allowed to tell me? It's bad, isn't it?"

Clark said, "No, sir. We just don't want to divulge any secrets about our technology."

"I'm sure," Rutherford said. "Secrets like how bad it is."

Terri twisted around in her seat to look in the back of the van. "Albert, would you tell . . . Albert, what are you doing?"

Rutherford glanced into the rearview mirror and saw Albert sitting in the minivan's rear seat, his oversized briefcase computer open with its screen casting light up onto his face. Multiple wires looped up from the inside of the case and over the back of the screen as he tinkered with something Rutherford couldn't see. Professor Sherwood sat crammed over to one side, pressing himself against the window to give Albert more space.

"What?" Albert asked. "Oh, sorry. I got a delivery from the rapid prototyping lab, and I'm just flashing firmware onto the ROM. It's funny, I had two prototypes I was so excited about the day before yesterday, and now I'm already on to the next thing. Here, Max, please pass these up to Rutherford. They're both for him."

Terri reached back and took two objects from Max. Rutherford reached over to take them, but something he saw through the windshield got his attention. He made a loud hissing sound, drawing a full lungful of breath through his teeth in roughly one second as he again nearly grabbed the steering wheel. Terri looked at his white knuckles and rigid posture as he stared through the windshield. "I'll hold on to these for now," she said, holding up a shotgun shell and an unwrapped all-day sucker. "You need to concentrate on not driving."

Albert said, "The lollipop's the replacement for your match. It's a tracking device. If you need to keep track of something, bite down on the sucker, then throw it at whatever is getting away. It'll stick and transmit its GPS coordinates. Just remember, and this is important: Don't lick it or put it back in your mouth after you've bitten it. It's got a very powerful transmitter and multiple glue packs. Both bad things to have activated in your mouth."

"Rutherford, keep that in mind," Terri said, as she held the fake sucker up for Rutherford. "Now put it in your mouth."

Sloan said, "Suck it, Rutherford. What? Don't look at me like that, Terri. How often do you get a legitimate business reason to tell a coworker to suck it? I'm not going to pass up an opportunity like this."

The rest of the team invited Rutherford to "suck it," as Terri handed him the sucker, which he joylessly put in his mouth.

Albert said, "And because you have the sucker to track things, you don't need the tracker dart shell for your pistol's shotgun barrels anymore, so I made that new one for you. It shoots Professor Sherwood's bee pheromone. If you blast someone with that, the professor won't have to spritz them with his spray bottle before he releases the bees."

"A nice idea," Professor Sherwood said, "but unnecessary, since Her Majesty needs no pheromone pre-spray."

Terri handed Rutherford the shell. "Load it up."

Albert said, "And now that all that's out of the way, I can move on to the real excitement. My newest invention!"

Rutherford let out a loud yelp, nearly dropped his partially loaded hand-cannon into his lap, and lurched forward, stopping his hands just before they grasped the steering wheel. He hovered there over the controls for a second, watching as the minivan swerved around the pedestrian who was strolling across the busy road while shouting obscenities at Rutherford, which they stopped immediately when they saw the enormous gun in his hand.

Terri asked, "Problem, Rutherford?"

"Yeah! We almost hit that guy, I panicked a little, and I nearly bit down on the lollipop."

Albert said, "Don't do that."

"I didn't! It'd help if I weren't riding in a van being driven by a guy I don't know, who, let's be honest, is probably working from a laptop in his bedroom. No offense, Clark."

Clark said, "I promise you, sir, I'm not driving your car from my bedroom."

"So you're what, in an office?"

"Yes, sir."

"A home office?"

After a long pause, the driver admitted, "Perhaps."

Rutherford slid the cartridge into one of the shotgun barrels, closed the chamber with a loud click, and holstered his gun. "Do you also sleep in this home office?"

Terri said, "Rutherford, please stop insulting Clark. Let him focus on his work, and you focus on yours."

Clark said, "Thank you."

Rutherford muttered, "Okay. But notice he didn't deny sleeping in his office, or using a laptop."

Albert said, "Here's my other new toy." He held up what looked like a used take-out container from a Chinese restaurant that had been crushed into a roundish mass about the size of a baseball.

Everyone else stared at the container. Nobody said a word.

Albert said, "I know it doesn't look like much. It's a prototype."

Sloan said, "A prototype made of garbage?"

"No," Albert said. "A prototype made to *look* like garbage. Inside it's packed with memory wire, microphones, accelerometers, and twenty tiny fish-eye cameras. They create a full three-hundred-sixty-degree panorama. Half of the image is of the ground, but still, that could be useful for following footprints."

Sloan said, "So it's electronics covered in garbage."

"It's not garbage! Garbage only becomes garbage once you no longer have a use for it. I'm using it here as camouflage. It's not garbage."

Sloan asked, "Where'd you get the take-out box you're using as camouflage?"

"That doesn't matter."

"Out of the garbage?"

"Never mind that. I got the idea the day before yesterday at the Hindman murder scene. We were in this restricted area, surrounded by cops keeping people out, but a piece of trash rolled right through the middle of the place and nobody seemed to notice."

Max nodded. "Whoever first admits to spotting a piece of garbage will be obliged to pick it up."

"Exactly. Then I looked at the murder watch with the memory wire and I got an idea." Albert continued to hold up the clump of cardboard, pushed forward to be over the seat space between Max and Sloan. With his other hand he poked at his laptop screen. The carton almost leapt out of Albert's hand and fell to the empty seat below. It rolled forward, up the seat's natural incline. It dropped to the floor, where it went under the front passenger seat.

Max and Terri shouted in surprise.

"What?!" Rutherford whipped his head from side to side like a barn owl trying to get water out of its ear. "What's going on?"

Sloan's artificial voice said, "Laughing. Laughing."

Terri leaned way forward, twisting herself to watch for the crumpled container to emerge from beneath her seat. When it finally did, and brushed against her ankle, she shouted again and drew her feet up onto the seat.

It rolled back under her seat into Sloan's footwell. Sloan reached down and picked it up, pinching it by the very tips of her finger and thumb despite the fact that she was wearing gloves.

"Gross," she said. "It's all fuzzy now."

"Lint must've stuck to the old cooking oil," Albert said. "Just makes it look more like trash, but if it starts to interfere with operation, I'll cover it in a clear coat or something. Oh, let me show you the best part."

He poked at his laptop screen again. The container flattened out as if someone had stomped on it repeatedly.

Albert said, "Pressed thin like this, we can slide it under doors and into windows."

Sloan held it close to her helmet's visor. "You can see the little lenses at the corners of some of the folds, but only if you look for them."

Terri asked, "And you can get usable video and sound from that thing?"

"It isn't broadcast quality," Albert said, "but it's more than good enough for surveillance."

"Well that's excellent, Albert. Well done."

"Thanks, Terri. I'm pretty proud of it. I call it *the wad*."

Terri said, "Please don't."

"It's just a working name. I'm sure we'll come up with something better. "CyberWad. TechnoWad.""

Terri closed her eyes. "Albert, my problem with the name wasn't that I thought the word *wad* needed a modifier."

The minivan pulled up to DeBeul's crummy electronics shop, squeezing itself into a surprisingly tight parallel spot almost directly in front.

As the van came to a stop, Clark said, "Thank you for traveling with TurkMO today. I hope you had a pleasant ride." The word *ride* was drowned out by a loud woof.

"Is that a dog?" Rutherford asked. "Do you have a dog in the office?"

"Yes, sir. I'm allowed to."

Rutherford asked, "Aren't you worried about it interfering with you while you drive?"

"Brunhilda wouldn't do that. She's old and lazy. She just stays curled up here next to me on the bed."

"On the bed?"

Terri said, "Come on, Rutherford."

"I was right!"

"Time to go."

"Look," Rutherford said. "It's cool. We got here. But unless he has some sort of office bed, I was right!"

Terri said, "We're going, Rutherford. Clark, thanks for the ride."

The team piled out onto the sidewalk and filed into DeBeul's shop. The air inside still smelled of hot dust and burnt plastic. DeBeul sat behind the counter, peering down at a pile of circuits, smoke trailing from the tip of his soldering iron as he gesticulated in concert with his shouts. "Damn it, I told you to de-solder the contacts for the capacitors!"

There was a distant crash, then the apprentice yelled from the back room, "I did!"

"There are still blobs of old solder on the contacts."

"You told me to de-solder the connections. I did. You didn't say to clean off all of the old solder."

DeBeul sat up and turned to face the door to the back room. "When I tell you to do something, I assume that you'll understand that I mean for you to do it well, to do it right! As if any reasonable man would assume that I meant for you to do a half-assed job. Oh, wait. I'm sorry. I just had one of those experiences where you say something out loud and realize as you're saying it that it's nonsense. This is my fault. Any reasonable person would have assumed that I wanted a lazy, half-assed job done of it *because* I asked you! What else could I have possibly expected? From now on, whenever I tell you to do something, I'll remind you to do it right, since doing quality work runs counter to every instinct you have, you lazy little oaf!"

"You're calling me lazy? All you do all day is boss me around, and now you can't be bothered to get up off your ass and come in here to shout at me."

"You work for me. You should have anticipated my need and come in here to get shouted at. Now pick that up!"

"Pick what up?"

"Whatever you knocked on the floor!"

"You don't even know what it is!"

"I know it doesn't belong on the floor, or I wouldn't have put it up on whatever you knocked it down from. Now pick it up, and since it seems I must include this part, pick it up *right*! I want it fully up off the floor!"

The apprentice groaned.

Max cleared his throat. DeBeul turned and smiled. "Max, you and your friends have come for another visit. How lovely."

"It's not a social call, Boris."

"More unsubstantiated accusations to share? I always enjoy those."

"No, I have something much more troubling. Evidence."

"What? Evidence? That I did something illegal?"

Rutherford glanced at Albert, hoping to communicate to someone how ridiculous he found DeBeul's professed innocence, but he saw that Albert was preoccupied, having pulled the wad from his pocket. Albert nodded to Rutherford and dropped the wad to the ground, where it landed lightly, with no sound.

DeBeul shouted, "Hey, pick that up!"

From the back room, his apprentice said, "I did!"

"Not you!" He pointed at Albert. "You, young man, what do you think you're doing, dropping your trash on my floor. This is a respectable shop. You pick that up!"

Albert said, "Sorry," and picked up his creation while everyone in the room silently watched.

Sloan's artificial voice repeated, "Laughing," in the team's earpieces.

Albert muttered, "Deployment's an issue."

Max said, "Boris, the memory wire used in the rigged watch, it was traceable back to the manufacturer."

"So? Proves nothing."

"That led us to the store that sold it."

"So? Still proves nothing."

"They have a record of selling a spool of it to you, at this shop."

DeBeul's eyes grew wide. "That . . . that proves something."

Max said, "I know."

"Max, I have a code of conduct, a sense of what is right and what is wrong, and I would never even consider killing someone with a device I made using traceable parts."

"I know that, Boris. That's what I told my colleagues. *He would never commit a crime like this, so clumsily.*"

"That's good to hear," DeBeul said.

Max said, "Let's talk this through. You know this kind of work better than anybody. Based on what you've seen of their handiwork, what do we know about the killer?"

"They are mostly incompetent. Their work setting me up was brutish and dumb. Their wiring was sloppy and derivative, built entirely on other people's creative work. The mechanism they built and the method of death was flamboyant, too clever by half, but crude and nasty. And the fact that they tried to set me up shows that they are aware of my work, know of my location, and for some reason want to see me inconvenienced."

DeBeul thought for a moment, then began shouting so he could be heard anywhere in the building. "We're looking for someone with experience in electronics, but with limited knowledge and skill. Someone who seems dedicated to making me unhappy."

DeBeul rose from his stool and turned to face the door to the back room as he shouted, "Someone unbelievably lazy, with an inflated sense of her own abilities, but lacking the skills and intelligence to properly hide her tracks. Hmm. I wonder, do I know anyone like that?"

From the back of the building Rutherford heard running footsteps and a door slamming.

"The back alley only lets out one way." DeBeul pointed to the right. "She drives a blue Toyota hatchback she can barely keep running. You'll have no trouble catching her. Happy hunting. Oh, Max?"

As the team headed for the door, Max paused. "Yes?"

DeBeul smiled. "If you happen to run into any mutual friends of ours, tell them I said hello."

THIRTEEN

They ran out of the shop and into the van. As the others fastened their seat belts, Terri pressed the TurkMO button.

Rutherford pulled the lollipop tracker from his mouth. "You think that's smart?"

Terri said, "Yes. You'll be free to jump out for a foot chase."

Rutherford said, "If it comes to that."

Terri glanced at him.

"Okay, *when* it comes to that."

The usual chimes played, and a man's voice said, "Thank you for using TurkMO. I'm Kenny, your remote driver. Where can I take you?"

At that moment, a dented blue hatchback emerged from the alley. The apprentice hunched over the wheel, as if leaning forward would make it move faster. She stopped at the alley's exit, searching for a place to merge into traffic. Looking up the street for an opening, she saw the team in the van, ready to pursue her. She floored it, forcing other drivers to slam on their brakes as she swerved, tires screeching, into the street.

Rutherford pointed with the slobber-covered lollipop. "Follow that car!"

Kenny's disembodied voice said, "Which car?"

"The blue Toyota hatchback that just took off."

"Where are they leading you?"

"What?"

"The driver of the Toyota. If you tell me where you're trying to go, I can find a way without following them. We may even beat them there."

"I don't know where she's going. I just need you to follow her."

"Sir, if I suspect a customer is stalking someone, I'm obligated to report it."

"I'm a cop. She's a suspect."

"Seriously?"

"Yes."

"What did she do?"

Rutherford growled, "Never mind." He pressed the TurkMO screen again, started the minivan, and moved the vehicle back and forth a few times to wiggle it free of its parallel-parking space, coming perilously close to a collision with each move. He stomped on the gas and the van roared out into the street. Thanks to the nature of Downtown LA traffic, the apprentice had only gone about half a block and was still clearly visible, stuck several cars back from the intersection, waiting for the light to change.

The minivan was also clearly visible to her, because as soon as the team began an active pursuit, the hatchback lurched to the left into the opposing lane of traffic.

Terri said, "Rutherford, we've—"

"Gotta chase her. On it."

Rutherford fought back all of his instincts and steered the minivan into oncoming traffic, dimly aware that behind him, Albert was throwing camera drones out of an open window to catch the chase's conclusion, whether that turned out to be a foot chase, a fistfight, or a fatal head-on accident.

The hatchback left an empty wake thanks to the other drivers naturally attempting to get out of the way of the maniac driving the wrong way down the street. This empty area allowed Rutherford to gain on her. A few drivers tried to retake their original lane after the maniac in the hatchback had passed, only to see an even bigger maniac in a minivan following her, and decided to stay in their relatively safe lane.

Professor Sherwood yelled from the back of the van, "Deploying Her Majesty!"

Terri said, "NO! I don't want to—"

Rutherford glanced in the rearview mirror and saw the professor looking down at a two-stick aircraft radio controller he held in one hand while using the other to push a thick, clear hose extending from his portable hive-suitcase out the window. Small black shapes streamed down the tube and out of the van, into the open air. Off to the side of the van, Rutherford saw Her Majesty: a quadcopter similar in design to Albert's camera drones, but with specially shielded propellers, and a compartment on its belly that held the hive's queen. The rest of the bees gathered around the queen instinctively and would follow her wherever the quadcopter went, essentially becoming a remote-controlled swarm.

Terri said, "Professor, I wanted to wait to use that thing until you had more practice."

"This will be good practice," the professor said.

"Using it on a case isn't practice," Terri said. "It's using! Look, Professor, can you fly that thing?"

"Yes. Of course."

"Albert, can he fly it?"

Albert said, "Sure, it's easy to fly, as long as he keeps the autopilot turned on."

Sloan said, "That's an interesting statement."

The hatchback screeched through an intersection and around the corner to the left, its front wheels struggling to both pull and steer the car through a much tighter, faster turn than the engineers who built it ever had in mind. It drifted outward into the proper lane for its direction as it disappeared around the corner. Rutherford still had a lot of ground to gain and worried he might lose her, until he heard the crash.

Rounding the corner while leaning on the horn and weaving through the drivers on the cross street, Rutherford saw the hatchback with its front end wedged under the back of a black SUV, the bumper of which had gone through the hatchback's front window and now hung over the dashboard. The apprentice shoved the deployed airbag out of her way, kicked her mangled door open, and burst out onto the street, waving a pistol.

The drones reached her well before the minivan. They approached her in a straight line, then orbited around her, getting great footage from every angle of her attempts to shoot them out of the sky. After missing two drones, nicking one just enough to make it deviate from its flight path, and causing everyone in earshot to freak out and run for cover, she did the same herself, running off of the street and between two buildings.

Terri said, "Ruther—"

Rutherford grunted, "Yeah, I get it. *After her,*" around his fake sucker as he brought the minivan to a sliding halt behind the wrecked hatchback. He leapt out and took off after the apprentice on foot. Rutherford hated the grungy jeans and the bulky leather jacket he was forced to wear, but whenever he engaged in a foot pursuit, he was glad that he got to wear sneakers. He ran straight for the gap between buildings where the apprentice went.

Rutherford said, "I don't like running with this in my mouth. If I fall, I'll choke."

Terri said, "True. Try holding it in your hand."

Rutherford grasped the stick with his right hand and held the sucker at eye level. To adjust his balance, he stopped swinging his left arm, holding it up and out to the side. He ran five steps like that before every member of the team told him to put the sucker back.

"Yeah," Rutherford said as he tucked the sucker into his cheek. "I think I was flouncing."

Terri said, "Run! Run!"

"I'm running as fast as I can!"

Professor Sherwood said, "Don't worry. Her Majesty is right behind you."

Rutherford ran faster.

In Rutherford's earpiece, Albert said, "You're almost there. She's in that alley."

Rutherford said, "Cool."

"She's around the corner," Albert said.

He was only steps away now. "Yeah, I know!"

Rutherford rounded the corner, then came to a halt, his feet sliding on the gritty pavement, managing to stop just in front of the apprentice. She stood in the middle of the narrow gap, her gun pointed at Rutherford's face. He put his hands up.

"I'm saying she's waiting right around the corner," Albert said. "Well, you see for yourself now."

"Yeah," Rutherford said.

"Pull Her Majesty back. Rutherford's too close to the target," Terry shouted. "Max, get out there."

"Hands up," the apprentice said.

Rutherford raised his hands even higher. The non-bee-encrusted drones positioned themselves, one behind and to the left of her, one behind and to the right of him, and the third above and beside them, getting a shot of them both.

Sherwood said, "I can block off the other end of the alley, around the corner."

"Good idea," Terri said. "Please do. Hey, looks like a civilian's approaching."

In the earpiece, Max gasped, "Shit! Oh no! No no no no no!"

"Why couldn't you just arrest DeBeul?" the apprentice asked, tears welling up in her eyes.

Rutherford said, "Because he didn't do it."

"He's done plenty of other stuff!"

A deep, amiable voice with an aggressively charming Australian accent said, "She's got a point there, friend."

The apprentice looked over Rutherford's shoulder. Rutherford started to turn to look himself but stopped when the apprentice shifted her focus back to him, jabbing her gun at his face as if being shot from five inches closer would make him five inches deader.

In the earpiece, Max moaned.

The owner of the voice stepped up to stand beside Rutherford. He was tall, with jet-black hair graying at the temples and a wide, contagious smile. Rutherford figured he was in his sixties, and judging from his build and posture now, he must have been pretty close to the perfect male specimen when he was younger.

"Hands up," the apprentice shouted.

The Australian lifted his hands to shoulder height with his palms facing forward. "Okay, okay. They're up."

In his ear, Terri and Sloan both said, "Max?"

"Yes. Right," Max said. "Don't worry, Rutherford. Stay calm. I'm coming."

The Australian winked at Rutherford and smiled at the apprentice. "Look, it's a tough spot you're in. But you can handle it. If you just back away, you can keep your gun on us, get around the back of this building here, and you'll have a nice head start on us. You'll probably get away."

Rutherford knew it was nonsense. At most that would get her a lead of a couple seconds.

The apprentice, it seemed, wanted to believe, but couldn't quite bring herself to. For reassurance, she glanced over her shoulder at the back of the building to see if the Australian gentleman's story checked out.

The instant the apprentice diverted her attention, the Australian lunged forward in a blur of motion. He reached up with both hands, grabbed the gun in one hand and her wrist in the other, then pulled with a pronounced twist and a sound like several kernels of popcorn popping at once. He took a bouncy step back, holding the pistol by its barrel. It seemed to disappear in his massive hand. He flicked his thumb across a switch on the side and whipped his wrist as if pounding a gavel. The magazine full of ammo dropped from the pistol grip and fell to the pavement. He then shook the gun once, violently, working the slide and ejecting the bullet in the chamber.

The apprentice looked at the Australian, then at Rutherford, then at her hand. It was still outstretched as if she held the gun, but all four of her fingers bent away at unnatural angles. Some twisted at the first knuckle, some at the second, but all four looked badly dislocated. The sight of her hand made Rutherford queasy. He couldn't imagine what it felt like.

She began screaming. Her hand shook, making her fingers wiggle, causing her to scream more.

The Australian said, "Relax, kid. A good doctor'll fix you right up."

She continued screaming as she looked up from her hand to the Australian and kept the screaming up as she tried to punch him in the face with her other hand.

The Australian tossed the unloaded gun to Rutherford in a high arc, grasped her forearm, planted his other hand on her collarbone, and pulled. A single, sickening pop stopped her screaming and her attack.

The gun hit Rutherford in the chest and fell to the ground as he watched the attack, too stunned to move.

The Australian let go of her arm. It dropped to her side, hanging slightly lower than it should.

She let out an appalled squeaking noise that grew louder when her arm moved, like a high-pitched Geiger counter. She tried to cradle her dislocated left shoulder, but when she tried to grasp it with her right hand and its multiple dislocated fingers, she froze, and her quiet squeal of pain and horror grew louder.

The Australian said, "Best stop now, love, unless you want me to go for the elbow."

Behind them, from the sidewalk, Max said, "Chaz."

The Australian turned around. "Max!"

Max took a long, deep breath. "I was afraid DeBeul called you. He told me to say hello, by the way."

"You had to know we'd meet again, Maxie."

"Look, I'm working right now, and I'd rather not do this in front of my colleagues."

"Of course! We can rendezvous later. Where are you staying?"

"We'll meet back here."

The Australian, Chaz, looked around at the gap between the two buildings. "Sure. Seems secluded enough. When?"

"Soon."

Chaz said, "Eager."

Max said, "I want to get this over with. Two hours. Long enough to get the young lady to a doctor, then to jail."

They all glanced at the apprentice. While they were distracted talking among themselves, she had slowly edged backward toward the corner of the building. When they looked at her, she took off running as quickly as her multiple dislocations would allow.

Chaz started to chase her, but Max said, "Don't bother."

Rutherford added, "She won't get far."

"Why not?" Chaz asked.

Both Rutherford and Max said, "Bees."

In the distance, around the corner, they heard the apprentice shriek in alarm.

Max said, "We meet two hours from now, right here."

Chaz said, "Alone?"

Max said, "Alone."

Chaz looked at Rutherford, then glanced at the gun lying on the ground. Rutherford quickly bent down, snatched up the gun. He nodded, trying to convince everyone, himself included, that he was on the ball.

Chaz turned to Max. "You could bring the kid along if you'd like."

FOURTEEN

Two hours later, Albert sat in a waiting room chair at the emergency room, his laptop balanced on his lap. He muttered, "The car stopped."

Sloan sat beside him, leaned over with her helmet almost resting on his shoulder, watching the screen. Sherwood sat on Albert's other side, leaning over slightly to see the computer. Rutherford stood a few feet back, behind their row of seats, phone to his ear, occasionally peering over Albert's shoulder while talking to—or more accurately, receiving a talking-to from—Vince Capp.

"I'm sorry that the footage wasn't usable," Rutherford said. "But it wasn't my fault that Australian guy intervened."

Capp said, "No, but you could have asked him to sign a release."

"Max was adamant that I shouldn't have anything to do with him."

"Where is Max right now?"

Rutherford glanced at the screen of Albert's laptop. "From the sound of things, on his way to either be beaten to death or kill the guy in self-defense."

"Oh. Geez. Well, if Max survives, tell him I had faith in him and have him call me. If the Australian wins, have him sign a release. Anyway, I'm not calling to talk about the footage. Terri tells me she had to goad you into initiating the foot chase again."

"What? She told you that?"

"I had to goad her into it. Was she lying?"

"Not technically, I suppose. I hesitated, like, half a second at most."

"Okay, so you hesitate half a second, then she has to spend time goading you, then I have to spend time goading her into telling me about goading you. Then I have to spend time goading you into admitting that she had to goad you. Do you see how your half second of hesitation costs us a lot more time than that, just in time spent goading alone? Believe me, you don't want to know how much all this goading costs at my billable rate as a consultant."

"No, sir. I'm sure I don't." Rutherford glared across the lobby at Terri, standing near a window, oblivious to the rest of the team while concentrating on her own phone conversation.

"Yes," she said. "I understand that you can't have clients asking your drivers to break the law. Honestly, at the time our man thought your driver would welcome the opportunity."

A shrill blast of sound came from her phone.

Terri said, "No, I'm not saying that we think your drivers are criminals. The opposite . . . I'm sorry, but we were unaware you had considered using prison labor for your remote drivers. Yes, I can see where that would be attractive for your business model . . . No, I understand why you chose against it. I'm just saying many people would welcome the opportunity to participate in a police-sanctioned chase. I think we just need a clearer picture of what help your drivers are and aren't allowed to give. I could have Mr. Capp discuss it with TurkMO's other principals."

Albert, still staring down at his computer, said, "The wad is deployed."

Sherwood said, "Terri's right. That isn't a great name."

Albert said, "It's memorable."

"Yeah," Sloan said. "That's not always a good thing."

Rutherford heard Capp's tinny voice ask, "Are you listening to me, Rutherford?"

"Yes," he blurted. "Yes, sir. I'm sorry. I drifted there for a second. I'm just worried about Max. I've never seen him like this before."

"Like what?"

"Concerned."

"Yeah, that isn't a good sign. I'd hate it if something happened to Max. He's irreplaceable."

"I know."

"You aren't."

"I know."

"So we need you to step up. Show some initiative. Take some risks. Even if what you do turns out to be a mistake, that would be better than having you make no mistake because you're doing nothing."

"Are you telling me that it's better to ask forgiveness than permission?"

"I really couldn't say. I'm a billionaire. It's been decades since I've needed either of those things from anyone."

Albert, Sloan, and Sherwood leaned in closer to the screen. The computer's speakers relayed the sound of a car door closing. In the image, an ordinary sidewalk with a brick wall in the distance stretched and loomed, shot from such a low angle that a piece of gravel looked like a boulder. Two gigantic-looking human feet attached to treelike legs strode off into the distance.

Albert smiled. "He didn't notice the wad dropping out of the car. We're in business." He slid his finger forward on the laptop's touchpad. The image remained stable, rolling forward, following Max as he crossed the sidewalk and entered the alley.

Rutherford turned his focus back to Capp.

"Rutherford, "I'm gonna go now, but I just want to reassure you that you're allowed to take risks. I have a terrifying army of lawyers who can get you out of almost any trouble you could possibly get in, as long as it's not anything indefensible, or it doesn't become more expedient to sacrifice you for the team."

Rutherford said, "I appreciate the reassurance."

"Responding to me with sarcasm isn't the kind of risk I meant."

"Noted, sir. Sorry."

Capp hung up. Rutherford put his phone away and stood behind Sherwood, Albert, and Sloan.

They watched on the computer as the wad followed Max around the corner, into the alley. Albert panned back and forth to get a good view of the two men present. Max stood with his back to the camera. The distinguished Australian man, Chaz, stood facing him from several yards away. Both looked like skyscrapers when viewed through the wad.

Chaz asked, "Aren't you happy to see me, Maxie?"

"How can you ask me that after Kraków?"

"I made a mistake, Max. Things got out of hand."

An orderly approached Terri, and Albert muted the laptop's audio so they could hear the update.

The orderly told Terri, "Mrs. Wells. She's coming out of X-rays now. She'll be in a private exam room until they get done treating her injuries. From the looks of them it won't take too long, so if I'm going to get someone in there to talk to her, it's gotta be soon."

"Thanks. One second please." Terri favored the orderly with one of her thousand-watt smiles and turned back to her phone.

She ended the call and approached the rest of the team. Sloan straightened her posture and looked away from the computer. Rutherford looked at his shoes. Sherwood looked the other direction and up, as if the joint where the wall met the ceiling was fascinating.

Terri said, "Okay, you heard the man. We're up. What were you all watching on the computer?"

Albert said, "Oh. Uh, it's the feed from the wad."

"See how terrible that sounds? Terri leaned around to look at the screen. "That's Max! He told you specifically to stay out of this."

Rutherford said. "But the wad was in the car anyway, and we're worried. If this Chaz guy turns out to be dangerous, we want to be able to help Max."

"If that Chaz guy is capable of hurting Max, there wouldn't be anything you could do but act as a witness."

Sloan said, "And that's what we're doing."

"You're nosy. It comes with being detectives, I suppose. Sadly, being clever does too, and the excuse you came up with is valid. Albert, stop watching the feed, but keep it recording. Sloan and Rutherford, go ask the suspect a few questions before the cops get to her or she has a chance to lawyer up. This gentleman has agreed to take you to her in exchange for some unofficial remuneration."

"No, I want money," the orderly said. "You promised me money."

"And you'll get it."

In the team's earpieces, Sloan said, "I hope he spends some of it on a thesaurus."

Terri said, "Off you go. And, Rutherford, where's your lolly?"

"In my pocket, wrapped in a napkin."

"Suck it, Rutherford." Terri smiled. "You were right, Sloan. It *is* fun to say that."

The orderly led Rutherford and Sloan through a set of swinging doors into the sterile inner workings of the hospital. Before the next set of doors blocking the path ahead, a police officer stood with his back to the hallway, leaning on a counter behind which a very pretty nurse stood, smiling and batting her eyelashes. The orderly nodded at her as they passed. She winked at the orderly and raised her eyebrows at Rutherford while the oblivious cop kept talking. Once they were safely beyond the unmanned checkpoint, the orderly said, "She's getting sixty percent of the bribe, but when she distracts a guy, he stays distracted."

They walked through the hospital-standard byzantine maze of hallways. Rutherford wondered if architects deliberately made hospitals confusing. Perhaps they figured that if you barely understand the staff's directions to the restroom or the radiology department, you would be less likely to doubt their judgments about your cardiovascular system.

Rutherford and Sloan walked in silence down the hall, but in his ear, Rutherford heard Sloan's computer-generated voice ask, "Is everyone listening?"

The rest of the team answered that they were. Albert added that he was recording the audio from their microphones.

"Good," Sloan said. "The apprentice's name is Lea Gladki. She's injured. She's clever enough to get herself into a really interesting mess, but she's not quite clever enough to get herself out. Right now she's scared and in pain. If we can give her the idea that we might be a way out, maybe we can get the truth out of her."

Rutherford said, "I don't see where we need much information beyond a confession here. We know she's the one who's killing Watsons."

"No," Sloan said. "We don't. We know that she rigged the watch that killed Emery Hindman and the circuit that locked his car doors. We don't know that there was ever really a plan to kill other Watsons, that she was the one who came up with the plan, or that she's the one who sent the watch to Hindman. We know she made things, and what those things did. That's all."

"If she isn't the killer, why'd she run?"

"Because she also knew that she'd made things, and what those things did. That was enough incentive for her to run. Here's the plan, Rutherford. You're going to be firm, but fair. You want her to think you're serious, but that you haven't entirely hardened in your thinking yet. If she thinks you're just looking to pin the whole thing on her and go home early she'll shut up. If she thinks you're buttering her up to manipulate her, she'll shut up. Firm but fair. Under no circumstances do we try any kind of obvious coercion or anything physical. She'll clam up faster than . . . I don't know, a clam? One of those giant ones that grab scuba divers. They seem pretty fast."

Rutherford said, "I think those might be oysters."

Albert said, "Scallops, maybe?"

"They could be scallops," Professor Sherwood said. "The shells do tend to have scalloped edges."

Terri cut in. "Focus, people. Rutherford, you have your orders. Firm but fair, and no strong-arm tactics."

Rutherford said, "You know me. I don't go in for the rough stuff. Never have, never will."

Terri said, "True, but it's always worth being clear."

The orderly looked back over his shoulder at Rutherford. "Man, you always walk around in public talking to yourself?"

Rutherford had been so caught up in the conversation he forgot that all of the voices other than his were in his earpiece. "Yeah. Sometimes it's helpful to go over the case out loud."

"I get why you'd talk about not using strong-arm tactics, but why've you been talking about oysters?"

Sloan said, "I can't wait to hear you explain this."

"I can't divulge the details of an ongoing case."

Sloan shook her head. "What a cop-out."

"Well, you have your partner right here. Why not talk to her about the case?"

Sloan looked at the orderly, then at Rutherford, then she shrugged.

Rutherford said, "Does she seem like the talkative type to you?"

The orderly looked at Rutherford as if he were crazy, stupid, or both, but Sloan said, "Laughing."

FIFTEEN

The orderly led them to a closed door, where he paused with his hand on the handle. "The doctor's in there, but he won't hassle you. I cut him in. He says you can stay while he's treating her, but after that you've gotta scram. Cool?"

Rutherford said, "Cool."

Inside, a doctor milled around at a counter in the corner while DeBeul's apprentice, Lea Gladki, sat on an exam table in a hospital gown. Her left arm was cradled in a sling, with her shoulder still looking misshapen. Her intact left hand held an ice pack covering the fingers of her right. She looked to the door as it opened and scowled as soon as she recognized Rutherford and Sloan. "Oh. You. Here to look at your friend's handiwork? What's the fun in police brutality if you can't come and gawk at the results, eh?"

Rutherford said, "Look. First off, that watch you made killed a man, horribly, because you designed it to. Then you threatened to shoot me in the face, so maybe a little less self-righteousness, okay? Second, that guy who attacked you wasn't a friend of mine. I'd never met him before, and he's probably trying to beat one of my teammates to death even as we speak."

The doctor said, "I was just telling Miss Gladki, whoever did this wasn't all that brutal about it. I mean, don't get me wrong, I wouldn't want him to do it to me, but the X-rays show no broken bones, no vascular or soft tissue damage to speak of. Just clean, resettable dislocations."

Rutherford pulled the fake sucker from his mouth and gestured with it. "Ms. Gladki, we've met, but I never got the chance to introduce myself. I'm Detective Rutherford, this is my associate, Ms. Sloan. I know they read you your rights at the scene, so I'm not going to beat around the bush here. What do you have against Watsons?"

Gladki snorted. "What? What's *Watsons*? Is that a restaurant or something?"

Rutherford said, "No it's not a restaurant. It's your victims. The guy you killed was a Watson."

The doctor approached Gladki carrying a tray containing alcohol swabs and a hypodermic needle. "Okay," he said, "we're going to start with the fingers. First I'll give you some injections for the pain, then I'll perform a reduction on your dislocations. Ready? Now, you're going to feel this."

The doctor stuck the needle into Gladki's index finger. She let out a long hissing noise, then said, "When you said the shot was for pain, I thought you meant the shot would kill the pain, not cause it!"

The doctor removed the needle. "Because you're feeling a little pain now, you'll feel a lot less later."

"This isn't a little pain."

"Yes it is. It feels terrible, but it's over very quickly. It's a little intense pain."

She snarled silently at the side of the doctor's head, then turned to Rutherford. "I don't know anything about anyone named Watson. The guy I killed's name was Hindman."

Rutherford said, "So you admit you murdered Emery Hindman."

The doctor said, "Here comes another."

"Another? I thought you said a little pain now and a lot less later."

"Yeah, well, we aren't done with the 'a little pain' yet."

"How much more is there?"

"A little more." The doctor inserted the needle into the mass between her knuckles.

After a long, inarticulate grunt, Gladki looked at Rutherford. "Yeah. I did it."

The doctor said, "And just a little more," and plunged another needle into her hand.

This time she growled while looking at the side of the doctor's head as if she wanted to bite off his ear. When the pain passed, she glared at Rutherford.

Rutherford said, "Hindman was on a TV show based on Sherlock Holmes. He played Watson."

As Gladki said, "Oh," the doctor administered the last injection, so her 'oh' became a strangled shout of pain.

The doctor said, "There. That's all the injections for now."

Gladki said, "Thank God!"

Sloan said, "Amen! It hurt just seeing that!"

Terri said, "It wasn't fun hearing it."

Sherwood said, "I had no problem with it. Working with bees, I've gotten used to sharp, stabbing pain."

Albert asked, "And that's a good thing?"

Rutherford remained focused on Gladki. "But you knew Hindman was a Watson, because that's why you killed him."

"Why would I kill some guy for playing Dr. Watson?" Gladki asked.

"You tell me."

"I wouldn't."

Rutherford furrowed his brow. "You wouldn't kill him for that, or you wouldn't tell me why?"

The doctor said, "Now that I've given you the anesthetic, I'm going to start performing the reductions."

Gladki said, "Okay."

The doctor grabbed the bent portion of her index finger and quickly twisted it back into place. The sound made Rutherford and Sloan cringe.

Gladki squealed with pain. "You said you were gonna do a 'reduction'!"

"I did," the doctor said. "I've reduced the amount the finger is dislocated by. It's a euphemism. They can be one of a doctor's most important tools."

"Well I'd prefer the truth, okay?!"

"Fine. I'm gonna jam your middle finger back into place."

"Wa—"

The doctor torqued her middle finger straight in a swift, violent motion.

"You said a little pain earlier for a lot less later. This hurts like hell!"

"But," the doctor said, "it hurts a lot less than it would without the anesthetic."

Gladki panted as she looked at Rutherford. "Look, I don't know anything about any Watsons. I killed Hindman because I was paid to."

"By who?" Rutherford asked.

"Some guy. I assume it's a guy. Never met him."

"How'd he hire you, then?"

"He found me on the internet."

"How?"

Gladki snapped, "I assume on a computer. He could have used his phone, but most people don't like to do anything that important with a tiny little on-screen keyboard."

The doctor laughed. "Hey, that was pretty good."

Gladki smiled. "Thanks, Doc."

He jerked her pinky back into place. She shouted directly in his face.

Sloan said, "It wasn't a great joke, but she didn't deserve that."

Rutherford asked, "Why'd you take a job designing a device to kill some guy you never met? You have your whole future ahead of you."

Gladki said, "Working as the apprentice to an awful, cheap pig who made his living killing people with devices he designed. What exactly do you think my future was going to hold? Years more of his abuse followed by a lifetime of exactly what I'm under arrest for. I figured taking this contract and framing DeBeul for it was sort of an attempt to graduate early. If I'd just quit and done something else, all my work and all that abuse would've been wasted, and DeBeul would just call me a quitter and go on as if nothing happened. If I took the contract and the police were stumped, great. If they weren't stumped, I frame DeBeul and he gets his sweetheart deal with the witness relocation program revoked, which is also great. At worst, I figured I'd get caught doing what DeBeul used to do and I'd negotiate a deal like he has for myself. I'm his apprentice. I know most of what he knows."

Sloan said, "Poor kid. Poor, dumb kid."

Albert asked, "Is your sympathy for her situation or the medical procedure?"

"Both. They're just two of the putrid vegetables in the rancid stew she's made of her life."

Terri said, "She is a murderer."

"Yes, she brought what's coming on herself," Sloan said. "Makes it more pathetic, not less."

Rutherford told Gladki, "They already have a deal with DeBeul, and he knows everything that he knows. The feds don't need you."

Gladki asked, "What do you mean?"

Rutherford said, "DeBeul's killed God knows how many people, and been involved in tons and tons of crimes. He can inform on hundreds of criminals and help them on a lot of cases. You know some of his techniques, and you've killed one guy.

You can't get a deal like his. You're not nearly evil enough. You're just a little evil, so you'll probably go to jail for life."

Gladki looked at Rutherford as if she were four and he'd told her that there was no Santa Claus, because Santa was murdered by her parents, after her grandparents told them to.

The doctor started removing her sling. "Okay, now we just reduce that shoulder dislocation, and you're done."

"What, wait, no, one second." Gladki turned to look at the doctor, then back to Rutherford. "You don't really mean that, do you? They're gonna cut me some kinda deal, aren't they?"

Sloan opened the door. In his ear, Rutherford heard her say, "We're done here. I don't want to see this."

Rutherford stepped toward the door. "I don't know. They might have something. Maybe they'll keep you on as DeBeul's apprentice."

She stood up from the examination table. "What?! No! I'd rather go to jail!"

Rutherford turned his back and heard a loud pop and a blood-curdling scream. He took a breath to compose himself, then stepped out into the hall with Sloan, closing the door behind himself.

Every staff member and patient in the corridor stared at Rutherford and Sloan. The orderly who'd led them in locked eyes with Rutherford and shook his head in disgust. "I thought you don't go in for the rough stuff."

Rutherford and Sloan decided to show themselves out. As they walked down the hall, Rutherford said, "I don't buy it."

Sloan asked, "You don't buy what, her confession?"

"Her story."

"Her story that she did it, and is guilty?"

"I believe she killed Hindman, but I don't think she's just a hired gun for one job. I think she's behind all of the killings."

Sloan said, "There's only been one killing. So far the only crimes we have are one murder and a threatening note. Do you think she just confessed to the murder but made up a story so she won't go down for the note?"

"I just don't believe her story, Sloan."

"Why not?"

"It's dumb. It's a dumb story. She hates her boss so she framed him, and her fallback if it goes wrong is to try to cut a deal like his? It's dumb."

"She hates him. Hate makes you dumb. She was desperate to be rid of him. Desperation makes you dumb. Committing murder is inherently dumb, and smart, sane people who aren't desperate rarely do it. The risk-to-reward ratio is all out of whack. Sure, you get the pleasure of killing this idiot you hate, then you have to hide what you did for the rest of your days or your life will be ruined. Any smart person who thinks about it calmly will see that it's better just to avoid the person. Divorce them, get out of business with them, whatever. Or ruin their lives by staying married or in business with them."

"But she made the watch, Sloan. She's sane and she's clever."

"Technical smarts don't necessarily translate to other areas of a person's life. How many inventors came up with a world-changing device that made some businessman rich while they went bankrupt? It's an old, old story. At least as old as the Guttenberg Bible, because that's what happened to Guttenberg."

Rutherford shook his head. "I see what you're saying, but usually the simplest answer is right, and in this case the simplest answer is that the person who did the killing sent the note. I'm telling you, she's in this alone, and the proof will come when there are no more murders."

In Rutherford's earpiece he heard Terri say, "It's an interesting theory. We'll discuss it in the car."

Rutherford asked, "Where are we going? The killer's in custody and the Watsons are all safe."

"No, they're not. I just got word that another Watson was murdered, twenty minutes ago, while the young woman you're sure is the murderer was in custody."

Rutherford said, "She killed Byrne? She must've gotten him this morning."

"It wasn't Byrne. It was Menard, the cartoon voice guy."

Sloan said, "Oh, no."

Rutherford nodded. "She must've mailed him another device."

"No," Terri said. "He was strangled."

As he and Sloan passed through the glass doors to the waiting room, Rutherford asked, "By a device?"

Terri stood in the middle of the waiting room. "By a murderer, with the murderer's hands, all the way across town. She's a killer, but she's not our only killer. Now we have to get a move on. Albert, check on Max."

Albert opened his laptop and peered down at the screen. "The GPS says he's still in the alley, but the wad doesn't see him. I'll look around . . . there they are."

Terri, Sherwood, Sloan, and Rutherford crowded around the screen. Max and Chaz appeared to be rolling on the ground.

Rutherford said, "Max has him pinned."

"Yeah," Albert said. "But he tore Max's shirt off in the struggle."

Sloan said, "He isn't struggling."

They leaned in even closer, not saying a word, then they all drew back quickly at the same time. Terri reached out and gently closed the laptop. "We'll, uh, um, we'll give them their privacy."

Rutherford said, "They're in an alley in broad daylight."

"Yes, they have little enough privacy without us taking more."

SIXTEEN

Rutherford sat with his hands at ten and two on the steering wheel and his right foot near the gas pedal, but the remote driver did the real work, which was a good thing. Rutherford's attention kept drifting to the rearview mirror. In it, he saw the backs of Terri and Albert's heads, and Sloan's helmet, as all three of them sat twisted around backward looking at the rear seats. All the way at the back of the minivan sat Sherwood, Max, and Chaz. Sherwood looked uncomfortable, pushed all the way to one side with his buzzing Samsonite suitcase on his lap. Chaz sat in the middle but leaned heavily to his right, draping himself over Max like a cape, gazing at him adoringly. Max smiled widely, his eyes slightly glazed as he jabbered at length about anything and everything that came into his head.

"That was the Carter administration, so our relationship with the US government was very different than it had been under Ford, what with Ford being a puppet."

Sherwood said, "Doesn't surprise me to hear that. Who was pulling his strings?"

Max laughed. "Oh, there were no strings. It was a series of electrodes implanted—"

Chaz put a finger over Max's lips. "Shh, Maxie. You're rambling about classified information again."

Terri said, "You mean some of the things he says are true?"

Max asked, "I did get off track there. Where was I?"

Chaz said, "You were telling your friends how we met."

"Ah, yes. That was the very end of the seventies. I had just left the Korps Commandotroepen and joined the AIVD to do my duty as a Dutchman."

Chaz said, "And my betters in the Australian Secret Intelligence Service had recognized my talents and put me to work for the good of the Commonwealth."

Max said, "Seducing male intelligence operatives from other countries to supply Canberra with blackmail material."

Rutherford asked, "Australia did that kind of thing back then?"

Max and Chaz both laughed, then Chaz said, "We bloody well didn't want to be the only ones who weren't. And don't judge me too harshly. I didn't do your friend Max here any harm."

Albert said, "He didn't fall for it."

"No," Chaz said. "He dove into it headfirst."

Max shrugged. "No reason not to. What Chaz and his handlers didn't know was that my superiors simply didn't care."

"We should have guessed. 'They're cooler about that kind of thing,' was practically the Netherlands' tourism slogan."

Max said, "That's because we're cooler about everything. Sex, drugs, wind power."

Sloan said, "Everything but tulips. You have a history of getting a bit aggro over those."

Max said, "Quite true."

Chaz asked, "What's true?"

"Oh," Max said. "Sorry, Chaz, I sometimes forget. Sloan said the Netherlands once got pretty crazy over tulips. See, she speaks with the aid of an electronic device. We hear her through our earpieces."

"Oh! I just reckoned she was shy."

Albert said, "You know, Sloan, it would be easy for me to rig up a speaker or something so everybody can hear you."

Sloan said, "It would be easy, if it weren't for the resistance you'd get from me, because I don't want everybody to hear me."

Max leaned his head toward Chaz and said, "She says she doesn't want everybody to hear her."

Chaz said, "That's understandable. Keep the cards close to the vest. Good for you, girlie."

Sloan said, "He calls me 'girlie' again and I'll say quite a few things he won't want to hear."

Albert said, "It would make your life easier, Sloan. You wouldn't have to have us talk for you anymore."

"See," Sloan said, "that would make life easier for all of you, not me."

Rutherford shifted his sucker from one side of his mouth to the other and said, "You sure did a number on Gladki, Chaz. You dislocated every finger on her hand in one smooth motion."

"You should tell them about your fighting style, Chaz." Max said. "They've heard all about mine. They'll find your approach interesting."

Chaz said, "Well, see, back in the midnineties, Max and I had reconnected again after one of our silly fights. I don't even remember what now, do you, Maxie?"

Max darkened. "Yes."

"Anyway, Max and I got back together, and I saw his new method, where he tried to make it look like he's wasn't fighting at all."

"So he didn't always fight like that?" Albert asked.

"Hell no! He used to be brutal! People who saw him fight once are still terrified of him to this day! He had this thing he invented called the one-two punch."

Albert said, "That's where you hit someone with a jab then a cross. Max invented that?"

"No," Chaz said. "Max had his own version. He discovered that if he hit some bloke hard enough in the breadbasket at just the right angle, he could make the poor bastard do a number one and a number two."

Max looked at the floor. "I was a very different person back then."

Chaz said, "Then Max told me he didn't want to hurt people anymore, and I thought, yeah, I can understand that, but it wasn't really for me. I decided I'd split the difference. I wanted an injury that was easy to inflict, treat, and recover from, but would be so gruesome that my victim would stop fighting. I immediately started learning everything I could about dislocations. I got the idea from Max."

"He dislocated someone's arm in a fight?" Albert asked.

Chaz laughed. "No, his own. You could argue I did it. And we weren't fighting."

Chaz laughed loudly. Max chuckled uncomfortably and said, "Please, Chaz. These are my coworkers. They don't want to hear that kind of thing."

"We're all adults here, Maxie. When did you get so stodgy? We'll have to work on loosening you up." Chaz aggressively tickled Max's ribs. Max giggled and squirmed, trying to get away from Chaz's intruding hands. Sherwood pressed himself harder into the wall.

Terri said, "It's been great meeting you, Chaz, but we have a crime scene to get to. Where should we drop you off?"

"Oh, don't go to any trouble for me. I'm happy to tag along."

"I'm sorry, but we have a murder to investigate."

"I know," Chaz said. "Sounds like fun."

Max said, "Chaz, dear—"

Chaz interrupted him. "Oh, come on, Maxie. You, me, a crime scene. It'll be like old times!"

Rutherford asked, "You used to solve crimes together?"

Chaz laughed. "Yeah, sure. We *solved* crimes."

"Hush now, Chaz. We're professionals, doing the most serious business."

"And I wouldn't dream of interfering. I'm not asking to come into the crime scene with you. I'm happy to wait in the van. I don't have any other plans, and if things go south and you want my opinion, or need anything dislocated, I'll be here."

Max gave Chaz a skeptical look that melted into an indulgent smile, then he sighed and turned to Terri. "Would you mind, Terri? I'll take responsibility for him, and he might actually be useful."

Sloan said, "'He might actually be useful.' With a sales pitch like that, how can you say no?"

SEVENTEEN

As the team piled out of the van in front of Capstan Studios, Rutherford heard Max say, "Wait here, and be good."

Chaz raised one eyebrow. "I'll wait right here for you, and when you return I'll be very good."

Sloan said, "Gross."

Max shrugged nervously. "That's just Chaz."

"You're saying Chaz is gross?" Sherwood asked.

"Yes," Max said. "He can be."

Sherwood said, "I guess you take the bad with the good."

Max smiled. "Sometimes, the grossness is the good."

Sloan, Terri, and Rutherford all said, "Gross."

Rutherford saw what appeared to be a CartFulls cargo truck parked up the street with its back roll-up door hanging open. Inside, technicians in purple lab coats worked in a cramped but well-equipped-looking mobile lab. He didn't see Claire among them, and told himself he was glad about that, until they entered the recording studio lobby and found, to his delight, that she was waiting inside. He thought he saw her scan him quickly from head to toe, but then she looked away, and Rutherford was unsure if it had happened in the first place or was just wishful thinking.

Beyond a small reception area, a long hallway teeming with police and crime scene investigators stretched off into the distance. Detectives Frederick and Burski saw the team enter and moved to meet them halfway.

Terri said, "Claire. Good to see you again."

Claire thanked her, smiled, and nodded at every member of the team except Rutherford, and led the team down the hallway toward the detectives. "Welcome to Capstan Studios. It's a general-purpose recording facility. They have four different studios of various sizes where they record everything from commercial voice-overs to music."

Detective Frederick smiled. "Good afternoon."

Terri said, "Good afternoon."

Detective Burski said, "I suppose it is a good afternoon. It seems wrong to say so; after all, a man is dead. But that is true of every afternoon. The only thing that makes this afternoon unusual is that we all know who the departed soul was, and knowledge, no matter how sad, is a good thing to have. Let's go get more."

Burski turned and walked away. Frederick smiled at the team, shrugged, and went off after his partner, motioning to the others to follow. They made their way back into the farther reaches of the studio, passing grief-stricken employees, most of whom took the time to say hello to Max and Sloan as they passed.

Terri said, "They seem to have taken to you here."

Sloan said, "Yeah, well, everybody loves Max, and my look didn't put them off at all. I figure it's because they record a lot of rock and pop acts here. I'm no weirder than most of them, and a lot less demanding."

They approached the real center of activity: a restroom with the door hanging open and a dead man on the floor. Detective Frederick gave them the details. "The victim is Mac Menard, age forty-eight. He played a lot of teenagers in movies through his twenties, then transitioned into voice work. He'd just finished a recording session and came to use the restroom before he left. That's when he was attacked. Ligature marks and the state of the scene suggest that he was strangled from behind after a brief struggle."

Max said, "Poor Mac. Now he'll never finish that puzzle he was working on."

Sloan put a hand on Max's shoulder. "He was a good man. He led a good life. Jen loved him. His coworkers respected him. And while he didn't finish the puzzle, at least he saw the picture on the front of the box."

Max said, "A basket of pug puppies."

"Yes."

Sherwood came forward and raised his buzzing wand to take a quick reading of the area.

Sloan said, "Ask Detective Burski if he's ruled out suicide or the wife."

Rutherford asked, "Detective Burski, you think this was suicide or the wife this time?"

"I've ruled out suicide, obviously," Burski said. "If a guy managed to strangle himself with his own two hands, that'd be one for the record books. I've also eliminated his current wife, but he had an ex, and I never totally rule them out."

Sloan said, "Fair enough."

Burski continued. "I would also consider his coworkers, but I find coworker-on-coworker homicide is rare. Too much evidence, too great a risk of getting caught, and the chance that they might get stuck with the victim's workload is usually enough of a deterrent to put the murderer off."

Frederick said, "But, we suspect the killer was a man, thanks to the second crime down the hall."

They all followed Detective Frederick.

"The employee who found the body also remembered catching a glimpse of the janitor," Detective Frederick said, "but he can't have, because the janitor was unconscious in here."

Frederick stopped at an open utility closet. A purple-coated CartFulls tech took pictures of the scene. Yellow plastic evidence markers sat inside a storage bin with its lid hinged open.

"From what we gather, the killer snuck onto the premises and holed up in this closet until the janitor came in. Then he chloroformed him, stole his coveralls, and dumped him in that bin in his underwear. He put the coveralls on over his clothes and went out to find and kill Mr. Menard."

Burski said, "We dusted for prints, but there were too many of them. Lots of people have been in and out of this closet, doing God knows what."

Sherwood asked, "Did the janitor see who attacked him?"

"He says no. We'll ask again later when the shock's worn off. They took him to the hospital to check him out."

Rutherford said, "I hope they gave him some clothes."

Sloan says, "He's in a hospital. They would just take the clothes back and stick him in one of those gowns that tie in the back."

Albert asked, "Does the studio have any kind of security system?"

Claire said, "An alarm and some cameras. We're going over the footage. I was about to go see what we've found when you arrived."

Terri said, "Lead on."

As they walked, Max pulled out his phone. Rutherford, walking behind him, reflexively glanced at Max's screen and immediately regretted it. "What the hell, Max? He's sending you dick pics?"

Immediately Sloan and Albert crowded around the phone to register their disgust as they all stared at the image.

Max said, "We left the poor man alone in the van. He has to do something to amuse himself."

Terri winced, "Are you saying he took a seminude photo in the van?"

Sloan said, "Two more have come in while we've been talking, so I'd say he's still taking them."

Terri said, "Max, we're going to have a talk about this later. Then we'll never mention it again. Also, I'm going to want to stop at a store to get some Clorox wipes."

At the back of the building in what looked like a storage room, one working computer sat on the one relatively tidy desk among stacks of dusty storage boxes. Burski, Frederick, Claire, and the entire team crowded around, filling what little floor space existed. The CartFulls technician sitting at the keyboard said, "Here's the footage from the camera above the back door, one hour before the attack."

On the screen, a well-built man in a black suit approached, stopped before he got close enough to be identified, and ducked behind a garbage can. After a moment, a small black object protruded from around the can's side. The man's head also poked out into the open for a moment, then there was a flash of light and the feed went dead.

The tech said, "The security system shows the back door opened fifteen seconds later. We went out back and found that the camera had been shot, which was what we expected."

Sloan said, "Sounds like a pro to me."

"Then," the tech continued, "just about the time the witness says he caught a glimpse of a janitor, the side-door camera caught this."

Black-and-white footage showed a well-built man in coveralls darting out the door and walking toward the alley behind the studio. His face was not visible, and he was only in view for a few seconds.

Rutherford said, "That's it, huh, footage of him sneaking in and escaping? He could be in Mexico by now."

The technician said, "We'll check to see if any other buildings around here have security cameras. Aside from that . . ." The technician looked up at Claire as he trailed off.

Claire said, "There might be other resources we can draw on. I need to make a phone call."

Claire pulled her phone from her pocket and headed out to the hallway. Rutherford watched her go, then said, "I have a call I should make too."

Rutherford watched as Claire walked down the hall, talking on her phone. He went the other direction, pulled out his phone, and looked at a gold record hanging on the wall as he waited through five rings. He was about to hang up when the ringing stopped and a voice said, "What?" The tone was that of a teenage boy answering an urgent knock on a locked bathroom door.

Rutherford said, "Hey, Randy?"

Randy asked, "Who's this?"

"Rutherford. I was the detective keeping an eye on Byrne yesterday."

"Oh. What's up?"

"Well, remember how you asked me to keep you updated on the case?"

"Yeah, so I can stay clear of Byrne if an attack is coming. Since you're calling me, I guess there's been some movement?"

"It hasn't made the press yet, but there's been a second murder. I'm at the crime scene right now."

"Oh. Cool. Well, not *cool*. You know what I mean. Any leads?"

Rutherford said, "Yeah, it looks like we've got multiple killers. One person's probably behind it all, but they're hiring professionals to do the dirty work. We caught the first one."

"But they didn't identify the client?"

"How'd you guess?"

"You're calling me from a crime scene, instead of holding a press conference about how you prevented a murder."

"Oh. Good point."

"Don't get discouraged, kid. Keep at it. If a nail doesn't go in on the first whack, swing harder."

"That . . . *might* be good advice."

"Oh, it is. You've got to double down. Go hard, kid. You can't pussyfoot around."

Rutherford cringed and let out a little moan. "I've never really liked that phrase. *Pussyfoot*."

"Yeah, I know what you mean," Randy said. "I'm not into feet either."

Rutherford ended the call, turned to go back to the room with the security system, and stopped short, finding Claire standing directly behind him.

"Have you got a second?" she asked.

"Yeah."

"Good. Come in here." She glanced down the hall furtively, then stepped through an open door. Rutherford followed her. She closed the door behind them and turned on the lights. Rutherford saw that they weren't in a small room but a large booth. A single stool and a music stand sat in the middle of the floor. An articulated arm extended from the wall suspending a shiny, old-school microphone like Frank Sinatra would have used. Three walls were covered with carpet, and the fourth held a double-paned window onto a pitch-black room.

Claire said, "I need to make something clear to you."

Rutherford said, "Okay."

Claire's mouth pressed into a tight straight line. Her eyes narrowed. "I'm into you, and I have been since the moment I laid eyes on you."

Rutherford blinked. "I'm glad we got that straight."

"But it. Us. You and me. It's never going to happen."

"And now I'm confused again."

"I've dated your type before. Too many times. Bad boys. Rebels. Those are both just romantic ways of saying *assholes*."

"They don't sound that romantic."

Claire put a finger over Rutherford's lips. "Stop! Stop with the smart-aleck remarks. It won't work. I've been through this before. It's fun for a while. A lot of fun. I mean, lots and lots of mind-blowing . . . *fun*. But it always ends with me getting hurt. I don't want that anymore. Now I'm looking for a nice guy. Someone kind. Someone responsible. Someone clean. Someone I can go antiquing with. That's not you, is it? So you can see, it's not going to happen with us."

Claire turned to open the door. Rutherford asked, "What if I told you I can be that guy? Would that change things?"

She shook her head. "You can't pretend to be something you're not to make me interested in you. It just won't work."

Rutherford asked, "Are you sure about that?" But she was already out the door.

Rutherford sat in silence for a moment, then a man's voice said, "That sucked."

The light on the other side of the window came on, revealing a young man with a soul patch long enough to hold a braid, sitting behind a mixing board. "Sorry. I didn't mean to eavesdrop, but you came in so fast, and it would have been awkward to interrupt. You okay, man?"

"I'll be fine."

"Yeah. You will. Hey, you want a recording of the conversation? I can make you a copy real fast."

"You recorded us talking?"

"Yeah. I didn't mean to. I only started rolling because I thought you were going to have sex."

"That's not better."

Rutherford stepped out of the recording booth and again stopped short to avoid running into Terri, who was standing in the hall waiting for him.

"What were you and Claire doing in there, Rutherford?"

"Talking, Terri. That's it."

"And why should I believe you?"

The next door down the hall opened. The recording engineer stepped out and handed Rutherford a thumb drive. "Here you go, man. Better luck next time."

Rutherford looked at the flash drive, then handed it to Terri.

EIGHTEEN

The building sat among a sea of large stores, mini-marts, and fast-food restaurants. It consisted of a box made of cement intersecting with box made of metal, both wearing a low, flat box made of glass as a hat. It looked cool and modern, but not so much as to arouse any curiosity. The purple CartFulls cargo truck and the sensor-encrusted TurkMO minivan pulling into the parking lot drew far more attention than the building.

As the minivan came to a stop, the cabin filled with the sound of seat belts, door latches, and people grunting and grumbling as they exited.

Rutherford turned to Terri. "We're here."

She sat in the front passenger seat, eyes closed, head bowed, one hand over her earpiece listening intently with a delighted smile on her face. She turned and looked at Rutherford, but instead of saying anything she chuckled slightly, shook her head, and put a hand on his forearm, telling him that she would not get out just yet, and that he shouldn't either.

Rutherford looked into the back of the van. The rest of the team, and Chaz, sat motionless, frozen partway through the process of exiting, watching Rutherford and Terri.

Rutherford said, "You all go on. We'll be out in a minute."

Albert asked, "What's she listening to?"

Rutherford said, "Nothing."

Sherwood said, "Well she's listened to *nothing* four times now."

"And she keeps giggling at it," Chaz added.

Terri looked up at Rutherford, shaking her head and fighting back a laugh.

Rutherford gritted his teeth around his fake sucker. "Just, please, get out. We'll be with you in a second."

The team reluctantly stepped outside. Rutherford and Terri sat in silence for a moment, then Terri began laughing. Rutherford made a show of being irritated for a few seconds but gave in and laughed as well.

Terri wiped a tear from her eye. "It's not really funny. I feel so bad."

Rutherford said, "I appreciate that."

"Not for you. For Claire. Poor thing. She wants a relationship with a guy like you, but won't get it because she's fighting her natural attraction to the kind of guy you're pretending to be."

"It's just, if she got to know the real me—"

"Oh, you'd be exactly who she's looking for. But she'll never know it because she's avoiding you because she's too attracted to you."

"It's galling to have someone decide they know all about me based on my appearance, you know?"

Terri nodded. "As a black woman, I know exactly how you feel. But because I'm hearing that complaint from a white man, I feel very little sympathy."

"Understandable. So what do I do?"

"Your job. I'm your supervisor. Any time you ask me what to do I'm going to say: *your job.* If I don't, I'm not doing my job."

"But what do I do about Claire?"

"You're pretending to be the kind of guy she usually dates but doesn't want to. In reality, you're the kind of guy she wants to date but usually doesn't. The only way I can see it working with Claire is if she gets the image you portray cemented in her head, then sees the real you and it comes as a revelation."

"And how does that happen?"

"By accident. You can't make it happen."

"Yeah, I get it; you can't force this kind of thing."

"True, but what I meant was that *you* can't make it happen. As your supervisor, I forbid it. You can't force it because I won't allow you to."

Rutherford and Terri got out of the van to find that Claire had gotten out of the CartFulls truck and was waiting with the rest of the team.

Terri said, "Sorry for the delay. We needed to talk."

Claire said, "No problem. Whatever it was, I'm sure he deserved it."

Rutherford decided to let the comment pass. He pointed at the CartFulls truck pulling out of the parking lot. "They aren't staying?"

Claire said, "We might be here a while, so I sent them off to have dinner before we go back to the lab."

Albert said, "And Chaz decided to eat with them."

Sloan said, "Because a few of them were pretty cute."

Max said, "He said he was hungry."

Sloan said, "And I believed him."

Max did not smile.

Albert said, "And we got word that the killer sent a new note. It should be in your inboxes."

Rutherford pulled it up on his smartphone.

Two days ago, I killed a Watson. I promised another dead Watson every day. I missed yesterday. I'm sorry for this embarrassing mistake. What can I tell you? Good help is hard to find. Rest assured, with today's dead Watson I am back on track. I will find a way to make up for the dead Watson I owe you.

Rutherford said, "Weirdly apologetic for a killer. And service oriented. Maybe our guy works in customer support."

Sloan said, "That'll drive you to kill."

Claire led the team to a single glass door on the side of the building, tinted so aggressively that it looked like glossy black paint. Small, white vinyl letters displayed the street address, and the name "SKeyeBALL Inc."

Inside they found a small lobby: plain, white textured walls and a polished concrete floor surrounded a very professional young woman in a suit so smart looking it would have been bullied in gym class. She sat at a gray metal desk across from a long table with dividers creating individual workstations, like in a library, or the room where one would take the written driver's exam. Each cubby held a tablet displaying a field of tiny black text on a white background.

The young woman stood up. "Welcome back, Dr. Romero. And welcome, Ms. Wells. It's a pleasure to meet you and the rest of the Authorities. We all hoped to collaborate with your team someday. I can confirm that the facility in which you stand is operated by SKeyeBALL Incorporated. I will be unable to disclose any further information until you and each of your associates: Mr. Warmenhoven, Mr. Mok, Detectives Sloan and Rutherford, and Professor Sherwood, have digitally consented to the comprehensive nondisclosure forms on the table in front of you."

Terri asked, "Um, I'm sorry, what was your name?"

"I didn't say. I cannot disclose that information at this time. Please consent to the nondisclosure agreement. It's quite comprehensive."

"I see. We work for Vince Capp. Can I please send a copy to our legal team so they can clear us to sign your form?"

"I'm sorry, but I am unable to provide you with any written copies of the comprehensive nondisclosure agreement. The terms of the nondisclosure agreement are covered by the non-disclosure agreement."

Claire said, "I've signed the nondisclosure agreement and I can tell you—"

The young woman behind the desk tensed noticeably and looked pointedly at Claire, who watched the young woman as she continued, cautiously.

"I can tell you that it's worth it. I'm certain these people can help with your problem . . ." Claire trailed off as the woman behind looked concerned. "In a manner that I am not currently at liberty to divulge."

The woman at the desk smiled and nodded, satisfied.

Claire looked at Terri. "Please, read the agreement for yourself. It's worth it, I promise."

Terri sat down at one of the cubbies. Everyone else sat as well.

Terri read as quickly as she could while still fully comprehending the thick legal jargon. When she was done, she looked up over the walls of her station to find everyone else staring at her.

"You've all already signed?"

Sloan said, "Laughing. No. We all gave up on reading it after the first paragraph. Now we're waiting for you to tell us whether we should sign it or not."

Terri eyed the woman at the desk, who still stood, watching and listening.

"I haven't signed it yet," Terri said, pointedly, "so I can still tell you that it says basically that we are free to use any information we gain from SKeyeBALL's proprietary technology and methods, but that we are unable to divulge what that technology is, what those techniques are, or what the experience of gaining our usable information was like, which I found weird, but what else is new? I'm going to sign it. None of you have to, but I won't be able to tell you anything about what I see or hear other than what information I get about the killer."

The team signed the digital NDAs.

NINETEEN

Once the team signed the NDAs, the woman behind the desk instantly brightened. "Thank you. I'm sorry for the formality, but trade secrets, or secrets of any kind, are hard to keep these days, as we know all too well. I am now able to tell you that you may call me Ms. Hurley. Please follow me."

She opened a wooden door at the back of the room. Beyond it, Rutherford saw glossy wood walls, pools of mood lighting, and thick, cream-colored carpet. Built-in chairs and couches lined the walls. A circular conference table dominated the center of the room. Two attendants in crisp suits like the one the woman from the lobby wore stood at the far end of the room. Both smiled and nodded. One greeted Claire by name and welcomed her back. Ms. Hurley closed the door, sealing the team in. Rutherford noted that while the door seemed cheap and insubstantial with a crummy brass knob on the outside, that was a veneer over one side of a heavy, solid door with chunky, polished steel hardware.

Ms. Hurley said, "Dr. Romero called ahead and told us the nature of your issue, so I propose that I explain our operation and we get to business. Can I offer any of you coffee? We have a full espresso bar."

Rutherford said, "I would love a latte. Do you have oat milk?"

Claire glared at him. "Don't make fun."

Terri also glared at Rutherford. "We'll forgo the coffee, thank you. Time is of the essence."

"Of course." Ms. Hurley stepped forward and pressed a button mounted to the underside of the table. The wood grain on the tabletop vanished, revealing that the surface was not wood polished to a glass-like smoothness, but a glass screen displaying an image of wood grain. The image faded to a slowly spinning blue sphere: the top three-quarters appeared to be made of a flexible fabric, pulled tight by inner ribs and air pressure like a blimp. The bottom quarter was solid, with eight struts extending upward beyond the sphere like arms, each ending with a small propeller. Small glass lenses dotted the bottom of the sphere and arms.

Ms. Hurley said, "Ladies and gentlemen, I give you the device for which our company is named. The SKeyeBALL autonomous balloon is designed to fly at a steady altitude of five thousand feet, circling over a metropolitan area, remaining clear of any air traffic or restricted airspace, of course. The individual units are small, one meter across; inexpensive; and easy to mass produce in volume. At any given time, dozens of units loiter silently and invisibly above Los Angeles, and several other major American cities, providing constant surveillance of the ground below in all directions using their thirty-two high-resolution camera sensors. The data is time-coded, compressed, and streamed in real time to our collection center. There we sync and combine the feeds from all of the active SKeyeBALLs over the city to create a searchable high-resolution video of the entire city, taken from multiple angles, with redundant coverage of every square foot of public space. Now let's track down this suspect of yours."

Ms. Hurley looked upward at the wall and nodded.

Rutherford followed her gaze and saw short, wide windows set near the ceiling. People sat beyond those windows. He couldn't make out any identifying details, but the color and angle of the light on their silhouettes told him that they were looking at computer monitors.

Ms. Hurley said, "Dr. Romero already gave us the address of the recording studio, so we will start there."

An image of the city from above filled the surface of the table.

"This is the view from the unit closest to that location right now. We'll select the recording studio."

A green dot appeared down at ground level. The view of the city zoomed in toward the dot, bringing the streets up quickly enough, and at a steep enough angle that Rutherford felt as if he were falling. The zoom stopped with an aerial view of Capstan Studios, the entire building highlighted in green. Police cars, officers, and caution tape surrounded the area.

Mrs. Hurley said, "Now we go back to the approximate time when the murder took place, which Dr. Romero told us earlier was shortly after two."

The cars and pedestrians in the vicinity of the studio began moving backward at a cartoonishly high speed. The point of view shifted as the SKeyeBALL balloon circled the city. Larger buildings blocked the studio, but the point of view jumped to a different unit that still had it in frame. Rutherford watched as the team's TurkMO minivan, the CartFulls truck, the police, and the paramedics departed and arrived in reverse, eventually leaving the studio alone and unremarkable among the other buildings. All motion slowed. A man in a janitor's coveralls walked backward around the building and into the side door. The footage stopped, then started again in its normal direction and speed. The man walked out the door, turned the corner as if he knew exactly where he was going, and began to dart out of sight around the corner. The image froze. The green highlight left the building and transferred to the man.

"If this is your killer, we can follow at high speed until we catch up to him in real time, and we will, but that just tells us where he is. We find it's instructive to start by following him back in time to where he started the day. That often tells us *who* he is."

The image reversed and sped up again until a man in a black suit and red tie walked backward out of the back door, ducked behind a garbage can, aimed a silenced pistol toward the building, made a muzzle flash, then put the gun away and continued backward up the alley to a sleek, black sports sedan parked on the street. Again the green highlight transferred, this time to the car as it reverse merged into the backward traffic.

Ms. Hurley said, "Now we let the algorithm trace it backward to his point of origin."

The view zoomed back out to a bird's-eye view of the city, with a tiny car-shaped green dot working its way through intersections and traffic lights to the freeway. The vantage point shifted several times as the green streak backed out to the suburbs. All motion stopped, and the view zoomed in to show a still image of the black sedan pulling out of a house at the end of a cul-de-sac.

"We can easily look up the address of that house, and the algorithm follows all the angles of the car's route to see if we get a clear shot of the license plate, but in the event that we don't, if the public records show that the owner of that house is a man of his height and build who owns that make and model of car, that's at the very least what the police call *a good lead.*"

Sloan said, "This explains that crazy nondisclosure agreement. It's no wonder they're so serious about keeping their secrets. Their business is exposing everyone else's."

Rutherford asked, "Claire, you said you've used this place before. What does CartFulls need with something like this?"

"It has a lot of uses. Catching vandals. Tracking shoplifters or armed robbers. Recovering stolen shopping carts."

Ms. Hurley said, "Tracking consumer habits."

Claire's expression soured. "That's not my area."

"Demographics?" Rutherford asked. "Like who bought what on what day?"

Ms. Hurley laughed. "No. The cash register tracks that. A lot of deep information can be gleaned from watching consumer behavior outside the store. What neighborhood are they from? What kind of car do they drive home in? How nice of a home do they drive to?"

Rutherford rolled his eyes. "Ah, yeah, I gotcha."

"Where do they work? Where do their kids go to school?"

"Okay."

"Do they stop at a bar for a drink on the way home?" Ms. Hurley continued. "How long did they stay at the bar? How well do they drive when they leave? How well do they drive in general?"

Terri asked, "And CartFulls tracks those kinds of things?"

Claire said, "I honestly don't know."

"But," Mrs. Hurley said, smiling pleasantly, "enough other major retailers do that CartFulls would only be putting themselves at a disadvantage if they didn't."

Rutherford said, "But they must just pick one or two representative shoppers a day. They can't really be doing this with everyone. That'd be impractical."

Albert said, "How much work did it take them to track our killer? They highlighted his car and the computer tracked it. The only reason it took as long as it did was that they had to slow it down so we could follow it. It sees a certain shape and color, goes back one frame and looks for that same shape and color nearby. They're just reading the video footage, not altering it, so lots of computers can access the data at once. Tracking every car in a parking lot is just a matter of throwing processors and memory at a problem, and those get cheaper every day."

"How much cheaper?" Terri asked.

Albert said, "In the seventies, a box of floppy discs that all together would hold a total of just over a megabyte cost fifty bucks. That's not adjusted for inflation, mind you. What's a sixteen-gig thumb drive cost now? If they aren't tracking all of us all the time already, they will be soon."

"We see it as a growth industry," Ms. Hurley said.

Terri said, "This can't be legal!"

Rutherford spread his hands over the projection of the city. "Look at it, Terri. It's all streets, roads, and roofs: public space. It's as legal as having a camera on an ATM that also catches the far side of the street."

"Quite right," Ms. Hurley said. "Our system cannot see what people do in the privacy of their own homes, or inside their places of business. We leave that to other vendors."

"Well, if this technology is available, why are there any unsolved crimes anymore?" Terri asked.

"Civil authorities are unable to access our service. They have restrictions that private and corporate entities do not."

Professor Sherwood said, "They answer to voters. Companies don't."

Claire said, "That's true. Also, SKeyeBALL's service is really expensive."

Mrs. Hurley said, "We prefer to call it *exclusive.*"

Terri sighed. "I suppose if someone's going to sell my privacy, I'm glad they're getting a good price for it."

Max said, "I sympathize, but in all honesty, worrying about losing your privacy is like wringing your hands because unicorns are going extinct. You're lamenting the loss of a thing that never existed. I know better than most."

"Because you used to work in intelligence."

"No, because I grew up in a very small village. Everybody knew everyone else's name, age, home address, dating history, and childhood nickname. If I wanted to purchase condoms I had to either buy them from a pharmacist who went to church with my parents or get a ride to another town, in the car of someone whose parents went to church with my parents. Between law enforcement, corporations, and your neighbors, you have to assume you have no privacy. And of the three, I prefer corporations."

"Good God, why?" Albert asked.

Max said, "If you pay someone for sex and the law finds out, they arrest you. If you pay someone for sex and your neighbors find out, they judge you. If you pay someone for sex and a corporation finds out, they offer to rent you a room."

TWENTY

Rutherford drummed his fingers on the steering wheel of the parked minivan and looked out at the suspect's neighborhood: a planned community originally built in the late fifties as affordable housing on the outer edge of town for young families. Then for several decades the city expanded, lot sizes contracted, and inexpensive contemporary architecture became midcentury design. Now the same neighborhood was an expensive, conveniently located enclave of classic houses "restored" to a better standard than their original construction, sitting on professionally landscaped lawns that looked like small parks.

"We're in position near the suspect's house," Rutherford said, tilting his head toward the in-dash information console, as if being a fraction of an inch closer to the microphone would make his voice clearer on the other end. "You'd love this place, Claire."

Claire asked, "What's that supposed to mean?"

"Just that it's a nice neighborhood."

Claire said, "Whatever. The house and car are both owned by a Casper Morrison, but we're pretty sure it's a fake name. We've found no connections to any of the victims, but that's no surprise, since he's probably a hit man. SKeyeBALL is still tracking the suspect. After he left the scene of the crime he went home, changed clothes, then went to a gym. Now he's at a gun range."

"Thanks, Claire," Rutherford said, "that's helpful."

"It might not seem like much, Rutherford, but it's all the information we have, and it's a heck of a lot more than you'd know without us."

"Yes, that's what I'm saying." Rutherford took a sip from a cardboard to-go cup, inadvertently making an audible slurping noise.

Claire said, "Oh, was that you drinking your *oat milk latte*?"

Rutherford said, "They didn't have oat. I had to settle for soy."

"Uh-huh. We'll keep watching. If it looks like he's coming back home we'll give you as much warning as we can."

"I'm sure you will."

"We will, Rutherford! Why's everything a fight with you?"

Rutherford bit his lip. "I honestly don't know. Thanks, Claire. Good work."

Claire ended the call.

Rutherford twisted around in his seat to look at Terri sitting beside him, and the rest of the team, including Chaz, in the rear.

"None of you wanted to help me out there?"

Sloan said, "No, we didn't. It's too much fun to watch you flounder." Instead of playing in the team's earpieces, her voice boomed out of every speaker in the van's sound system.

Terri said, "Albert, the Bluetooth interface you whipped up for Sloan's voice seems to work, but there needs to be some way to turn down the volume."

Albert said, "Sloan has total control over the volume. She's choosing to talk loud."

Sloan poked at her smartphone's screen. Her voice, now much quieter, came only from the speaker in the door next to Terri. "Yes. And I can use each speaker independently."

Terri flinched. "We may want to lock her out of all of that, Albert."

Through the two front speakers, Sloan said, "No, I think it's fine like this."

Sloan's voice came entirely from one of the rear speakers. "Yeah, Sloan's right."

Albert said. "I see what you mean. I'll try to find a solution that has fewer distracting options."

All of the speakers played Sloan saying, "Boo! You're both spoilsports."

Terri said. "Now, back to the matter at hand."

Rutherford said, "Catching a murderer."

Terri said, "No. Not quite yet. First we have to deal with you, Rutherford. You're clearly going way out of your way to ingratiate yourself to Claire. You've got to stop that."

"I was just trying to be professional, Terri."

Terri said, "No. Your default setting is *professional*. You do that by accident. You were trying to be pleasant to her because you want her to like you. Part of your job is to project a certain image, and that image is not of a man who is desperate to be liked."

Chaz said, "Don't knock yourself out trying too hard, kid. At lunch, her workmates seemed to think you're in with a chance there."

"What else did they say?" Rutherford asked.

"A couple of them said I'm in with a chance too, with them. But they didn't say it with words. Actions speak louder, if you know what I mean."

Max said, "Chaz!"

"Oh, don't be jealous, Maxie."

Sherwood said, "He's joking. I'm sure he wouldn't do anything inappropriate with a work colleague of yours whom he just met."

Max said. "No, he would."

Chaz nodded. "One hundred percent, and Maxie and I both know that's the deal, so I don't see a point in him getting jealous about it."

Terri said, "We're here to do a job. We need to stop focusing on Rutherford's love life or Max's love life, and start focusing on the killer."

Sloan said. "We know nothing about the killer's love life."

Terri said, "Not helpful, Sloan."

"But," Sloan continued, "we know that he killed Mac Menard. At the moment, we don't have anything admissible. We need to find something, or at least find probable cause for the police to go in and find something for us. I suggest Rutherford goes over to the suspect's house and deploys the wad."

Terri said, "Don't call it that. Now, Rutherford, I don't want you anywhere near that house when the owner comes back."

Albert handed Rutherford the crumpled-up Chinese food take-out box. "Here you go. I suggest you try to jam the wad through the mail slot."

Professor Sherwood said, "Terri has a point. That does sound terrible."

"If there's no mail slot," Albert continued, "try to slide it under the door."

Rutherford said, "Will do," and exited the minivan.

Rutherford knew that what he was about to do was not, strictly speaking, *legal*. He didn't feel great about it, but he was doing it to capture a killer and save lives. He didn't want to compromise his principles, but how many dead Watsons were his principles worth? He knew of two more Watsons, which felt like too many, not to mention all the other targets this particular hired assassin would kill in his career.

In his head, he heard Capp telling him, *Show some initiative. Take some risks.*

He also heard Randy say, *Don't pussyfoot around.*

He reached the end of the cul-de-sac and paused on the sidewalk, looking at the suspect's home. The wall-sized front windows allowed views through the house and the wall-sized back windows to a deck, a safety railing, and blue sky in the distance. Looking around the door he saw the predictable security camera and motion sensor. He looked around to see if anyone was watching, then pulled out his oversized gun. He quickly aimed, squeezing one eye shut, and pulled the trigger on the left shotgun barrel, which he'd taken care to load with a special shell Albert had designed to neutralize security cameras. Instead of a loud bang, it made the hollow *thunk* of a compressed air charge. A small, light, slow-moving black mass sailed through the air and hit the camera's lens, flattening out into a shapeless blob and sticking in place.

Rutherford slid the gun back into his shoulder holster. "I've shot the goo and am preparing to deploy the wad."

"Now you're doing it on purpose," Terri fumed.

Rutherford said, "Yes. Yes, I am." He double-timed it up the walk and across the flat rectangular lawn.

He held the crumpled take-out box by one corner. It unfolded itself into a wrinkled flap of slightly thicker than usual waxed cardboard. If he looked closely, he could see the tiny pinhole lenses in all the points where three or more fold lines converged.

The metal flap covering the mail slot would not open, but it moved just enough to tell Rutherford that the hinge remained intact. The cover must have been bolted shut on the inside and only left in place for aesthetic reasons. He knelt down and tried to slide the cardboard slab under the door, but it was hung far too precisely, and weather stripped too thoroughly.

Rutherford said, "Mail slot's blocked, and it won't go under the door. We need another option."

Terri said, "Okay, Rutherford. Come on back. We'll try to come up with another way in. I dunno, maybe a chimney or something."

Rutherford said, "Or I could pick the lock."

Terri asked, "You know how to pick a lock?"

"Yeah. Kinda. I understand the basics. I'm sure Max or Chaz could talk me through it."

Max said, "No, Rutherford, you would not be able to pick a lock without practicing first. It's all done by feel and knack. Chaz or I wouldn't be able to talk you through it. I'm afraid one of us would have to do it for you, and . . . Chaz, you can't just shove the seat forward. There's a lever. Albert's sitting in that seat! The man is not a taco!"

Terri said, "Chaz! Chaz! Max, where's Chaz going?"

Max answered, "Where do you think?"

Rutherford turned around to look up the street and saw Chaz running straight down the middle of the road.

Rutherford stepped aside as Chaz slid to a stop in front of the door, pulled some shiny strips of metal out of his wallet, and winked at Rutherford. "Just gimme a tick, kid, and I'll have this open for you."

Terri said, "No! Rutherford, stop him! He's breaking the law!"

Rutherford said, "Terri says to stop. She says you're breaking the law."

Chaz said, "Of course I'm breaking the law. I broke the law when I stuck the pick in the lock. If I stop now, I'll be a criminal and a quitter, and that just ain't me. Half of it, at least."

Rutherford said, "Terri, I don't like it either, but I think we have to do this. Yes, it's illegal. But it was illegal to put the wad in the house to begin with. Heck, it was illegal for me to trespass to insert the wad."

Terri groaned.

"You're groaning because you know I'm right."

"No, Rutherford. I'm groaning because of what you just said."

Chaz said, "There's the dead bolt. Now to work my magic on the knob."

Terri groaned again.

Rutherford said, "Two people are dead and someone else is going to die in the next twenty-four hours if we don't stop it. The only lead we have is this guy. Capp would tell us to do everything we can."

Terri asked, "Sloan, what do you think? Would Capp want Rutherford to pick the lock and plant a surveillance device, knowing it's illegal?"

Sloan said, "No. I mean, he wouldn't want him to only do that. Capp would be fine with picking the lock and planting the wad, but since Rutherford is breaking the law anyway, Capp would want him to go in and snoop around while the place is empty."

Rutherford said, "Damn. She's right."

Professor Sherwood said, "You can't fight crime with crime."

Sloan replied, "Says the man who fights crime with bees."

Rutherford said, "Capp would say that you can fight crime with crime, if your crime's not as bad as theirs, or your legal team is much better than theirs. Just this morning he told me to take more risks, and that his lawyers could help smooth things over as long as we get results."

Max said, "Terri, Rutherford can do things a robot can't."

Terri said, "That's true. He can get arrested. He can lose his badge. He can lose his job because he's no use to us anymore."

Albert said, "It's an unnecessary risk. If the suspect comes home, the wad can roll under a piece of furniture and just sit there eavesdropping for hours."

"I can hide under furniture and listen."

Albert said, "Not as well."

Chaz gently twisted the doorknob. The door swung open. "There we are. All yours, kid."

Chaz swatted Rutherford on the butt and ran off down the street toward the minivan.

Terri shouted. "Do not go in there. Just throw the wad. Throw the wad, Rutherford. And the rest of you, stop smiling!"

Max said, "No risk, no reward."

Terri said, "Also, stupid risk, no reward."

Rutherford tossed the wad down onto the floor. "Okay, I've deployed the device. Terri, I don't want to go in there. But part of doing a job is doing the parts you don't like. If this guy gets away or gets off and another victim is killed, will it make you feel better about it because at least we didn't trespass *all that much?*"

Sloan said, "We have Claire and SKeyeBALL watching the guy. If he comes home, we should have plenty of warning."

Terri sighed. "Okay, do it. But I don't like it."

Rutherford said, "None of us likes it."

TWENTY-ONE

Rutherford closed the front door behind him and surveyed the living room. The furniture looked expensive, stylish, and unused. The couch cushions were perfectly rectangular. Neither the end tables nor the coasters had beverage rings. Only one chair directly across from the TV had any noticeable wear. Rutherford had seen this kind of thing before. The home stayed impressively clean and nice because nobody but the owner ever came in to be impressed by it.

Rutherford said, "Doesn't look like I'll get much in the living room. Moving on to the kitchen."

As he walked out of the living room, he looked behind him and noted the wad, crumpled into a ball and rolling along in his wake.

"The kitchen's spotless. Pots and pans hanging from a rack, organized by size. Knives in a knife block. They all match. Except one, a big cleaver, stuck in the butcher block. Nothing unnerving about that."

Sloan said, "Look in the fridge."

Terri asked, "You think there'll be body parts in there or something?"

"No, but if we don't look, and it turns out there were body parts in there, we'll feel like idiots."

Rutherford carefully tore a paper towel off of a roll and used it to open the fridge without leaving prints. "No body parts. Expensive beer. All the usual condiments, but only one of each, even mustard, which is weird for a guy. Nothing suspicious though."

Rutherford closed the fridge and went through a door at the back of the kitchen.

He said, "This is the cleanest garage I've ever seen. No storage boxes. No old golf clubs. The floor's pristine. He has a special plastic pan he parks over in case of oil drips. There are tools hanging on the wall, organized like the pots in the kitchen. They've been used, but they've also been cleaned afterward. He has a huge dispenser full of black latex gloves. That can't be a good sign. I'm going back in. I'll head upstairs."

Rutherford took a pair of the gloves and pulled them on as he walked back through the kitchen and living room to a set of floating stairs protruding from the back wall. He was halfway up when Albert said, "Hey, Rutherford. Could you help me out with the stairs, please?"

Rutherford went down and picked up the crumpled to-go container, then tossed it on the landing as he crested the stairs and walked to the door at the end of the hall. As he suspected, this was the main bedroom. A sharp-cornered rectangle of a bed with a padded leather headboard and footboard took up one wall. A dresser and a white three-foot-tall statue of a matador on a plinth flanked the door to the hall. The wall behind the bed held an archway to the en suite bathroom and the door to the closet. The far wall was mostly taken up by a window to the front yard and the street below. On the last wall, across from the foot of the bed, was a giant painting of a matador fighting a bull, stretching almost from floor to ceiling. Rutherford looked at the wall, then ducked out to the hall and looked at the distance to the stairs, then back at the wall.

"Something's off; it looks like there's space behind that wall."

He looked closely at the painting's frame, moving around to the side, examining how it met the wall. "I think the picture's hiding a door. I don't see any switch or latch mechanism."

Albert said, "Look at the statue. That's where I'd hide it."

Rutherford crossed the room, examining the statue. He noticed a thin line at the shoulder. "I see a seam. I think the arm's been tampered with. One second."

Rutherford grasped the arm, gently twisted it one way, then the other, and when he felt some movement, twisted harder.

The arm came off in his hand.

In his ear, he heard everyone in the minivan giggle and Sloan's artificial voice say, "Laughing. Laughing. Laughing."

Rutherford took a moment to glare down at the wad on the floor before he went back to the painting. He gripped the frame and gently pushed. The painting slid to the side, revealing a rectangular hole large enough for a man to step through.

The walls of the hidden space held countless guns, knives, swords, bludgeons, arrows, darts, and a fine selection of weapons Rutherford had only seen in obscure kung fu movies. They all hung neatly, categorized by type and size exactly as the pots, knives, and tools on the first floor had been. The only flaw in the organizational scheme was an empty spot the perfect size for a silenced pistol.

He turned and looked down at the wad, sitting in the middle of the floor. "You seeing this?"

Before anyone could answer, an alert sound played in Rutherford's ear, followed by a voice similar to Sloan's repeating, "Group call incoming. Dr. Claire Romero. Group call incoming."

Terri said, "Let me do the talking. She can't know what Rutherford's doing."

Rutherford said, "Thanks."

"It's to protect her, not to help you!"

Going from stern to casual in the space of two seconds, Terri said, "Hello, Claire."

"Hi, Terri. Just calling with an update. Two things. One: We found some blood under one of the victim's fingernails. Not much, but enough to get a DNA match for Casper Morrison. That's enough for the police to pick him up. They're headed your way right now."

Terri asked, "Why come here? Why not go get Morrison where he is?"

"Yeah," Rutherford added, very interested in the answer himself.

"That's the second thing. Morrison's heading home. Stay put and you should get a first-class view of him getting arrested."

"Where exactly is he right now, Claire?"

He left the freeway right before I called the police. Looking at the map—oh, he's making good time! He's turning onto the street where you're parked right now."

Terri said, "Really! Oh, yes, I see his car. Oh, good!"

Rutherford leapt out of the gun closet into the bedroom. Through the window he saw a black sedan rounding the corner at the far end of the cul-de-sac.

Sloan said, "This neighborhood has surprisingly good freeway access."

Terri said, "We're gonna go now. Thanks for the update, Claire. Bye," and hung up.

Rutherford said, "Gotta get out of here!"

"Yes," Terri agreed. "Uh-oh! He's looking at us!"

Chaz shouted, "Everyone make out!"

"No! Just act casual."

The sound of closed-mouth moaning, heavy breathing, and smacking noises filled his earpiece as Rutherford looked into the gun closet for anything he had disturbed.

Terri said, "Max, Chaz you don't have to . . . Oh whatever. Sloan, you said we'd have plenty of warning!"

"I said we should have plenty of warning, and I was right. We should have."

Rutherford slid the painting back into place, covering the door. The breathing and smacking in his ear continued as he scanned the bedroom. The severed arm of the matador lay on the floor next to the plinth. He picked it up and made for the hallway, but froze when he heard the garage door opening.

Going over the layout of the house in his head, Rutherford realized that his route to the two downstairs exits that weren't the garage still led him within view of the door to the garage.

Terri and Sloan both said, "Hide."

Max and Chaz continued heavy breathing.

Terri shouted, "Will you two stop?"

The wad, controlled by Albert, rolled under the bed. Rutherford dropped to all fours to scuttle under himself, but found that the bed's side rails hung too close to the ground, leaving only a four inch gap. He'd have to lift the bed to get under there, and then he'd have a hell of a time trying to get out without help.

Albert said, "I told you, you can't hide under furniture as well as the wad."

Rutherford said, "Now is *not* the time."

Sloan said, "You might be dead later."

Downstairs, he heard the door to the garage open and close. The killer was in the house, between him and all the exits.

Rutherford sprang back to his feet and looked at his options. He could hide in the bathroom or the closet, but the killer might plausibly come directly into any of those rooms if he came upstairs, and Rutherford would be cornered. He looked at the secret gun room. He'd still be cornered, but he'd be armed to the teeth. But if he managed to slide the painting in place behind him, he had no guarantee he could slide it back out of the way from the inside.

Professor Sherwood asked, "Shall I send Her Majesty in?"

"What?" Terri asked. "No! Why? They're inside. What are you going to do, make the swarm hover outside the window?"

"Hmm. Good point. Maybe we should add something that can break windows so she can gain entry. Maybe a pellet gun. Nothing dangerous."

Sloan said, "No, nothing dangerous, just bees and the broken glass."

A sound Rutherford couldn't immediately identify drifted up from downstairs. Rutherford moved closer to the open bedroom door to hear it better. In his ear, his teammates back in the van tried to identify the noise.

Albert said, "High pressure gas escaping?"

Max said, "A great amount of fluid spraying onto a concrete floor?"

Sloan said, "Something very large sizzling in a whole lot of very hot oil?"

Terri said, "It's nothing good, that's for sure."

The hissing remained, joined by distant yelling and whistling. By the time the drums and guitars kicked in with a simple mambo beat, Rutherford knew he was listening to a concert recording filtering up from the first floor. The singing kicked in with a chorus of female voices singing "la la la" in an almost mocking tone.

Albert asked, "Is that the Spice Girls?"

Sloan said, "Yes. That is the Spice Girls."

"Huh," Terri laughed. "Like I said, nothing good."

Rutherford opened his mouth to tell them how happy he was that they weren't letting his deadly peril interfere with their enjoyment of the music, but the sound of footsteps on the stairs flushed all other thoughts from his mind. He dove to the floor on the far side of the bed and pressed himself against the bedframe, making himself as small and hard to spot as possible. As he hit the ground, his lungs expelled most of their air, blowing the fake lollipop from his mouth. Rutherford cursed, reached up, and lifted the now fuzz-encrusted sucker from the carpet. His left eye could see under the bed to the far side of the room and out the door into the hall.

The wad rolled over under the bed and parked next to Rutherford's head. Sloan said, "There's another thing you can do that the wad can't: panic."

Rutherford saw Casper Morrison's feet and lower legs, dressed in slacks and shiny black shoes, as the man walked into the room. Morrison sang along with the *la la las* in a quiet, absentminded way.

He stopped in his tracks in the middle of the room; the only part of Morrison that Rutherford could see—the feet and ankles—remained still. As the *la la las* ended, his voice trailed off. For what seemed like an eternity, Morrison stood there, still and silent, leaving Rutherford convinced that he'd been spotted and would soon be murdered.

The feet turned, and Morrison stepped toward the matador painting. Rutherford saw the bottom edge of the painting slide to the side, then Morrison stepped into the secret room as he inarticulately sang along with the rhythm and melody of the song without enunciating most of the words.

"Mu mu, muh mu, sad and low. Mu mu, muh mu, mu you wanna go."

Sherwood said, "His back is to the room. Might be a good time to go."

From inside the secret room, Rutherford heard, "Mu mu, muh mu, positivity."

Max said, "No. He could turn around at any second. He'd see Rutherford, and he'd have his choice of a hundred weapons to kill Rutherford with."

Sloan agreed. "The best chance Rutherford would have in that case is if the guy froze up from option paralysis."

The halfhearted singing grew louder as Morrison stepped back out of the hidden room. "Ha blah blablablah, spice up your life. Ha blah blablablah, spice up your life. Hi yi yi yi yi." Morrison walked across the room into the master bathroom. Rutherford heard the clink of a toilet lid raising.

Morrison's singing grew a bit louder in the resonant tiled space of the bathroom. "Ha blah blablablah, spice up your life. Ha blah blablablah, spice up your life. Hi! Yi! Yi! Yi! Yi!"

Finally, predictably, Rutherford heard the somewhat muffled sound of a stream of urine hitting the water in the bowl.

Terri said, "He's going to the bathroom. Is this Rutherford's chance?"

The wad rolled closer to the bathroom door while remaining hidden beneath the bed.

Max said, "Feet. Looks like he's sitting, so he can probably see into the bedroom."

Chaz said, "Well, we know he'll be a while."

Max said, "Maybe. Maybe not."

Chaz said, "He's clearly taking a dump."

Max said, "Could be a whiz."

"What kind of man sits to whiz?" Chaz asked.

Sherwood said, "The kind who cleans his own bathroom."

Max said, "Either way, a man is seldom more dangerous than when you interrupt him on the toilet."

Albert said, "The bathroom sink is to the side. When he washes his hands, he'll be turned away and the wall will cut off his peripheral vision. That's your best time to go, Rutherford." He rolled the wad toward the side of the bed, parking it right next to Rutherford's arm.

Sherwood asked, "What if he doesn't wash his hands?"

Sloan said, "Rutherford will have to hope Morrison is a kicker, not a slapper."

Morrison sang along with the song, "Yellow man in Timbuktu. Ha blah blablah, blah blah blu."

Albert said, "Oh, *that* line he sings perfectly!"

The stream lessened, then died completely. A slight break in the singing and a flushing sound told Rutherford that Morrison was done with the toilet for now.

After a brief pause, he heard the bathroom faucet.

Everyone in the van shouted, "Go!"

Rutherford grabbed the wad and made for the door, trying to find the middle ground between tiptoeing fast and running quietly while holding the lint-covered lollipop in his left hand and the wad, now re-formed into a take-out box, in his right. The sound of the running faucet continued as Rutherford speed-snuck down the stairs. As he rounded the bottom of the staircase and crossed the living room, his fast steps subconsciously synchronized with the beat of the concert video on the TV. He slid out the front door and pulled it shut behind him. He turned around and stopped in his tracks, dumbfounded, as six police cruisers tore up the street at him, lights flashing but sirens silent. They fanned out and parked spread across the bulb at the end of the cul-de-sac. The cars disgorged two officers each, all of whom drew their weapons and aimed them at Rutherford. They all shouted at the same time, but not in unison. Rutherford picked out the words "Freeze," "On the ground," "Hands on your head," "Don't move," and "Drop the lollipop and the takeout!"

Two officers took the lead and ran up the lawn to the porch. Rutherford put his hands over his head. "I'm a police officer. I'm reaching for my badge."

He slowly brought his left hand down, hooked a finger under the chain around his neck, and pulled it upward until his badge popped out of his T-shirt. He tossed it to the nearest officer, who examined it for a moment then said, "Looks legit."

The cops all relaxed, exhaling heavily as they put their guns away. Rutherford started to relax too, but tensed back up when he heard the door behind him open and the Spice Girls playing in the background.

Rutherford spun around.

Casper Morrison asked, "What the hell's going on out here? I didn't order Chinese."

TWENTY-TWO

Rutherford again found himself sitting in the driver's seat of the parked minivan, drumming his fingers on the steering wheel, looking at Casper Morrison's house, which was now swarming with police. A steady stream of officers carried out weapons from the hidden gun closet.

Terri stood in front of the house, talking to Detectives Frederick and Burski. Frederick did most of the talking, but only looked at Terri occasionally as he talked. For the most part, his gaze, or to be more accurate, *his glare* was aimed straight at Rutherford. A few times Frederick pointed at the house, the other police, and one time up at the sky (though Rutherford suspected he was pointing at God), but it was clear that Rutherford was still Frederick's primary topic.

Off to the side, across the street and a few cars down, Max and Chaz stood, having what had become an ugly public spat next to a second TurkMO remote-driven minivan Max had called to take Chaz somewhere that Terri would find him less of a disruption to the team's work. Chaz took this as a rejection, not just of him professionally by the team, but romantically by Max, and he clearly believed both were unwarranted. He felt everyone involved was lucky he was present, and foolish for sending him away. He explained why at great length and escalating volume. Max stood by, listening, occasionally saying a quiet word or two before Chaz interrupted to reiterate his case.

Albert said, "Poor Max. He knows he has to send Chaz away, but you can tell he really doesn't want to."

Rutherford said, "He probably knew it would play out like this."

"It had to happen," Sloan said. "And Max knew it. It sucks, but as long as he stands far enough back that Chaz can't dislocate anything or make out with him, he should be all right."

"Hey Rutherford, I've been thinking about your predicament with Dr. Romero," Albert said.

Rutherford said, "I must remember to thank Terri for briefing you all about this."

Sloan said, "We already did. Profusely."

"Do you want to hear what I think or not, Rutherford?" Albert asked.

"Sure. What the hell?"

"I think you're pretty much screwed."

Rutherford said, "Great. Thanks for that."

"But you're screwed in a really interesting way."

Professor Sherwood sat alone in the rear seat and remained fully reclined, but he raised his voice to be sure Rutherford heard. "Yes! In my years working on a college campus with student lab help, I've seen many a romantic conundrum, but nothing that comes close to the no-win scenario you're in. It truly is fascinating."

Albert said. "The professor's right."

Rutherford said, "He agreed with you, and now you're agreeing with him agreeing with you."

"Yes," Albert said. "Because we're both correct."

Rutherford said, "I don't know about that."

Albert said, "We'll explain it to you."

"Must you?"

Professor Sherwood said, "Perhaps not, but we will. First, the basic givens of the situation. For your work, you pretend to be a bad boy, something you very much are not."

"Was the 'very much' really necessary?" Rutherford asked.

Sloan nodded. "If anything, he undersold it."

Sherwood continued. "Dr. Romero is drawn to bad boys, but she is weary of the downsides to dating them, so she wants to avoid bad boys and instead date a good boy, which you are."

Rutherford said, "I'd prefer it if you said *good man*, or maybe *good guy*."

Sloan said, "The opposite of bad boy is good boy. Deal with it."

Sherwood said, "You're what she wants, but she can never know, because you have to pretend to be what she doesn't want."

Sloan shook her helmet. "Professor, as the only woman in the car, I have to say I think you're looking at it backward."

Rutherford said, "Good!"

Sloan said, "Laughing. Sorry, Rutherford. It's not good. Claire wants what she wants. She's into bad boys because bad boys are what she's into, and she thinks she's into you because you pretend to be what she's into. She doesn't really want a good boy, like you, but she's decided that what she wants is bad for her. She's looking at dating a good boy because her brain tells her one would be good for her, but she doesn't really want it. To her you look like a donut, Rutherford. But you are kale."

Quietly, Rutherford said, "*I'm kale.* That's the worst thing anyone's ever said to me."

"Yes," Sloan said. "It was harsher than I meant it to be. Forget kale. You're skim milk. No, a juice cleanse. I'm just making this worse."

"What you are," Albert said, "is the greatest logic puzzle I've ever come across. You might be exactly what she wants while repelling her by pretending to be the opposite. Or you're exactly what she doesn't want and attracting her by pretending to be the opposite. In a sense, you're both of those things, at once!"

Professor Sherwood said, "Kind of like how light appears to be both a particle and a wave."

Sloan said, "No, he's either one of those things or the other, but we can't tell which, so both options are equally possible."

Professor Sherwood said, "Like Schrödinger's Boyfriend."

Sloan said, "Maybe. I don't know Schrödinger, or who he's dating."

Albert said, "She's right. The only way to find out would be to run an experiment. Actually, have him and Romero go on a few dates, then afterward ask her why she dumped him."

Rutherford said, "She might not dump me."

Sherwood said, "That's the spirit."

Albert said, "We'll never know, because your job depends on keeping up your cover, even to her."

Sloan leaned forward and placed a hand on Rutherford's shoulder. "Look at it this way. Your situation is confusing and complicated in a way that makes successfully starting a relationship with Dr. Claire Romero highly unlikely."

After a long pause, Rutherford said, "But?"

Sloan asked, "What?"

"*But?* Usually, Sloan, when someone starts a sentence with 'Look at it this way,' then says something negative, they'll say *but*, and end by putting a positive spin on it."

"Oh," Sloan said. "I'm not going to do that."

"Then why start with 'Look at it this way' if you're just going to be negative?"

"Because that's the way I want you to look at it, Rutherford: negatively."

Terri continued her conversation with the LAPD detectives, but Frederick seemed to have tired himself out. He stood slightly slumped and clearly displeased, still glancing over at Rutherford every few seconds, while his partner Burski did the talking. Finally, she said a few words and walked back to the minivan.

She sat in her customary front passenger seat and faced forward as she filled the team in.

"Detective Frederick is absolutely convinced that Rutherford broke the law somehow."

"What did you tell him?" Rutherford asked.

Terri said, "A lie. I told him you didn't break the law, which was a lie, Rutherford. People, I know that occasionally we might need to step outside the lines to do this job, but today we went much farther than I'm comfortable with."

Rutherford asked, "Did he believe you?"

"He pointed out that the black rubber gloves you were wearing when they apprehended you matched the ones in the dispenser in the garage. So, no. I don't think he believed me, but he can't prove anything, and I doubt he'll try since it would jeopardize his case."

Sloan asked, "What's Burski think?"

Terri closed her eyes. "Let's see. He thinks that the idea that the suspect was obviously making a good living from the business of killing had an appealing but tragic symmetry, as if he was stealing the life and vitality of his victims and trading them for creature comforts and consumer goods. The irony being that it could be argued that the things he purchased and thus needed to maintain were in fact robbing him of his own vitality, and slowly swallowing his life."

Albert asked, "What's going on with the case?"

"Morrison's lawyer showed up just behind the cops. Turns out Morrison's been on the LAPD's radar for a long time. They have a whole string of cold cases where practically no evidence was left behind, but they suspected were all done by the same perpetrator. They've been calling him 'Mr. Gas.'"

Rutherford nodded. "Gas: the silent killer."

Sloan said, "That's a nice idea, but you know they called him that because he's silent but deadly."

"It's weird," Albert said. "When I was a kid we said 'silent but violent.'"

Sherwood said, "I wonder if that's a regional thing, like soda versus pop."

Terri said, "Morrison's offered to testify against a bunch of his former clients in return for a reduced sentence and a minimum-security prison."

"Pity his poor cell mate," Sloan said. "*So you're an embezzler? I'm a contract killer. You don't mind if I play some Spice Girls, do you? Come on. Sing along with me.*"

Outside, Max finally had enough and began shouting at Chaz, who stood silently, listening with his fists clenched. The sound of Max losing his temper caused the rest of the team to forget their conversation.

Rutherford said, "Wow! That's the maddest I've ever seen Max."

"Yeah," Terri said. "He might be angry enough to hurt Chaz in a way that actually looks like an attack."

Sloan asked, "So, Morrison's giving up clients. Does that include our Watson killer?"

Terri shook her head. "Of course not. He says he doesn't know who hired him. He took the job through a kind of bulletin board on the dark web where people who want to hire a killer can find people who will kill for money."

"Does it have a name?" Sloan asked.

"No. Just an IP address."

"Good," Sloan said. "Then I'm going to call it *Threatsy.*"

"You do that. It's all anonymized. The client pays in cryptocurrency. There's no way to identify who hired him."

"On Threatsy?" Sloan asked.

"Sure. On Threatsy."

Outside, Chaz finally had enough and started shouting back at Max. Max, however, did not stop shouting himself. The two of them stood, face to face, shouting for several seconds, then Max pointed an accusatory finger at Chaz. Chaz reached out to grab the finger. Max yanked back his extended digit just in time, making Chaz grasp at thin air. They both stopped shouting immediately, Max looking at Chaz, hurt and upset. Chaz looked back, only slightly chagrined.

Sloan said, "It would have been nice if Morrison could have identified his client, but it's not all bad. At least our next step in the investigation is fairly clear. We work the case like detectives, looking for things or people the two victims have in common to find someone who had a motive."

"Like what?" Sherwood asked. "We haven't found any yet."

"We haven't looked for any. We've been too busy staking out productions and meeting Max's old associates."

Terri asked, "What do you have in mind, Sloan?"

"All of the people threatened have a job in common. One way or another, they play Dr. Watson, so they're all successful professional actors. That means agents. That means publicists. That means lawyers. That means fans. If any of those people are shared by all the known Watsons, or even just the two victims so far, that's a lead. For that matter, they all got cast in their parts. Maybe some other actor was up for all the parts, or, again, just the two victims' parts, and lost out. We have no leads, but if we put our heads down and go through the background information, we might be able to find one."

Rutherford said, "And while she does that, I could try something more direct."

Terri said, "The most direct way to see if a gun's loaded is to look down the barrel. That doesn't mean it's the best way. But what do you have in mind?"

"I post to this dark web bulletin board posing as a killer and hope the perp tries to hire me."

Terri asked, "And what do you think of that, Sloan?"

"I don't like it, and I don't think it will work, but we should probably do it."

Terri said, "No. Rutherford, even if you get hired to kill someone, there's no guarantee you'd get hired to kill a Watson. Besides, the client hired Morrison anonymously. If they hire you, they'll do it anonymously and all you'd accomplish would be to confirm that we are indeed looking for someone who's anonymous."

Rutherford said, "I'll act interested in any job I get offered, then I'll push all of my clients for a meeting. What have we got to lose?"

Terri said, "What have we got to lose? By deliberately meeting up with murderers? Well, the first thing that leaps to mind is *your life,* Rutherford. We could lose your life. Catching a murderer by pretending to be a murderer. I don't like it."

Albert said, "They say it takes a thief to catch a thief. Maybe the same holds true for murderers."

Terry twisted around in her chair to look at Albert. "They say it, but it isn't true. Lots of thieves are caught by people who aren't thieves. It doesn't take a murderer to catch a murderer."

Sloan said, "It would take a murderer to murder a murderer. If I needed someone to murder a murderer, I'd send a murderer."

Rutherford said, "I won't be meeting with murderers though. I'll be meeting with people who want to hire murderers. They are, by definition, not willing to kill someone themselves. Heck, this'll probably be the safest I've ever been in this job."

Sloan said, "Terri, I feel like we need to approach this from more than one direction because my hunt for a connection might not pan out. It's possible that the person behind this just has a strong grudge against one Watson, but is killing all the others to cover for it, like when a guy gets a little drop of pee on his pants so he splashes a bunch of water on it."

Rutherford said, "I told you, that bathroom had crazy water pressure and the sink channeled it right at me."

Professor Sherwood pointed forward. "Uh-oh."

Rutherford turned around to look out the front window again and saw Max and Chaz hugging.

Terri moaned. "Ugh. Did Max cave?"

Sloan said. "No. Never."

Sherwood agreed. "More likely they're fighting in a way we can't even perceive."

Albert squinted and turned his head sideways. "Yeah, Chaz might be trying to dislocate Max's spine."

The hug ended with a quick kiss. Max stood by smiling as Chaz got into the second TurkMO minivan and rode away. Max returned to the team. He and Albert did a quick dance that resulted in Albert sliding into the back row next to Sherwood, and Max sitting in the second row next to Sloan. Rutherford thought Max looked drained, as if being around Chaz had aged him at an accelerated rate.

"I want to apologize to all of you," Max said. "Chaz has always been a reliable source of distraction. I should have never allowed him near our work. I am sorry."

Terri said, "We understand, Max. We all just want you to be happy. So, where will Chaz go?"

"Seattle. He's going to stay at my house until I get back. Then we'll see what happens. Where are we with the case?"

Terri said, "Morrison's going to prison, but he can't identify his client."

Rutherford said, "So I'm going to go undercover as a contract killer to get the same person to try to hire me."

Max shrugged. "That's not a terrible idea."

Rutherford smiled. "Thank you!"

Terri said, "That wasn't actually much of an endorsement, Rutherford."

Sloan said, "And it came from a man who just agreed to turn Chaz loose in his home for a few days while he's out of town."

TWENTY-THREE

Rutherford had spent most of the afternoon hunched over the computer with Albert, and he was now spending his evening standing in front of a 7-Eleven, sipping from a straw stuck in a plastic cup the size of Abe Lincoln's hat. Albert and Professor Sherwood sat in the front seats of the TurkMO minivan, witnessing and recording every second of the nothing that had happened since Rutherford's arrival.

In his earpiece, Rutherford heard Professor Sherwood ask, "Are you sure that in front of a 7-Eleven was a good place to meet with people who want to hire a murderer?"

Rutherford said, "It's perfect. Why, what would you suggest?"

"I don't know, an alley? An abandoned warehouse?"

Albert said, "A lonely road out in farm country, right next to a suspiciously convenient hole and a pile of loose dirt?"

Sherwood said, "Oh, that's a good one."

Rutherford said, "All those places seem like they'd be good for clandestine meetings because that's where you've seen these kind of deals go down in movies. But meeting in places like that makes criminals nervous because they've seen the same movies, and in them someone always gets twitchy or tries to pull a double-cross and there's no help or witnesses around. They'd rather hide in plain sight where the other guy won't want to try anything. A place where everyone can see but nobody's paying attention. That's why the sidewalk in front of a convenience store is perfect. Nobody wants to hear anything you have to say in front of a convenience store. Tons of spur-of-the-moment illegal transactions happen here."

Albert said, "I bet most of them are just agreements to buy minors some beer."

"Yeah," Rutherford said. "And that familiarity makes the criminals more comfortable."

"If you say so," Albert said. "All I know is sitting here, staring at the front of a convenience store, is making me want a Slurpee."

"See, I never went in for Slurpees. It's nothing but a big cup of ice with a little sugar syrup mixed in. I don't want to pay for that."

"Isn't that exactly what that pop you're drinking is made of?"

"I had to buy something, or they would've shooed me away."

"Yeah, but you chose a soda over a Slurpee. Why is it better?"

"It's carbonated?" Rutherford winced at the weakness of his own argument. "No. Here's my problem with the Slurpee, and snow cones for that matter. They want you to think they're like ice cream, but they aren't. They're just ice and Kool-Aid."

"Ah," Professor Sherwood said. "It's the dishonesty of it that bothers you."

"Yes."

"It's a funny thing for you to be irritated by," Sherwood said, "since you pretend to be something you aren't for a living."

Albert said, "Maybe that's precisely why it bothers him. He feels like the law enforcement equivalent of a Slurpee, and he resents being reminded of it."

Professor Sherwood said, "It's funny. When you look at a place like this, they probably make most of their money selling flavored water. Seems silly."

"Yeah," Rutherford said, looking at his giant beverage. "I see what you mean. I probably should have got a coffee instead."

Albert said, "Hey, Rutherford, I see someone walking up the sidewalk. Middle-aged white man. Seems out of place."

Sherwood said, "He could be our guy. He could well have parked somewhere near, but not at the store. He wouldn't want his car showing up on any security cameras."

Albert said, "He just looked right at you and tensed up, Rutherford. He seems a bit nervous. He's veering into the parking lot."

"Gotcha." Rutherford put a great deal of effort into scanning the area with an air of casual confidence. He wasn't sure he pulled it off. He saw an average-sized man with a stocky build and a pronounced belly wearing a white hooded sweatshirt, hood up, and jeans. The man walked with his head down. The streetlights reflecting on the man's glasses hid his eyes, but Rutherford could tell the guy was sizing him up.

Rutherford didn't hide the fact that he noticed the guy but tried to act indifferent to his arrival.

The man walked up to Rutherford and stood next to him, about five feet away, facing the same direction in an extremely formal imitation of casualness.

They stood like that for a moment. Rutherford took a sip from his drink, then asked, "You the guy?"

The man in the hoodie said, "Maybe. You the guy?"

"Possibly. So, we both might be the guy. Small world. Are you here looking to get a job done?"

"You could say that, I suppose. That's one way to put it."

"What kind of job?" Rutherford asked.

The man laughed nervously. "Um. I guess that depends. I can think of a few different kinds of jobs I'd like to get done. At least three."

"That doesn't help me much." Rutherford took another sip.

The man in the hoodie said, "How about this. Why don't you tell me what kinds of jobs you're willing to do, and how much you charge, then I'll choose what I want."

Rutherford sighed. "You're a cop."

"What? No! What makes you think—"

"I'm a cop too. Detective Rutherford. Seattle PD, here on a special assignment. I'd show you my badge, but I don't want to break cover."

"Yeah, I get it. Detective Engel, LAPD. I'm out trolling for prostitutes."

"Good to meet you, Detective. And the preferred term these days is *sex workers*."

"Yeah, maybe in the Seattle PD. So obviously you're posing as one to catch johns."

"No! What makes you think that?"

"The outfit. The beat-up leather jacket, the tight jeans, the way you keep suggestively sucking on that straw."

"I'm posing as a contract killer. I'm meeting someone about a murder."

"Oh." Engel looked Rutherford up and down. "Huh. Well, you probably scared off all my prostitutes."

"Sex workers. Tell you what, I'm looking for a specific perpetrator here. If anyone who isn't him tries to hire me, as a killer or a sex worker, I'll give you the collar. Fair?"

"Yeah, that works for me. I'll be inside. I think I'm gonna get a taquito. Good hunting." Detective Engel went into the convenience store where the lone cashier was watching an episode of the original *Transformers* TV series.

Once he was alone, Rutherford asked, "Guys, I don't look like a sex worker out here, do I?"

Albert said, "No."

Sherwood said, "I don't think so?"

Albert added, "I guess not."

Sherwood asked, "I mean, how would I know?"

Albert said, "That guy was a cop. He'd know better than either of us."

Sherwood said, "And he thought you did, so, yes, you probably do."

Rutherford scowled in the direction of the darkened minivan. He started to take a sip of his beverage, but he stopped before his lips touched the straw. He paused for a moment, puckered, stopped puckering, puckered again, stopped again, groaned, and threw the drink in a nearby trash can.

"Aw," Albert said. "You just wasted, like, a gallon of pop. And if you're not having a drink, you should put the sucker back in your mouth."

"I seriously doubt that the sucker would help fight off the sex worker vibe. Besides, I don't wanna have that thing in my mouth twenty-four seven. It's gotta be bad for my teeth."

"It's not real," Albert said. "It doesn't have any sugar."

"No, but it's a hard object. My teeth are probably grinding against it."

Albert said, "You know, you might be right."

"So what can we do about it?"

Sherwood said, "Apply the scientific method. You've posited a hypothesis. Long-term oral insertion of the fake sucker might damage your teeth. Now, we test the hypothesis."

Rutherford said, "You mean we wait and see if my teeth get messed up."

"Yes."

"Well, I'm not putting it in my mouth tonight."

Albert said, "Terri was clear. If you're not eating or drinking the sucker goes in."

Sherwood asked, "Are you hungry? You could go inside real fast and buy a corn dog."

"That won't make me look more like a killer, or less like a sex worker."

"You could try to eat it menacingly," Albert offered.

"How do I do that?"

"I don't know. Chew slowly while making eye contact."

Rutherford said, "You're just messing with me now."

Sherwood said, "Correction. we're just messing with you, *still*."

Albert said, "It gives us something to do while we sit here watching this plan fail."

Rutherford said, "It hasn't failed yet."

Sherwood said, "It's failing, even as we speak."

Albert said, "It's started failing, and is continuing to fail, but it isn't done failing quite yet. It's still got some failing to do."

"Come on guys, this may not be going well, but it was a good idea."

"I wouldn't go that far," Sherwood said. "It was definitely one of the two best ideas we had, but that doesn't mean it's good."

Albert said, "And of the two ideas we had, Sloan took one for herself and gave you the other. Do you really think she would have given you the better one?"

"Max said it was a good idea."

"No," Albert said. "He said it wasn't a terrible idea, and he's not thinking straight right now."

"You both thought it was a good idea."

Albert said, "No I didn't."

Professor Sherwood said, "Not even a little."

"You volunteered to help."

Albert said, "We volunteered to watch. That's a very different thing. Hold that thought, here comes another bogey. Opposite direction from the last."

Rutherford stood with his hands in his pockets, glancing occasionally at the stranger as he approached. He looked to be in his midtwenties, dressed much as Rutherford was, with a black leather jacket and jeans. As before, he walked up beside Rutherford and stood there, facing the same direction.

Rutherford asked, "You the guy I'm supposed to meet?"

The other man said, "Maybe. Do you meet guys here often?"

"No. Not here."

The other man nodded. "How long have you been in this line of work?"

"Long enough," Rutherford said. "I have plenty of experience. I know what I'm doing, if that's what you're worried about."

"I don't doubt it, man. No offense meant. I bet you have some crazy stories you could tell."

"Some."

"I'm curious, how'd you get into this work? Did you need the money for rent, did you get addicted to something, or did, like, a boyfriend put you up to it?"

Rutherford stared at the man for a moment, then looked across the parking lot at the minivan. In his ear he heard Albert and Sherwood laughing.

Rutherford said, "Okay. We have two problems here. One is that you are clearly some kind of journalist."

The other man put his hands up, trying to calm Rutherford. "I'm not here to judge you, man. Just to tell your story. I'll can come up with a pseudonym for you, you know, a fake name, and I'll buy you a hot meal."

"And our other problem is that I'm a cop."

The reporter kept his hands up, in fact raising them a bit higher. "Hey, man, officer, man, there's no law against asking people questions. I didn't offer you any money for sex here. You can't claim I did!"

"Relax. You didn't. I wouldn't. I'm not after you."

"Okay. Good. Thanks. Sting to catch johns, I suppose."

"No! I'm not a prostitute. I mean, I'm not posing as a prostitute. I'm a hit man, waiting for my client."

"Really! Huh. That sounds like a pretty good story too. But I should point out, the preferred term is *sex worker*."

Rutherford took a deep breath before saying, "Of course you're right. Look, if you wanna hang out inside, where you won't scare off my client, there might be an exclusive in it for you. There's another cop you could ask some questions."

"Done. Thanks." The reporter paused as he entered the convenience store. "You know, you might look less like a sex worker if you had some obvious reason to be hanging out at a convenience store. Maybe a drink or something."

"Thanks."

The reporter went inside. As the door swung open, Rutherford heard the undercover cop say to the cashier, "Megatron has the advantage, because he has a gun mounted to his arm. Prime has to carry a gun and pull it, quick-draw style."

The cashier said, "But Megatron's gun is so big and bulky, it makes his gun arm useless for anything else."

"He doesn't need that arm to do anything else," the cop said. "He can use the gun mounted to it to threaten anybody to do anything he wants."

"They teach you that at the police academy?"

"Shut up." The door swung shut.

Rutherford muttered, "This sucks."

In Rutherford's earpiece, Albert and Professor Sherwood agreed.

Rutherford smiled. "Still, it's better than how Sloan's spending her evening, going through old records."

Albert said, "She's not going through the records herself. It turns out CartFulls has a forensic accounting department."

Rutherford said, "No way."

Professor Sherwood said, "Indeed. It makes sense. The lab started to investigate theft. It follows that they'd have people who also investigate embezzlement."

"Yeah," Rutherford said. "I suppose. So Sloan's working with them?"

Albert said, "More like they're working for Sloan. She told them what to look for, they got to work, and now she's got the night off to brainstorm."

"How do you know this, Albert?" Rutherford asked.

"Terri told me."

"Terri called? Why didn't I know?"

Albert said, "She didn't call. She's been checking in with me and the Professor by text since we started. Just to see how it's going."

Rutherford asked, "What have you told her?"

Albert said, "The truth."

Rutherford muttered, "Damn. And she's with Sloan, then?"

"And Claire," Albert said.

Professor Sherwood added, "They're having sort of a *girls' night.*"

Albert said, "Terri wants me to tell you: now that your drink is done, put your sucker back in your mouth."

"Well I'm not going to. Not tonight."

"She won't like that."

"Only if you upset her by telling her I said it. If she puts up a fuss, say that they want a loose cannon. I'm being a loose cannon."

Professor Sherwood said, "That's too loose. You're disobeying orders. That's firing cannonballs into the rigging of your own ship. You need to aim the cannon."

"You can't aim a loose cannon. That's the whole point of a loose cannon. If you aim it, it isn't loose."

Albert said, "I think this analogy has failed us."

Rutherford said, "No. The analogy's good. They want a loose cannon that they can control. They want a wild man who behaves himself. They want a guy who plays by his own rules, but his rules are their rules too. What they want is logically impossible."

Sherwood said, "No, Rutherford. The idea of a loose cannon comes from the navy. Some ships had a loose cannon. It didn't just fire at random, it was a cannon they could wheel around and fire at anything they wanted regardless of what direction the ship was pointing. Terri and Capp want a guy who plays by the rules, but thinks of moves they wouldn't. They want a loose cannon that will at least try to fire at the enemy."

"So you're telling me that they want me to give them the benefits of having a free-thinking, fast-and-loose wild man on the team, but without any of the problems that come with them."

Albert said, "Yes."

"They want the best of both worlds. They want to have their cake and eat it too."

Sherwood said, "Yes. Just like every other employer on earth. They want you to do things they can't or don't want to do themselves while giving them the least possible amount of trouble."

Albert said, "Hey, I think we have someone. He parked a sedan on the other side of the street; now he's coming in from your left. He keeps looking over at you."

"Yeah, I see him. He's crossing the street."

Albert said, "Tsk, jaywalking. I shouldn't be surprised that he has no respect for the law, since he's out here looking for a sex worker."

Rutherford growled.

"Or a murderer," Albert said, laughing. "There's definitely a small chance that he's looking to hire a murderer. I bet you could get a sex worker to kill someone if you offered them enough money."

"Yeah," Sherwood agreed. "And you might get a killer to have sex with you, though you'd need to be very brave to ask."

A man in his fifties walked across the parking lot. His wool overcoat, slacks, shoes, graying hair, and deeply lined face spoke of a man who made good money and spent none of it on moisturizer.

He stepped up onto the curb and stood facing Rutherford directly. "Are you the one I'm supposed to meet?"

Rutherford tried to phrase his sentence in such a way as to not sound like a sex worker. "I'm here to meet someone. It might be you." Rutherford was mad that he had failed so badly. He tried to make it better. "I'm a contractor. I'm here about a . . . contract."

"I'm here about a contract too. Pest control."

Rutherford nodded, relieved. "Yeah, I'm who you're meeting. You bring the half up front? If not, there's no point in talking."

The client said, "I've got it."

"Good. Tell me about the pest."

The client continued. "It's someone I work with. A woman. We, uh, we had a thing. It started out as just a bit of fun, but then she asked me to leave my wife, and I told her that couldn't happen. Now she's—"

Rutherford said, "Yeah, I get the picture. It's pretty standard. In the business we call it a 'Full Landau.' Will you excuse me one moment, please?"

Rutherford turned away from the confused man, opened the door to the convenience store, and leaned in.

Inside, the reporter had joined the detective and the cashier's conversation. The cashier asked, "But think about it. Which would you rather be, a truck with a mind of its own or a gun with a mind of its own?"

The reporter said, "Easy! The truck! It can drive anywhere under its own power and run over anything it wants. The gun needs someone to aim it, unless the truck just happens to roll into the crosshairs."

The policeman said, "But in general. Which would you rather have, a truck or a gun?"

"The truck! The truck's more useful. Nobody asks you to help them move because you own a gun."

The cashier said, "That's more of an argument for the gun than for the truck."

Rutherford said, "Hey, guys, I've got someone out here who's a good candidate for your, uh, particular professional skills."

The client said, "Hey, hold on. I'm not looking for anything weird. Just someone to kill my mistress."

TWENTY-FOUR

Rutherford stood in the corner of the soundstage, working to prevent the murder of Russell Byrne in the only way he could: by watching the parts of a TV production that the entire crew works very hard to never let anyone see.

At the center of the huddle of cameras, lights, a large green screen, and a few minimal set pieces suggesting the edge of a large water tank, Russell Byrne and his costar, Chris Wolfberg, performed their dialog.

Byrne said, "The oversized paw prints lead right up to the water's edge, Holmes."

"Yes," Wolfberg said. "Golden Labs love the water, clearly even when suffering in the grip of lycanthropy."

Kyndra Perrin, sitting to the side, watching the camera feed on a large monitor, yelled. "Cut. That'll do. The next setup is just pulling in for close-ups of Wolfberg. It shouldn't take long to rig, so make sure it doesn't. Actors, stay close. Detective Rutherford, stay out of the way."

The crew rushed in every direction. Rutherford looked at Perrin through the bustle and said, "I am out of the way."

Her eyes narrowed to slits, and she slowed her speech as if explaining to someone so dim-witted that they needed their condescension delivered underhand so they could catch it. "I know that you're out of the way. That's why I said 'stay'. If I'd thought you were in the way I'd have said *get*. Really, though, the last guy was killed in a bathroom. You should be staking out the urinals instead of disrupting my set."

"Not necessarily. The first victim was killed in his car."

"You waiting in Russell's car would work for me too."

Rutherford said, "Mr. Byrne is here. That makes this the most likely place for someone to try to kill him, right now."

Perrin laughed. "Shows what you know. A working set is a terrible place to try to kill an actor and get away with it. It's well lit, the actors are the center of everyone's attention, and the place is full of witnesses and cameras."

Rutherford said, "Yeah, but it could be done so it looks like an accident. An electrician could drop a light on him, or an effects guy could blow him up."

"And risk getting tossed out of the union? No murder is worth that."

"You think a lot about your actors getting killed, don't you?"

"Every director does." She turned and walked away but looked back at Rutherford as she went. "If I ever teach at a film school, I'm going to devote an entire lecture to it."

Rutherford walked to the nearest exit door and opened it just a sliver. After his eyes had adjusted to the light, he saw a police officer stationed there, since they were now at every door for any building Byrne was likely to enter.

Beyond the officer, Max stood against the wall, talking into his phone.

"No," Max said, "please don't transfer me. I've been waiting on hold and climbing the limbs of your phone tree for over two hours. Yes, as soon as I got back from lunch I called.

If you transfer me it'll just be another half hour on hold to talk to another person who wants to transfer me."

Randy rounded the corner of the building. He eyeballed Max as he passed, but Max didn't notice, focusing on his desperate effort to convince the person who was currently not helping him to continue to not help him.

The police officer guarding the door nodded to Randy. Randy said, "Uh-huh," without even looking at him and walked through the door.

"Hey, Rutherford."

"Randy."

"Anyone kill Byrne yet?"

"No." Rutherford squirmed a bit as several members of the crew looked at him and Randy.

Randy said, "Good."

Rutherford relaxed a bit.

Randy said, "I'd hate to have missed it. So what's the deal with your guy out there?"

"Max? When we went to lunch he found his credit card was missing. When he tried to cancel it, they told him someone else has been using it. He's been hashing that out ever since."

"Well I can see why he's distracted, then. Still, he didn't even see me. For a detective he's not real observant."

"Max isn't a detective. He's head of personal security for the team."

"And his credit card got stolen?"

Kyndra Perrin announced that they were ready to try again. The hubbub around the set slowed, and the murmuring fell silent. She called "Action."

Byrne said, "The oversized paw prints lead right up to the water's edge, Holmes."

Wolfberg said, "Yes. Golden Labs love the water, even when suffering in the grip of lycanthropy. Clearly, the were-dog either jumped or fell into the tank with the great white shark."

Byrne said, "Or perhaps he was pushed."

"Don't be silly."

"Sorry." Byrne cleared his throat. "There are no tracks leading out, so it seems the dog—"

"Were-dog."

"—was eaten by the shark. Problem solved."

"Yes, Watson, so it would seem. Unless the were-dog managed to bite the shark before the shark bit her!"

As the actors continued, Randy asked, "So where's this other detective you apparently work for?"

Rutherford whispered, "At another set."

Randy said, "What? Is there another Sherlock Holmes show?"

A young man with a tablet PC and an oversized pair of headphones shushed Randy, who nodded and held up a hand as if to tell the young man that he understood and would handle the situation. The young man turned back to face the actors.

Randy said, "They already killed the Watson from the show with the Indian, and the one from the cartoon. Then there's us, and that's it, right?"

Rutherford held up a finger, signaling Randy to wait until the take was over.

Slightly louder, Randy asked, "Right?"

The assistant with the tablet computer spun around and shushed them again. Randy looked around, anger in his eyes, as if looking for whoever was making all the noise, making a shushing sound himself.

Wolfberg continued a line Rutherford hadn't caught the start of.

"—with rows and rows of werewolf fangs instead of shark teeth."

Mercifully, the director said, "Cut."

As the crew milled around, Rutherford said, "They're at the set of a late-night talk show. *The Wee Smalls with Mia Paul.*"

Randy said, "Heard of it."

"She and her announcer have a comedy bit they do every couple of weeks where they dress like Holmes and Watson and use deductive reasoning to explain why whatever celebrity's in the news did whatever stupid thing got them there."

Randy stroked his chin. "Hmm. Yes. I see why you think Byrne's a better target. At least he plays Watson full time."

On the set, Byrne looked past the woman touching up his makeup and asked his costar, "How did it feel that last time?"

Wolfberg said, "Like we professionally executed the script we were given."

Byrne sagged, "To think that I'm starving myself and working with a personal trainer five nights a week to look good for this."

"No," Wolfberg said. "You're starving yourself and working out so you can surprise people with how ripped you look when you take off your wet suit to hopefully drum up some thirst clicks and get you a better gig when this ends."

"It's that obvious?"

"Only because most of us have similar plans. How's training with Hogan going?"

"She's killing me. I'm sore in places that a month ago I didn't know were places. But I'm seeing the results."

"Good. And, uh, any progress on the personal front?"

"I put out some feelers, to see if she's interested."

"And?"

"Beyond our professional arrangement, she has no interest in me or my feelers."

Wolfberg and the woman doing Byrne's makeup laughed. Byrne didn't.

Perrin announced that they would start again from the next line, called for quiet on the set, making sure to look in Rutherford and Randy's direction, then said, "Action."

Byrne said, "But even if I believed in were-sharks, or were-anything, the creature would be completely contained inside the tank."

"Hopefully, Watson. But we can't be sure how the lycanthropy would affect a shark. For all we know it grew canine legs."

"A land shark!"

"A land *were*-shark. And the worst part is we won't know for sure until the next full moon."

Randy elbowed Rutherford. "Come on. We've got an errand to run."

Rutherford whispered, "Can't. Gotta watch Byrne."

"Let Max."

"He's busy."

"He's right out there, and there are a million cops around."

"But Byrne's in here."

"What about that other old guy? The professor. I saw him playing with his suitcase near the craft services table."

"Yeah, he has to stay there. That suitcase is full of . . . things they don't want on the set."

"Tell him to ditch the suitcase and get in here. Then you can come with me."

"No, Randy. I can't."

Perrin yelled "Cut," then turned, looked directly at Randy, and pointed at Rutherford. "You'll leave if he goes with you?"

Randy said, "Yup."

Byrne said, "Go, Detective. It's worth the risk."

TWENTY-FIVE

Rutherford and Randy stepped out of the soundstage into the daylight. The late-afternoon sun had dipped behind the administration building across the street, casting the entire canyon between the buildings in shadow. Rutherford pressed his earpiece into his ear. "Sorry, Professor. Yeah, I just have to step away for a few minutes, thanks for covering. Sorry you'll have to leave the suitcase, but I pity anyone who tries to mess with it. Byrne says he'll be fine until you get here. Thanks again."

Max pressed his phone to the side of his head. "If the card was used last night or today, at all, then it was stolen. Where was it used?"

Rutherford said, "Max, I need to go take care of something. The Professor's coming to cover."

Max nodded. "LAX, Sea-Tac, and Nordstrom? I . . . I think I may know who has it."

Randy said, "Come on. Time's a-wastin.'"

Rutherford said, "I have one more quick call I need to make while we walk."

"Whatever. Just make it fast."

Rutherford pulled up his contacts and selected Terri. After a few seconds, she answered.

"Hello, Rutherford. I should warn you that you're on speakerphone. Claire and I are both here."

"Understood. You're over at the CartFulls lab this morning, right?"

"That's why you're on speakerphone."

"Have to keep your hands sterile in the lab?"

"No, I'm just sticky. Their lab is attached to the back of a CartFulls store, and the break room's stocked by the store bakery every morning."

"Sounds nice. Tell me, did we get any kind of access to Mac Menard's financials?"

Claire said, "Yes, we have bank records going back five years. The boys in forensic accounting haven't gotten to it yet."

Rutherford said, "Cool. Can you search for the name *Hogan*?"

After a small amount of typing and a few seconds of silence, Claire said, "Hogan Fitness. I've got it right here. Four payments, a couple of years ago."

Rutherford said, "Both our victims worked out with Amanda Hogan. I just found out Russell Byrne is currently a client."

Claire and Terri both said something Rutherford suspected was congratulatory, but he couldn't know for sure since they were drowned out by Randy shouting, "Hogan, the one from the billboards? The one with the butt?"

Claire said, "Typical. I'm going to go get a donut."

Randy said, "Is she the one with the butt? Rutherford, tell me she's the one with the butt."

Terri asked, "Who is that?"

"Randy, the show's police consultant."

Randy asked, "Is she the one with the butt?"

Rutherford said, "Just shut up about her butt. Besides, everyone has a butt."

"Everyone has a butt. She has *the* butt. Rutherford, we need to go question her."

Terri said, "Randy sounds like an idiot, but an idiot with a point. We should question her, as soon as possible, but not about her butt. Sloan's across town guarding the talk show with Albert, and I'm at the CartFulls lab. Max and Sherwood should be able to manage there at the studio. You can go talk to her yourself. I'll contact Sloan and get back to you. We'll eavesdrop over your earpiece. You did good, Rutherford. I'll let you know what Sloan says." Terri ended the call.

Randy asked, "So that was the chief detective you were reporting to?"

"No. Sloan's the chief detective. That was Terri, our supervisor."

Randy winced. "Yeesh. Oh, man. Rutherford, that's terrible. I mean, I knew you were a sidekick, but to be an *underling's* sidekick! No wonder you don't get any respect."

Just around the corner from the soundstage, a row of reserved parking spots lined the side of the road. In among the sports cars and sedans sat a single dark-blue Chevy truck from the 1970s, which was *jacked up* both in the sense that it sat high on oversized tires, and that it appeared to have substantial collision damage and noticeable panel rust.

Rutherford said, "Your truck?"

"Yup. Ain't she a beaut?"

Rutherford did not tell Randy if he considered the truck to be *a beaut*, and also chose not to ask why it was parked in what was marked as Russell Byrne's parking spot.

Randy climbed in, but before Rutherford could enter, Randy had to lean across the seat to clear away several old soda cups, beer cans, and an old gray hoodie that looked like it had been used to clean the truck's dipstick. He swept the refuse off the seat and into the passenger side footwell. When Rutherford sat down and put his feet on the floorboards, they submerged ankle deep in the trash.

The doors, shocks, and seat springs all squeaked. The interior smelled like dust and motor oil. The starter took a couple of seconds to do its work but eventually the engine came to life with a deafening roar.

Rutherford asked, "What've you got in this thing?"

Randy said, "A hole in the muffler." They snaked through the grid of roads running between the soundstages. Thanks to the heat, the bouncing, the trash, and the deafening noise, it felt to Rutherford as if he were riding around the studio lot in a clothes dryer full of garbage. After a minute, Rutherford leaned toward Randy and shouted, "What's this errand we're running?"

"We're going to go question this Hogan chick."

"No, seriously."

"We're going to seriously question her. You'll do all the talking while I determine if she's being truthful by observing whether or not she clenches her glutes as she answers. It's what we in the business like to call *a tell.*"

"No. I mean, yes, I'm going to go interview Amanda Hogan. But that's not what you wanted me to come help you with."

"True, but the first thing'll only take a second. Then we go question what's-her-butt."

Rutherford could only imagine what a guy like Randy might do while questioning Amanda Hogan, and that was the problem: He could only imagine it. Here was a chance to see firsthand what a guy like Randy would do; a golden opportunity, since Rutherford was paid to do the things a guy like Randy would. Rutherford would need to make sure Randy was on his best behavior, which would alter the experiment, but he didn't mind. He doubted he could emulate Randy's worst behavior without suffering a terminal bout of shame, possibly due to blushing so hard that his brain got starved for blood.

"Maybe . . . *maybe* you can drive me there, and I can introduce you, but I do all the talking, and you need to promise to be on your best behavior. Better than your best behavior."

"I can be professional."

"Can you, Randy?"

"Relax, kid. Hey, look me in the eye. I give you my word, I'll be professional."

"Okay."

"I can go?"

"Yes."

"Ha! You doubted me, then I spend ten seconds acting like a stiff, and I had you fooled! And I'm not even trying to screw you! Wait until you see me turn on the charm."

Randy backed the truck into a space next to a seven-foot-tall chain-link fence on the far end of the studio lot from where they started. "Come on. We're here."

They dropped down out of the cab. Randy pointed to a spot directly behind the truck bed. "You stand there and be ready."

"For what?"

"Anything. That way you're covered no matter what happens." Randy hunched over and ran along the fence a few steps until he reached a gate, where he fiddled with the padlock.

Rutherford looked to the other side of the fence. He saw lumber, plywood, a small cement mixer, and various other bits of construction-related materials. Randy opened the gate, then closed it behind him without relocking it. He began to search the area, skulking around with his back severely hunched, occasionally lifting the edges of tarps to peek at whatever lay beneath.

"What are you doing?" Rutherford asked.

"Just looking for some stuff. Ah! Bingo." Randy folded back the corner of a tarp, revealing a stack of large, flat, yellow bags. Randy lifted one of the bags with great effort and carried it to the fence opposite Rutherford. He raised the bag up over his head and rested it on the top edge of the fence over Rutherford's head. "Catch."

Randy tipped the bag over the fence. Rutherford put his hands up but was unprepared for the weight. His arms buckled and only just managed to slow the bag's fall as it came down on his head, neck, and shoulders. He staggered backward and managed to get his arms curled under the bag, stopping its downward motion at his waist.

Randy said, "Put it in the truck, and don't break the bag. You don't want to get this stuff on you."

"What is this?"

"Quick-drying concrete mix." Randy grunted as he lifted a second bag.

"And your friend gave you permission to take it?"

Randy smiled as he lugged the second bag to the fence and lifted it above his head. "I didn't say he was a friend, and he said I could take it." Randy tipped the second bag over the fence. This time Rutherford expected the weight, and while he still nearly dropped it, he hid the struggle better than before.

Randy went back among the piles of supplies, looking for something else, smiling the whole time, obviously pleased with himself. "I got to talking with one of the set carpenters. He found out I was a cop."

"You're not a cop anymore."

"But I was. So he tells me that they have a security problem. They're shorthanded and have a bunch of sets going up, so the material lot is unguarded. He said all day, anyone could just wander in and take whatever they want. He asked me to help him figure out how to secure it. I told him I would, next week. In the meantime, I figure *anyone* includes me." Randy picked up a four-foot-by-eight-foot sheet of particleboard and nearly ran with it to the fence.

"But—the lock?"

"That model's notoriously easy to open. All you need's a ballpoint pen."

"How'd you know they used that lock?"

"I told him to. All part of my help."

Rutherford said, "You're stealing stuff."

Randy slid the sheet over the top of the fence toward Rutherford. "If you wanna look at it that way, then *we're* stealing stuff."

Rutherford leaned the plywood up against the gate and backed away from it as if it were radioactive. "I'm not helping you steal stuff, Randy."

"Not anymore. You're pretty much done now. And I don't like to think that I'm stealing, per se. I prefer to think I'm taking my consultancy fee in advance, in the form of materials."

Rutherford asked, "If that's the case, why not ask the guy if you can come take a few things?"

"Kid, there's no point in asking permission for something you already know you're gonna do, especially if you're pretty sure they're gonna refuse." Randy grabbed a couple of five- or six-foot scraps of two-by-four. "If they say yes, you've gained nothing. And if they say no, it just makes them madder when you do it anyway."

"But if you know they're against it, you probably shouldn't do it."

Randy slid back out through the gate, tucking the two scraps of lumber under his arm as he closed the door and the padlock behind him. "No, kid. You gotta learn this. Everybody's against everything. People fear progress and they resent doers. Any time someone starts to accomplish something, most people's impulse is to shut that shit down. Human nature. It's easier to prevent something than it is to do something, and just as satisfying. Think about it, kid. You've seen it yourself."

Rutherford started to disagree, then thought for a moment and went silent.

"Take it from me, kid. I've been around. I have all the answers, and they're all no." Randy chucked the wood into the bed, slid the plywood Rutherford had leaned against the fence in on top of it, and climbed back into the cab.

Rutherford opened his wallet, pulled out a fifty, and surreptitiously wedged it between the padlock and the hasp. That done, he got back in the truck.

Randy said, "Now to go meet lady butts-a-plenty. This is turning out to be the best day ever. We can stop on the way and I'll buy you a drink."

"I'm on duty."
"Coffee's a drink."
"Oh. True."
"And so is the bourbon I'll be having."

TWENTY-SIX

Most cars use a soft suspension, a plush interior, and noise insulation to make the passenger forget the outside world. Randy's truck employed the opposite approach. It made Rutherford forget the outside world by calling attention to itself with violent bouncing, shrill squeaking, and a constant engine roar punctuated by occasional backfires.

Randy glanced over at Rutherford and shouted, "What're you thinking about?"

Rutherford bellowed back, "How I'm going to explain why I let you come along."

"Why explain at all?"

"Because they're going to ask."

Randy scowled. "And you have to answer?"

"Yes."

"Just tell them you wanted to bring me along."

Rutherford shook his head. "They'll ask why, and I'm right back where I started."

"People boss you around a lot, don't they?"

Rutherford said, "Some people. My bosses."

"How many bosses have you got?" Randy asked.

"I've never counted."

"You know why people tell you what to do? It's because you do what they tell you. It encourages them. Follow my lead, kid. Stop obeying orders. Eventually they'll all give up."

"Aren't you worried about getting fired?"

"My current employers didn't hire me for my obedience."

"Why did they hire you?"

"For my discretion. Back when I was a cop, I learned a few things about a couple of the studio executives. When I left the force, I looked them up to have a little talk, reminisce about the old days, let them know how good my memory is. Now they keep me on the payroll, and as long as I don't talk, they don't care that I never do anything else."

"Extortion?"

"Extortion's what they call it in court when you get caught. What I'm doing is blackmail. Kid, two stiffs committed a white-collar crime. They need to be punished, and some good should come of it. If I turn them in, they'll either pay a fine, which the government will waste, or they'll pay a scumbag lawyer and go free. My way they pay more, they suffer for longer, and the money goes directly to the cop who caught them—me. Isn't that for the best?"

"That's self-serving bullshit."

"Which is the best kind of bullshit there is. Bullshit's everywhere, kid. I left the force because I was sick of dealing with the wrong kind."

"Too many orders from your bosses?"

"Bingo! The way I see it, kid, you can follow the leader or you can lead the followers."

"Why'd you decide to become a cop in the first place, Randy?"

"My old man. I used to watch him when I was a kid, and I decided when I grew up I wanted to arrest people, like him."

"He was a cop?"

"No. A criminal."

"Oh."

Randy went quiet for a second before continuing. "My mom died when I was young. Dad crawled into a bottle and lived there, like a genie in a lamp you didn't want to rub. Eh, you don't wanna hear this."

Rutherford did want to hear exactly this. He'd hit a nerve. The things that made Randy tick. These were the insights Rutherford would need to imitate him. That said, he knew that pushing too hard would shut Randy up, possibly forever. Instead, Rutherford decided to take a different tack. Keep him talking, just about something else.

"You got a girlfriend?" Rutherford asked.

"Nah, I just got out of a relationship."

"What was she like?"

"She was a dancer."

"What kind of dancer? Ballet? Modern?"

"Mostly pole. Sometimes lap."

"Oh."

"She dances at a club called Diamond Noir. She works under the name Ana L."

Rutherford let out a small groan.

Randy said, "She spells *Ana* with one *n*."

"I see."

"It spells—"

"I know what it spells. What's her real name?"

"How should I know? You're one of those *ask about the stripper's life* guys, aren't you? Man, I don't get it. You're hanging out with Superman. Why do you wanna hear about Clark Kent?"

The truck leaned alarmingly to the outside of the turn as Randy steered into the parking lot of a fitness center that looked small and no nonsense, in a high-end kind of way. The sort of place where people pay a substantial amount of money to come in and work out regularly and discreetly, as opposed to most health clubs, where members pay a discounted price to occasionally come to be seen using a stair-stepper placed right in front of the window, but more often just drive past and feel guilty for not going in.

Randy parked at a diagonal angle that allowed two corners of the truck to impinge on the spaces on either side. He turned the key to kill the engine, but the poorly tuned V-6 hesitated to go into the light, shuddering and sputtering for nearly ten seconds before giving up with a final, plaintive backfire.

Randy said, "Before we go in—"

Rutherford said, "I never said you were going in."

"And I never said I wanted your permission. But before we go in, I gotta take a whiz. Be back in a sec." Randy opened his door, slid down out of the cab, and walked toward a row of bushes at the edge of the parking spot. Rutherford asked, "Why don't you ask to use her bathroom when we go in?"

Randy said, "I wanna make a good first impression. And I notice you acknowledge that I'm going in."

Once Rutherford finished grumbling, angry with himself for getting outwitted by a man who was preparing to urinate into a bush, he initiated a conference call with Terri and Sloan.

Rutherford said, "I'm at Hogan's gym. I'm about to go in and question her."

Terri said, "Good. I called ahead. She's expecting you. It seems like she wants to cooperate."

Sloan said, "We'll listen in and make suggestions and help you if there are any surprises."

Rutherford said, "About that. I won't be going in alone. I brought Randy with me."

Sloan said, "Okay, I didn't expect the surprises to come from you."

Rutherford said, "Randy's a former cop. He's got experience. And don't worry. I can keep him under control."

Terri said, "You shouldn't have brought him, Rutherford."

"I wasn't going to, but he decided he was coming along, and I kinda couldn't stop him."

Sloan said, "Didn't you just say you could control him?"

Terri said, "I haven't met this guy, Rutherford. Where is he?"

Rutherford sighed and held his phone out the truck's window so they could see Randy, still urinating into the bush.

Terri said, "Well, he's not going to intimidate her with his class and refinement."

"And from the looks of it," Sloan added, "he doesn't drink enough water."

Rutherford said, "I know what you're thinking, but you want me to act like a certain kind of cop. This is a chance for me to see how that kind of cop acts."

"Keep a tight rein on him," Terri said. "We'll be listening."

Rutherford climbed down out of the cab as Randy began bounced up and down slightly and zipped up his fly.

Rutherford said, "Shall we?"

Randy started walking toward the door. "Hell, yeah. Just relax, kid, and watch the master work."

Rutherford jogged a couple steps to catch up. "No. Randy, I'm going to do the talking."

"Sure, kid, sure. Until it's time for me to go in for the kill."

"No, until it's time for us to leave. I'm a police officer, Randy. You aren't. Not anymore."

"But I was a cop for longer than you've been one, and I did a lot of stuff you never have."

"Stuff you got fired for."

"This is your chance to learn from a master interrogator. Rookies worry too much about what questions to ask, but the secret is to be a good listener."

Rutherford heard Sloan's voice in his earpiece say, "He's actually right about that."

Rutherford ignored her. "Randy, you're not listening to me."

Sloan said, "And you're right about that. This is quite a debate you've got going. You're very evenly matched."

Randy reached the door and started to press the intercom's buzzer, but Rutherford placed himself between Randy and the button.

"Randy, be quiet. Be quiet and listen to what I'm telling you."

"Okay, kid. What do you want to say?"

"Be quiet."

"You said that."

"Not just out here while I'm talking. Be quiet in there. For any of this to be admissible, I have to take the lead. You can make polite conversation and ask the occasional follow-up, but that's it. If that's a problem, you can get back in your truck and go back to the studio. Understand?"

Randy laughed. "Sure, kid. No problem. You're in charge."

Rutherford nodded, acknowledging that he heard Randy and believed him. In his ear, Terri said, "He's lying."

Sloan said, "Obviously."

Rutherford turned around and raised his hand to press the buzzer, but hesitated when Terri said, "It's your call, Rutherford, but you can still make him wait outside."

Rutherford whispered, "It's no problem. I can handle this."

Randy put a hand on Rutherford's shoulder. "It's all right, kid. You psych yourself up as much as you need. You'll do great."

Sloan said, "Laughing. Laughing. Laughing."

TWENTY-SEVEN

Rutherford pressed the buzzer. After a moment, he heard a woman's voice. "You have an appointment?"

"Hello. I'm Detective Rutherford. I'm here to meet with a personal trainer, Amanda Hogan."

"Yes, please come in."

A click told Rutherford the door had been unlocked.

Inside they found a beautiful, welcoming lobby where an even more beautiful, slightly less welcoming young woman directed them to the cardio area. They walked through the expected maze of welded-steel torture devices, all painted glossy black with contrasting gray vinyl pads that complemented the paint and rubberized floor covering. A driving beat accompanied by just enough other coordinated sounds to technically qualify as music played loud enough to be heard, but not so loud as to drown out the industrial pumping and clanging sounds of various machines, or the grunts of the people powering them. At the back of the room a middle-aged man dripped with sweat as he ran on a treadmill. Amanda Hogan kept pace on the treadmill next to him, looking cool and dry. She nodded at Rutherford, said something quietly to the man, stepped off her treadmill, and walked toward Rutherford and Randy.

To see Amanda Hogan in person was to get the impression of an anatomy chart of unrealistically idealized human musculature, rendered in three dimensions and animated. She wore yoga pants and a T-shirt with her logo printed on the chest, but on a person in her shape, almost anything she wore became revealing.

Randy let out a single, low moan that weakened and ended in a sobbing noise.

Sloan said, "Judging by that man's pitiful whimpering, I'd bet she's just as irritatingly hot in person as she is on billboards."

Terri said, "I hope she has a silly voice to make up for being beautiful."

Rutherford said, "Be professional," to all three of them.

Terri said, "We are. This is okay. We're both women, complimenting another woman."

Sloan added, "Behind her back, as is customary."

Randy just said, "No, I don't wanna."

Just before she reached Rutherford, Hogan looked back over her shoulder and shouted, "Keep running, Michael. I can hear it if you slow down."

Rutherford said, "Ms. Hogan, thank you for agreeing to meet with us. We won't take up much of your time. I'm Detective Rutherford. This is my associate, Randy McCormick."

She shook both of their hands. Randy chose not to let go. Instead he leaned in closer, motioned toward the man on the treadmill with his eyebrows and asked, "Is he someone famous?"

In a hushed tone, Hogan said, "It's rude to ask that."

Randy said, "Yeah, but is he?"

Rutherford asked, "If you have to ask if someone's famous, isn't that your answer?"

Hogan shushed Rutherford, quickly looked back to see if the man on the treadmill had heard, said, "Keep running, Michael," and gently pushed Rutherford and Randy into an empty office: a small room with a bare desk and no chair, with a large window looking out onto the gym floor. She pushed the door almost fully shut but stayed near so she could hear the sounds of the machines outside.

Rutherford asked, "What?"

"Detective, the only thing ruder in this town than asking if an actor is famous is suggesting that he isn't."

Rutherford said, "Sorry. I hope I didn't offend him. We'll get out of your hair pretty fast. We'd like to ask you a few questions."

Randy raised an eyebrow at Hogan and asked, "What's up?"

In the earpiece, Sloan said, "Or just one incredibly vague question."

Terri said, "But, in a sense, we are trying to figure out what's up."

Hogan blinked at Randy instead of answering. Rutherford stepped in. "We were already aware that you worked with the first victim, Emery Hindman. We only recently learned that you also worked with the second victim, Mac Menard."

"Yes," Hogan said. "But only for a little while, years ago. Nice man."

"And you're also working with Russell Byrne, whom we view as one of the two remaining potential targets."

"Yes. I am working with Russell."

Rutherford asked, "That strike you as odd, Ms. Hogan? All the trainers in this town, and all three of these guys have worked out with you?"

"I can see why you'd think so, but it's not that weird. Many of the male film and TV actors in town have had at least one session with me. Most drop out fast when they realize that I'm not going to date them, but I am going to work their asses off. That's why I charge for the first five sessions up front. The rest stick with me until they reach their goal or they can't take it anymore."

Rutherford smiled. "The billboards bring in the business?"

"That, and I have great word of mouth. If a client sticks with me, they get results and I get the credit. If they quit, they don't get results, and the story is that they failed because they didn't stick with me. Either way, I come out looking good."

Randy said, "I'll say."

Sloan said, "Of course he will."

Randy tilted his neck and pursed his lips appreciatively. "How do you get those yoga pants to fit like that?"

Hogan said, "They stretch."

Randy nodded. "I bet they do."

Rutherford said, "Of course they do. They're yoga pants. That's the one thing they're designed to do."

Randy rolled his eyes. "I wouldn't know. I don't do yoga."

Hogan's eyes bulged in mock surprise as she looked Randy over. "No! You're kidding! You got in that shape not doing yoga?"

"Yup," Randy said, sniffing loudly. "That's why I'm man shaped."

Rutherford said, "There's nothing wrong with a man doing yoga. Lots of *man . . . shaped* men do yoga. I've done yoga."

Randy shook his head. Hogan looked at Rutherford's body, raising one eyebrow.

Rutherford looked back at Hogan. "Not a lot of it, and not particularly well."

She smiled.

He turned to Randy, "And I didn't wear pants like hers when I did it."

Randy asked, "What did you wear?"

Sloan said, "That's the first good question he's asked."

Rutherford looked Randy in the eye, but he said, "Shut up," to both him and Sloan.

Hogan held up one finger, indicating that Rutherford should hold on for a second. She pulled the door further open and leaned out, looking to the back of the gym and shouted, "Keep running, Michael. I'm still listening."

Rutherford asked, "Have you ever worked with a woman named Justine Warner?"

Hogan let out a heavy breath through her nose that was almost a laugh. "No."

"You're sure?"

"I'd remember. Most of my clients are men."

Randy said, "Hey, I'll tell you something about me you don't know. I played football in high school."

She looked Randy up and down. "High school was a long time ago."

Randy said, "Which just makes it more impressive that I've kept myself in such good shape."

She pointed through the window at a bench press machine less than five feet away. "Show me."

Randy stood perfectly still for several seconds, the smarmy smile frozen on his face, before finally saying, "I don't have to prove anything to you."

"Then why'd you bring it up?" she asked.

Randy froze again.

Sloan said, "I hope she isn't our perpetrator. It'll be hard to become her best friend if she's in prison."

Terri said, "But still worth the effort, I think."

Rutherford asked, "You worked with Mac Menard. Why did a voice actor need a trainer?"

Hogan shook her head. "It was years ago. He was trying to get back into film work, the poor guy. He was up for the lead in one of those avenging-middle-aged-man movies."

"Which one?"

"*Blood Relation*. At the time it was going to be called *Release My Niece*, but they decided to change the title when Mac lost the part to Liam Neeson. They were afraid it would make the ads sound silly. 'Liam Neeson: *Release My Niece*.'"

Sloan said, "Now in wide release."

Terri added, "Hailed as a masterpiece. I'm really enjoying this."

Sloan said, "Yes. It's like *Mystery Science Theater 3000*, but instead of a terrible movie we're heckling Rutherford's life."

Ignoring the voices in his ear, Rutherford said, "One more thing, Ms. Hogan. You knew all three of them. Can you think of any reason someone would want Mr. Hindman, Mr. Menard, and Mr. Byrne dead?"

"No. Mac was a dear man. Emery was a bit dumb, but nice. Byrne's a little hung up on his mother, but that's no reason to kill someone."

Randy said, "Eh, in Byrne's case, it might be enough, but whatever. Now that all that's out of the way, are you busy tonight?"

She said, "No, and it's going to stay that way. I like my men to be at least in half as good a shape as I am."

Randy laughed. "Afraid I can't keep up with you, baby? There's an easy solution for that. I just won't move much. Gotta conserve my strength."

"Okay," Hogan said, opening the office door and ushering the men out. "We're done."

Randy said, "Not just yet. One last question. Why are you hiring people to kill your clients instead of doing it yourself?"

"All right, out. Both of you. Detective, I hope you catch whoever's doing this before anyone else gets hurt, but if you want to talk to me again it'll be with a lawyer present."

"If you're not guilty, why do you need a lawyer?" Randy asked.

"To sue you for sexual harassment."

Rutherford glared at Randy. "That's understandable, Ms. Hogan. Thank you for your time. We'll be on our way."

As Rutherford and Randy headed toward the exit, Randy shouted, "Yeah, I'm sure you have a lot of hard work to watch. Keep running, Michael!"

Between heavy breaths, Michael yelled, "Go to hell!"

Randy gave a thumbs-up and said, "Right on," as he went out the door.

Outside, Rutherford squinted into the sky as he pulled out his sunglasses. "That went badly."

"Yeah," Randy said. "And it was all your fault. You're a terrible wingman, kid."

"I wasn't there to be your wingman, Randy. I was there as a cop. I'm justice's wingman."

Sloan asked, "Did you say that kind of thing when you were in uniform? And if you did, how much crap did the other cops give you?"

Rutherford disregarded her and addressed Randy. "Does that 'I'll tell you something about me you don't know' gambit ever really work?"

Sloan and Terri both said, "No."

Randy said, "Yup. It gives you a chance to say something that will impress them and makes you seem mysterious and intriguing. It works every time."

Rutherford said, "It didn't work that time."

"That's just because it was a ruse, kid. If I was really putting the moves on her, she and I'd be back in the storage room right now, and you'd be covering for her, telling Michael to run. I distracted her with my charm to make her put her guard down."

"Her guard seemed pretty up to me."

"Yes," Randy said. "But a different guard. She was too busy denying her attraction to me to also lie convincingly."

"Do you think she did it?"

"No." They reached the truck, and Randy hoisted himself into the cab. "When I asked her why she was hiring killers she was genuinely offended."

"I agree," Rutherford said, climbing into the passenger seat.

Randy said, "Which means she answered the question truthfully, and proves my distraction worked. You're welcome." He turned the key in the ignition. Conversation in the truck stopped while they listened to the starter struggle to turn the engine over, only succeeding after five seconds and some muttered obscenities from Randy.

Rutherford shouted, more to Sloan and Terri listening in than to Randy, "But she's still a connection between three of the Watsons. We should still look into her life, her routine, the people around her."

"Yeah," Randy said, pulling the truck out onto the street. "You should find out who she's dating. Who she's sleeping with. Try to get pictures if you can."

TWENTY-EIGHT

The sniper walked a serpentine route to his sniper's nest, making sure not to retrace his steps from last time. Normally he wouldn't be caught dead anywhere near a place where he'd recently caused someone else to be caught dead, but he had failed in his previous attempt, and now he needed to come back and try again; to take the deadliest of mulligans.

His client had taken his failure badly. No surprise there. People who hire contract killers don't tend to be the forgiving type. In the end, the sniper was given a second chance. This was fortunate. The more typical reaction to a failed contract would be for the client to hire a new killer and give that killer two assignments: the one that was botched and the one who botched it. In his line of work, when you got fired it was usually with gunfire.

His plan remained the same, even though the situation had changed. The successful killing the day before altered the landscape and made his failure sting even more. It salved his ego that the most recent murder was carried out by a seasoned pro, the man the police code-named Mr. Gas. He had admired Gas's work and hoped one day he might team up with Gas on a job, or assassinate Gas after a protracted game of cat and mouse. Now Gas was in police custody, and the two of them would never get the opportunity to trade respectful compliments and/or gunfire.

Gas's successful kill and ignominious capture meant the police were on high alert. He saw noticeably more officers this time. Wardrobe, makeup, and the soundstages where *No Matter How Improbable* filmed—any building or trailer Russell Byrne set foot in throughout the day—had armed officers guarding every entrance and exit. Little did they know that he would strike from a building Russell Byrne never entered or exited.

He reached the admin building with its shining glass windows and metal awnings. His entry point today would be the same as before, the emergency stairwell exit door. Though he had failed to kill anybody, the getting-in and getting-out portions of his previous incursion had been a complete success. For a moment he regretted not permanently disabling the lock on his last visit, but he had never really considered it, and wouldn't on this visit either. To do so would be the act of a pessimist, and hired assassins are a surprisingly optimistic lot. Defeatists tend to avoid a career where failure means imprisonment or death.

Just like before, he crouched in front of the door, toolbox resting on the ground nearby, as he worked on the lock.

Unlike before, someone came out of the door, hitting him in the head and sending him falling back on his rear. He sat on the cement path, blinking and marveling at how easily the handles of his lock pick and torsion wrench could have stabbed one or both of his eyes out. He filed that information away in case he was ever hired to kill a burglar and make it look like an accident.

The unexpected door opener stood in the doorway and looked down at him: a tall, thin woman attempting to compensate for a bland tweed suit with an extravagantly colored blouse. "I'm so sorry!"

He clambered to his feet, palming the lock picks. "No problem."

"What were you doing?" she asked.

"Fixing the door."

She swung the door back and forth on its hinges. "It seems to work fine."

"Yes. Now." He stepped forward and held the door open for her, though she had already technically passed through it. She smiled and walked away. He hoisted the toolbox up off the ground and darted inside, closing the door behind him.

He felt like a salmon returning to his spawning grounds. Although instead of coming to create life, he intended to end it, and instead of swimming upstream, he was running upstairs.

He double-timed it up four stories and slipped out onto the roof without being spotted or heard by the office workers. Some in his line of work looked down on their kind. He felt an odd kinship with them. He was also a professional, diligently doing his job, earning his pay. And while he did not envy them their need to conform to societal norms and outdated ideas about right and wrong, he wouldn't have minded access to their health benefits.

He threaded his way through air handlers, ducts, and conduits, back to the exact same spot as before, along the roof's edge, looking down on the kill zone.

He knelt down, opened his toolbox, and pulled out the false top, revealing the hidden trays beneath. His heart still quickened at the sight of his custom-made sniper rifle, the parts all precision machined from the finest steel and then blackened to make them more resistant to corrosion and nestled in their own little foam cutouts. He sometimes suspected that he got less pleasure from killing for money than he did from the trappings of his profession: the specialized gear, the exquisite planning, the attention to detail. More than once he'd looked at Martha Stewart and seen a kindred spirit; someone who, with a bit of training, could have become a fine assassin herself instead of a mere client.

He looked at the washer that had tripped him up last time, then picked up the stock. He glanced at the washer again as he pressed the black steel spring into place, keeping it pressed down as he lifted the lower receiver and slid it home. He again looked at the all-important washer as he mounted the scope.

Breathing slowly, keeping his heart rate low, he pulled the gun barrel from its compartment, the screw-down bezel sliding freely along its length. He tucked the barrel under his left arm so that it would be easily accessible once the washer was in place. The stock and receiver assembly held firmly against his body, he gripped the washer tightly and pressed it into place on the circular indentation where the barrel would attach.

A sigh of relief escaped his lips as he looked down at the washer that had caused him trouble the last time, now exactly where it should be. He chuckled quietly as he grasped the hilt of the barrel and raised his arm. He heard the sound of metal sliding on metal, followed by the faint ringing of a small metal object vibrating while in free fall. After a quarter of a second, the ringing stopped with a clink and a faint rumble, like a coin rolling on pavement, which faded to silence.

Holding the barrel out in front of himself, he saw at a glance that the screw-down bezel was missing.

He whispered, "Oh, fudge!"

He spun around in place, looking down at the black roof beneath his feet, and saw no sign of the equally black bezel. He spun a second time, then a third in the opposite direction. He looked at his watch, then over the side of the building at the street-level door four stories below.

He didn't have time for this.

Moving on autopilot, his hands grabbed the magazine and locked it into place as he dropped to his knees, frantically looking at every square inch of rooftop in his line of sight. He then placed the partially assembled rifle on the ground and dropped lower to his hands and knees, pressing his cheek to the hot roof and closing one eye to look under the ductwork and sheet-metal HVAC machinery. He saw no sign of the bezel.

"Oh, fudge!"

In the distance, he heard talking. He sprung to his feet and peered over the roof's edge. Crew members were beginning to emerge from the soundstage door. He screwed the silencer onto the barrel while running around in irregular circles, looking over as large a portion of the roof's surface as he could. He snatched the receiver and stock from the ground and held it in one hand and the barrel and silencer in the other while continuing to run in circles and spin in place, looking for the missing bezel, muttering, "Oh, fudge! Oh, fudge!"

Below, a bearded man in a sweater came out of the door, followed by Russell Byrne and an older black man in a nylon windbreaker carrying a suitcase and some sort of metal detector. The window of opportunity had opened and would only remain open for a few seconds.

He gritted his teeth, held the stock to his shoulder with his right hand, used his left hand to press the barrel into its socket, and sighted through the scope. He could see Byrne's head lined up in the crosshairs, but he could also feel the barrel wobbling slightly in his grip. In his mind's eye, he saw the explosion that would likely cost him several fingers if the bullet tried to enter a barrel that was anything less than perfectly aligned. He pressed harder with his left hand, but that made his aim less stable and still didn't feel like a safe firing condition. He watched helplessly through the scope as Byrne entered the makeup trailer and his window of opportunity closed for another day.

Moaning, "Oh, fudge," he stared down at the stretch of road where numerous people who were not his target walked. He sagged and looked at the two halves of the rifle in his hands, momentarily at a loss. He bent down to place the barrel-silencer assembly on the ground while he dismantled the stock and receiver. As he leaned forward, he again heard the sound of metal sliding on metal, the slight ringing of a metallic object vibrating as it fell, and the clink of it hitting the ground. He saw the washer he had carefully placed in the barrel socket hit the roof on its edge and start to roll away. Moving quickly, he stomped down on it, trapping it before it disappeared, but it felt like a hollow victory.

TWENTY-NINE

Randy smiled as he wrestled the bucking beast of a pickup truck into Byrne's studio-assigned parking spot around the corner from the soundstage. "There. I got you back in time to watch that turd Byrne get his makeup scraped off and go with him to his performance art piece, which I've seen, and it isn't art, or much of a performance either. The word *piece* does fit, depending on what you mean by it."

As they climbed down out of the truck, Rutherford asked, "You don't like Byrne much, do you?"

"There are the keen instincts that make you a natural-born assistant detective."

"That's harsh." Rutherford took a few quick steps to catch up as Randy walked toward the soundstage.

"Don't get me wrong, kid. You've got skills. It's your instincts you've gotta work on. You've gotta learn to be more direct with suspects, and chicks for that matter."

"No. And how would you know? And anyway, the way you approach a suspect and the way you approach a woman you like are totally different."

"Not for me they aren't. With one you want a confession, with the other you want sex. Either way, you're trying to get something and they're trying to avoid giving it to you."

"I hope that's not true."

"I watched you with Hogan. She was both a suspect and a chick, so she was the perfect example. You were tentative."

"I wasn't trying to hit on her."

"Not in any way she would have noticed, anyway. There's a word for guys like you, guys that beat around the bush."

"Gentlemen?"

"Lonely. You waste so much time worrying about how girls feel, you never get around to actually feeling them. You have to tell a woman that you're interested."

"I know that."

"And you have to tell her that she's interested."

"Do you?"

"Yes. If you don't, she might not notice."

As they rounded the corner, Rutherford saw crew members milling around outside the soundstage and Max talking on his phone next to the makeup trailer instead of the soundstage door, both signs that production had wrapped for the day, uneventfully.

It took two full steps for Rutherford to notice that Randy was no longer beside him. He turned and saw that Randy had stopped walking alongside him. "What's wrong?"

Randy said, "Nothing. It looks like filming's done for the day, so I am too. I think before I head home I'm going to drive over to the carpentry department, talk to my buddy."

"And see if they've noticed any of the stuff you took is missing?"

"Bingo."

"Maybe you should walk over."

"It's all the way across the lot."

"If they haven't realized that stuff is missing already, they might when they see it in the bed of your truck."

Randy held up a finger. "That's a good point. That's a very good point. I think I'll walk it. Good catch, kid. We'll make a lead detective out of you yet." Randy pulled out his phone and began tapping out a message as he walked off around the corner.

"By having me help you get away with crimes?" Rutherford asked.

Randy looked back over his shoulder to say, "What better way to learn?"

Rutherford headed toward the makeup trailer. As he weaved his way through the various techs and stagehands carrying random set pieces and expensive-looking film-related gizmos to and fro, he briefly made eye contact with the showrunner, Kyndra Perrin, as she walked the opposite direction. She smiled and pointed at him. "I just wanted to tell you that you did some good work today, and I appreciate it."

Rutherford said, "You mean the part when I wasn't here, don't you?"

She didn't bother to look at him as she passed, saying, "Damn straight," then walked away, two assistants following.

Rutherford approached Max, who was standing near the door to the makeup trailer, talking into his phone. A uniformed officer guarded the trailer door and had obviously spent quite a while listening to Max's half of the conversation. The officer rolled his eyes, effectively communicating to Rutherford that it was not going well.

"Yes, Chaz," Max said, "I know you need to eat. I didn't know that you needed me to buy you food. And how did you manage to max out the card if all you bought was groceries?"

Rutherford stood beside the little folding steps outside the makeup trailer as he reached up to the doorknob and opened the door to stick his head in.

Professor Sherwood sat in a hairdresser's chair along the back wall, his constantly buzzing suitcase resting on the floor between his feet. Byrne and his costar, Wolfberg, sat in the makeup chairs farthest from the professor's case. Two makeup artists, one man and one woman, circled around them using various sponges, creams, and moistened towels to remove the thick layer of foundation necessary to make people look presentable in high def. Last time Rutherford was on hand for the makeup removal, the trailer had been filled with conversation. Today, everyone was quiet, listening intently to Professor Sherwood.

"Don't let the buzzing disturb you. It's only so loud because you can hear it through the air holes. I chose the size of the holes very specifically so that the bees could get enough air, but it would be rare for one to squeeze out."

"Rare?" one of the makeup artists asked. "How rare?"

"Very rare. Only a few get out every day. Say, did you know beeswax is used in many cosmetics?"

Rutherford closed the door, secure in the knowledge that nobody would attack Byrne, or make any false moves at all, as long as the professor was trying so hard to make everyone in earshot less fearful.

Max held up his phone and shook his head. "He got mad and hung up on me."

Rutherford squinted at Max. "*He's* mad at *you*?"

"Yes. You Americans have a phrase, you say *pet peeve*, I think?"

"Yeah."

"Well, Chaz's pet peeve is when I find his actions unacceptable. He hates that."

Rutherford said, "He didn't seem so crazy yesterday. I mean, he seemed crazy, but not this crazy."

"We were together yesterday," Max said. "My life is fine when he's either in the same room as me, or if he's completely absent. It's when we're in contact but physically apart that we fight."

"You can't confront him to his face," Rutherford said, nodding. "Too worried you'll upset him, so all the fights happen over the phone."

"No," Max said. "It's not that. It's just, when we're together we can't fight. We're too busy having sex."

The uniformed officer who couldn't help but overhear asked, "The sex is that good?"

"Very much so, yes, but the real issue is that there's so much of it."

"I know how that is," Rutherford said.

Max said, "No, you don't."

"No, I don't," Rutherford said. "But I imagine it's terrible."

"Again, no you don't. You think it sounds great. And it is, but too much of anything is bad for you. People need water, but can easily drown."

"I always hoped a guy with your, uh, let's say *maturity* wouldn't have to deal with this kind of drama, you know?"

Max shook his head. "Rutherford, older people are not immune to bad relationships. Quite the opposite. When ours go bad they're infinitely worse, because we have the experience to know the best ways to torture each other. But we shouldn't be wasting any more of our time on the job talking about Chaz. The sun is going down soon. It appears we may have gotten through another day without an attack. How was your interview with the trainer?"

"It was interesting," Rutherford said. "I don't think she did it. She didn't say anything that explicitly eliminated her from suspicion, though. She's got connections to both of our victims and Byrne, but she has nothing tying her to Justine Warner, the Watson from the talk show. Of course, that doesn't necessarily mean anything. Miss Warner hasn't been attacked—"

Rutherford stopped short, interrupted by his and Max's phones going off at the same moment. Rutherford looked at his phone and said, "Yet. I was going to say she hadn't been attacked *yet*."

THIRTY

Rutherford drove to the theater where *The Wee Smalls with Mia Paul* taped so that they could speed. Even so, with the typically heavy Los Angeles traffic, the relatively short trip took them a half hour, every second of which of which Max spent on the phone with Chaz.

They reached downtown Hollywood to find a crowd of people, plenty of police cars, and no parking spaces. Rutherford pulled the minivan up to the front of the theater and hit the TurkMO button. A voice from the dashboard said, "Thank you for using TurkMO. I'm Carl, your remote driver."

"Hello, Carl. Can you park the car for us? Traffic's pretty bad."

"No problem, sir." In the background, Rutherford heard a pounding noise. The driver continued, "The meter fees will be applied to your account."

Rutherford said, "That's fine."

The pounding sound continued, and a distant voice shouted, "Who are you talking to in there? You're playing that stupid driving game again!"

The driver said, "It's not a game, Dad. This is my job!"

"Yeah, the only job you have is the con job you think you're pulling on your old man!"

The driver came back to the microphone. "I'm very sorry about that, sir. You should go. This isn't going to stop any time soon. Just use the app to summon the van when you're ready to leave."

Professor Sherwood tapped Max on the shoulder. Max looked up, but continued talking into the phone. "No, I'm not being cheap, Chaz. That card had a three-thousand-dollar limit and now it's full. What did you buy? . . . It *is* my business, I paid for it . . . No, that doesn't mean you don't have to repay me. You definitely have to repay me."

Rutherford pointed to the theater. "We're here." He pulled his fake lollipop from the sandwich bag he'd taken to carrying it in and popped it into his mouth while he, the Professor, and Max watched as the minivan drove off with no passengers to hunt for a parking space. They made their way through the crowd to the theater entrance, Max continuing his phone conversation as Sherwood led him along.

They reached the front of the crowd, which appeared to be at least half made up of professional journalists holding cameras, the other half being ordinary citizens using their phones as cameras. The crowd ended at a line of police tape and two officers blocking the door. A quick flash of Rutherford's Seattle PD badge and an explanation that they were part of the consultant team here to help Frederick and Burski got them in. Albert met them in the lobby.

Max said, "Okay, Chaz. I have to go. I'll call back as soon as I can . . . I have to work . . . wait, what do you mean my other credit cards?"

Albert and Sherwood exchanged looks that said, *What's going on there?* and *Don't ask,* respectively.

Albert beckoned Rutherford, Sherwood, and Max to follow him through a door that led to a long, undecorated hallway.

"What happened?" Rutherford asked.

"We definitely have our attempted Watson murder for the day."

Professor Sherwood said, "I'm glad it was just an attempt."

Albert said, "Yeah, well, it wasn't a particularly good one."

Behind Rutherford, Max said, "In the pack with the passports and the handguns? Chaz, you know full well that's my burn bag!"

Albert said, "The show had just wrapped up taping for the day. Decent monologue, but the sketch after the first commercial fell kinda flat."

Max said, "And there was cash in there too. Thirty thousand in dollars, euros, and gold ingots. Don't think I've forgotten."

Rutherford said, "Why don't you hang out here until your call's done, Max? We'll yell if we need you."

Max nodded, looking equal parts grateful and sad. "So you're claiming you just happened across my burn bag when you were what, just innocently rummaging around in the secret hiding spot beneath the discolored floorboard, under the refrigerator?"

Rutherford and Albert walked on.

Albert said, "Mia Paul and Justine Warner were in the hall outside the dressing rooms. That's where we're going. They were saying goodbye to the guests when all of a sudden, some dude runs in wearing a yellow tracksuit with a black stripe down the side. You know, the Uma Thurman look."

Rutherford said, "Bruce Lee wore it first."

"Yeah, but Uma wore it best. Either way, it's a terrible thing to have on if you're trying to blend in. But he wasn't, since he just sprinted in, tossed a homemade throwing star at the victim, missed, whacked her over the head with a pair of ratty nunchucks instead, then tried to fight his way out."

"Seriously?" Rutherford asked.

"Seriously," Albert said. "She's at the hospital, getting stitches and a penlight shined in her eyes. The assailant's still here, though. The police have been waiting, hoping the crowd outside will dissipate, but that doesn't seem to be happening. Terri took a TurkMO here, beat you by a few minutes. Claire and her CartFulls team are going over the scene, not that we need forensic evidence."

The door at the end of the hallway led into a large open area where several hallways and rooms converged. Rutherford could easily picture the area bustling with activity before and during tapings. Right now, however, the room contained mostly cops and purple-clad CartFulls techs. The primary sound in the room was a muffled stream of high-speed syllables pouring out from one of the dressing rooms. Three police officers, each with various scrapes and bruises, blocked the door.

Rutherford asked, "What happened to you guys?"

They both looked at Rutherford, making sure he knew that they heard his question and did not intend to answer. Rutherford craned his neck to look past them and caught a glimpse of the assailant, sitting in a sweat-soaked yellow tracksuit, talking at an elevated volume and speed.

"Sun Tzu said if the head is armored, attack the tail," the assailant said. "If the tail is armored, attack the head. If both the head and tail are armored, attack the middle. He didn't say what to do if the whole thing is armored. Maybe attack something else, I guess."

The hallway outside the dressing rooms widened into a sort of lobby. Sloan and Terri stood, talking. Rutherford, Albert, and Sherwood joined them, then detectives Frederick and Burski walked over. After a round of greetings, Rutherford asked, "What have we got here?"

Detective Burski shrugged. "It's a talk show. They're all the same, really. The host pretends the guests are impressive, because they're the best guests they could book. The guests act like being on the show's a huge honor, because it's the best show they could get booked on. At home, people try to be satisfied with the show, because they can't think of anything better to watch. It's all an exercise in cooperative mediocrity. Everybody participates but nobody is satisfied. It's a fine metaphor for something, but fittingly, I can't be bothered to think of what."

Rutherford said, "I was asking about the case."

Burski smiled. "I know, but I wanted to talk about something interesting instead."

Frederick said, "There isn't much to talk about with the case. We need your help even less than usual on this one. Multiple witnesses, the victim survived and can identify the assailant, and we already have him in custody."

Rutherford asked, "Can he identify the person who hired him?"

Frederick said, "A man in a gray hooded sweatshirt. Hood drawn tight. Didn't see his face. Mostly the guy just goes on and on about kung fu, which he doesn't actually know, by the way. He thinks he does, but he just watched a bunch of old movies until he had the general idea."

Sloan said, "I call his fighting style Gist Kun Do."

None of her teammates acknowledged her joke.

Rutherford said, "The officers over there seem a little banged up. He can't be totally incompetent."

Frederick said, "No, he is. He just made up for his lack of technique with speed and manic energy."

Rutherford nodded. "Meth?"

"No, he's too big a poser for meth. He drank a bunch of energy drinks full of ephedra to psych himself up."

One of the uniformed officers approached. "Excuse me, Detectives, can I bother you for a second?"

Frederick and Burski followed the officer away. Rutherford turned to the rest of the team.

Sloan said, "I'm beginning to see your point, Albert. It would be good if I could talk directly to the detectives without one of you having to repeat what I've said."

Albert said, "Yes, but to be honest, I don't think they would have laughed at your *Gist Kun Do* joke either."

Rutherford said, "As for the case, I think this clears Amanda Hogan. She has no connection to Justine Warner, so that's a pretty strong suggestion she isn't behind this."

Sloan said, "It was the best lead we had, but it was always shaky."

Terri said, "Of course, now we have no suspects. Unless any of you have an idea."

Rutherford said, "I don't have any evidence to back it up or anything, but the showrunner for *No Matter How Improbable*—Kyndra Perrin—her attitude doesn't sit right with me. She's hostile to the point of being abusive. She really doesn't want us on her set."

Terri asked, "Professor, when you were on set, did you have your suitcase full of live bees with you?"

Sherwood said, "Of course."

Terri asked, "And Albert, didn't you spend your day on her set conducting robotics experiments on trash?"

Albert said, "They weren't experiments on trash. I was building a prototype . . . *out of* trash."

Terri said, "And Rutherford, your whole deal is designed to draw attention. I know, I helped design it."

Rutherford said, "Yeah, I see your point. She has reason to worry that we might be a disruption, but she's weirdly aggressive about it."

Terri said, "She's a woman who has made it to the position of director and showrunner. Maybe she's weirdly aggressive in general. Fighting her way up the ladder might have just made her an asshole."

Rutherford grimaced. "Can a woman be an asshole?"

Sloan said, "Laughing. I promise you, I can be as big an asshole as any man. I'd be happy to arrange a demonstration."

"No," Rutherford said. "That's not what I mean. Is it, I don't know, *proper* to call a woman an asshole?"

"I know what you mean," Sloan said. "You're thinking there are gender-appropriate insults to use on women. I'd like you to think about that for a moment. Gender-appropriate insults. Does that sound right to you? The words you're thinking of. Bitch. The c-word. Even 'witch.' Because they're only used to describe women, they sort of suggest that the only reason the person you're insulting is acting in the manner you wish to insult is because she is a woman. She isn't a specific, awful kind of person; she's a specific, awful kind of woman. Women are just as capable of being assholes as men. I've met some who are more capable. And we won't have true equality until everyone understands that women can be assholes, just like men."

Rutherford said, "I never thought about it that way, Sloan. I promise, next time we argue, I will call you an asshole."

Sloan said, "Don't you dare."

Detectives Frederick and Burski returned. This time, Dr. Claire Romero came with them. Frederick said, "We're going to try to get the perp out of here in a minute. If you want to question him, you'd better do it now. He'll be busy getting booked once we get him back to the station. He's been talking nonstop since he got here, but he hasn't said much useful."

Rutherford glanced furtively at Claire, then said, "I'll go talk to him." He started toward the door.

Terri said, "I don't know if it's worth the trouble, Rutherford. The guy's just babbling."

Rutherford said, "Then there's no harm in trying. What's the worst that can happen, he'll tell us more nothing?"

Rutherford turned away and approached the huddle of uniformed officers. As he got closer he began to make out parts of the would-be assassin's monologue.

"A true warrior must know their weapon as intimately as if it were a part of their own body. One can only gain that knowledge if one crafts the weapon themselves. I understand how my shuriken flies because I remember the paint can lid it used to be."

The contused and bloodied officers blocking the door stood aside. As Rutherford stepped into the dressing room, he noticed that the officers inside the room were wearing full riot gear, including helmets.

The assailant sat on the front edge of an easy chair, his hands cuffed behind him, leaning way forward with his weight spread evenly between his tailbone and the balls of his feet. He had no body fat and muscles like twisted rubber bands just on the verge of breaking. Sweat rolled down every inch of his exposed skin and soaked through his bright yellow tracksuit. His eyes almost glowed with energy. His words spilled out of a wide grin, a noticeable amount of saliva flying out with them.

Rutherford stood in the now open doorway and smiled down at the perpetrator.

The perpetrator smiled back, leaned forward to lift his rear from the chair, and slid his wrists under himself until his handcuffs hit the backs of his knees. He rolled back in the chair, pulled his legs tight into his chest, and stretched his arms so that the handcuffs passed under his feet, leaving his hands still bound but in front of his body instead of behind. The surrounding cops dove for the chair, but the assailant had already moved on. Two of them grabbed at empty air while the third managed to touch the man's shoulder, but he was so drenched in sweat that the officer couldn't get a firm grip.

The assassin darted forward, planted his back foot, and channeled all of his momentum into punching Rutherford in the chest with both of his cuffed fists while shouting, "Wha KAA!"

An explosive cloud of breath and spittle blew the sucker from Rutherford's mouth. It bounced off the suspect's face and fell to the floor. Rutherford fell backward out of the doorway, grabbing at his attacker more out of an instinct to stay upright than any attempt to counterattack, his hands sliding on the sweat squeezing out of the would-be killer's clothing and coating his skin. He finally got a solid grip on the chain of the perpetrator's handcuffs. As Rutherford fell onto his back, he pulled the other man down on top of him.

As the would-be-killer's chest pressed into Rutherford's face, a wave of stale sweat seeped out of the man's shirt and onto Rutherford's eyes, nostrils, and mouth. At first having another man's sweat sting his eyes troubled Rutherford, but soon the smell and taste of the perspiration led him to actively focus on the pain in his eyes as a welcome distraction. Unpleasant as the moisture was, it provided lubrication, sparing Rutherford a nasty rug burn as the man slid forward, his weight still resting on Rutherford's face. In the distance, Rutherford heard Terri's voice shout, "Albert! Albert!"

Albert said, "I'm filming with my phone."

Terri said, "Good."

Rutherford lay there for a moment as the prisoner wallowed on top of him, struggling to get to his feet. With his face pressed into the man's gut, Rutherford threw both arms around his midsection in a bear hug to prevent him from fleeing. The suspect finally got up and managed two waddling steps, dragging Rutherford between his legs. Rutherford hung on as best he could, but he fell away as the cops dove into a classic dogpile, an instant too late. Most of them landed on Rutherford in the split second after the assassin had run away, using Rutherford's shoulder and head as starting blocks. The assailant squirmed and slid free of those trying to stop him and barreled through the double doors into the hallway where Max was continuing his phone call.

"No, it wasn't thoughtless," Max said. "You clearly put thought into this, Chaz. Please hold."

As the assassin attempted to run past, Max dropped his phone into his sweater pocket and took a half step into the man's path, balled up his right fist, and brought it down at a steep angle. The blow connected with the escapee's gut right below the rib cage and pressed back and downward toward his tailbone, as if Max meant for his fist to emerge from the man's anus. The force of the punch brought the man to his knees; he slid down and then sprawled on the linoleum floor, moaning, "What? What the hell? No, I didn't?! Oh no!"

Max pivoted neatly, looked down at the man in handcuffs floundering around on the floor, then pulled his phone out of his pocket and pressed it back to his ear. "I'm back, Chaz."

The assassin rolled over and arched his back to keep his rear off the floor. "No! I don't understand! I don't do this! Not since I was a kid!"

Max stepped around him and walked down the hall in search of quiet and privacy. "Yes, I'm angry. Of course I'm angry. You knew I'd be angry and you did it anyway. That's what makes me angry."

The uniformed officers all rushed forward, surrounding the prisoner, but none of them were in any hurry to touch him. He just stayed on the floor, whimpering and muttering, "Not since I was six, and never both at once!"

Rutherford scrambled to his feet, his face dripping and the collar of his shirt damp with sweat that wasn't his. He mumbled a half-hearted thanks as one of the officers handed him his sucker.

Detective Frederick asked, "What the hell just happened?"

Rutherford, sensing an opportunity to regain some semblance of cool, arched an eyebrow, and said, "The one-two punch." To heighten the effect, he nonchalantly popped his sucker into his mouth. For several seconds he stood silently grimacing as he regretted that decision, then he spat out what he hoped were carpet fibers. He glanced at the rest of the team. They all looked horrified.

Claire said, "I need to go," and walked away quickly, looking as if she might be sick.

THIRTY-ONE

The next day, Rutherford and Terri sat on folding chairs in a dark corner of the soundstage, ignored by the cast and crew, but watching with great intensity so that nothing would escape their notice.

Terri said, "Great googly moogly, this is boring!"

Rutherford said, "I've noticed. Take heart. We're almost done. There's a little under fifteen minutes to go before Byrne's hard out."

Terri rolled her eyes. "Thank heaven."

"Then we watch him get his makeup removed and it's off to the gallery to witness his one-man performance art piece."

Terri sighed, "And suddenly fifteen minutes doesn't seem like long enough."

The crew swarmed around, making tiny adjustments to the set, the lights, and the actors, trying to correct one minor problem that Kyndra Perrin had with the previous take, and seemingly millions of other problems they hoped to fix before she noticed them.

Across the stage, along the far wall, Albert sat at a folding table staring at his computer screen. Rutherford pulled out his phone and tapped on Albert's icon.

"Hey Albert. How goes wad patrol?"

"Same as it has been," Albert said. "Just running laps around the outside of the soundstage. Haven't seen anything yet. I have discovered a design flaw, though. If I come across a conscientious employee, they'll pick the wad up and throw it away. Then I have to go dig it out of the garbage."

"Yeah, that is an issue. I just wanted to let you know, Byrne's quitting time is coming up, so you might want to call the wad home."

"Will do."

Rutherford terminated the call.

Kyndra Perrin shouted, "Okay, let's give it another try."

The crew scattered like cockroaches when the kitchen light comes on, leaving the actors alone on the set. Perrin watched her underlings scurry in every direction with an air of satisfaction, or at least less dissatisfaction. Her gaze drifted across Terri.

Terri said, "If we're in the way we can move."

Perrin said, "Thanks. You're not in the way."

Terri smiled.

Perrin looked at Rutherford and said, "You are."

Rutherford said, "I'm standing right next to her."

Perrin rolled her eyes. "Yeah, well, if you were standing where she is, you wouldn't be in the way."

As Perrin turned away to focus on her work, Rutherford muttered. "I don't get it. She likes you, but she hated me on sight."

Terri said, "Maybe not. Maybe she's trying to flirt with you."

"By constantly picking at me? Women don't really do that to flirt, do they?"

"Not that you've noticed, clearly."

Rutherford looked at Perrin for several seconds, then said, "Well, anyway, I couldn't date a suspect."

Terri said, "She isn't a suspect."

"We don't know a motive, but her behavior has been suspicious."

"I just gave you one possible explanation, and I'm not even a detective."

"I don't get you sometimes, Terri. You put the kibosh on me and Claire, but this you encourage?"

"I'm not encouraging anything, or discouraging anything, just pointing out a possibility. And I didn't put any kibosh on Claire. She came with a kibosh pre-installed."

Up on the set, Byrne, Wolfberg, and a gorgeous young actress in a lab coat and glasses stood on the same water tank set they'd filmed on the day before. Byrne wore a full wet suit and held a speargun loaded with a silver-tipped spear. Wolfberg wore the same suit he'd been wearing in every other scene.

Byrne reached around behind himself, essentially twisting his own arm behind his back to pull down the zipper on his wet suit. "Good lord, Holmes, I was lucky to get out of that tank with my life!"

"Yes, but your salvation might be the rest of the world's damnation. To save your life, Dr. Chandler let the shark out into the tidal pool."

Byrne peeled off the top of the wet suit, allowing it to fall around his waist, revealing his surprisingly large shoulders and chest, and a perfectly defined six-pack, all glistening in the studio lights.

The actress said, "It escaped. The gates to the open ocean were closed, but I didn't know that the were-shark could jump higher and farther than a regular shark."

Wolfberg said, "Nobody blames you. The fact remains, the aquatic lycanthropy will spread. If we don't find the were-shark and kill it before the next full moon, we'll have multiple were-sharks on our hands. Or, at the very least, badly maimed were–sea lions."

Perrin said, "Cut." As usual, the set suddenly burst with activity.

Randy, who had been standing on the opposite side of the stage, made a beeline for the set to offer the young actress guest starring in the episode his suggestions, only some of which, Rutherford suspected, had to do with her performance as an actor, since she was not playing a police officer.

Randy had said hello when Rutherford arrived that morning, but he carefully kept his distance from the rest of the team. Only when Rutherford was off by himself had Randy come over and shown an interest in the investigation.

Rutherford said, "The guest star is drawing Randy away from backing us up."

Terri said, "I wouldn't trust him to back up a thumb drive."

Rutherford said, "Sure, we wouldn't hire him if he applied for a job, but he has law enforcement experience and he's here already. We might as well use him."

"Rutherford, you crack me up. You want everybody to like you, even people you don't like. Either way, I don't really think the ingenue over there is making him keep his distance. I am. Guys like him tend to stay away from strong, assertive women."

"Why is that?"

"Because we tell them to."

Perrin said, "We're about to go. Make sure Russell's lubed and zipped up."

A tech with a squeeze bottle squirted a large dollop of clear gel into his hands and smeared it on Russell Byrne's arms and shoulders, then helped Byrne pull the top of the wet suit back on over his torso, and went around back to zip it up.

Byrne said, "Is there something we can do about this zipper? I look like an idiot reaching around back there to unzip it."

Perrin said, "The whole point of this is to make Watson look strong and masculine. If you start the scene by turning your back to Holmes and saying 'unzip me,' it'll ruin the effect. Everyone, we're going to tweak the lights, try the scene just one or two more times, then we'll call it, since Russell has his hard out."

Rutherford said, "That means Byrne'll be on the move. I'll pop outside real fast."

"What happens if someone makes a move on Byrne while you're out?" Terri asked.

Rutherford made eye contact with Randy across the room as Randy talked to the attractive young guest star. Rutherford pointed to himself and the door. He pointed at Randy then at his own eyes and the set.

Randy nodded and gave a thumbs-up.

"You and Albert are here, and you're not the only ones paying attention. There are cops around, and Randy is on it."

Terri said, "If by *it* you mean the sex offender registry."

"I'll be outside for like a minute. It just makes sense to make sure everyone's ready."

Rutherford had taken his second step toward the door when he heard Kyndra Perrin, speaking up to be heard from a distance, ask, "Leaving, Detective? Please say yes."

Rutherford said, "Yeah, I'm going outside to get things ready. You're probably rid of me for the day."

Perrin said, "You ever heard the old saying, 'I hate to see you go, but I love to watch you leave?'"

Rutherford said, "Yeah?"

Perrin said, "Well, I'm happy to see you go."

Rutherford furrowed his brow, trying to figure out what that meant as he stepped out into the sunlight.

THIRTY-TWO

Multiple police officers stood near the door, and all the other entrances and exits to the sound stage and the makeup trailer. Max sat under a small tree across the street, talking on his phone.

Sherwood sat a dozen yards or so farther down the strip of lawn in the shade of the office building across the way, wearing his portable mesh hood and gloves, his vintage Samsonite suitcase open on the grass as he tended to the small hive of bees he kept inside. The police and the studio crew all kept their distance. Office workers inside watched him through the window.

Back on Rutherford's side of the street, Sloan leaned against the makeup trailer, discussing the case with Detectives Frederick and Burski, speaking to them through a battery-powered Bluetooth speaker the team had hastily purchased at a CartFulls on the way to the set that morning. Albert had suggested several high-end models with other useful functions or integrated light shows, but she insisted on a cheap one from the clearance section, as it was a life-sized human skull with red glowing eyes and a jaw that opened and closed in time with her synthesized voice.

As Sloan and the cops all seemed on guard, Rutherford walked across the street to get Max ready for action.

Max took no notice of him.

"You don't have to keep saying it was an accident," Max said. "It's a fire in my house. I don't have a fireplace, so I assume it was an accident. It was, wasn't it?"

Rutherford looked up at the tree and the office building with its rows of windows and metal louvers that probably looked very modern in the late nineties before the sun faded them and architectural styles changed.

Max held up a finger, putting Rutherford off for one moment while he tried to wrap up his call.

"Of course, I care if you were hurt," Max said. "Chaz, the first thing I asked was if anyone was hurt. You're included in anyone."

Rutherford asked, "Is he hurt?"

Max mouthed the word *no*. "Chaz, I told you not to smoke in my house . . . Yes, I know you always smoke after sex. I guess I didn't tell you not to have sex in my house. So I suppose my mattress is ruined."

Rutherford said, "Byrne should be coming out any minute. Be ready."

Max nodded, "My dining room table? I should ask how a cigarette could set an oak table on fire, but I guess that's academic. Besides, if I'd ever found out you had sex with someone else on my table I'd have to get rid of it anyway."

As he walked away, he heard Max say, "Why? Because I eat off of it! The table! Don't get cute. I'm not in the mood."

Rutherford got as close to Sherwood as he dared without protective gear. The professor sat, legs folded, his windbreaker zipped up and his protective hood and gloves on despite the warm LA afternoon. A cloud of bees surrounded him and crawled over his open suitcase. Inside the case, Rutherford could make out the plywood support structure of the hive, the mechanical forms of the case's ventilation system, and the currently dormant queen-carrying quadcopter.

Rutherford cleared his throat. "Professor, Byrne should be coming out any minute."

"I'll start gathering the swarm. Thank you." Sherwood lifted a rectangular form the size of a shoebox; bits of the underlying plywood and metal mesh of which it was constructed were exposed beneath the writhing, buzzing coating of live bees.

"How are your friends?"

"Good, thanks for asking."

Rutherford said, "I'm sorry they wouldn't let you in the stage today. I told them the bees wouldn't get out unless you wanted them to."

Sherwood said, "Oh, it's not that. It's the buzzing. Their microphones pick it up. Apparently, the sound crew spent all day yesterday trying to track it down. It sounded just like interference through an exposed wire. They thought they had it fixed until I came back in this morning."

"Oh. That's unfortunate."

"Yes, but it can't be helped. I don't want to prevent them from doing their work. I prefer the fresh air anyway. It gives them a chance to stretch their legs . . . wings." Sherwood turned the wood-and-mesh box over so that a large hole cut into one of the wooden sides pointed straight down at the open suitcase. He shook the box once, sharply. A black mass of bees fell out of the box in one large clump, landing in the suitcase with much louder buzzing and a sound like dry leaves rustling. He ran a gloved hand along the box's flat sides, wiping away big masses of bees that also fell into the case.

Rutherford asked, "Doesn't that make them mad?"

"Probably," Sherwood said. "But I'm wearing the proper protective gear."

Rutherford was not wearing the proper protective gear, and he chose to go back across the street to where Sloan, Frederick, and Burski were talking. As he approached, he heard Sloan's voice coming from the plastic skull, the clacking of its mechanical jaw clearly audible.

"Why would someone hate Watsons?" she asked. "Is it the character? I mean, what is Watson? He's a doctor. He's a writer. He's a sidekick; a hanger on. He and Sherlock are seen as a team, so Watson gets half of the credit, but he does less than half of the work. Who would be mad at someone like that?"

Detective Burski asked, "Have we questioned Paul Simon?"

The skull said, "Laughing."

Rutherford said, "How are things over here?"

Detective Frederick said, "Quiet."

Rutherford said, "I can see that. And nobody's made another attempt on Justine Warner?"

Detective Burski said, "No, but I don't see how they could. She has an army of police guarding the entrances to the entire hospital, her wing, and her room. She has a team of doctors and nurses monitoring her vitals and waiting to treat her for the slightest ailment. And last I heard, two high-ranking claims adjusters from her producer's insurance were there, watching like hawks to make sure their company's liability doesn't increase by even a single cent. She is safer now than she has ever been in her life, possibly the safest person in the city, specifically because someone wants to kill her."

Rutherford asked, "Speaking of that, have you three come up with any new ideas about the case?"

"Just that I hate it, but that's not new," Sloan said, turning the skull so that its glowing red eyes appeared to be staring at Rutherford.

Rutherford asked, "Do you have to point the skull at me when you talk?"

"No," Sloan said, the plastic jawbone clacking with each syllable. "I don't have to point the skull at you. I choose to point the skull at you. I have to do something to cheer myself up, because, as I said, I hate the entire situation. I hate what we've been reduced to. I want to prevent crime, not ambush it after the fact. We're all standing around hoping that someone tries to kill Byrne. If they succeed, then get away, then this is all for nothing.

If they try, fail, and get away, same deal. If they don't try, we have nothing to go on. In those last two scenarios, we have to come back tomorrow and go through all this again. And even if they do try and we catch them, they aren't who we really want, just a hired stooge. Our hope is that they'll lead us to their client, which none of the other stooges have done. This is a horrible, ugly piece of police work with a whole lot of ways to fail and only one slim chance that we might succeed."

"And," Rutherford said, "Byrne's the last Watson they haven't tried to kill, unless there's a high school play we don't know about. So, if we don't get some traction this time, we probably won't get another chance."

"Yeah," Sloan said. "The murder spree ending would be bad news for us. I hate this case."

"Well, I came out to tell you Byrne will be done soon."

"How soon?"

The door to the soundstage opened.

Rutherford said, "That might be him."

Frederick sneered and shook his head. "Thanks for the timely warning."

Only two people came out of the door. The attractive young guest star walking from the set to makeup, and Randy following in her wake.

Randy said. "You did pretty good. I've seen every guest they've ever had on the show and you can tell when someone's really about to make it big. If you want to talk about what you can do to get over the top, I'm free for—"

As they passed, Rutherford said, "Hey, Randy, got a minute?"

Randy said, "No, I'm talking serious business with the young lady."

As she climbed the steps into the makeup trailer, she said, "No, that's all right. Talk to your friends."

Randy said, "No, you're more important." But the trailer door slammed shut like a period on the sentence, so he turned to glower at Rutherford.

"Why you gotta cock block me like that?"

"Why are you out here?"

Randy pointed at the now closed door. "Have you seen her butt?"

Rutherford said, "Yes."

Despite her helmet, Rutherford became aware of Sloan looking at him, both with her eyes and the skull's red LEDs.

Rutherford said, "I mean, no."

Randy arched an eyebrow.

"Yes," Rutherford said slowly, "I have seen it, in that I am a detective, and nothing escapes my notice, but . . . I mean, however, I did not find it germane to the case we're working on, or the task of protecting Russell Byrne. Speaking of which, Randy, you said you'd stay in there and keep an eye on him."

"I never said that."

"You nodded!"

"Oh, you mean when you made all those hand signals? Is that what you meant? I thought you were telling me to check out her rack. I did, by the way. It's great too."

Rutherford tried not to lose his temper.

Randy smiled. "Relax, kid. Everything's cool. Everyone on that set is either with the show or your team. If someone's gonna take a shot at Byrne today, they aren't going to do it in there."

Rutherford said, "Here's hoping you're right. Hey, how'd it go with the guy from the carpentry department yesterday?"

"Eh, I might as well have driven over. He wasn't there."

"Oh, so you walked across the lot for nothing."

Randy smiled. "Not entirely for nothing. I found fifty bucks! Some dummy just tucked it into the padlock!"

THIRTY-THREE

The sniper held true to his rule of avoiding taking the same route twice by walking straight to the admin building. Once there, he knelt off to the side of the stairwell door and picked the lock at arm's length. It took longer in that awkward position, and at one point the air pressure inside the building made the door move, causing him to flinch and drop his picks.

Once the door was open, he tore off a length of duct tape and slapped it over the edge of the door, holding the bolt in so the door couldn't lock behind him. The precaution took only five seconds, but the self-loathing he felt after doing it lasted the whole walk up the four floors of stairs.

He skulked across the roof, looking in every nook and cranny for the black steel bezel he'd left behind last time. Now that he didn't need the piece, he hoped it would be easily found, but the beautifully knurled and threaded black steel ring still eluded him.

He reached his sniper's nest at the corner of the roof, dropped the toolbox, and sat down with his legs crossed.

He practically tossed the tray of decoy tools aside, sick of the sight of them, and carefully lifted out the foam inserts carrying the sinister black rifle parts. His pleasure in their appearance was more than a little spoiled by the shiny, purple, anodized-aluminum replacement bezel, the only compatible one his gunsmith could come up with on such short notice.

He rose to one knee and looked down over the short wall at the edge of the roof. Below, he saw the makeup trailer and the soundstage door, flanked by uniformed police officers. Other people milled around: two cops in suits, some dude in a leather jacket, and a woman in a black pant suit and a motorcycle helmet. As he watched, a woman in a white lab coat and a man in a cheap nylon jacket came out of the soundstage. None of them mattered. He only cared about one person: his target. Another person's well-being had never mattered so much to him in his life. For the good of his career, his self-esteem, and his faith that there was any justice in the universe, Russell Byrne had to die.

Sitting back down on the roof, he lifted the rifle barrel and the stock. He tried hard not to look at the shining purple bezel as he tucked the barrel under his left arm, but he made sure the offending bit of hardware was above his armpit this time, not below it. He held the rifle stock in his left hand, then reached over with his free right hand to pick up the lower receiver.

He couldn't wait to take the shot. That single split second, a simple squeeze of his right index finger, meant more to him than any Christmas or birthday had when he was a child. It wasn't just his wish for this job to finally be over and behind him, though that was part of it. He longed to complete the plan as he originally envisioned it: a single shot from a silenced rifle from an unexpected angle at an inconvenient time. From the victim's point of view, there would be no warning, fear, or pain.

His was a strange business. The greatest honor was to get no credit for your work. The greatest assassin in history was the one who killed Jimmy Hoffa. Everyone knows Hoffa was murdered, but nobody knows how, by whom, or where he ended up. The worst assassin was Lee Harvey Oswald, who despite killing his target and pulling off an amazing shot, was so inept that most people know his name but don't believe he did, or was even capable of doing the job.

There was no greater satisfaction than to glide in and out, invisible as a whisper, silent as a shadow, leaving nothing but confusion and a corpse in your wake. When he left, nobody would know where he went, just as, right now, nobody knew where he was.

He thought about these things as he compressed the spring to slide the rifle's receiver into place. The thoughts all disappeared from his mind in an instant when he felt his finger slip from the spring, and just like all other springs used in the assembly of complex machines have done since the dawn of time, it vanished with a quiet *sproing*, flying off into the air too quickly for him to see where it went.

He cringed, said, "Oh, fudge," and waited, listening for the sound of an impact.

He had a vague sense that the spring might have shot straight up into the air. If he was very lucky, it would come down and hit him on the top of his head, meaning he would know exactly where it was. It would also count as fortunate if the spring landed anywhere on the roof. If he never heard anything he'd have to assume it had gone over the side, leaving him with a non-functioning rifle and another failed attempt. He couldn't imagine anything worse, until he heard the loud ping of the spring hitting the steel-louvered awning mounted above the top floor's windows, five feet below him.

"Oh, fudge."

He looked down, over the edge of the roof, hoping to see the spring lying on the awning where he might be able to reach it. He didn't see the spring, but he heard it as it hit a different louver, then another, then a brief silence as it fell to the next layer of awnings followed by another musical series of pinging noises as it worked its way to the ground, visiting at least three louvers on each layer of awnings on its way.

He stood at the edge of the roof, looking down in utter disbelief. The thought occurred that he might be able to go retrieve the spring in time, but then he looked across the street. Everyone there—the suit cops, the leather and nylon jacket guys, even the lady motorcyclist—they were all looking at the rough area where he figured the spring had landed.

The light reflecting off the woman's helmet seemed to twinkle and flash with a purplish hue. All their heads tilted upward, following the path the spring had taken until they all stared directly at him. He looked down at himself and saw that he had the easily identifiable stock and barrel of a sniper rifle in his hands, and the sunlight was reflecting off facets of the shiny purple replacement barrel bezel.

THIRTY-FOUR

Between the white, cloudy background and the bright point of purple light, it took a second for Rutherford's eyes to adjust well enough to see what was on the roof of the admin building, and another for him to believe what he was looking at when they did. There, clear as day, was a man in workman's coveralls holding a partially assembled sniper rifle. At almost the same moment, it clearly dawned on the man that he was being seen, judging from the way he shouted "Oh, fudge," and ducked out of sight.

At almost the exact instant that the figure with the disassembled rifle dropped from view, the door into the soundstage opened and Byrne stepped out into the open.

Detective Frederick shouted, "Sniper! On the roof!"

Rutherford spun around to see Byrne, standing in the doorway looking stunned and confused. Behind him Wolfberg stopped short to keep from running into Byrne's back, then was violently shoved to the side. Kyndra Perrin grasped Byrne's shoulders and jerked him back into the soundstage. She pushed Byrne to the ground, shouting, "Get down, you idiot!"

The people inside, Terri and Albert among them, scattered as Byrne fell flat on his back. Perrin threw herself on top of him, twisted around, and shrieked, "Rutherford, go get the guy! Wolfberg, close the damn door!"

Detective Frederick shouted into his radio, "Suspect on the roof of the building next door. Repeat, sniper on the roof."

Sloan thrust her plastic skull high for all to see and said, "Rutherford, Max, go get him."

Rutherford was already three steps into his sprint before her speech synthesizer had finished the sentence. He heard Detective Frederick following behind, calling all the officers on his detail. He also heard Max, receding into the distance, talking into his phone. "I must go. It's important."

The tone that denoted a conference call played in Rutherford's earpiece. The party line went live, catching Albert midword.

"—ploying the drones."

Terri said, "Good. Send them to the roof."

"And recalling the wad."

"Fine. Whatever."

Professor Sherwood said, "I'm deploying Her Majesty!"

Terri said, "Fine. Send her up to the roof. It's as isolated a test as we're likely to get."

Rutherford ran toward the corner of the building. Just behind him he heard Detective Frederick yelling into the radio as he matched Rutherford's pace. "Keep Byrne inside. Two uniforms each on all the building's exits. Everyone else at the main entrance with me. Suspect's trapped. Can't get out past us. Then we search floor by floor."

In the distance, Rutherford heard the harmonized whine of multiple small electric motors as Albert's drones and Her Majesty rose to the building's roof.

As he rounded the corner of the building, Rutherford saw an unmarked door, most likely an emergency exit, which he knew from his training was often at the bottom of a stairwell. He skidded to a stop on the gravel-strewn asphalt. Detective

Frederick ran past him, glancing back as he went, but not slowing down. It surprised Rutherford to see Randy run up behind him.

"What?! Why are you stopping here, kid?"

Rutherford said, "A door!"

"Good catch. I'll guard it, you go."

"Maybe I can get in here. Might be stairs to the roof."

"No, it'll be locked. You gotta—"

Rutherford tried the door, which opened easily. "Someone put tape over the lock. Might have been the sniper."

"Then he'll probably come out this way," Randy said, speaking up to be heard over the approaching drones. "I'll wait. You go get more cops."

"No. You wait here. I'm going in."

Albert said, "I can see the roof from three angles. He isn't up here anymore."

Terri said, "So the sniper's in the building."

Rutherford said, "I'm definitely going in."

Randy standing there with him, and Terri and Sloan in his earpiece, all said "No."

"Bad idea," Terri said. "That's a hired murderer. He's trapped in the building with nowhere to go. The wise move is to wait for him to try to exit and catch him then."

Randy also continued talking, but Rutherford didn't catch what he said, as he was focusing on Terri's voice. He pointed to his earpiece with one hand and flapped his other open and closed to simulate a mouth. Randy stopped talking after a few irritated curse words.

Rutherford said, "He knows he's trapped in a building full of civilians. He could take hostages. He could try to shoot his way out. He could kill one of them and assume their identity. Someone needs to go in after him. I'm a trained cop with a huge gun."

Sloan said, "He's got a point."

Rutherford said, "Believe me, I don't want to go in, Terri, but Capp would want me to."

Terri said, "Be careful. At least take Max."

"He's not here. No time to wait."

"Albert, where's Max?"

"His phone shows as busy. I'll patch in manually."

After a click and some static, they heard Chaz's voice: "—always something more important than me."

Terri shouted, "Yes! There is! Max, we need you!"

Max started to answer, but Chaz talked over the top of him. "Have they been listening this whole time? That's just—"

Albert disconnected them.

Rutherford entered the building and stepped to the center of the stairwell, looking up the rectangular shaft. Three-quarters of the way up, Rutherford saw a man's head peek over the handrail and look down. The man saw Rutherford and said, "Oh, fudge!" His head disappeared as he retreated to the outside of the stairwell and out of sight. A half second later Rutherford heard a door open and close.

Rutherford said, "I just saw him. He's on the third floor, I think."

"I'll bring the drones down," Albert said. "Maybe I can find him through the windows. Rutherford, if I find him I'll direct you to him, and film him attacking you when you get there."

Rutherford said, "Good idea," as he sprinted up the stairs. Only when he reached the top of the first flight and rounded the corner to attack the second did he notice Randy following.

"What are you doing?" he asked, still running up the stairs.

"Figured you'd need backup," Randy panted.

"Thanks."

"You're welcome. Now slow down!"

Rutherford rounded the corner past the second-floor door and began his two-steps-at-a-time ascent to the third. He stopped by the door, pulled out his gun, checked to make sure that the pistol and the two shotgun barrels were all fully loaded, re-holstered the weapon, shifted his fake sucker from one side of his mouth to the other, then watched as Randy staggered up to the stairs to his side.

Rutherford prepared to pull the door open. "Ready?"

Randy barked out a series of deep, wracking coughs, but waved for Rutherford to go ahead.

The third floor consisted mostly of a large open space divided by a great many cubicles. From the door Rutherford could see a wall; a long, straight walkway; the low plane formed by the tops of the cubicles; and a wall of windows. Albert's drones hovered outside. With each passing moment, more of the workers in the cubicles stood up to look out the windows at the drones. Behind them, capitalizing on the distraction, a man in workman's coveralls carrying a large toolbox headed toward the marked exit at the far end of the floor. He was three-quarters of the way there, a good fifty feet away from Rutherford, and walking so casually as to accidentally call attention to himself.

Rutherford shouted, "Hey!"

Everyone turned to look at him, except the workman, who flinched, but pretended not to hear.

Rutherford drew his oversized three-barreled pistol. "You, with the toolbox, freeze! Police!"

The people in the cubicles saw Rutherford's gun and let out a variety of alarmed sounds as they ducked back below their cubicle walls. The guy with the toolbox turned around slowly, looked at Rutherford long enough to decide if he'd shoot an unarmed man, tucked the toolbox under his arm, and crouch-ran to the side, disappearing into the cubicle maze.

Rutherford ran forward, pointing his pistol at the ceiling. He had only covered half of the distance to where the workman had stood when he heard breaking glass. An entire panel of the windows shattered, causing several of the employees to yelp in surprise. A breeze and the harmonized whine of Albert's drones filled the office. Rutherford reached the point where the workman had been and turned down the same access path through the cubicles the workman had ducked down. He saw the workman, still carrying his toolbox, jump out of the window. Rutherford felt a sick moment of panic, thinking the workman chose to jump to his death rather than be captured. The workman only fell two feet, landing on the awning below with a thud that resounded almost musically in the metal louvers. He looked back, smiled at Rutherford, and began walking carefully along the awning.

Rutherford ran up to the edge of the open space where a window had been. He poked his head out and looked at the workman, then pulled his head back to look at Randy. Randy glanced at the escaping suspect, then down at the awning, then back at Rutherford with a shrug.

Rutherford said, "He broke the window!"

Professor Sherwood said, "Oh did he now?"

"Yes, and he went out through it, onto the awning! He's getting away!"

In his earpiece, Sloan asked, "Where's he going to go?"

Rutherford said, "Like I said, away! Somewhere! I dunno. We can't risk him escaping! Guess I should follow him."

Terri said, "That's a terrible idea."

Rutherford said, "I know! But should I do it?"

Sloan said, "We know what Capp would say. It would make great video."

Rutherford looked down through the awnings at the ground three floors below and muttered, "To show at my funeral."

Sloan said, "Capp wouldn't say that last part. He might think it, though."

Professor Sherwood, with a smile you could hear in his voice, said, "Stand back, Rutherford. No need for you to go out there."

Terri shouted, "Professor?!"

Rutherford heard a buzzing from above.

Sherwood said, "Don't worry, everybody. Her Majesty's coming!"

Looking up, Rutherford saw a black drone-shaped mass at the center of a dark cloud coming down the side of the building as the buzz grew louder. Rutherford pulled his head inside, ran away from the window, dragging Randy by his jacket collar, and shouting, "Everybody run! Now!"

The workers just stared at him.

Outside the broken window the buzzing grew louder, and the light dimmed. Rutherford pointed toward the noise and yelled, "Bees!"

People seemed to appear out of every nook and cranny just to sprint to the doors at either end of the room, screaming the whole way.

Outside, over the buzzing, Professor Sherwood's amplified voice said, "Attention, criminal, do not panic. Throw down your weapons, put your hands where I can see them, and state, in a loud, clear voice, if you are allergic to bee stings."

The workman scrambled back in the window, waving his free arm madly while carrying his toolbox in the other.

Albert said, "Okay, You chased him in. Good work, Professor."

"The autopilot refuses to enter the window," Sherwood said. "Changing to manual control."

Albert and Terri both shouted, but Rutherford paid no attention, instead focusing on Her Majesty as she flew in through the window with remarkable speed and unsteadiness, seemingly dragging a swarm of agitated bees with her.

Professor Sherwood said, "How hard can it be? Wha?! Whoa!"

The drone darted toward one wall far too fast, then stopped, overcorrected, and whizzed back to the other side of the room with equal speed. The swarm of bees, thick enough to read as a dark blur, followed along in its wake.

Professor Sherwood said, "I've got it! I've got it! Whoa, uh, yikes! Okay, I'm good!"

Her Majesty's altitude rose and fell constantly, varying from nearly grinding on the ceiling to almost hitting the cubicle walls. As the drone flew in over the desks, papers blew up in its rotor wash, adding an extra note of chaos to the people fleeing. Thousands of confused bees flew in every direction in their attempts to follow the erratic drone.

Randy asked, "What in the *hell*?!"

"Her Majesty," Rutherford said.

Randy asked, "What does it do?"

Sherwood said, "Where is he?! Let me see him so I can land this damn thing! Okay, there he is!"

The drone darted forward, crashing directly into the workman and latching onto his clothing with built-in claws. Instantly the bees converged on him. He spun, flapping his free arm wildly and shrieking until he dropped his toolbox, which broke open on impact. Tools and rifle parts spilled onto the floor; the workman stepped on several tools, tripped, and fell hard. The bees piled up into a round, black lump on his back as he lay motionless, screaming.

"That," Rutherford said. "It does that."

THIRTY-FIVE

The paramedics treated the sniper's broken femur and multiple bee stings out of the back of an open ambulance as their patient lay handcuffed to a rolling gurney. Up on the admin building's roof, forensics techs from both the LAPD and CartFulls went about their business, searching the scene of the multiple attempted crimes with a fine-tooth comb.

Professor Sherwood was away, gathering his swarm, and Terri was off coordinating with the police and the CartFulls forensics team. Rutherford, Albert, Sloan, and Max stood by, listening as Detectives Frederick and Burski questioned the sniper.

"You claim you were bird-watching?" Burski asked. "Through a sniper rifle?"

The sniper smiled, sickeningly. "In a sense, Officer, the scope on a sniper rifle is nothing but a badass telescope."

"It was loaded."

"A *really* badass telescope."

Detective Frederick said, "Look, I get it. You still think you're gonna get away with this, but you're not. We've got you. But we don't really want you. We want the guy who hired you. The sooner you flip on him, the less time you'll spend in jail."

The sniper shook his head. "If I were a professional killer, which I'm not, but if I were, I'd never meet my clients in person. Anybody I meet also meets me. Anybody I can identify can identify me. But, of course, I don't have to worry about that, on account of I'm a bird-watcher."

Burski said, "I can see why you wouldn't want to admit to being a sniper. It's such an ugly business. Brutish. Crude."

"No," the sniper said. "Sniping is an art."

"I thought you were a bird-watcher," Detective Frederick said.

"I am, but I have the highest respect for snipers. Their work requires cunning, patience, and skill. Like bird-watching."

Burski laughed. "Oh yeah, cunning, patience, and skill. You have to hide, wait, put the crosshairs on the target's head. All you need is cowardice and a low enough mental capacity to be impervious to boredom."

The sniper said, "It takes a lot of strategy and technical knowledge."

Burski said, "You have to decide what part of the head to shoot them in, and which part of the gun to shoot them with. A million options there. The only difference between a sniper and a mugger waiting around a corner to bash you in the head is that the mugger is comparatively brave."

"A head shot from a sniper rifle is a clean kill."

"Anyone who calls a head shot a clean kill has never had to mop up after one."

"It's instant and painless. It's downright friggin' merciful!"

Max said, "Now, now. I know something about this subject."

The conversation was far too heavy for Rutherford's taste. He was relieved to hear Max step in to steer it in a more pleasant direction.

Max continued, "A head shot can be instant, but it isn't always. I have personally seen people hang on for quite some time after taking a bullet to the head."

Rutherford no longer felt any relief.

Max closed his eyes, as if struggling to remember, or not to. "Eyes wide open. Disoriented. Distressed. In horrible pain from a ghastly head wound. Only able to communicate by moaning, if that's even what he was trying to do. No, a bullet to the head doesn't guarantee a lack of suffering. I've given a lot of thought into how not to hurt people, and I've decided that most of the steps we say we take to make death painless for the person dying really just make it more satisfying for the spectators."

Burski said, "Go on. That idea really strikes a chord for me."

Sloan held her talking plastic skull up at eye level for all to see as she said, "Shocking."

Max said, "Think about hanging. Why would breaking the spine or closing off the windpipe and carotid artery mean instant brain death? Same goes for beheading. If there's a brain, and blood in that brain, there may be consciousness. There is only one truly reliable way to guarantee an instant, painless death."

"Well? Go on," Burski said. "Don't keep us in suspense. What is it?"

Max said, "A hat made of high explosives."

Burski let out an appreciative moan.

Max nodded. "The entire head is vaporized faster than the time it takes for a nerve impulse to travel from the skin to the brain."

Sloan said, "Note that he did not say *would be, hypothetically,* or *in theory.*"

After a long silence, the sniper said, "Shit. That's dark."

Sloan added, "And that's coming from a professional killer."

A woman cleared her throat. The team and Detective Frederick turned around to see Claire with her tablet computer and clear-plastic evidence bag. Terri stood next to her. Rutherford couldn't be sure, but judging by her eye movements, he suspected Claire had been looking him over before he turned around.

Rutherford looked at the two of them and chose to address Claire first. "Find anything interesting?"

Claire blushed, but quickly went back into professional mode. "I'm sure we'll find plenty of evidence buried under your wreckage. You do make a mess, don't you Rutherford."

Rutherford clenched his jaw, biting down on the stick of his sucker. "Someone's gotta do it."

Claire tilted her head. "Do they?"

Rutherford clenched his jaw harder. "Don't they?"

Claire said, "That wasn't an answer."

Rutherford raised one eyebrow. "That wasn't a question."

Claire stared at him and exhaled heavily, then turned to Terri. "We only just started surveying the scene, but one of the techs did find this." She held up the plastic evidence bag containing a black metal ring. "It looks like part of his rifle. The grade of steel, finish, and machining all match."

The sniper asked, "Where'd you find that?"

Detective Frederick turned to the paramedics. "We're done with him for now. You can take him to the hospital."

As they pulled the sniper's gurney into the ambulance and closed the door, he said, "I mean, it's not mine. I don't know what it is, but seriously, where the hell was it?"

Claire said, "We're just getting started here. Between the roof, the stairwell, and the mess in the office, we're going to be working for a while."

A voice said, "You've got the weekend."

Kyndra Perrin walked forward, two assistants with tablet computers struggling to keep up. "I guess it's lucky you caught the guy on a Friday afternoon. Gives you two days to work the scene."

Claire smiled. "I suppose that's true."

Perrin did not smile. "Still, that's no reason you shouldn't get cracking."

Claire said, "Right," and walked away.

Perrin looked at Rutherford. "It's funny, all this time you've spent guarding Russell and I end up having to save his life myself."

Rutherford said, "You threw yourself between Russell and a guy who was standing really far away holding an unassembled rifle. You didn't block any bullets. Technically, you just committed assault."

"But," Terri said, interrupting, "it was very impressive, the way you risked your life for one of your actors."

Perrin continued, "We still have multiple episodes left to shoot. We'd have to delay production, pay everyone their union minimums during the downtime, reassemble the writers' room to come up with an explanation for Russell's absence, and adjust all the remaining scripts."

Terri said, "And, of course, the emotional toll on you and the cast and crew would be terrible."

"Not a factor," Perrin said. "Hiding their actual feelings is literally an actor's job. As for the crew, they aren't on camera. They can cry all they want. As long as they don't sob loud enough for the boom mic to pick them up, we're good."

Max said, "You didn't actually have to say any of those terrible things."

"Leadership requires honesty. It saves trouble and time. For instance, Rutherford, you and I are never going to be a thing, because it would never work." Perrin walked away, accelerating to a brisk pace quickly enough to force her two assistants to struggle to keep up.

Rutherford said, "It never occurred to me that it might work in the first place."

Sloan said, "Which is one of the reasons that it wouldn't."

Terri watched her go. "I see what you mean about her now, Rutherford. She'd totally be capable of hiring a hit man."

Albert said. "But she risked her life to save Byrne, so I guess that rules her out."

Sloan said, "Yeah. We catch another murderer, and we lose a suspect. I hate this case."

Albert asked, "So, what's our next move?"

Sloan said, "Byrne's performance art piece is canceled. The police are escorting him home and will be all over his house all night. Not that anyone's likely to take another shot now that we caught the bird-watcher, and the sun's going down soon. I think the best thing would be for all of us to just have a meal, unwind a bit, and get a good night's sleep. Tomorrow we split back up into two teams and guard the two remaining Watsons, unless any of us comes up with a better idea."

Terri said, "Or at least a new idea."

Rutherford said, "Any new idea would probably be better than what we have, so you're both right."

Terri said, "Okay. Now that we know the plan, which is 'steady as she goes,' we can move on to staff issues. Max, what's wrong with you."

Max said, "Terri, I'm just trying to—"

Terri stuck a finger in his face. "Shh! That was not a question. It's the subject. I'm about to tell you what's wrong with you. Max, the quality of your work has fallen through the floor. You were hired because you're a friendly, nonthreatening presence who also happens to be an expert at subduing criminals while de-escalating the situation. That's a rare skill set. Only you have it. And that's why you're so vital to our team."

Max said, "Thank you."

"But ever since Chaz showed up, you're distracted, you're unreliable, you lash out with far more viciousness than is called for, and you spend all day on the phone with your boyfriend. If we needed that skill set, all we'd have to do is go to the nearest high school and hire the first girl we find wearing black lipstick."

"I have not been so good at my job lately. I see that."

"But that's not the upsetting part," Sloan said, holding up the plastic skull. "Max, none of us likes seeing you tortured like this. We want you to be happy. Chaz is making you miserable."

Max said, "I'm touched to hear you say that. Even if it is filtered through a novelty Halloween decoration."

Terri said, "Sloan, we all have earpieces. Put the skull away."

Sloan said, "Spoilsport," but she turned the skull off.

Max shook his head. "You are right, of course. Chaz . . . it's complicated. Chaz is like chocolate cake."

Rutherford said, "Cheap and easy to get?"

Max said, "No. Well, yes, but also, chocolate cake is the worst thing in the world for me, but if it's available I will keep eating it until I finally either remember my self-respect or I feel so sick that I have to stop. Usually, it's the second one. Next time we talk I'll tell him I can only talk on the phone once a day, and when we get back to Seattle I will end it. It's funny. Just saying that out loud made me feel a bit better."

"Why wait? Why not end it now?" Rutherford asked.

"You've heard how he's treating my belongings. That's his behavior when he's in a relationship with me. Try to imagine how he'd behave as my angry ex."

Terri said, "That's good thinking. I'm glad we had this talk. And as for you, Rutherford, I'm unhappy we're about to have this talk."

"What?" Rutherford gasped. "What did I do? We caught the sniper. I did some stupid things, but I consulted with you first. If Her Majesty hadn't stopped me, I would have gone out and probably gotten into a slap fight on that awning. I thought you'd be pleased."

Terri said, "That's all fine. I'm talking about after, with Claire. All that 'someone's gotta do it' stuff. I told you to stop trying to impress her."

"What? But! I wasn't," he sputtered. "What I said shouldn't impress her. It shouldn't impress anyone! It was nonsense!"

Terri rolled her eyes. "Oh, come on. Then what was with the squinting and the gritted teeth?"

"I was wincing. I hated hearing that drivel coming out of my mouth. But I say it because it's the image you want me to project."

"Not to her. Not knowing what we know about her tastes."

"So what do you want me to do instead, Terri? Be myself?"

"No. Absolutely not."

"So what can I do then, Terri?"

"I don't know, Rutherford. How about you just avoid her?"

Sloan said, "Yeah, ignore her. Give her the cold shoulder. That always makes people less interested."

Terri said, "You aren't helping, Sloan."

"Yes, but the difference between you and me is that I know it, Terri." Sloan pointed at Rutherford. "The kid's in an impossible position. He's damned if he does and dammed if he doesn't."

Terri said, "Yes, but either way, it's my job to do the damning."

Sloan said, "I know that, but I'm saying that damning him isn't getting you the result you want."

"Then what do you want me to do, Sloan?"

"The same thing you want him to do."

"What's that?"

"I have no idea, but I'll criticize you when you don't do it."

Rutherford said, "Thanks for the backup, Sloan. But I do wish you wouldn't talk about me like I'm not here."

Sloan said, "I'm pointing at you. I've been pointing at you this whole time. I'm literally demonstrating that you're here."

Terri said, "And when someone's defending you, don't criticize how she does it."

Sloan said, "Thank you."

Terri said, "You're welcome."

Rutherford put his hands up defensively. "Oh, so now you're both mad at me?"

Sloan said, "Yes. Maybe we should get Claire in on this conversation. That might set her straight."

THIRTY-SIX

When the huddle broke, Rutherford took less than four steps before Randy swooped in, draping an arm over his shoulder. "Come on, kid, we're going drinking."

Rutherford said, "I don't think that's a good idea."

"Kid, if people waited until it was a good idea, nobody'd ever get drunk. Get in the truck. I know just the place."

Two hours later Rutherford sat in a torn, sticky booth, drinking bad beer from a foggy plastic glass while music he didn't like played on a terrible sound system.

Randy sat across from him, nursing his own beer, head bobbing to the beat while he played the tabletop like a bongo drum.

"How can you stand to listen to this?" Rutherford asked. "The speakers are all blown out."

"Kid, a roached-out stereo is the best way to listen to Willie Nelson. His voice already sounds like a bad speaker, so it makes no difference for him, but it makes the rest of the band match."

Rutherford took a drink of warm, flat beer, gripping it with two hands for added stability. He put down the glass and felt some relief in seeing that only about a third of a glass remained. Randy saw it too, and he quickly picked up the plastic pitcher and poured the last dregs into Rutherford's glass, nearly filling it. He shook the pitcher in an apparent effort to make sure Rutherford got every last drop, but more beer landed on the table and Rutherford's lap than in his glass.

"Johnny," Randy shouted as he placed the empty pitcher with two others on the end of the table. "Another round of your cheapest!"

The bartender said, "Yeah, sure, Randy. Just stop yelling."

Randy replied, "Sure thing," raising his voice another decibel.

Rutherford figured Randy was something of a regular. All of the waitresses knew him by name, and avoided him. "Do you have to specifically order the cheapest thing they have, Randy? This stuff is half water."

"That's right, kid. Smart! Keeps you hydrated. Prevents a hangover. You have a point, though. We could stand to kick things up. Johnny! Four shots of Jäger, *mach schnell!*"

Rutherford asked, "No, I don't think so."

"I know so," Randy said. "You've heard the old saying. 'Beer before liquor, never drunk quicker.'"

"Is that how it goes? And is speed really the goal?"

"Why are you picking at me, kid? I'm not what's bothering you," Randy said. "You're mad at the case, not me. I can see you're really beating yourself up because you haven't nailed this guy. But I gotta tell you, I think you're looking at this thing all wrong."

Rutherford shrugged. "Well, I mean, sure. We've caught four contract killers. That's great. But our goal is to get the person behind the killing. We haven't made any progress on that, and if Byrne or Warner gets killed, it'll be on us."

"That's not what I meant, and I disagree anyway. Kid, the biggest mistake people like you make is when things go wrong, they ask, 'Is this my fault?' when they should be asking, 'Is this my problem?' You think it's your responsibility to catch this guy. Why?"

"Because it's my job."

Randy asked, "But is it? Have you ever given any thought to what your job really is?"

"Doing what my bosses want."

"No. Your job is to get what you want. Your bosses want you to do things, but that's what *they* want. Getting what they want is their job, not yours. Your job is to get what you want and when you get down to it, all you want is for them to keep paying you. That's it. When I was a cop, I was told to follow rules and do paperwork. Instead, I went after the bad guys any way I saw fit and left the paperwork to someone else who was into that kinda thing. As long as I was getting results, they had to pay me and they couldn't fire me."

Rutherford stayed quiet for a long moment, allowing his thoughts time to swim to the surface through the alcohol. "But they did fire you."

"Yeah, but I'm the exception that proves the rule."

"I've never understood how an exception can prove a rule."

"But it does," Randy said. "Every single time."

The bartender walked up to the end of the booth. "Another pitcher of our cheapest beer, and four shots of Jäger." He put the pitcher and glasses down hard enough that each spilled slightly on the table, then walked away without asking if they wanted anything else.

Randy shouted after him, "You're not working very hard to earn your tip, Johnny."

The bartender said, "You never tip."

"You're not giving me much reason to start." Randy slid his two shots over closer to himself, then pushed the other two toward Rutherford. "Okay, drink up."

Rutherford shook his head, and instantly regretted it. "Thanks, but, no, I don't think I should. I'm not feeling great."

"That's why I ordered Jäger. It's medicinal."

"Is it?"

"I guess. It tastes like medicine. Come on. We'll finish up what we have here, then we'll call it a night, I'll drive us back to my place, and you can sleep it off on my couch."

"You shouldn't drive."

"I'm fine."

"You're drunk. Your judgment's off."

"That's your opinion, but you're even drunker than I am, so I can't trust your judgment, can I? Now down the hatch."

Rutherford tossed back one of the two shots and grimaced. "It's like a cross between black licorice and fire."

"Yup," Randy said. "No matter how bad things get, having a mouthful of Jägermeister makes all your other problems seem small."

Rutherford shrugged and took his second shot.

Randy shook his head. "Look at my job now, kid. They hired me to use what I know about police work to make their show about arresting ghosts and aliens more realistic. Nobody can do that, and the audience doesn't even notice that I don't try. The job I really do is to keep the producer's career-destroying secrets. Turns out I'm good at it, as long as I'm well paid."

"You're forcing them to pay you through blackmail."

"And it's working. You're asking your employers to keep paying you by doing anything they want. Is that any easier? Kid, I'm just one man, with one life. I don't have the time or the ability to make everybody on earth happy, so I say why not start with myself."

"Then move on to other people when you're happy?"

"I don't know. I'll cross that bridge when I come to it."

"That's a pretty selfish way to go through life."

"Yes it is, but it's honest. All I really care about is me. All you really care about is you. And if you think I'm wrong, the only one you're really fooling is yourself."

"Then why did you help me today?"

"I didn't. I haven't told you yet, but you're paying for the drinks."

"No, I figured that. And that's not what I'm talking about. I mean, when you ran up into the building with me to get the sniper."

"I wasn't helping you. I was following you because you had the right idea. Be direct. Go where the action is. While the cops cover the exits and wait for him to come out, we go knock some heads and get our names on the news."

"But what if we'd ended up fighting him?"

"I would have fought hard, after you tired him out, and taken as much credit as I could for catching him and saving you."

Rutherford said, "But that's not how it works, Randy. No. We get the most done when we work together. I try to make you look good and you try to make me look good, and that way we both look good."

Randy laughed. "That's a great approach, for you. Go for it. I fully support you working to make me look good, but I'll go on working to make me look good, and with the two of us working together, I'll look great."

"But in the long run you'll look terrible, Randy. There's no *I* in team."

"That's right. There's no *I* in team. That's why *I* am not in a team. Not having an *I* is *team's* problem. *I* is already a word all by itself. *I* is fine on its own. The last thing *I* needs is a *T*, an *E*, and an *A*, let alone some stupid *M* hanging around, getting in the way. And I'd point out, those letters also spell *meat*!"

Rutherford grimaced. "What's that have to do with anything?"

Randy let out a heavy sigh that seemed to deflate his entire body. "I don't know. Probably nothing, but it seemed worth mentioning. Kid, you're like my mom. She was a team player. Always wanted to help people. Always wanted to do good.

At least that's what I'm told. I barely remember her. She died in the back of a crashed ambulance. She and the driver were doing their best, trying to get an overdosed addict to the hospital. My mother bled to death in a twisted wreck surrounded by first aid supplies. Nobody gave a shit. Most of the reporters didn't even bother to get her name. They just said, 'The driver and paramedic also perished.' She got *Professor and Mary Ann-ed* in her own obituary."

Rutherford stared across the table at Randy, not knowing what to say.

"I'm sorry," Randy said. "I got off track there. What were we talking about?"

"Your mom."

Randy waved his hand. "No, before that."

"My job, but it's not as important as—"

"Your job! That's right. My point is: You need to stop worrying about giving other people what they want, and focus on taking what you want. For example, right now, I want to take a whiz. Am I going to ask you to give me a whiz? No. It's on me."

"It's on you?"

"The responsibility, not the whiz. Though that would keep me from having to get up."

* * *

Rutherford stumbled into his hotel room, relieved to be back at what, while he was in Los Angeles, qualified as *home*.

Randy had insisted on having Rutherford come sleep it off at his place, but Rutherford refused, citing the hotel's housekeeping staff, who could clean up any mess he might make. Of course, housekeeping was not on duty at the moment. Still, he was willing to bet the daily maid service had at least provided him with a clean place to vomit. He doubted Randy's home could offer the same.

Once Randy accepted that Rutherford wasn't going to crash on his couch, he insisted on driving Rutherford to his hotel, but Rutherford chose the remotely driven TurkMO van instead.

Seeing that Rutherford didn't want his help, Randy stated that he was going to drive himself home. Rutherford made it clear he wasn't going to let that happen either, called him a cab, waited until he saw Randy get in, and paid the cabbie cash in advance. He felt satisfaction in knowing that he had been a good friend to Randy, if not a particularly trusting one.

Rutherford sloughed off his clothes and folded them out of muscle memory. He looked down at his nice, warm, comfortable hotel bed and knew instantly that he wanted no part of it. Instead, he lay in his underwear on the cold tile bathroom floor, letting it leach the excess heat from his body. He had never been room-spinning drunk before and did not like it. In addition to all the usual reasons that alcohol poising is not fun, the room was spinning counterclockwise, which he found particularly nauseating, as if clockwise would be less sickening for some reason he couldn't quite articulate.

He felt the cool tile pressing into his hot, sweaty back and pictured all the thousands of travelers' bare feet that had touched that very floor just that year. The image made him feel like throwing up. He thought more about it in hopes of forcing himself to purge the poison from his body. He went so far as to picture wet feet, sore and sweaty from a long day of travel or tourism, in dirty socks, perhaps extra painful due to some fungus or toenail infection.

That almost got him there, but not quite. As a Hail Mary, he turned his head to the side to smell the floor.

As was typical of his life, just as he achieved his goal, the thought that went through his head was: *big mistake.* As he threw up into the hotel toilet, he marveled that he hadn't even sniffed the tile; turning his head did the trick.

When the well had seemingly run dry, he flopped back down onto the cool floor.

This was the worst. Rutherford couldn't understand why on earth anybody would ever do this more than once. He'd be willing to bet Randy had, but Randy's self-punishing tendencies made a certain amount of sense. The poor man's mother died in an ambulance accident.

Rutherford tried to imagine what that would be like, but he couldn't. He couldn't even imagine how he'd have handled it if his mother was merely injured in an ambulance crash. He pictured himself as a child, having a panic attack as they wheeled his unconscious mother out of one smashed ambulance, directly into another ambulance, which then sped away.

It occurred to him that Byrne's mother died in an ambulance accident too. He would have thought Randy would like Byrne better, having that in common. Unless that was why Randy hated him. He resented that their mothers died in the same. . .

He never finished the thought. The idea that both mothers' accidents had been the same in some ways triggered a torrent of ideas and connections that streamed through his brain too quickly to keep up. True, the speed was decreased by his current drunken state, but so was his ability to process it all, so the overall effect was the same as any other flash of inspiration, just slower and sloppier.

A simple web search would give Rutherford the one piece of information needed to tell him if his theory was sound—or just drunken lunacy. He rose to his hand and knees, then used the toilet rim and the sink to pull himself to his feet. He stood straight and tall for less than one second before he decided this wasn't the time. He bent over like a question mark and used one hand to work his way along the wall while keeping the other close to his mouth. He saw no way that trying to cover his mouth while throwing up would lead to a positive outcome, but it felt like the thing to do.

He slumped his way back out to the bedroom, found his smartphone hidden deep in his stack of neatly folded clothes, and completely messed up the whole pile clumsily digging the phone out of a pants pocket. He slunk back to the bathroom, bending over a little further with each step until he didn't so much lie down on the floor as he rolled over onto it, sliding slightly in the slick of his own drunk sweat.

He tapped the microphone icon and blurted out, "Catalina Byrne, ambulance accident, names, paramedic, driver."

The first several search results proved fruitless. He searched further. His condition did not help, but after what felt like an eternity, he found the names of the driver and paramedic. The driver was named Franklin Barker. The paramedic's name was Emilia McCormick. She left behind her husband Randolph, and one son, Randolph Junior.

In that instant, Rutherford knew with absolute certainty exactly what he had to do.

He put his head over the toilet bowl and threw up again.

THIRTY-SEVEN

Rutherford willed himself awake at seven, his head throbbing so painfully that it made him resent his own heartbeat.

He ran through what he could remember of his thoughts from the previous evening and found that they still held up when he analyzed it with, while not a properly functioning brain, one that was at least impaired in a different way than it had been the night before. He slid up to a seated position, completely untucking the bottom sheet of his hotel's bed in the process. He put any thought of fixing it out of his mind. He had limited capabilities and something much more important to accomplish.

He thought there was a chance that Randy might be behind the killings, but he had doubts. The Watson killings required a great deal of planning, effort, and selfish disregard for other people. Rutherford had trouble believing Randy was really capable of that much planning and effort.

Then again, other people did all the work, and in retrospect it didn't seem all that well planned. Two out of four of the hit men turned out to be incompetent; half of the attempted murders failed; and in the end, the person writing the note and calling the shots got all of the attention and none of the consequences. That definitely sounded like Randy's handiwork.

He knew what he needed to do, but not how to do it. Two options occurred to him. He could call the team, tell them Randy (the guy he'd befriended and taken advice from) was their man, have them contact the police, hope everyone got their ducks in a row quickly, try to capture Randy before anything tipped him off, and everybody would all share in the glory. His other option was to just go over on his own, catch Randy unaware, bring him in before the police were done with their morning briefing, claim he'd been onto Randy for a while but only just got his proof, and be back in Seattle, hailed as a hero, by nightfall.

The team option was a bit embarrassing, less dangerous from a safety perspective, but more dangerous from a risk-of-failure point of view. Going in alone would be dumb and selfish, but more likely to succeed and would make him look good. It ran counter to every instinct Rutherford had, and was exactly what Randy himself would do.

* * *

The TurkMO drove up the long dusty driveway, which was really just two long ruts that wound between the trees.

Rutherford leaned back in the steeply reclined driver's seat and took a gulp from a bottle of fruit punch sports drink.

The thousand-and-one strings rendition of what Rutherford eventually recognized as "Black Hole Sun" quieted as the remote driver asked, "Are you feeling any better?"

Rutherford said, "I am, a little. Thanks."

"My pleasure. They train us with a whole list of suggestions to help deal with hangovers. They figure once we go public, something like sixty percent of our business will be alcohol related."

Rutherford tipped the bottle back and drank the last little bit of fluid as the van rocked its way up the unpaved driveway. "There. All done. I don't think I spilled any in your car."

The driver said, "Don't worry about it, sir. It's not my car, and I don't have to clean it."

The driveway led to a double-wide trailer, sitting three feet above the ground with a long-faded wooden lattice skirt hiding the axles and the plumbing. All the shades were drawn and there was no sign of life. Randy's truck sat out front in an area that was either an abused and patchy lawn or a neglected, weed-bound parking lot. The truck's presence puzzled Rutherford, since he'd sent Randy home in a cab the night before. The truck should still have been parked at the bar. He hadn't expected Randy to have an easy means of escape, but it didn't matter now. The die was cast.

As the TurkMO came to a stop, Rutherford glanced at the dashboard clock. It read twelve minutes after eight. He popped his sucker into his mouth and stepped out of the minivan, holding a small box of donuts wedged into the bottom of a plastic shopping bag with assorted napkins, sporks, and other items that looked like trash even when brand new.

Randy leaned out of the front door, wearing jeans and the kind of white cotton tank top that comes as packs of six in a zip-top bag.

As Rutherford walked toward the trailer, the TurkMO drove away. Randy asked, "Your van isn't waiting for you?"

Rutherford said, "It isn't the team's loaner. It's a TurkMO I called for a quick lift. I'll get another when I'm ready to go. I swung by CartFulls and grabbed some donuts."

"Huh. CartFulls. They're the ones with that whiney shopping cart. 'I love CartFulls! I got a great deal on a forty-pound box of...'" Randy trailed off, shook his head, and gave up imitating a cheerful tone of voice as he continued. "Oh, I dunno, some bullshit."

Rutherford let out one laugh followed by a long groan. "Ugh, don't make me laugh, man. My head can't take it. Hey, how'd your truck get here?"

"I drove it here."

"But I put you in a cab."

"And I had the driver circle the block once and drop me back off."

"He agreed to that?" Rutherford asked.

"Sure, when I said he could pocket the money you paid him."

The wooden steps and porch wobbled under Rutherford's weight.

"I see why you needed the building materials."

Randy disappeared into the trailer, raising his voice to be heard through the open door. "It wasn't for the porch." He left the door wide open. The sun was out, and the lights in the trailer were off, so inside Rutherford only saw a bit of the floor and a dark void.

Rutherford stepped through the door and onto an area rug, which gave way beneath him. He plummeted and pitched forward. His right leg disappeared into the space below, splashing into some unseen thick fluid. Scrambling for any means of breaking his fall, he dropped the CartFulls bag and tried to catch himself. His rib cage bashed painfully into the front edge of the hole, knocking the wind from his lungs. He finally came to a rest with both legs soaking up to the knees in the viscous mystery liquid below. Rutherford stopped there, the floor pressing against his chest, with one arm pinned to his side and both legs sunk into the mystery sludge under the floor. His other hand was free above the hole in the floor, clawing at the carpet to keep from sliding in further.

Randy stepped forward, laughing and pulling a rumpled Hawaiian shirt on over his tank top. "The building materials were for the floor. You see it needs some work."

Rutherford raised his free hand so that Randy could help him up. Randy took his hand and pushed Rutherford down further into the hole.

Randy said, "There. That's better."

Rutherford said, "What the hell, man?" and started to pull his trapped left arm out of the hole, but stopped when Randy pointed a black nine-millimeter pistol at his face.

"Chill," Randy said. "Don't move a muscle."

Rutherford stopped moving.

Randy held out an open hand next to his pistol. "Give me your ear bug."

Rutherford pulled out his earpiece and put it in Randy's outstretched hand.

Randy said, "Good boy. I'll let you keep the lollipop."

Randy dropped Rutherford's earpiece into an old Lay's potato chip bag, which he wadded up. Rutherford winced, partly because he knew the mylar in the bag would block radio signals, and partly from picturing his earpiece covered in grease and crumbs.

Randy pulled out the box of donuts Rutherford had brought, leaving the bag and everything else in it behind on the floor. "Now, while you stand down there, I'll just have a seat up here. There's no reason for both of us to be uncomfortable while we wait."

Randy pulled a white resin lawn chair out from under the dining table and sat down facing Rutherford, gun still pointed down at him.

Rutherford said, "You know, putting an unbuttoned Hawaiian shirt on over a disgusting pitted-out undershirt isn't an improvement."

"Sure it is. It draws the eyes away from the stains. Besides, bad taste is more socially acceptable that bad hygiene."

"You've got both, and the shirt might hide the sight of your pits, but it doesn't hide the smell."

From his spot right by the still-open door of the trailer, Rutherford could see the kitchen, dining area, living room, and the hall leading off to the bathroom and bedrooms. Piles of trash and clutter filled every corner and covered most of the furniture. It was all much as Rutherford expected, except for the old engine hoist and hand truck sitting in the living room between the couch and the TV.

Rutherford asked, "What am I standing in?"

Randy said, "A plywood form full of wet concrete. Thanks again for helping me load the truck. Looks like you're finally going to live up to your stupid nickname, 'Cement Shoes.' Yeah, I looked you up the morning we met."

"Nobody really calls me that."

"Yeah, I noticed. Maybe they will now."

THIRTY-EIGHT

Rutherford wiggled his feet around, trying to feel any change in the concrete's viscosity. He asked, "So this stuff hardens, then what? You plan to put a stopper in the sink and flood the kitchen? Or are you gonna put me in the back of the truck and drive me to the Santa Monica Pier?"

Randy took a bite of a donut and answered with his mouth full. "I'm going to hoist you up out of that hole and lug you out back to the swimming pool."

"You have a pool?"

"Yeah. That surprise you?"

"I just didn't peg you for a swimmer."

"For a long time I used to take a dip every day instead of bothering with a shower. I stopped when I realized that it doesn't really work. First I smelled like armpit, then I smelled like chlorine, then in the end I smelled like armpit and chlorine."

Rutherford looked around at the trailer interior. "The pool, it's one of those round above-ground ones?"

"Oval. So what?"

"Nothing. Pool maintenance seems like more work than you'd want to take on."

"That's why I don't do it. The water's dark green and sticky. Did you know water could be sticky? It's so gross. You'll see for yourself."

So, your plan is for me to stand waist deep in swamp water?"

"I'll put you in the deep end, dumbass."

"Your above-ground pool has a deep end?"

"Yes!" Randy spat pieces of donut as he shouted. "It's a fully legitimate swimming pool! They dig a hole for the deep end, then they build the above-ground pool on top of it. You're such a snob. A snob with an inferiority complex. How does that work? You think you're better than everybody, but you also think everybody's better than you. Look, kid, your part in my plan is to stay still until the cement dries. The only difference between you being conscious and unconscious is whether or not I have you to keep me company while I wait, so be nice or I'll use you to play the world's easiest game of whack-a-mole."

"How long of a wait are we talking about?"

"That's quick-drying concrete, so it could be as little as ten minutes. But I'm going to call it thirty, just to be safe."

"You don't really want to kill me. That's why you're stalling."

"I'm not stalling. I'm drawing it out. You're gonna sit here and think about what's coming to you, then I'm going to dump you in the pool at just the right part of the slope into the deep end to have your eyes above the water so I can see the fear in them while you drown."

"What you'll see is me tilting my head back, so my nose is above the water."

"Nose plugs." Randy reached into his jeans pocket and pulled out a pair molded from light-blue plastic with a cute, little plastic fish glued to the front, clearly meant for children. "The final indignity."

Randy laughed hard. Rutherford just stared at him, disgusted. When he'd finished laughing, Randy asked "What's the matter? Got nothing to say?"

"I was just trying to decide if I should tell you that you're an idiot, and that if I tilt my head really far back and pucker, I'm pretty sure I can still keep my mouth above water."

Randy's smile disappeared. He sat silent for a moment, tilted his head back, puckered, then said, "You shouldn't have told me. Now I'll just dump you in the deepest part and be done with it. And I'll still make you wear the nose plugs."

"Yeah, I figured. I'm gonna fight you all the way out to the pool."

"I'll tie your hands, and your feet will be in concrete. What can you do?"

"I'll scream bloody murder. Someone will hear me and come help."

"You came up that driveway, you know I have no neighbors. I have two square miles of land out here. It's the one thing my old man gave me besides my weekly beating. He bought it with the settlement from mom's accident. Thought he was going to get rich in real estate. The city was already butting up against the property boundaries. He figured it was just a matter of time before he got a big fat offer. Didn't happen. They just built around us. Turns out nobody wants the land—the soil's all contaminated with hazardous chemicals."

"Who'd he buy the land from?"

"A chemical disposal company."

"Uh-huh. Randy, your plan still won't work. My backup will be here way before the concrete's dry."

"Backup?" Randy asked through a mouthful of donut. "For breakfast with a buddy? You're not quite that big a wuss."

"We both know I'm not here for breakfast. I'm here to arrest you for hiring killers to eliminate actors who play Dr. Watson."

Randy's eyes widened. He sat silent for a moment, then tilted his head back and laughed.

Rutherford said, "Don't try to deny it."

"I'm not, kid. I'm just surprised you figured it out. This certainly explains you not asking why I'm killing you. I thought you took that surprisingly well. So, what tipped you off?"

"There were lots of clues. When I called you from the recording studio after the second murder you seemed really interested to hear that the murder was successful. The guy who tried to kill Justine Warner said she was hired by a man in a gray hooded sweatshirt, just like the one I found on the seat of your truck. When we went to interview Amanda Hogan, you got us back just after the sniper was supposed to take another shot, giving you an alibi, if he had done his job. But the puzzle piece that made everything else fall into place was last night, when you mentioned that your mom died in an ambulance accident with someone who overdosed, and that there was press involved. I remembered that Byrne's mom also died in an ambulance accident after she overdosed and got a lot of press. I figured out they were the same accident, which gives you the one thing nobody seems to have: a motive."

Randy laughed, spraying more donut in Rutherford's direction. "So you figured it out because I got drunk and told you. Great detective work there."

"You didn't tell me. You let a little detail slip."

"The little detail that I had a motive."

"I had to put two and two together!"

"Yeah, sure, after I gave you a bunch of twos."

"Hey. Wait a minute. You didn't know I figured it out until now?"

"Nope."

"Then why are you trying to kill me?"

"You just said yourself that I've been killing Watsons."

"Yeah. So?"

"There you go."

"What do you mean?"

"You really need me to say it out loud, kid? I'm killing you because you're a Watson."

"I'm not an actor. I don't play Watson."

"You don't need to be an actor, you're a real-life Watson."

"No, I'm a detective. Watson's not a detective. He's just someone who tags along."

"A detective wouldn't need me to spell this out for them."

"I'm not a Watson!"

"You're such a Watson! You're the biggest Watson. Sloan's a detective. You're her Watson."

"I am not!"

"Watsons never think they are."

"Well, look, we aren't going to see eye to eye on this point."

"Not with you stuck down there in that hole." Randy popped the last hunk of a donut into his mouth.

THIRTY-NINE

Randy dug into the box for another donut and pulled out a cruller. He took a moment to examine the signature ridged top, raised an eyebrow, smiled, and said, "Ooh, fancy."

Rutherford said, "It's called a cruller."

Randy said, "I know that. They're one of my favorites. They're like the Ruffles potato chip of donuts."

"I'm sorry, Randy, do you think Ruffles are fancy?"

"Yeah. Compared to plain Lay's. What?! Ruffled shirts are fancy, why wouldn't chips be? Shut up!"

"So the friendship, the advice, going out for drinks last night, what was all that, Randy? A ruse?"

"More of a ploy. I got you drunk last night thinking I'd bring you back here and kill you with no resistance. It's worked for me before. Of course, I didn't use it for murder, never on a dude, and certainly never on such a damned goody-goody. When you wussed out, I thought I was going to have to come up with a new plan, then you called this morning asking to just come on over yourself."

"I also called the cops."

"I'm sure that's what you want me to think, but I ain't buying it. Kid, you've been trying to be more like me ever since we met. I mean, I get it. If I were you, I'd want to be more like me too. You'd try to take me out in a way I'd respect. You knew I would go in alone, so you came in alone, and now you're going to die alone."

"But why, Randy? Why kill Watsons anyway? I can see why you'd want to kill Byrne. The way you see it, his mother killed herself, took your mother with her, and got more famous for it while your mom got forgotten. You both grew up without mothers, but it set you off in life on the wrong foot while Byrne kinda benefited and doesn't even seem grateful."

Randy chewed his donut. "Yup. And also, he's an ass."

"But why kill the other Watsons?"

"Because I didn't just want Byrne to die. I wanted to profit from it. I wanted money, fame, and revenge—the whole shebang. To manage that, I needed a hook. A theme and a published list seemed like just the ticket. If you publish a list of people you're gonna kill but don't kill them, you're just a nut. Publish the list and kill one person, you're a nut who just got lucky. You need at least two to get any real attention. The plan was to kill some other Watson first to throw the cops off, get away with it, send out my note threatening all the others, then the next day, send a sniper in after Byrne. I directed the sniper when to shoot, where to shoot from, and what way to go to get in and out. Then I figured I'd watch Byrne get shot, intercept the sniper, catch him single-handedly, hit the news, do the talk shows, agree that my catching Byrne's killer was an ironic twist that makes a great story, get some geek to ghostwrite a book, and spend the rest of my life going on the news networks as an expert every time there's a shooting. Easy street."

"And all it took was two innocent lives."

"I owe Byrne. No, Byrne owes me! As for Hindman, I didn't feel great about that, but I met him once, buying groceries at Ralph's. He blew me off."

"And that cost him his life?"

"My mom tried to help people, and that cost her *her* life."

So then what about the other two Watsons?"

"The sniper said he had technical problems. He needed to try again, and I had to scramble. I found three killers when I was planning things, so I hired the one I hadn't used—"

"The most expensive one."

"Yes. Shut up. Anyway, I sicced him on the cartoon guy, Menard. My hope was that the damned dippy sniper would do his job, I'd pinch him, and it'd be over. But he screwed up again."

"And for Justine Warner, you were out of time and money and had to go with the first guy you found."

"Then the sniper screwed up *again*, and that brings us to where we are. The only way I can see to salvage this mess is to take out the ultimate Watson in the most awful way I can. Killing the Watson of the superfancy detective trying to catch me should fit the bill. Then I skip the country, sell my story, and get rich and famous that way. I won't get revenge, it won't be the whole shebang, but I figure I can settle for the partial shebang."

"You're not going to get any part of the shebang, Randy. You killed two innocent people and injured a third for nothing."

"Don't give me that. They weren't innocent."

"Why? Because they took an acting part similar to the one the guy you hate has?"

"They took an acting role as someone who fights crime, but they get more attention than real cops. Hell, the Watsons don't even play crime fighters. They play people the crime fighters explain stuff to. Byrne's mom played the dispatcher on a show about an ambulance company, but her death was a tragedy, and nobody cared about the actual ambulance crew she took out with her. The plan wasn't to kill all the Watsons, but if I had to kill someone, they were a pretty good choice. The world's got too many posers. Actors pretend to be heroes while real heroes are ignored. You pretend to be a detective to get press for your team. Even back when I was on the force, all of the raises and promotions went to the fake little weenies like you who obsessed over their paperwork and labeled all their evidence perfectly while the real cops, like me, the hard-core ones who did what had to be done, we got fired."

Rutherford said, "You weren't a real cop, you certainly weren't *hard core*. You didn't care enough about being a cop to even bother doing it right. You didn't do what needs to be done. *Paperwork* needs to be done. *Labeling evidence properly* needs to be done. You only wanted to do the parts of the job you liked. I've tried to be more like you and it's awful, but I do it because it's my job. That's what makes me good at it. I do all the things I believe in and am good at: following protocol, acting like a professional, real detective work, but I'm willing to do the parts I don't like. Running. Fighting. Driving fast."

"Oh, come on. You love it and you know it."

"No. I hate it. It's embarrassing. Randy, any time a situation ends with a chase or a fight, that's a sign of failure."

"And I suppose now you're going to arrest me, even though you hate to."

"Not at all. I'm really enjoying arresting you, and I'm gonna love sending you to jail."

"Oh yeah," Randy said, chewing a donut while looking down the barrel of his pistol at Rutherford stuck in the hole in the floor. "You've got me right where you want me."

"I don't have you in a headlock or anything, but my backup will get here any second, because I do things the way they should be done, even if that's the hard way. Things like calling all the other members of my team, telling them you're our guy, and resigning myself to the idea that they'd make me wait to come get you until the LAPD is in position. Luckily, they surprised me and agreed that we could stall you while the cops got rounded up. That's why most of them are in our loaner van at the end of your driveway, recording this conversation."

"Bullshit."

"No. Sorry, Randy. I mean, I'm not sorry, I'm pretty happy with how this has played out, but I recognize that it's not a pleasant situation for you."

"I don't believe you."

"You will, eventually. You should just give yourself up now and make things easier on yourself, but you won't. I'll end up having to chase you, and we'll both be all over the internet by nightfall."

"I took your earbug. If you're wearing a wire, the microphone's probably under the house with the rest of you."

Rutherford shook his head. "It's not on me, and it isn't just a microphone."

The empty plastic CartFulls bag the donuts came in lay on the floor near Rutherford. It stirred on its own. A flattened Chinese take-out box crumpled itself into a ball and rolled out of the bag.

Rutherford said, "Allow me to introduce the wad. It's designed to look like trash. I only brought the donuts as camouflage, though looking around your home, I shouldn't have bothered. The fact that the trash is in a bag makes it stand out in this dump."

A distinct buzzing sound drifted in from the distance, growing louder.

Rutherford said, "You've heard Albert's drones before. The rest of the team's probably driving up right now."

Randy stood up and leaned far to one side, then the other to see as much of the area outside the open door as he could. The drones were getting louder, but there was no sign of cars yet. "Okay, kid, you got me to confess. Good for you. It'll be a little harder to escape. What's to keep me from putting a bullet in you anyway?"

Rutherford said, "I said most of the team was waiting at the end of the driveway. Luckily, Max likes a good hike."

Max, wearing khakis and a tan cardigan—his version of desert camouflage—pivoted into the doorframe from the spot right outside the door where he'd been hiding. While Randy was still stunned, Max leapt forward, over Rutherford's exposed head and arm, making Rutherford cringe and let out an alarmed yelp.

Randy stood and thrust his pistol forward. Max pushed the gun to the side, grabbing its barrel in an iron grip. He looked at the firearm and said, "Ah, Beretta!" His free left hand came up in a blur of speed, poked at a lever on the gun's side, and the entire upper slide came off in Max's hand, rendering the rest of the firearm useless except as a poorly designed boomerang.

Max stood there smiling at the still-stunned Randy until the floor, unsound to begin with and weakened by the hole in which Rutherford was stuck, gave way under Max's weight. Max fell backward, his mass and momentum widening the hole. The linoleum warped into a pit that Max fell into, landing flat on his backside next to Rutherford in the dirt beneath the mobile home.

Randy threw the useless remnants of his pistol at Max, who caught it and quickly reassembled the gun. Randy yelled, "Shit!" He grabbed the nearest item at hand—his chair—and threw it at Max. Being made of light plastic, it did not hurt Max in the slightest, but it might have prevented Max from taking aim with the gun, if he had even tried. Randy ran to the living room and opened the window. Rutherford bit down on the sucker in his mouth, then took it out and threw it. Randy saw it coming and turned in an effort to dodge, but the sucker hit the back of his Hawaiian shirt and stuck there. Randy paused to reach for it, whining, "That's just petty," but saw Max beginning to climb out of the floor and decided to leave the sucker where it was and flee through the open window.

FORTY

Max managed to stand on the dirt beneath the mobile home, thigh deep in the ruined floor. He offered Rutherford a hand to help pull himself out of the deeper hole full of wet cement.

Rutherford lifted his left foot out of the heavy gray glop. "Thank you."

As Max stepped up onto the porch, Rutherford went the opposite direction, toward the kitchen counter, wet cement slopping from his foot with every step. The floor cracked and warped under his weight.

"Man, he really did need to make repairs."

Max asked, "What are you doing?"

Rutherford snatched a crumpled potato chip bag from the counter, pulled it straight, and shook his earpiece out into his hand.

"I knew it. Greasy!" He grimaced but put it in his ear anyway. "And the crumbs!"

They both climbed out of the ruined trailer onto the wobbly deck in time to see Randy's truck barreling down his long driveway, Albert's drones following behind. The team's TurkMO van pulled aside as it came from the opposite direction, allowing Randy to pass.

The TurkMO pulled up, the driver's seat empty, with Terri riding shotgun and Sloan, Sherwood, and Albert in the rear. Max dove through the sliding side door while Rutherford took the driver's seat. He hadn't even closed the door before Terri said, "After him."

The remote driver said, "Yes, ma'am!"

Albert shouted, "Wait!"

"What?" Terri asked.

"The wad's on its way out. It'll be here in a second."

"We aren't waiting for your wad! Driver, go!"

The minivan pulled a tight, fast, U-turn that Rutherford feared might tip it over, but the van stayed on its wheels and fishtailed down the driveway at top speed.

Rutherford flopped back and forth in the seat, trying to steady himself by gripping his shoulder belt with both hands while the steering wheel spun in front of him like a circular saw blade. He looked at the dashboard, alarmed, and seemed on the verge of complaining when Terri spoke up.

"Rutherford, our driver today is Hal."

Hal said, "Heya, sport."

Rutherford said, "Hi."

Terri said, "Hal's a retired stunt driver. Mr. Capp had him hired for special situations like this. He wants to market the use of remote pursuit drivers to police departments. They'll get access to expert drivers for much less money, and people like Hal will get to use their skills in a safe environment."

Sloan said, "Safe for him."

Rutherford braced himself against the dashboard and the door handle, keeping his hands well free of the steering wheel as the van bounced up off of Randy's dirt driveway onto the tarmac highway and slid through the two eastbound lanes in a hard left turn to chase Randy in the two westbound lanes.

Albert said, "The drones have him. They're locked onto the signal from the tracking sucker. He's about two hundred yards ahead, and we're gaining on him fast."

Hal said, "Of course we are. Your boy doesn't know who he's dealing with."

The woods on one side of the road stopped abruptly at the edge of Randy's property. Businesses lined the sides of the street ahead and traffic filled the lanes. The van swerved into the slow lane to get around a box truck, then dodged around a sedan that attempted to pull out of a parking lot. In the distance Rutherford saw Randy's truck, moving fast but not making it look easy. Soot poured from the exhaust. The truck's body bounced on the suspension's rusty leaf springs. Every swerve made the whole vehicle lean one way, then tilt back the other. The drones flew along a couple hundred feet or so behind and fifty feet above the ground—close enough to keep him under surveillance, but far enough back that he wouldn't hear them over his faulty exhaust system.

Hal said, "We're nearing the ambush point."

"Ambush point?" Rutherford asked.

Terri smiled. "Hal's not the only stunt driver looking for steady work."

Hal said, "That I am not! Passing the ambush point in three, two, now."

Three empty TurkMO vans merged onto the highway from the parking lots of three different businesses. Two joined traffic slightly behind Randy and accelerated to catch up. The third was several car lengths in front of Randy and drove slowly to make traffic flow around it as Randy drew closer. Soon, the two rear vans drew along either side of Randy's truck, keeping him from changing lanes. The van in front slowed until Randy had no choice but to tailgate him. Randy leaned on his horn, but the vans took no notice. Hal sped forward, nuzzling up to Randy's tailgate. Acting in unison, the vans all slowed to twenty-five miles per hour.

Rutherford said, "This is great! We can just lead him off the road and trap him."

Terri said, "Yes."

Rutherford looked out the side window and saw one of the drones flying alongside the van in a perfect position to film the van's hood. "But that's not what we're doing, is it?"

"No."

Rutherford leaned forward to look at the distance between the front of the van and the rear of the truck. "Yeah, okay, I get it." He rolled down the window, unfastened his seat belt, and put both hands out the window to feel for a handhold on the roof.

Terri said, "The vans are going to keep the speed under twenty-five."

"Great. That way, if I fall under one of them, it'll run over me slowly."

Hal said, "Use the rack on the roof to work hand over hand onto the nose, take your time, and when you're ready, take the jump. Don't sweat it. I've done this gag a thousand times, both as the jumper and driving either car."

Rutherford said, "I bet you've never done it in a minivan."

"You'd be surprised. We do a lot of stunts in these things. Lots of crashes. Productions can get 'em for cheap and they're great for rollovers. They go ass over teakettle at the drop of a hat."

Rutherford said, "Oh. Good." He pulled himself out the window until he sat on the door.

The drones flew around in front of the van, high over Randy's truck, framing Rutherford so that their shots wouldn't show the vans, but they would catch the pavement rolling past beneath him to give any future viewers an exaggerated sense of speed. In the cab of the truck, Randy craned his neck to look at Rutherford, equal parts amazed and furious.

Rutherford crouched on the window frame, gripping the roof rack with both hands. He worked his way hand over hand to the front corner of the heavy-duty gear rack. Carefully planting his left foot on the van's stubby nose, he followed with the other foot, spreading his hands and feet wide for maximum stability. Rutherford found himself face-to-face with the sensor package bolted to the roof. Specifically, he saw his own distorted reflection in a large camera lens. His face seemed huge, his body a tiny appendage extending below, and the world seemed to rocket past him from all sides. He stood, temporarily mesmerized in the moment, but was snapped back to reality by Terri's voice in his earpiece. "Hal says you're blocking his view!"

Rutherford moved to the side, clearing the camera's line of sight, and pivoted carefully until he was hunkered on the van's hood, leaned forward into the wind, his right arm stretched back, gripping the rack for dear life.

Randy's truck was only three feet ahead, four at the most. If the vehicles were stationary it would have been trivially easy to jump from one to the other, but they weren't, and it wasn't. Either vehicle could slow down, speed up, or swerve with no notice. Rutherford would be leaping into a twenty-five-mile-per-hour headwind, and if he leaped too high, his face could collide with one of the three camera drones, leading him by a few feet, flying backward to frame the most dangerous-looking shot Albert could muster.

Looking at the truck bed, he saw Randy staring back at him through the rear-view mirror. They briefly made eye contact. In an instant he knew that Randy knew what he was about to do, he knew what Randy would do to try to make it difficult for him, and they both knew that it wouldn't stop him.

Rutherford leaned forward into the wind, let go of the roof rack, and leapt from the van. Randy, as Rutherford predicted, pressed the gas pedal to the floor, creating a terrible noise, a noticeable puff of black smoke, and a tiny amount of extra speed.

Rutherford adjusted for this as he instinctively calculated his jump to get him off the van's hood and onto the truck's back bumper. Then the truck rear-ended the TurkMO van in front of it, about which both Rutherford and Randy had forgotten. The truck's acceleration came to a screeching halt, and the truck actually slowed. Instead of landing on the back bumper and grabbing the tailgate for support, Rutherford kicked the back of the truck, hit his shins on the tailgate's top edge, and fell face-first into the bed with the assorted trash deposited there by Randy and people who couldn't find a garbage can in various parking lots over the years.

He rose to a crouch and sprang forward to grip the top of the truck's roll bar. He found that it wobbled under the slightest pressure. Looking down to the roll bar's base he saw that it was haphazardly bolted into the bed, with several of the bolt holes empty and the remaining bolts both loose and covered with rust.

"The roll bar isn't welded in?" Rutherford shouted.

The cab's sliding rear window vent was open, to compensate for the lack of air-conditioning, so Randy heard him. "Welding cost more!"

"But if it isn't welded, it's useless!"

"It still looks cool!"

"Whatever," Rutherford said. "Just give up, Randy. You can't get away. Stop the car, we'll have a quick fistfight for the cameras, and that'll be that."

"Yeah? What makes you so sure I can't get away?"

"I'm in the truck with you, for one thing. Unless you think the cab is fast enough to outrun the bed, you're done."

"There are still ways to lose you."

Randy stomped on the brake. Rutherford flew forward until his belly hit the roll bar, forcing the air from his lungs. He bent forward like a child doing somersaults on a schoolyard monkey bar until his face slammed into the truck's roof. He bounced back, rotating in the opposite direction, and felt some of the rusty bolts holding the bar break loose. Then the team van rear-ended the truck, instantly accelerating it to its former speed, causing Rutherford to pull back on the bar with more than his full weight. The remaining bolts snapped, sending him and the bar clattering back into the truck bed in a tangled heap.

Randy hit the brakes again, making Rutherford and the roll bar slide forward, then made a hard right turn. Rutherford managed to sit up enough to see out of the bed. The three vans boxing in the truck on its front and sides continued down the road, caught unaware by the sudden deceleration. Randy had cut behind the van on his right and aimed for a parking lot along the side of the road. Sadly, there was no parking lot entrance handy—only a curb, a sidewalk, a ditch, and another curb.

The truck bucked as if it had been hit by a meteor from below somehow. Rutherford, the roll bar, and the sun-bleached trash all flew up above the rim of the truck bed, completely out of control, then came down hard just in time for the truck to cross the sidewalk and reach the ditch and the second curb. This time the push upward came with an alarming crack. Rutherford landed on his front next to the half of the roll bar that remained in the bed. The rest hung over the side and dragged on the pavement, making a shower of sparks and a ringing sound.

The truck shook violently as Randy powered forward. Rutherford suspected they had popped both front tires and probably bent the rims in their impact with the curb. Looking back at the road behind them, Rutherford saw the team's van stopped, its front end smashed and leaking coolant. The side door slid open and Max burst out, running in pursuit of the truck. The other three TurkMO vans were driving ahead to make the turn into the parking lot at the nearest actual entrance, hundreds of feet down the road.

Turning to look forward, Rutherford saw a vast sea of pavement sparsely polka-dotted with cars out by the road, but densely packed near the two entrances of a CartFulls superstore.

Randy aimed the shuddering, staggering truck for the store as best he could, but the truck's damaged suspension had other ideas. Rutherford noted the stricken vehicle's speed, direction of travel, and the line of parked cars looming ahead, and hurdled the tailgate. He hit the ground and tumbled to a stop just as he heard the truck hit a parked car. Rutherford turned to look at the damage and was unhappy but also unsurprised to see the truck's door hanging open and Randy running away toward the store. His distance from the crash and lack of injuries both suggested that Randy had jumped out of the moving truck before it stopped.

The thought *I gotta catch him* occurred to Rutherford's brain after he'd already taken three steps in pursuit of Randy. They appeared to be headed toward the store entrance. Maybe Randy meant to lose Rutherford in the maze of aisles. Maybe he intended to take hostages. He didn't appear to be armed. Maybe he hoped to find a weapon inside the store. It was hard to say.

Rutherford knew two things for sure: he didn't want Randy to enter the store, and given Randy's head start, it was going to be a tall order to catch him in time.

Randy rounded the corner at the end of the row of cars and had a straight path directly to the doors. His only obstacle was a long row of purple shopping carts, all nested into each other to form a single unit, rolling along at a walking pace. It was steered by a parking lot attendant in a purple smock at the front of the chain and propelled by a purple motorized pusher at the rear. A normal pedestrian would walk around them or wait a few seconds for them to pass, but Randy was no ordinary pedestrian. He reached out, planted a hand on the top of a cart, and attempted to vault over the moving cart train. His hand slipped and his arm disappeared elbow-deep into a cart. He stopped mid-vault and lay, confused and panicked, on the top of the carts. His panic grew when he tried to pull his arm free and couldn't.

Rutherford maintained his sprint. One of Albert's drones raced ahead and circled overhead, filming Randy as he tried to free his arm while the parking attendant shouted at him to get down off the carts. Rutherford knew that Randy was caught, and that the other two drones were behind him, ready to film the arrest. Capp's words came to him: *Fighting on top of anything that looks like a train is a plus.*

Rutherford aimed for a spot a dozen or so feet back from Randy, planted a hand, and leapt up onto the chain of carts in a manner that he hoped looked like Spider-Man. The cart train tipped up on one side and hovered there for a few alarming seconds, but it fell back onto its wheels.

Rutherford said, "No dice, Randy. This is the cash-only line."

Randy shouted, "What? What the hell are you talking about?"

In his ear, Sloan said, "He's right. That was a weak line."

Terri said, "Yes, but the instinct was good. Keep trying, Rutherford. Max?"

Max replied, "Almost there."

"Good. Get up to the front and make sure that kid keeps those carts moving. That's your main job. After that, help Rutherford."

Rutherford looked out into the parking lot and saw Max running in his beige ensemble. Max turned slightly away from Rutherford to run toward the attendant, who, as Terri feared, stopped the cart train and yelled, "Hey, get off there, you idiots!"

Rutherford ran along the tops of the carts, hands out, making a show of maintaining his balance as the drones dropped altitude to catch less of the background and hide the lack of motion.

"You're under arrest, Randy. I've got you." Rutherford glanced at the camera drones, making sure he was framed well. "You're in the bag. But will that be paper or plastic?"

Sloan said, "Woof. Not much better."

The carts nudged forward. Looking to the head of the line, Rutherford saw the lot attendant shoving some cash into his pocket as he guided the carts. Max stood where he was, literally waiting for the fight to come to him.

"Randy," Rutherford said. "Give it up. You're trapped. Just wait a second and I'll get someone to help you to the car . . . like a bag boy, but a cop, helping you to the police car. Ugh, never mind."

Sloan said, "Laughing. Laughing. At you, not what you said, for the record."

Randy sagged, unable to pull his arm free. As he finally stopped straining against the carts, the pressure that pinned his arm released. Laughing at his sudden change in fortune, he sprang to his feet to fight Rutherford off. He put up his fists. Drops of blood flew from his arm in Rutherford's direction. Randy's right fist and forearm were a red, dripping mess; he had clearly cut himself quite badly trying pull himself free. Randy and Rutherford both let out cries of alarm and disgust.

The lot attendant shouted, "Oh, man, I'm gonna have to clean that!"

Max began walking alongside the row of carts, near enough to the action to step in if needed, but keeping enough of a distance to stay out of the drone's shots. "We'll throw in another fifty for the trouble," Max said. The lot attendant shrugged.

Rutherford pulled his comically oversized firearm from its shoulder holster and aimed at Randy. "It's over, Randy. You're past your sell-by date."

Sloan said, "I didn't know a joke could make me sad."

Randy stepped forward and took a swing at Rutherford with his bloody right fist, but his precarious footing and poor balance atop the rolling line of carts robbed the punch of any real force. Rutherford dodged it easily, more intent on not getting Randy's blood on him than evading any harm the punch might cause. Randy fell past Rutherford and off the carts. Max was right there to catch him.

"Oh, careful," Max said as he reached up to support Randy while burying a fist in his gut. Randy's fall slowed considerably, held aloft by Max's friendly hand on his shoulder and his less friendly one still pressing against his kidney.

Max said, "Okay, easy." Randy tilted backward, landing on his feet, both of which Max swept out from under him, sending him falling to the pavement. Max lunged forward and down to get under Randy and break his fall, also guiding Randy into a one-hundred-and-eighty-degree spin so that he slammed face-first into the ground.

Max crouched next to him, planting a hand between Randy's shoulders. "Stay still, friend. You may have a back injury. You mustn't move."

Randy tried to roll over. Max pressed his thumb into Randy's spine with a subtle twist of his wrist. Randy went limp and shrieked with pain.

Max said, "See?"

Rutherford jumped down from the carts and pointed his gun at Randy's back. "Randolph McCormick Junior, you're under arrest for attempted murder, solicitation of murder for hire, reckless endangerment, and destruction of private property. I can count at least six more charges off the top of my head, which means we can't use the express lane."

Max looked up at Rutherford, who smiled back down at him.

Terri said, "Okay, that settles it, we release the video without sound."

FORTY-ONE

Rutherford and Max apprehended Randy just before nine in the morning in Los Angeles. By four that afternoon, Rutherford and the rest of the team stood in a darkened hotel conference center, looking out on a small sea of cameras and reporters who watched a video projected on a screen behind Vince Capp. It was standard procedure for Capp to hold a press conference whenever the team broke a case. Usually the crime was in Seattle, only the local Seattle press outlets were interested, the team was in Seattle, and Capp was in Seattle, so the press conference was held in Seattle. In this case, the arrest took place in Los Angeles, the national press (all of whom had a major presence in LA) were interested, the team was in LA, and Vince Capp was in Seattle, so the press conference was held in Seattle.

Rutherford turned around. He hadn't actually watched the final edited and released video from the arrest yet. On the screen he saw Randy, his face heavily pixelated and his arm trapped by the shopping carts, desperately trying to pull himself free as Rutherford carefully walked along the tops of the carts toward him. He saw his mouth move, but no audio played. Instead, a subtitle read "Aren't you a little old to be riding in the shopping cart?"

The press tittered politely.

The rest of the arrest played out much the way Rutherford remembered it. The drones framed the action to make Rutherford seem heroic and ensure that Max's interaction with Randy at the end looked like assistance, not the devastating attack it was. The on-screen Rutherford jumped down off the cart train, pointed his immense handgun at Randy, and said something the viewer couldn't hear. A subtitle at the bottom of the screen said, "I love CartFulls. I got a great deal on a two-hundred-pound sack of crap."

The press laughed as the video ended and all focus returned to Vince Capp, who stood behind a podium next to the screen. "Once again, justice has been served by my team."

Sloan said, "And the passive voice has been used by him."

Capp, who had an earpiece and heard Sloan, smirked as he continued. "We've chosen not to show the perpetrator's face or mention his name. He committed his crimes to gain notoriety, and we intend to start his punishment by making sure that all of the attention goes where it belongs, to his victims. Emery Hindman and Mac Menard lost their lives. Justine Warner was attacked, but only suffered minor injuries, thank goodness. On a positive note, Russell Byrne, who it appears was his intended target all along, has already received offers for the book and film rights to his story. And I'd also like to thank the brilliant investigators of CartFulls forensics labs. Their assistance has been invaluable. We all know CartFulls is the place to go for cartfulls of savings, but it's time the world knows that they also solve cartfulls of crime."

Rutherford used the polite round of applause for the forensics team as an excuse to sneak a peek at Claire, standing on the far side of the stage with three members of her team. He could have sworn she had been looking at him but averted her gaze the instant he glanced her way.

"And," Capp said, "as always, I want to thank my team, the Authorities, for their excellent work, and to single out good old Cement Shoes Rutherford for his excellent detective work. It's good to know we can count on him to do whatever it takes to get results."

After that, Capp opened the floor for questions, most of which centered on why a major big-box store chain had a forensics lab. Once the questions were exhausted, Capp adjourned the press conference. The team and Claire's CartFulls crew walked down the hall to the second, smaller conference room Capp's people had reserved to serve as a green room and staging area.

Max hobbled along with the help of a cane in his left hand, as his right arm hung in a sling and his right index finger was in a splint.

Rutherford walked up behind him. "So you swung by home between the airport and here?"

Max said, "Yes. I wanted to get it over with."

"And?"

"I got it over with. It's over . . . with. I kicked Chaz out of my house and my life."

"How'd he take it?"

Max looked back over his shoulder at Rutherford, but didn't answer.

Rutherford smiled. "I'm surprised you had time to go see a doctor."

"I didn't. I had all this first aid gear already. This isn't the first time I've broken up with Chaz."

Albert said, "I can't believe Byrne's already getting offers for the rights to his story."

Terri said, "Well, the offers came from a publisher and a studio that Capp holds a stake in."

"How do you know that?" Albert asked.

"I'm the one who delivered the offers. That's how they were able to get to him before anyone else. It's called *synergy*."

Professor Sherwood asked, "Will Byrne's story be particularly interesting? I mean, all he did was have a guy repeatedly fail to shoot him. He didn't even notice it was happening."

"No," Terri agreed. "But they'll hire a writer to make up a different story that will be interesting."

"Would they really do that?" Sherwood asked. "Just make something up?"

Terri said, "They're writers; it's literally their job."

As they entered the second conference room, Rutherford saw a plastic-wrapped case of bottled water haphazardly torn open in the middle of the room as *refreshments,* a smattering of folding chairs, and a half-dozen or so young executive assistants not using them. As the team entered, the assistants greeted them with practiced smiles and dead eyes.

Rutherford grabbed two bottles of water, moved quickly to the side of the room, and nonchalantly began his visual search for Claire. He had a dim hope that, now that the case was over and they weren't technically working together, Terri might not mind if he tried to get something going. At the very least, he would just be handing Claire a bottle of water. He didn't see how Terri could object to that. He knew she would, though, and looked forward to watching her do it, like one would watch a pool hustler pull off a trick shot.

Before he could locate Claire, he heard his name, turned, and found himself face-to-face with Detective Frederick.

"Rutherford, could I have a word?"

"Sure, uh, Detective." Rutherford's attention drifted as he spotted Claire, but Terri immediately approached her and said something Rutherford couldn't hear. As the two of them walked back out into the hall, Terri looked Rutherford in the eye and smiled, making him profoundly uncomfortable. He turned his attention to Detective Frederick. "You want a bottle of water?"

Frederick said, "Yeah, thanks," and took the second bottle from Rutherford.

"I'm surprised to see you. I didn't know you were here."

"Yeah," Detective Frederick said. "Mr. Capp's company flew me and Burski up to be part of the press conference, but Mr. Capp vetoed us at the last minute. He said having members of the LAPD there would steal credit from your team."

Rutherford winced. "Oh, that's awful. We couldn't have done it without you. I'm sorry."

"No," Frederick said. "It's fine. You deserve the win. You got him, not us."

"Where is Burski?"

"Still in the press conference. A reporter asked him why we were here. He started going on about the urge to watch the hankie in the magician's right hand while the left reaches into a pocket to grab a ball. I figured he'd be occupied for a while, so I snuck away. Look, Rutherford, I copped an attitude when you showed up, but seeing how things worked out, I think I could learn a lot from you. I'd like to sit down, have a few beers, and pick your brains about how to be a better cop."

Rutherford laughed. Frederick watched him laughing, confused. After a moment, Rutherford sad, "Detective, the last thing you should ever do is try to act more like I do."

"You don't think I can?"

"I'm sure you can. It's not hard. Just don't think things through and let your hygiene slip. I don't think you *should*."

"But, it's like Capp said, you get results."

"I get lucky. I do the flashy stuff and steal the credit, but guys like you do the real work that puts bad guys away. You're by far the better cop. We need more of you, not me."

"Really?"

"Trust me. I know what I'm talking about."

As Vince Capp entered, the room erupted into applause. The bored, dead-eyed functionaries and gofers who had been awaiting his return instantly blossomed into enthusiastic disciples, elbowing their way in front of each other to praise their boss.

"That was great, Mr. Capp."

"You had them eating from the palm of your hand, Mr. Capp."

"That line you came up with, about the two-hundred-pound sack of crap? Genius!"

Capp smiled, but shook his head. "Thanks, but I didn't come up with it. That was one of the marketing copywriters' idea."

"Yes," the assistant said, "but you hired him!"

Capp said, "Her. If you'll excuse me for a moment, I'd like to have a word with the Authorities."

The lickspittles smiled, said that they'd be happy to, then glared at any team member they saw as they walked away. Rutherford, Sloan, Albert, Professor Sherwood, and Max all converged on his location, knowing that Capp saying he wanted to talk to them didn't mean he wanted to go out of his way to do it.

Capp said, "Now that the press isn't around, and you know I don't have to be positive for the cameras, I just wanted to tell you all how happy I am with your work. It took longer than any of us wanted, and it seemed pretty rocky for a while, but that's just the nature of the beast. Some cases are going to be like that. The point is, in the end you got the guy and did your jobs admirably. Professor Sherwood, don't think I didn't notice how well Her Majesty worked."

Professor Sherwood laughed. "Her Majesty was great. My piloting skills were not. I'm afraid that I'll need quite a bit of practice before we use her in public again, preferably somewhere far away from anybody who might get hurt."

Capp nodded. "Whatever you think is best, Professor. Albert, your camera drones did an excellent job of framing the action. They get better every time. And the boys in product development are very interested in your wad, though the marketing people ask that you either give it a different name or at least come up with an acronym to justify calling it the wad."

Albert looked up at the ceiling and mumbled, "Adaptive deformer, ambulatory disguise . . . I'll work on it. The *w*'s going to be a challenge, though."

Capp said, "I'm sure you're up to it. Max, Rutherford, that was some great work you did in the video, both of you. Max, nobody watching would ever know you were beating the snot out of that guy. Speaking of which, what the hell happened to you? Did the guy put up a fight after the cameras were off?"

"No, sir," Max said. "This happened later. It's personal."

"Oh, okay." Capp turned to Rutherford, dropping the subject so quickly and so fully that it was clear that he would never ask about it again, not only because it was none of his business, but because he also genuinely did not care. "Rutherford, fighting on the shopping carts, brilliant! That perfect mix of awesome and pathetic that you do so well."

"Thanks, but I can't take all the credit. You're the one who told me that fighting on top of anything that looks like a train is a plus."

"Yes," Capp said. "I did. And you took my direction and ran with it, which is great. That said, the marketing team is concerned. This is two of your videos in a row where you've fought on top of something moving. They want to make sure you don't go back to the well too often."

"They want me to fight while not on something that's moving?"

Capp said, "No, I mean, that's just fighting on the ground. How boring is that? Marketing would like you to look for some opportunity to dangle from something during a chase."

"Dangle?"

"Yeah. I know it sounds far-fetched, but if you look around, there are lots of things to dangle from. Helicopters, airplanes, bridges, tall buildings, even those signs over the freeway."

Rutherford said, "That sounds, uh, great."

"Doesn't it? It'll look amazing on camera. Really dangerous. I mean, really, genuinely, life-and-death dangerous. Of course, I don't want you to risk your life."

Rutherford said, "Of course not."

Capp added, "Unless there's a good reason. And maybe if whoever you're chasing is hanging there too you could get into some kinda kick fight."

Albert said, "I could build a safety harness into his shoulder holster. It could have steel cables that go down his sleeves, with a carabiner at the end. He could latch onto a helicopter's skid and just hang there all day."

Rutherford said, "Fantastic."

"Excellent," Capp said. "Nice and safe, as long as you detach before the chopper lands on you. Which, I guess would mean dropping before they land. Huh. Oh well, you'll figure it out. The marketing team is also delighted that the guy tried to drown you."

"They are?"

"Yeah, because he tried to use cement shoes. They had worried that the nickname 'Cement Shoes' wasn't getting any traction, but this shows the strength of the brand they've created."

"Yeah," Rutherford said. "Tell them I said thanks for that."

"Will do."

Capp slapped Rutherford on the back and turned away, clearing his throat. "Everyone, this is the team's first high-profile, national case, and again, I just couldn't be more pleased with how it's worked out. I say this calls for a celebration. Rutherford, party at your place."

Rutherford said, "Oh, I don't know. I'm not really prepared."

Capp said, "Wasn't a request."

Rutherford shouted, "Party at my place!"

FORTY-TWO

Rutherford pulled the team van into the marina parking lot. The SUV full of CartFulls employees pulled in behind him, followed by the highly modified UPS truck Vince Capp used as an oversized limousine. Catering trucks filled the marina parking lot. Caterers filing back and forth to Rutherford's barge clogged the dock. Life in the marina was completely disrupted. Rutherford knew his neighbors would not be happy with him. Maybe, if he was lucky, one of them would come complain in front of Terri and Capp, which would make him look good in their eyes.

Rutherford got out of the van, then watched as Sloan, Sherwood, Albert, and Max all spilled out the sliding side door, Max bringing up the rear and moving much slower than usual.

"You sure you're up to this, Max?" Rutherford asked. "Shouldn't you be in an emergency room?"

"Nonsense! I already popped everything back into place. All they'd do is give me aspirin and charge my insurance five thousand dollars."

"I don't know. It might be smart to get some X-rays."

"I'd never allow that to happen."

Rutherford said, "They're perfectly safe."

"For me, yes. But anybody who saw my X-rays would get a visit from some men with foreign accents and never be heard from again."

Rutherford and Albert laughed, but the laugh did not last long or end convincingly.

Professor Sherwood said, "So, if you're ever in an accident, we shouldn't let the doctors do an X-ray."

Max said, "No you should not, and if they try to CAT scan me, evacuate the building."

As they walked up the dock to the barge, they had to dodge the constant stream of caterers carrying tables, chairs, and food out to the barge, then returning, empty-handed, for the next load. They saw Terri sitting on a lawn chair on Rutherford's barge, outside the Airstream trailer that he called home. As they crossed the gangplank, the rest of the team exchanged greetings with Terri and moved on toward the food. Rutherford stayed back with her to talk a moment.

"You were here early," Rutherford said.

Terri said, "I had my reasons. I needed to talk to Claire, so I told her about the party and drove her over so we could talk on the way. See, Mr. Capp and I both think the partnership with her lab worked out well, and CartFulls got some nice free press out of it to boot. So we're going to be working with CartFulls a lot in the future, and we want Claire to be our liaison with her company."

"Oh," Rutherford said, "that's good."

"Yes, but she won't really be a member of our team, Rutherford. Just a contractor, and as I've said about a million times this week, you can't reveal your real personality or proclivities to anyone who isn't on the team or doesn't already know."

"I understand."

"If she ever figures it out on her own that you're not really a scumbag, and that you like all the same things, that's great. But she has to work it out herself."

"I understand."

"Good."

"So, where is she now?"

Terri pointed at the trailer behind her. "In there. When we got here, I suggested she powder her nose."

Rutherford looked at the trailer. "She's in my trailer?"

"Has been for ten minutes. I told her it was where you live, and that she shouldn't nose around in your stuff," Terri smiled. "I figure someone who went into forensic science won't be too prone to snooping."

"Terri. Thank you for everything."

Rutherford stepped into his trailer and saw Claire examining the contents of his closet. She stuck her head out, saw Rutherford, and said, "You!"

Rutherford held up both hands in surrender. "I just caught you going through my stuff. I don't think you're allowed to be mad at me."

She pulled a gray suit out of the closet and held it up on its hanger. "This suit, the label in it says H. Huntsman and Sons, Savile Row."

"Yeah. It's an estate sale find. I pretty much won the lottery on that one. I had it altered and it fits pretty well, considering it was made bespoke for someone else."

She put the suit back and took two very forceful steps to the kitchenette counter. Rutherford noted that one of the advantages of living in a very small space is that it makes it difficult for people to storm around.

She pointed at Rutherford's personal watch, sitting unworn on the counter, as opposed to the cheap digital work watch on his wrist. "And what's this?"

Rutherford said, "My Junghans max bill chronoscope. I have a soft spot for Bauhaus design. Are you all right, Claire?"

She marched back to the closet, reached up to the top shelf, and pulled down a woven hat with a flat crown, a flat brim, and a blue striped hatband. "And what is this?"

"A straw boater."

"I *know* it's a straw boater. The question is, why the hell do *you* own a straw boater, Rutherford?"

"To go with my seersucker suit."

She rifled through his closet again, pulled out a blue-and-white striped sleeve, and looked questioningly at Rutherford.

He shrugged. "Sometimes I feel jaunty."

She looked around the spotless trailer with its tidy bathroom and the impeccably tasteful bedspread and pillows. She pointed at a stack of Blu-ray cases next to the TV, squinted at them, and said, "Wes Anderson. That's everything Wes Anderson has directed."

"Yes."

"Including *Bottle Rocket*."

"Yes."

"I thought you were making fun of people who like Wes Anderson. You really are into all this stuff."

"Yes."

"But the leather jacket. The torn jeans!"

"I hate them. I'm paid to wear them. It's my uniform, but they make me feel dirty. I mean, they are dirty, but I feel it on the inside."

"But if you had a choice?"

"If I'm wearing a shirt, pants, and a jacket, I figure it's just as easy to put on a suit."

Rutherford could have sworn that Claire teared up slightly. "I've never heard a man say anything like that before."

Rutherford said, "You've never talked to me. Not really. The real me."

"I see that."

Rutherford stepped closer to her. "You know, most guys who wear a leather jacket and jeans would grab you and kiss you right now. Forcefully."

"Yes, they would."

Rutherford stared at her for a long moment, then asked, "Would you like to go to dinner tomorrow night?"

"Yes," she said. "Very much."

ACKNOWLEDGEMENTS

This book fought me a lot harder than any pervious book I've written. I think it's probably because I wrote the first draft as the pandemic first started tightening its grip on the planet, and my general mood about how people reacted bled through into the tone and content of my work.

It was not good.

Missy, my wife of over twenty-five years and my primary test reader, put the first version of the book down halfway through after bursting into tears . . . not a good sign for a book that's meant to be a comedy.

So, in this case, my deep and heartfelt thanks go to Missy, and to my friend Rodney Sherwood, who helped talk me down from the edge and guided me back to a book that I hope is actually enjoyable to read.

ABOUT THE AUTHOR

After an unsuccessful career in radio, and a mediocre career in stand-up comedy, Scott Meyer found himself middle-aged, working as a ride operator at Walt Disney World.

In his spare time, he produced the successful web comic *Basic Instructions*. He slowly built a following of fans all over the world, whom he begged to purchase his first self-published novel, *Off to Be the Wizard*. The book's success brought him a publishing deal.

Scott Meyer now makes his living as a novelist and a web cartoonist. He lives with his wife and two cats, all of whom try their best to keep him in line.